Choices...

Dear Carla,
Thank you for your continued support.
I hope you love Samantha and her choices.
Love
Sarah xo

SARAH ANN WALKER

Also by Author Sarah Ann Walker

I am HER…

THIS is me…

My Dear Stranger

LOST

Copyright © 2015 0614 Sarah Ann Walker
Cover Design: James Freeburg
All rights reserved.
ISBN-13: 978-09917231-40

This book is a work of fiction. Any reference to real people, or real locales are used fictitiously. Other names, characters, places, and incidents are the product of the author's imagination, and any resemblance to actual events or locales or persons, living or dead, is entirely coincidental.

DEDICATION

To Jakkob

Once again, you are absolutely everything to me.

I would give up every single pair of shoes I own for you in a heartbeat. Even the special red-soled ones I refuse to wear.

I love you.
Mommy
xo

Choices…

CONTENTS

Dedication   i

Acknowledgments

Choices...

Epilogue

ACKNOWLEDGMENTS

James, thank you for another *amazing* book cover. I love it.
To my parents, thank you for reading my books, even when you hear my voice in the characters, and the dirty parts make you cringe.
Brennah, thank you for giving me my handsome nephew Zakkary, and my 2 beautiful nieces Piper-Ireland and Teaghan.
Paola, thank you for being my longest, dearest friend.
Silvana, thank you for making me laugh, and for totally getting me.
Randi, thank you for your amazing support and friendship
Sam, thank you for being my BBE- Best Brit Ever.
Amy, thank you for pimping me endlessly and selflessly.
Christina, thank you for thinking I'm wicked awesome- right back atcha.
Kim, thank you for keeping my friendship even after I tested it with LOST.
Olivia, thank you for being my BIE- Best Italian Ever.
Brenda, thank you for holding my hand *way* too often.

A special thanks to Diana, Darcy, and the Twisted Sisters, and to Sandy, Michelle and Michelle for giving me an amazing opportunity to attend my first American Author's event- Lovely Ladies and Naughty Books, Bash at the Beach in Atlantic City, June 6th 2015. I'm so glad I finally met you all.

Thank you Deniro, Cheryl, Paula, Megan, Michelle, MTO Diane, Jen, Katica, Crysti, Glenda, Lou, Diane, Mark, Doug, Laura, April, Suzy, Carla, Coach & Christine, Alanna, Tracy, Suzanne, Elizabeth, Lustful Literature, Triple M Books, Chris' Book Blog Emporium, Mommy's Naughty Playground, Enticing Book Journeys, & A Pair of Okies, to name a few...

I want to thank all the readers and bloggers who supported me this last year. I wish I could name you all.

So many people have come into my life the last 2 ½ years. Some people who have legitimately cared, and some who just pretended to care when they wanted something from me. It's been an interesting lesson for me. For those of you who honestly care, I thank you, and I truly appreciate you in my life.

xo
Sarah

CHOICES…

CHAPTER 1

Walking up the side pathway with Heather, she's so ridiculous I can't keep it together anymore. The shock, the humiliation, the look on her face- *all* of it is killing me.

"It's not funny." Still pouting Heather elbows me hard in my side to make me stop laughing. "How was I supposed to know?" She asks seemingly totally offended by my laughter.

"How *couldn't* you know?" I return as I start laughing again for the tenth time since we left the restaurant.

"Did *you* know?" She stops at my apartment door.

Looking at Heather in utter disbelief, I can help respond. "My friggin' grandmother would've known. *Jesus,* Heather, he wasn't only gay; he was perhaps the funniest, most overtly flamboyant gay man I've ever met in my life. He puts Neil to shame," I say stunned at her naïveté. "I mean come *on*; there's maybe gay, there's gay, and then there's super gay. And Frederick from Marvolo's Bistro is *super* gay. Actually, he's probably the gayest gay man I've ever seen in my life," I giggle.

"Well, I didn't know," she says quietly as we make our way up the stairs to my apartment on the third floor.

Pausing on the stairs, I lean against the wall and try to reason with her again like I always do.

"Okay. Somehow you didn't know he was gay, even though he touched every single male shoulder in the restaurant while he took their order. He had the funniest lisp and almost valley girl speech pattern, *and* he had on pink ankle socks that matched his pink bow tie," I grin. "But still, even if you didn't know, do you always beg a man to take you to bed like that? *Seriously?* I can't believe you wrote that on our bill, 'I know you want to fuck me, so take me to bed,' with your phone number? Jesus Christ, Heather, have you never heard of subtlety?" Still giggling a little, I remember her stunned face when Frederick turned her down.

"It usually works," she whines walking away from me. "And I haven't been laid in like a month. So I thought I'd cut to the chase. And it usually works-"

"With straight men," I add while pushing open the third floor door.

Growling at me, she concedes. "Yes! With *straight* men. Shit... Did he have to be such an asshole about it? He could've just ignored me, or like lied and said he wasn't available or something. I mean, why be such a prick about it?"

Shaking my head, I start laughing again. Frederick *was* rude, but she kind of brought it on herself with her ridiculously blunt come on. Honestly, he couldn't have been more obviously gay if he offered blowjobs with an after dinner aperitif to all the MALE customers.

Turning to unlock my door I have to respond. "Well, I think he too was just being as blunt as you were. And really, he did say if you could get better looking, grow a dick and find a personality overnight he *might* be interested..." I say as seriously as I can until Heather's head snaps around to glare at me from the hallway. While I try desperately to hold in my laughter, thankfully, Heather cracks first as she pushes past me shaking her head laughing.

"Fine. That was a good one," she says and I can't stop myself. Laughing my ass off again, she joins me and blushes totally embarrassed by the loud, public, scathing turn down she received from a humored Frederick. He *was* kind of a prick for saying what he did so loudly, but still, with 'I know you want to fuck me, so take me to bed,' she kind of deserved it.

"Can we move on now?" Heather begs fanning her red cheeks before walking to my balcony for a smoke.

"Sure," I grin. "Neil, Daniel, and Olivia aren't coming for another hour, so I'm going to go get ready."

Pausing at the door, Heather looks murderous. "If you tell Neil and Daniel what happened, I'll kill you," Heather threatens pointing her smoke at my face.

"I can't promise that. If I get drunk enough it may slip. Sorry," I grin wickedly before walking to my bedroom as she calls out *Bitch* to my back. I am soooo telling them. Daniel is gonna shit, and Neil will torture Heather for months over this one.

We have all talked to Heather about her tongue, her poor choice of words, and her blatant obnoxiousness over the past few years, but she continues anyway. She's so funny and a real sweetheart, but at least monthly she puts her foot in her mouth so badly, she needs a shoehorn to remove it.

Choices…

And no one is safe from Heather's accidental foot in mouth disorder. She's made me cry a few times since we were 14, Olivia once or twice, and once she even made Neil choke up when she talked about agreeing with some woman on the bus who said being gay was, 'a lazy choice'.

Even as I stared at her bug-eyed, trying to get her to stop talking, she didn't notice my attempt and continued to the silence around her as we all listened in shock.

Oblivious to our discomfort, Heather said, 'gays were cheating the rest of us all out of love so they had *both* genders to choose from, and therefore more opportunity to find the right one.'

Sitting on the couch casually, totally unaware of the thundering silence around her, Heather continued talking about how gay people were taking all the good ones away from us straight people who have to actually *work* for love.

I remember being stunned, and almost kicking her before Neil choked up and ripped a piece out of her until she apologized. Listening to Neil talk about all the 'choices' he had as a teenager; bullied and ridiculed, hated and mocked, even being beat up once by a group of assholes because he was gay, I sat silently watching the sudden comprehension dawn on her face as he spoke.

I remember Neil's upset and Heather's shock and understanding as he explained his own reality growing up, which was far from a lazy choice, as she had first put it.

It was a rough night. It was dramatic and nauseating, and Olivia and Monica eventually left Daniel, Neil and I alone with Heather as we all explained sexuality and what *choice* really was.

God, she's so hard to explain. Heather is sometimes an idiot, but she's one of the kindest people I've ever known. She is endearing and sweet, and she gives thoughtful gifts just because. She knows everyone's birthdays and makes them special. She gives everything she has to anyone who needs it, and she's the best person to talk to when you're sad. She was always there for me when I was a teenager, and she was especially loving and supportive recently when I needed her after my break-up.

She just has NO filter. And sadly, she believes everything she reads on the internet or hears on t.v. and repeats it, usually without even thinking about whatever it means before she speaks.

But we all love her. And I've been her friend since high school, so I'll never give her up. We all seem to almost wait for the next stupid thing she's going to say though. It's like we prepare to be shocked and hurt by her. And once a month someone ends up yelling and fighting with her, she cries and apologizes, then we all move on until the next time. We do love her very much though, regardless of her monthly stupidity.

This funny at Marvolo's can't be ignored however. Heather laughs at all of us when we're idiots, so I'm sharing this one for sure. Plus, I think Neil knows super gay Frederick so this'll be hilarious for him.

*****

After a quick shower, and redressing in my bedroom, I decide on simple but sexy. A cute little red summer dress, with spaghetti straps and a square neckline. My cleavage will be minimal, but the dress is fitted to just above my knees with side slits, giving it a sexy appeal without looking slutty. Plus it comes off quickly overhead- *not* that that'll happen. But if it does happen, my dress can be easily removed if I want it to be.

Thinking about our night out tonight and the implied intentions, I really don't think I'll put out, but I need to know if I actually want to. It's time to test myself before I make my final decision tomorrow, I think.

Allan and I broke up over 5 months ago, and I've done the 'I want to be fabulous and single' thing for long enough. I've even done the 'I'm taking care of me now' thing, and the 'This is *MY* time' thing. I've watched the empowering chick flicks, partied with my girls, laughed with my boys, gained weight initially, and lost weight subsequently. And now I'm finally at the place where I forgive Allan. Thank god.

I was waiting for it to happen, and it took 5 friggin' months for me to get there, but it's finally here.

I know it's time to move on now. I went through all the post breakup steps. I cried. I asked why. I begged (only once) thank god. Then I got angry, demanded explanations, and I cried again when no explanations were given. I cried a few more times, tried to breathe, went out and did all the girls work that is required to move on.

And now finally, thankfully, I'm at the Allan isn't a *total* asshole and I don't hate him anymore phase, allowing me to finally move on.

Tonight isn't about hooking up with some random though, but it *is* about not turning down the potential to hook up with some random if I want to. I'm testing myself to see if I want something more before I commit again to Allan forever.

I've never done the bars out hook-up thing like Olivia does sometimes, and Heather does always. But tonight I'll at least figure out if I want to hook-up should a guy talk to me, instead of instantly giving some curt response to the offer of a drink, or to a hand touching my back at the bar with intention.

Tonight, Neil is damned and determined to get me laid by someone better than the 'button on a bag' that was Allan, so I may just go for it.

And yes, Neil once saw Allan naked in our apartment, and though scarred for life, Neil has never gotten over the tiny little nub penis as he called it in the middle of Allan's bag.

Sadly, Allan has become the 'Button on a bag', BB, or just *Buttons* to all my friends because of Neil. The term Buttons is too funny, but I'm not a mean person so it does freak me out a little if Allan ever finds out that Buttons is his nickname among my friends. I'll admit the nickname was kind of funny and even helpful though especially when I was still in my I hate Allan phase.

It's also totally true, incidentally. Allan actually cried the first time we were going to have sex. Seriously. In his bed, after much foreplay, which it turns out he was a pro at *because* of his button on a bag, he finally attempted to penetrate me and when I questioned what he was waiting for, he burst into tears, sat up on his shins, and pointed to his tiny penis with a shaking hand, which was a moment between us for sure.

The whole thing was so bizarre after dating for 2 months, I ended up just saying, 'you're amazing Allan. And I don't care about that.'

So after I told him I didn't care about his size, he exhaled and leaned back down to put his tiny penis inside me while I play acted the best most convincing orgasm ever. And for almost 4 years I continued play acting as well.

He had no idea for just under 4 years I didn't have even one orgasm through penetration with him, so he never questioned his sexual abilities with me. I didn't want him to because I loved him, and I really didn't care about an orgasm. I just cared about loving him.

Allan was my boyfriend from 19 to 23 and next month I turn 24, so I'm finally ready to face my adulthood with him a second time.

Allan helped me decide my future, and he supported me totally. After 2 useless years in University, when I had my strange epiphany that I wanted to become a Psychiatrist, Allan didn't laugh at me, or even pause. Allan kissed me, said I would be an amazing doctor, jumped on our University requirements comps and showed me the courses I had already taken toward my Med School eligibility in 3 years.

Allan was an amazing friend, boyfriend, and future for me. He may have ended up an asshole, but he wasn't an asshole until our end, and no one could argue that fact because all my friends loved him, too.

My girls thought he was amazing, and I know they secretly used Allan as the model for which they looked for their own boyfriends. And my boys loved him, totally. Neil approved of him and loved him from the moment Allan and I started dating, and once Daniel joined our little group, Daniel also thought Allan was amazing. Which he was.

Allan was the guy my girls called in the middle of the night to rescue them from a bad decision at some guys awful apartment. And Allan was the guy Neil talked to over a drink about finding the perfect man when he was single before he met Daniel. Allan was loved and accepted by everyone because he loved and accepted everyone. Well, except for me, evidently.

But I forgive him now which is better than still hating him. I forgive him finally, and though my friends all think I'm justified with my hate, I choose to let it go now. Allan begged me to make a choice, and I have.

When we broke up, other than Monica, my 2 other close girlfriends, Olivia and Heather, and Neil and Daniel sided with me. I won them in the breakup which was good for me, because I needed my friends at the time. My friends were there for me always just like I would have been there for them.

Monica and I never really recovered though. Eventually we didn't even survive the breakup, though we tried at first. Monica was the one friend who though my friend first, chose to stay in Camp Allan. She tried to stay on the fence in both camps, and she tried to be an in between friend. But it was always too hard for us avoiding the hurt, and the Allan triggers which caused nothing more than strained awkwardness between us. So I slowly lost her and our friendship to Allan.

From what I've heard Monica even thinks she's creating a real relationship with Allan, but she isn't. Monica thinks she has a chance with Allan, but Allan wants *me* back.

Allan came back 5 weeks ago. 4 months after the last time we were together, Allan showed up at my door begging for a second chance. Allan showed up and said and did everything I ever wanted to hear, especially after the first days following our breakup, but it was too late to go backwards with Allan. I was heartbroken by him and couldn't even imagine taking him back 5 weeks ago, no matter how hard he tried.

Desperately, Allan bought gifts, and flowers, and nostalgic little reminders of our years together. He offered makeup weekends, and endless apologies, culminating into more apologies, which eventually even turned into crying and begging to get me back.

Allan did and said everything I ever wanted, but it was too late at the time. Though admittedly, I did almost give in quickly.

After one spontaneous kiss, I almost gave in, slept with him, forgave him, and fell right back into the life I had always wanted and believed I was going to have with Allan for the rest of my life.

But the hurt suddenly slammed into my heart and mind as he held me, I stopped the kiss quickly, woke up to my reality, and pushed him out my apartment. I pushed Allan away and closed the door of the apartment I don't really like, but had to find quickly, because Allan ended us so abruptly by cheating with some woman I didn't know but hated as well.

And that was the unofficial end of Allan and Samantha, forever... until tomorrow night.

*****

"Why, don't you look slutastic," Neil smiles from my bedroom doorway as I turn to him.

"And don't you sound like the total cliché gay best friend," I grin back with a curtsy.

Walking into my room, dramatically jumping on my bed Neil replies, "Of course I do. I'm gorgeous enough to be a model. I'm gay. AND I'm your best friend," he says all *duh*. "Did you change your sheets for tonight?"

Ugh, he's so gross sometimes. "Of course I did. But only because it's Saturday, and I always change my sheets Saturday for laundry Sunday morning as you know. You're such a perv, Neil."

"You love it. You would do me in a second," he says as I smirk at him through the mirror. "Admit it. I'm sexy as hell, awesome, super cool, professional when I have to be, fabulous when I want to be, and totally doable," Neil says with another smug smile as he leans back placing his arms behind his head on my pillow.

"Yes, darling," I sigh dramatically. "If only you weren't with Daniel, oh, or *totally* gay, I would do you in a second. Good?"

"Yup. But your sarcasm doesn't hide the fact that you want me. Badly," he grins again.

Turning to my closest friend, I want to smack his grin off but couldn't possibly. Plopping on my bed beside him I can't help but give in as usual.

"You're right. You're my ideal, Neil. Except for the whole YOU ARE GAY thing. Um, do you realize we have this exact conversation every single time we all go out?" I ask as he nods.

"Yes, I do. It's so I get you all hot and bothered over who you can't have, so you go and do someone you actually can have."

"*Really?* So this isn't about your constant need to be told how gorgeous you are? This is all for me?"

Laughing, Neil sits up and side hugs me. "This is all for you, Samantha. I swear I don't even care that you want to do me. It doesn't affect me one way or the other. I don't-"

"You are so full of shit. You love all the girls wanting you. And it's sad really. Why do you care if-"

"Because he's an attention-seeking manwhore," Daniel suddenly says behind me in the doorway.

Grinning at Daniel, he too joins us on my bed, and suddenly I'm sandwiched between the two of them. Oh, the fantasies going through my head.

"Um, this is a little too much for me. I don't know if I can stop from throwing myself at you both. Right here, right now. I'm all hot and-"

When my hair is suddenly yanked backward until I'm lying flat on my bed they kiss each other. Right over my body Neil and Daniel give each other a beautiful kiss. Not all wet and tonguey- just lips on lips with a little movement of their heads until I'm the one who suddenly moans.

Breaking their kiss, Daniel grins down at me to quickly kiss my lips hello. "Hi baby," he breathes his minty gum breath, and I swoon.

"Okay, *this* is hot," I moan. "Please get off me, or I'm going to get off... *soon.*"

Jumping away, Neil fake gags and Daniel bursts out laughing as he collapses beside me for a hug.

"I love you, Sammy," Daniel breathes into my ear as I shiver. "We need to find you a good guy to love so Neil will stop obsessing over you, and so I can stop worrying about you."

"I'm trying, but it's only been a few months."

"Almost 6 months, honey. And you need to leave that prick in the dust. You're too special to be alone," Daniel says sweetly. Telling him the truth about Allan right now would make things awkward if I allowed it, so for tonight I've decided to keep my secret.

"Thank you, Danny," I grin because I'm the only person who gets away with calling him Danny, and I love it. Then again, he's the only one who calls me Sammy, so I guess we're even.

"Can we do the nasty one day so I can be your future baby mama when you boys decide to have kids?" I suddenly ask so seriously Neil turns from my mirror with horror on his face as Daniel laughs again and breathes *absolutely* against my cheek.

Shaking his head, Neil has clearly had enough of us. "Up! I'm fixing your hair. It's gotta be an up-do so the club boys have something to look forward to later. And you have to wear dark red lipstick on those awesome pouty lips of yours so they can imagine those sexy lips wrapped around their hard-"

"*NEIL!*" Both Daniel and I yell laughing.

"Get up, Samantha, or else," Neil threatens with a hairbrush. So naturally, I stand up.

As Neil works on my hair quickly and quietly, Daniel joins Heather in the living room. Watching him closely, Neil looks like he wants to have a heavy with me but keeps stopping himself. He's almost struggling with not speaking, but I don't want to help him. I don't want to talk about Allan anymore.

"I'm fine, I promise. Let's just go get this party started," I smile and shake my ass to the music we hear from the living room. Smiling, he bobby pins the last few strands of the sexy bun he created on my head.

"Can I ask you something?" Neil stops with his arms up high holding my bun in place.

"Of course, but please be gentle. I want to have fun tonight," I pout. Exhaling, Neil looks at me through the mirror and asks the same

question he's asked me a dozen times in the last 6 months. Though slightly amended, it's essentially the same question.
"Do you ever resent me telling you about Allan?"
"No."
"Not ever? I mean he wants you back, so he probably wouldn't have cheated for long. So maybe if I'd kept my mouth shut the night I saw him with that whore, you wouldn't have gone through this heartache, and then you'd be-"
"Still in love with a man who didn't love me enough to not cheat on me. Neil, *you* told me that. You're the one who talked me out of begging him to come back to me," I exhale. "Do you remember what you said after the first time he called me a few weeks after he cheated? When he wanted me back? Do you remember?"
"I do, but-"
Exhaling again, I shake my head as he stops messing with my hair. "That was the smartest thing you ever said to me. 'Ask Allan if he broke up with the whore or if she dumped him, because then you'll know why he's back.' And I did ask him, and you know he admitted she dumped him after only 2 weeks, and though it hurt like hell to hear the truth, you were right. Allan begging me to give him another chance was totally different when I knew he was dumped and alone, rather than if he dumped her to get back with me. You *know* this. So why keep asking?"
"I'm just sad that I may have pushed you to end something that you could've worked out. I'm gay, Samantha," he exhales. When I suddenly give him a *no shit* face he quickly continues. "What I mean is, I'm gay, so I'm super jaded about relationships. Gay men fuck anyone all the time. I'm almost 100% sure Daniel hasn't cheated on me, but-"
"He hasn't," I interrupt.
"Okay. But he's weird. And I haven't really cheated on him, except in the beginning, so we're weird together. There aren't many totally committed gay male couples in their late twenties, so I'm fairly experienced with shitty relationships before Daniel. And I *know* cheating. I've never not cheated, or been cheated on. So I feel like maybe I gave you gay advice instead of straight advice."
Turning to Neil, I need him to understand. "You didn't give me gay advice. You gave me *good* advice, and another reality to think about when I was just too sad to think for myself in the beginning."
"That sounds good, Sam. But if I hadn't seen him with that whore and

bust your door down that night to tell you for your benefit I thought, maybe he would've come around and told you, or stopped cheating with her, or maybe just-"

"*Never* told me," I snap at Neil. "And then I'd be blissfully unaware of the fact that the most amazing men we all knew and loved was a cheating asshole!" I can't help but yell. "Please stop all this shit. It just confuses me and I don't want to feel confused anymore. Allan cheated, broke my heart, I loved him, and eventually hated him, which you wanted me to do so I could move on. And now I forgive him, and I want to move on. So seriously, just stop," I exhale hard pulling away from Neil.

"But if I hadn't told you to not get back with him you might have been happy again, or maybe worked it out, or-"

Spinning to look back at Neil, I'm feeling pretty pissed. "Stop being such an arrogant asshole! I didn't stay away because YOU made me. And I didn't finally tell him to piss off months ago because you didn't want me to give him another chance. I did that because *I* wanted to, not because you told me to. I love you, Neil, but I don't *live* for you."

"You *don't*?" He suddenly smirks trying to break up the tension between us, and I can't help but smile back as I exhale all my anger.

"Well, not entirely. I love you, but I'm totally *in* love with Daniel. So there! I would do anything *he* told me to do. But unlike you, Daniel doesn't talk and advise endlessly. He listens and gives his opinion if I ask for it. You, however, never shut the hell up. And that's why Daniel is my favorite," I smile.

Shaking his head, Neil groans, "I'm not going to tell him you said that. His head'll explode."

"It doesn't matter if you tell him, he already knows. Now, finish my hair so we can we get out of my bedroom. Heather is probably already fantasizing about us screwing, and imagining a ménage scenario with Daniel right about now," I say grabbing my purse while straightening my comforter as Neil fake shudders before fixing the last piece of my hair. "Oh! And *pleeeeease* ask her how dinner was," I can't help laughing as I flip off my bedroom light and leave my room with Neil in tow.

*****

Walking to my kitchen with a clear view of my living room, Neil jumps on the couch beside Heather while I join Olivia and Daniel to make a drink.

"Was he any good?" Olivia asks deadpan.

"Nah. His parts don't work right with mine."

"Well, they work just right with mine," Daniel grins at Neil.

Shaking her head, Olivia begs, "Do we really need to have the all the good ones are gay discussion again? I mean, I get it Daniel. Neil is amazing, and you are to die for. Can we just move on?"

Giving Olivia a hug, I ask how Matt is, but when she suddenly looks a little pissed, I pause, raise an eyebrow, and wait for her to vent.

"Ummm... He's kind of an asshole actually. I think I'm dumping him tomorrow," she exhales slowly.

"Why's he an asshole?" Daniel turns toward her to give Olivia his beautiful I'm here for you and I'm totally listening face as she continues.

"I don't know, little things- like he's bossy and annoying. And he's totally about the guys, which is way too soon if you ask me. I mean, we're only 2 months in and he's already reverted back to guys' nights almost every night, and booty calls only when *he* wants them. So, I think I'm done."

"You should be done. Life is too short to put up with less than you deserve. And you're right, Liv. That's way too soon to already be out of the honeymoon phase," Daniel says with sympathy.

"I know. I may even pick up tonight since Matt told me he'd be out too late to hook up with me later. I just don't really feel a spark or anything anymore, so what's the point?"

"There's no point. Dump him. You're gorgeous, Livi. You need a guy who can't wait to hook up with you, not one who pencils you into his schedule," I offer.

"I know..." Olivia grins as I give her another quick hug smiling over her shoulder at Daniel for being Daniel.

Turning from everyone, I start pulling out the ingredients for our drinks. From the precut lemons and limes, the celery for Olivia's Caesar, to the maraschino cherries for my Vodka and Cranberry. Daniel starts pouring as Olivia starts mixing until we hear a loud burst of laughter from the living room as we all turn to Neil.

"Here we go," I grin at Daniel and Olivia.

Yelling from the living room, Neil's laughing too hard to speak or coherently ask for us, but I kind of hear my name. So turning back I grab my drink, Daniel's hand and make my way to my living room with a huge smile as Olivia follows us already giggling at Neil's laughter.
   "Yes, Neil?" I ask as straight-faced as I can.
   "Fred-*erick*?" Neil stutters laughing.
   "What about him?" Daniel asks quietly behind me with his hand on the back of my chair.
   "Not *me*!" Neil laughs. "Heather! And it was only once, Daniel. You *know* that, so let it go." Instantly, I feel the tension and physical heat behind me as I reach over my shoulder and squeeze Daniel's hand.
   Shit. If I had known Neil slept with Frederick, I never would've allowed Heather to tell her funny story. I maybe should've assumed he had though since Neil has slept with every gay man in the city, but I didn't know. And the last thing I want to do is upset Daniel.
   "What did you do, Heather?" Olivia asks already laughing.
   "Um, I tried to pick him up, but-"
   "*Frederick!?* The *gayest* gay man ever?" Neil howls.
   "That's what I said!" I can't help join in.
   "Any*wayyyyyy*..." Heather says glaring at me. "I tried to pick him up, but he was a total prick about it."
   "She actually wrote on our bill, 'I know you want to fuck me, so take me to bed,' with her cell number," I helpfully fill in the blanks to Heather's scowl.
   "*Really*?" Olivia asks stunned just as Daniel says, "Shut *up!*"
   Still squeezing Daniel's hand I lean forward and beg Heather to tell them what he said. Smiling and laughing, I prompt everyone to start harassing Heather until she finally caves.
   Shaking her head, she moans, "Fine! He said if I got better looking and grew a dick he might think about it."
   "And found a personality," I add seriously before anyone reacts. "What he actually said *wassssss*... If Heather got better looking, grew a dick and found a personality over night, he *might* be interested, then he turned and walked away laughing."
   And that's it. A one second delay. A one second pause before chaos breaks out. I'm dying, and so is everyone else. Olivia is snorting, Neil is crying, Daniel seems to have forgotten he doesn't like Frederick, and even Heather can't hold it in. Pissing ourselves laughing, I haven't felt

this light in almost 6 months.

"Wow, baby. That was *brutal*," Neil says hugging Heather tightly as she buries her face in his chest laughing.

Lifting her head again and wiping her mascara, Heather begs us all to let it go which we do, though admittedly it's hard. That one was way too good to pass up. And it's not like we would ever tell anyone outside our little group, so within our group it's just too funny to not enjoy.

We eventually move on though and talk about anything else to give Heather a break. And after 3 drinks, one argument over slutty clothes versus trampy colors, make-up touchups and bathroom breaks, we're finally ready to hit the club as our fabulous group of five.

CHAPTER 2

Walking into our side of the club, I'm immediately assaulted by sound, lights, bodies, and perfumed sweat. And I love it.

For me these few nights out are extra special because soon I'll be studying my ass off in Med School. Followed by more studying and interning while struggling to get sleep anywhere I can, making my crazy nights out quite limited for the next 5-7 years. Knowing my immediate future, I enjoy and appreciate these nights, because they are the last fun memories I'm going to make for years.

Looking around at everyone, this club is our absolute favorite. We can all just let loose and have fun here. We girls can pick up if we want, and the boys can just be a gay couple generally without any harassment or ignorance. Most men check out Olivia, Heather and me for potential. And most women check out Neil and Daniel with a mixture of first lust, then sad disappointment when they see they're a couple.

Seconds in, we five are already standing at the bar ordering, while Daniel looks for some form of table for us to lean against. Finding 5 chairs is absolutely impossible, but one or two chairs against a high table will usually suffice.

Grabbing my vodka and cranberry, Neil covers the first round, and we all know we'll trade off each round through the night. I already have a slight buzz from the 3 stiff drinks at my place, and with the heavy music thumping through my body, I know 3 more will probably get me nice and drunk, which I honestly look forward to.

Looking, Daniel points to an empty high table with only one chair, but we don't care. It's a table for drinks and purses, so we make our way over.

Walking, or more like *moving* to the beat of the music, I already feel the thrill of the night all around me. I'm going to see if I want to kiss someone tonight. I may even see if I feel the need to make out with someone to test my resolve. We'll see.

"I LOVE this place," Olivia yells across the table to all of our nods because it really is an awesome club.

The music is always loud with heavy bass beats to dance to, but they also pull out the staple old school 90's club songs throughout the night. You get slow alternative song remixes sped up, old school Blur, and of course Nine Inch Nails 'Closer' towards the end of the night. We may hear some techno, rave-like what the hell is this song, followed by either The Smashing Pumpkins 'Bullet with Butterfly Wings', or The Beastie Boys 'Sabotage', which though hard to dance to, is awesome to hear regardless.

"*He's* checking you out," Daniel leans into me while blatantly pointing to a guy 2 tables over. Looking, the guy smiles and raises his beer in a hello before gulping. Um, nope. He screams player.

"Not interested. He seems too smarmy. Like a total pig who already has 4 others lined up," I shake my head to Daniel as Heather stares at the guy still smiling at me.

"Don't you want a sure thing?" Heather asks pulling her eyes away from him slowly.

"I don't think so. Well, kind of, I guess. But I don't want a guy who carries his condoms on a pocket chain," I say as Heather and Olivia laugh. "Like Neil used to..." I add.

Smiling, Neil tips his head in deference as Daniel growls at him playfully. Neil really was a slut, so no one can argue or take offense, *especially* Neil.

"Let's dance," Heather tugs at me and I'm totally on board. I love dancing. I love moving and shaking, and laughing, and just everything about dancing. And when I'm with my girls, I'm happy to dance without reserve or self-consciousness.

"Watch our purses, boys, and watch the show we give," Olivia says with a cheeky grin before pulling me and Heather away from our table to the dance floor.

And then we dance. Hot, sweaty, close, and fun. Heather grinds on me at one point, and Olivia and I mock sexy tango to some weird techno Spanish sounding song without lyrics. We dance to maybe 4 full songs, and when I feel the first droplets of sweat on my forehead, I know I need a drink.

Grabbing Olivia's waist, I pull her as she takes Heather's hand and we make our way back to Neil and Daniel, who have a guy talking with them I don't know.

And he is a guy- a very hot, delicious, muscular, tall, *wow* looking guy. He's sexy in a total dirty boy kind of way in his t-shirt, jeans and shitkicker boots.

"Sexy..." Daniel breathes in my ear as I shiver again. I swear he does that on purpose because he knows I'll always shiver. He could say rectum for Christ's sake and I'd shiver like it's the most erotic word ever.

"Bitches. This is Slayer," Neil announces.

"*Slayer*?" Heather laughs. Ugh. Looking at formerly hot guy, he just lost all his hot points in a millisecond. I'm almost turned off enough to walk away for another round of drinks until he quickly speaks with a laugh.

"Hey. It's actually Matt," hot guy says looking at me, Olivia, and Heather. Oh, thank god.

"Well, *I'm* out," Olivia laughs. "I'm looking for a hookup to dump my own Matt with, so I'm going for drinks. Sam?" Nodding, I can't help but grin. As if Olivia needs another Matt in her life.

Walking away, I stop for a second to watch Heather working the tabletop already. Her cleavage is practically dripping on the table, and she couldn't be closer to Matt if she was in his lap.

"He's fucking hot. Like a gorgeous, tempting, dirty, sexy devil in low-rise jeans kind of hot."

"Yes, he is," I moan checking him out again.

"Did you see those abs through his t-shirt? I want to lick him from cock to clavicle, just to feel his ripped muscles on my tongue."

"Holy *shit,* Livi! I can't believe you *said* that," I choke as she howls with laughter.

"But *Matt*... Really?" Olivia practically pouts at his name.

"I know. What are the odds? But look at Heather. You'd have to compete with that, and I'm sorry to say it but you'd lose," I smile as we shove our way to the bar past endless people.

"I wouldn't lose!" She yells totally offended, but as she turns back to look, she concedes. "Okay, I'd totally lose. God, she's amazing," Olivia looks with awe at Heather working Matt.

Seeing Neil walking toward us, I wait for some lowbrow comment from him about fucking on tabletops, or whoring on the dance floor. And just as Olivia gets the bartender's attention so we're next, Neil grabs my waist from behind and whispers in my ear, "I think you may have missed your chance with Slayer," as I shiver.

Elbowing Neil to get off me as he laughs, I give him shit. "Stop breathing in my ear! You KNOW I can't handle that."

"Of course I do. That's why Daniel and I do it. It's funny to watch you shiver like you want to screw us both."

"You *know* I want to screw you both, so why keep teasing?" I pout as Neil starts laughing and hugs me from behind.

While Olivia starts ordering our drinks, Neil adds a Rye and Coke for Matt, I assume, and after a ridiculously expensive payout for 6 drinks plus a quick Jäger shot for the 3 of us, we each grab 2 drinks and make our way back to Heather practically screwing Matt on the table as Daniel stares at her looking horrified but somewhat amused.

"Thanks, ladies. And Neil," Matt smiles as we pass out drinks.

"Neil calls Matt Slayer because he's so hot he could slay women's panties!" Heather yells with a giggle. "And I'm going to let him slay mine before he *fucks* me!" She finishes in front of all of us *and* a shocked looking Matt.

Jesus! Heather is at her drunken finest again. At least Matt had the grace to look a little stunned by her announcement, even as Olivia sputtered her drink down her chin cracking up Neil and Daniel.

"Subtle, Heather," Daniel says deadpan, and then we all seem to have nothing more to say in our collective discomfort.

Turning to the dance floor, I practically gulp my Vodka and Cranberry, even as I feel the post Jäger Meister burn in my stomach. I'm going to be hammered in about 1 more drink, so I decide I want to get it now.

I'm not sure why Heather still makes me so uncomfortable with her behavior because really I should be used to her by now. I just don't like that blatant kind of sluttiness from her- I never have.

"Sorry, I'm gonna go back to the bar before I dance again. I figure I'll be finished this round by the time I'm served again anyway," I announce already turning from my friends.

Feeling Daniel with me I make my way back to the bar. Pushing and almost shoving people, I get there in an instant and start flagging the bartender again.

"Why does it bother me so much when she acts like that? And I'm not trashing my friend, or talking about her behind her back. It just bugs me," I whine to a listening Daniel.

"It bugs everyone. Well, not Neil because he *was* Heather before me," he grins. "But everyone else. I don't know why it bothers you so much, but her blatant sluttiness makes everyone at least slightly uncomfortable for sure. You're not alone, Sam," he says raising his hand higher than mine to get the bartender's attention instantly.

"I wish I could do that," I yell so he hears me.

"Act like Heather?" He asks with a raised eyebrow.

"No, ya moron- Get the Bartender's attention so easily," I huff as Daniel laughs.

"It makes us uncomfortable because she looks so desperate when she does it, Sam. We know how sweet and kind she is, but she's lonely, so she acts slutty to get attention."

"I know but-"

"Sam, she's not like you or Olivia. She's aimless. She needs attention because she's unsure of herself. And I think she's sad a lot of the time," Daniel says without trying to chastise me I know, but I still feel it.

Exhaling, I feel bad suddenly. "You just made me feel like such a bitch," I almost choke up.

"You're not a bitch at all. You just don't understand her. But I do. She's lonely, honey. So she takes random men to bed for momentary attention, and she tries to feel happy when she's their sole focus, even if it's only for the one night," Daniel says stopping to order our drinks. "Another Jäger?"

"Yes..." I whisper feeling ashamed.

I know I shouldn't feel bad because Heather's behavior every single time she sees a *walking* dick as she calls them *does* make me uncomfortable, but Daniel's right. She pretends well, but I know Heather is secretly sad and lonely, wanting someone to love her for more than just a night, which kind of breaks my heart.

Looking up at Daniel he smiles when he knows I feel bad and kisses my nose. "Take your shot with me. That should liven you up a little. You're not a bitch, honey, you're just not as confused or as unfocused in life as Heather is. You've experienced love, you've had a long term relationship, you have very close friends who love you to death, and you know exactly who you are. Heather has never had any of those things, so she's desperate to experience something more. That's why she acts desperate, even embarrassingly so."

Nodding, he's right. I know exactly who I am and what I'm doing with my life. I've already been accepted into Med School, and though I'll be buried in student loans for about 2 decades when I'm done school, I know I'm going to be a successful doctor because I want to be. I'll make myself succeed so I can help people.

After paying the bartender and tipping him generously for not making us wait, Daniel and I kick back our shots of Jäger, cringe and obsessively gulp down the horrid liquid, then we grab and carefully hold the 3 drinks we each have to carry through the throngs of people back to our table.

Arriving, Olivia grabs her drink, kisses my cheek, and looks like she's dying to get the hell out of there. And I can see why immediately.

Unbelievably, Heather's blouse is 2 buttons lower, showing not only *all* her cleavage but even her full bra down to the underwire and bow. Suddenly laughing, I see even the very gay Neil staring at Heather's boobs like he's mesmerized by them.

Knowing I need to intercede somewhat, I hand Heather her drink and ask if she wants to dance while she talks closely to Matt.

"Do *you* want to dance, Matt?" She asks instead not even looking in my direction as she rubs against him.

"Nah... You go ahead with your friends. I'll just watch and try to keep Neil out of trouble," Matt laughs as Daniel smirks a 'good luck with that' to a smiling, innocent looking Neil.

"Okay. But I'll see you soon, baby," Heather purrs before planting an unexpected kiss on Matt's lips. Horrified, I actually watch the shock cross Matt's face when she's suddenly kissing him until he pulls away to lift his drink to his lips with the weird fake smile of the totally uncomfortable.

"I have to pee," Olivia yells in our faces as she pulls Heather away from the table.

"Don't do it!" I yell back. "Don't break the seal or we'll be dancing in the bathroom every five minutes for the rest of the night. Just hold it, Livi. *Please?*" I beg until she laughs agreeing.

Stepping back on the dance floor with my girls, I realize I'm actually quite drunk. The music feels like it snakes through my skin, and thumps its beat with my own heart. I'm moving and dancing, but I'm hyper aware of the fact that one more drink will push me from quite drunk, to pukey hammered in a second. But then my song starts and I forget everything.

I love this song. It's not really my style of music, but I love it anyway. 'Fuck You' by Virtual Embrace gets me every time.

Moving my hips to the heavy beat with my arms raised, I fall into my own fantasy world. This song, though not a love song by any means, makes me think of dirty sex every time I hear it.

I picture moving my hips to this beat as I have hot, sexy sex. I picture being thrust into as the chorus starts. I imagine carefree, passionate sex, while mouthing 'fuck you, hate you," as I match thrusts with my own body. I imagine being lifted to bang hard against a door, or thrown on a bed to be thrust into as he kneels behind me grunting in time to my moans. God, this song is sexy as hell.

When it winds down to the slow finale, I finally open my eyes to Olivia's smile. Leaning into me she moans, "God, you're so hot you made *me* want to fuck you," and that's it. Grabbing her in a hug, I laugh my ass off at my tiny, sexy friend.

"Thank you, Darlin'. One more drink and I may take you up on that offer," I grin as she gives me a quick kiss giggling.

"Okay! I have to pee, too," Heather suddenly cuts in as we make our way through the crowd to the other side of the room listening to that stupid Farmer song I hate. What an awful contrast- 'Fuck You' which is sexy as hell, to that stupid farmer song that gets half the crowd dancing as the other half walks off the dance floor for fresh drinks.

Waiting in line, Heather adjusts her blouse, pulling it lower, actually tucking the open edges into the sides of her bra. It's a horribly desperate look, but somehow kind of hot on Heather.

"I know what you're thinking, but I don't care," she suddenly says to me and Olivia.

"What are we thinking?" I ask confused.

"That I look like a slut. But I don't care. Matt's hot, and I want to fuck him. So if lowering my blouse is the way to get him, I'm doing it," Heather smiles even as she pushes her boobs up almost under her chin.

"Why do you want him so bad?" Olivia asks gently.

"Why not? He's super-hot and really nice. He's got a job, he's finishing school. Plus, he knows Neil, and I'm super horny."

"You're always horny," I grin.

"I know. But I'm hornier tonight. He's hot, right?" And without much more prompting both Olivia and I nod.

"Good. I'm gonna make my move soon,"

"*Going* to?" I burst out laughing. "You've been all over him! Look at your boobs, Heather. What move could you possibly make?" I ask dumbfounded.

"I'm going to grab his dick and lead him to the doors. I'll call you in the morning and tell you how it goes," she smiles a near victory smile.

"What if he doesn't want to sleep with you?" Olivia asks even as I'm thinking the same thing remembering his discomfort when she kissed him.

"Yeah, *right*... He wants to fuck me," she answers with finality.

And that's it. We finally make our way through the line in the hallway to inside the washrooms, so we only have the 10 stalls to wait out. Which we do. Silently.

After we're done using the nasty bathroom, and refreshing our lips with the warm lipstick Olivia kept in her skirt pocket, we finally make our way slowly through the crowd back to our table.

Looking, I see Matt is nowhere to be found just as Heather catches on.

"Where's Matt?" Heather yells scanning the crowd to the bar.

"He had to go. He has a paper to finish for Monday morning, but he bought us a round of drinks before he left," Daniel says casually. Looking at Daniel, I realize he's *too* casual, so I know he's trying to lessen the blow to Heather.

"What paper?"

"He's working on his Master's thesis and he said he had inspiration to start a new subtopic."

"Was I his inspiration?" Heather asks excited.

"Maybe..." Neil smiles wrapping his arm around her shoulders.

Smiling back Heather finishes with, "Well, that sucks. But it's kind of cool, I guess." After she pouts, we each nod and smile back at her patiently.

God, I hate this feeling. *Clearly*, Matt blew her off, but Heather doesn't see it. And there's no way any of us would hurt her like that by telling her the obvious. I love her too much to be mean. Plus, that would be her second rejection in one night, which is too much rejection for *anyone* to handle, never mind a drunken, desperate Heather.

Finishing our newest drinks, I feel strangely soberish. My awesome drunk buzz is gone, and I suddenly feel little more than just tired.

"I think I want to get going soon," I say as Olivia agrees.

"But I haven't picked up tonight, Sam. And neither have you!" Heather yells almost as an accusation.

"It's okay. I'm kinda over it," I admit honestly. I don't really need to get laid- I just didn't want to turn down an opportunity should it present itself so I knew if I was making the right decision with Allan or not.

"Condom-chain guy is still looking at you," Neil helps.

"No way. Are you guys coming or staying?"

"Heather?" Daniel asks.

"You can go if you want. I'll just stay a little while longer."

"Not a chance, honey. We're staying if you are," Daniel says as Neil nods yes.

"Do you want to go?" Heather whines.

"Soon."

"Okay. Forget it. I'll just go when you're all ready," Heather pouts for the tenth time tonight.

Twenty minutes later after Neil and Daniel dance together to Closer, *of course,* Daniel fingers the air with a sexy little smile for me, beckoning me to him.

"My turn girls. I'm gonna show up Neil," I laugh as Heather tells me to work my drunken ass.

When I finally approach them on the dancefloor, Neil kisses Daniel and moves away as he high fives me with the down low handslap behind our backs ala Top Gun as I pass.

"He's all yours, baby. Show me what ya got," Neil purrs as he passes with a smug smile when I turn toward Daniel.

"You just wait, sweetcheeks. I'm gonna *kill* this," I grin as he shakes his head with a smile. I'm so going to win and he knows it.

Walking into Daniel's waiting arms we move closely together to the end of the current song until my favorite Portishead song 'Glory Box' starts and then I'm immediately swept into Daniel's arms to really dance.

Being dramatically spun and dipped nearly to the ground Daniel pauses over my chest and looks up at Neil and the girls with a wink and a beautiful smile that quite frankly would make anyone melt- male *or* female.

Laughing, he finally lifts me, raises my leg over his own thigh as he grinds against me until my leg slowly slides back down to the floor.

"You're such a flirt," I swoon as I'm spun around with my arms held tightly crossed against my chest by a swaying, grinding Daniel behind me.

"Only with you and Neil," he whispers in my ear to make me shiver before moving me to face him again. And then there's no more talking.

Dancing with Daniel is sexy and fun. He knows how to hold a woman, and he knows how to tease the shit out of her. In Daniel's arms, I'm fluid, wanton, sexy and weightless.

Daniel makes everyone feel beautiful when he's around. But in his arm's dancing, he makes you feel like you're the reason he lives. He teases and smiles, and just warms every part of your soul.

As Glory Box winds down, I notice more couples are watching us, and though a little embarrassed by the attention, Daniel just stares at me with his magical blue eyes like I'm the only one on the dancefloor.

Turning me again, Daniel lifts my arms overhead, slides his own hands down my arms, past my torso to my hips while nuzzling my neck, and then he spins me again as the song ends.

Finishing our dance with another low backward dip, my right thigh circles his waist for support as he plants a sweet kiss on my chest and cleavage. When Daniel finally lifts me slowly and turns us to look over at everyone- we see Neil actually standing on a chair by the railing clapping as Olivia and Heather clap and catcall the two of us as well.

"You are an *angel*, Daniel. And I *totally* won," I smile as he takes my hand grinning to lead me off the dancefloor.

"Yes, you did. Neil couldn't possibly bend as well as you do. And sadly, he's not *nearly* as flexible," he wiggles his eyebrows and laughs as we walk back to our friends.

"Thank you for the dance, Danny."

Smiling and planting a kiss on my lips, he replies, "Thank *you*, Sammy," as we join everyone at our table.

Bowing in acknowledgment of my dancing victory, Neil kisses me quickly then takes Daniel's hand from me with a growl.

"We're leaving. *Now*," Neil says almost dangerously, and I can't help but think of the very sexy sex they're about to have together.

"*Fuck*, I'm horny!" Heather suddenly yells causing me to laugh at her declaration. "You two shouldn't dance like that when I'm horny. I want to do both of you, but you won't put out," she grumbles to me and Daniel.

"Get over it, babe. He's mine," Neil threatens with a smirk as we all throw back the last of our drinks and start walking for the club exit and the waiting cabs to take us to our individual apartments.

As I settle in for the fifteen minute drive home I realize I didn't get laid, but I didn't shy away from getting laid either. I just didn't want to. I really am sure I want to try again with Allan. So even though I'm kind of horny *and* drunkish, I feel good about my night out. And undeniably, I had fun with my girls and boys.

Suddenly remembering Matt, I'll admit I'm intrigued by him though. He was unbelievably hot, he likes my boys, and he did look honestly embarrassed by being Heather's *walking* dick for the night.

I'll have to casually ask Neil about him to get the real scoop.

CHAPTER 3

Waking to the sound of my apartment doorbell buzzing I quickly look at my alarm clock totally pissed. Without even knowing who it is, I know exactly who it is- *Neil*. The fucking asshole.

Yes, we go for a jog every Tuesday, Thursday and Sunday morning. And yes, we started this 3 months ago when I seriously looked like I had gained weight after Allan- weight I could no longer deny or hide behind my ice-cream. But *still*... We were all out until almost 1:30 in the morning, and he couldn't let me sleep in just a little?

Wanting to scream in my bed I know there's no use ignoring him. The phone calls and texts will start, and so will the singing in the hallway followed by perfectly timed door knocks to the beat of a lame ass song until either I kill him or my neighbors do.

Shit! Throwing my warm sheets off to grab my housecoat, I stumble for the door until just as I get there, I already hear the song he's singing. 'Closer'? *Really?* Ugh...

"Okay!" I yell before unlocking and opening the door a little aggressively to Neil standing there with a huge smile on his face.

Shaking his head at me he looks disgusted. "Have I ever told you how much I hate that rattyass housecoat?"

Groaning, I try to remember why I love him. "Yes, you have. Every goddamn time you see me in it," I glare.

"Then here. Try this on," Neil grins pulling a big La Senza bag from behind his back.

"*Really?*" Okay, now I'm awake and excited. I love Neil gifts, even at 6:15 on a Sunday morning, exhausted, and fairly hungover. Neil gifts are always the best. But he really shouldn't have, and he knows I feel uncomfortable when he buys me stuff for no reason. "*Neil...*" I threaten.

"An early birthday present," he shrugs totally unrepentant.

Pushing past me, Neil also slips a coffee in my hand, kisses my cheek, and walks to his favorite chair in my living room.

"Go! You look hidddddd-e-ouso," he sings before kicking his feet up on the coffee table with a loud sigh.

Running for the bathroom, I pee quickly and rip open the bag to a gorgeous new housecoat. Actually, it's more like a black negligee that lands at my knees with ties in the front and dark blue piping all along the edges. But it's velvety, which feels amazing. So though it lacks the rattyass length of a normal housecoat, the velvety texture makes it feel super soft and comfortable to wear. Yay! I love Neil gifts.

Yelling from the bathroom before I brush my teeth, "You're totally forgiven for being here this early, Asshole!" I suddenly hear from behind the door, 'You're welcome, Fatass!' and burst out laughing.

I kept calling myself a fatass a few months ago, even though Neil and Daniel would argue I wasn't. So after a while I stopped saying it to them, and Neil and I took up jogging three mornings a week to aid my big booty, as my fatass was eventually referred to.

"Hurry up!" Neil bangs on the bathroom door. "I wanna see your sexy ass."

Smiling, I remember why I love Neil again. He is by far the bestest best friend ever, and he is amazing to me always.

Pulling open the door with a flourish and striking a pose, Neil acts appropriately. Clapping his hands together and beaming, his reaction is exactly what I needed.

"Oh, sweet, sweet, Samantha. Even with that hideous pink nightgown underneath, you look *amazingly* fuckable. Even to me," he grins.

"Thank you, darling. I needed to hear I was fuckable even to the gays," I smile giving him a huge hug. Whispering, "Thank you, Neil. I love it," I squeeze him a little tighter to me as Neil whispers back, 'You're so welcome, baby.' And that's it. We pull away smiling as Neil smacks my ass and tells me to get dressed for our jog.

"Can we leave in 20 minutes? I want to have some coffee first to ease my headache. Please?"

"Take a Tylenol," he pushes knowing I don't take any pills for any reason ever. Waiting, he finally agrees grumpily. "Fine. But I have a hot breakfast date with my horny naked boyfriend I don't want to miss, so hurry up."

And with that sexy announcement I turn for my bedroom to get dressed with yummy visions of their hot breakfast date running wildly through my head.

*****

"Have you spoken to your mom lately?" Neil asks as I plop on the couch beside him with my coffee.

"Nope. She's apparently drug free right now according to my dad, but I'm not engaging," I mumble tying my running shoes.

Nodding his head, Neil had the fortune, or rather *mis*fortune of meeting my crazyass mother over the years, and he's never forgotten her. Though true to form, Neil thinks of her with sadness and concern, rather than with the repulsion and loathing he should have based on her horrible appearance and nasty words to him the day they met years ago.

Bumping my shoulder with his own, Neil keeps trying. "Maybe you *should* engage so you can see where she's at?"

"What's the point? She's probably high out of her mind, and my dad, god bless him, is taking care of her basic needs as best as he can while in denial that she's actually high because *she* say's she isn't right now."

"But she's still your mother."

Turning to Neil, I try to remain calm. "Please... just leave it alone. I have nothing to give her right now, Neil. Any money I make this summer is paying my rent, and any additional money I make will pay for extras once school starts in September. My loans will make everything really tight next year, especially with this shitty apartment, and really, I just don't want to," I exhale.

"I know, honey. I just think maybe one day you'll regret not knowing her," Neil says as he leans into my shoulder, implying the worst case scenario.

"I doubt I'll ever miss anything with or about her. But at least one day if she lives long enough I may be able to get her the medical help she needs. I know my dad won't admit she's anything more than a casual drug user, but *I* know she isn't."

"Maybe you could talk to her and explain what you think so she-"

"She'll never listen or change. I don't think she's even capable of changing at this point. Think about it. She's a stay at home, *what*? She has nothing to do in her lovely home but get high. She doesn't go out except to meet her special *friends*, so she just coasts through life high, apologizing, pretending to try, and regressing in the next breath. There is nothing I could possibly say to help her or to stop her," I exhale an irritated breath.

"Maybe if you told her you forgave her for what she did, she'd want to stay clean for you," Neil whispers, treading lightly around the event I refuse to acknowledge or discuss.

"She didn't stay clean for me before then. God, she didn't even ask for my forgiveness that day, Neil. So my forgiveness will mean absolutely nothing to her now, I guarantee it."

"You never know, Sam. Maybe she's been struggling with what she did to you, so your forgiveness *would* actually mean something to her. Maybe she'd even get clean if she had a reason to."

"I doubt it..." I sigh, hoping he's done.

Thinking of my batshit crazyass mother always makes me feel shitty and sad, so a subject change is desperately needed.

"I'm meeting Allan for dinner tonight," I nearly whisper as he pauses with his coffee lifted to his mouth.

Nodding, Neil exhales then waits before speaking. "So you've made a choice?" He asks way too calmly, translating into Neil not approving but not admitting he doesn't approve either.

"I think so. He's been begging for months, and slowly I've forgiven him the more we talk and get to know each other again. I know what I'm going into this time though, and I know what I'll accept." Nodding beside me, Neil is shockingly silent still which kind of hurts.

Leaning into Neil, I need him desperately to be a part of this. I need Neil to support me, and I need him to be open to Allan back in our lives.

"We've talked endlessly about any future between us, and Allan understands that he had *one* fuck up. One only and that's it. I've explained I will never forgive or forget another and he swears he will never give me a reason to not forgive him a second time."

Still waiting for something from Neil, I'm desperate for his input. The silence, almost a distant ache suddenly between us is so rare I can't handle his silent disappointment any longer.

"*Please*, Neil? You and I are forever but I love him, too. And he swears he still loves me and regrets his mistake horribly. So I want to try again with him. I want to try to be Samantha and Allan again, but I do need your support. I wish I didn't, but I do. I love you too much to not have your support with this. It's too big a decision, and its forever, and it's something you will always have to be a part of with us."

"I've got you, baby," Neil whispers suddenly as I exhale a hard breath and squeeze his hand tighter. "I'll accept whatever you want, and I'll give him another chance at a friendship with me if you want. It's just hard knowing what I saw happen to you, and knowing the pain you went through because of him," he continues as I nod against him.

"But I love you, Samantha, no matter what. You know you're everything to me. So I'll support you giving him a second chance if you want me to. I don't think Daniel will be half as supportive though, so prepare yourself, honey. Daniel loves you so much, he absolutely *hates* Allan for breaking your heart the way he did," he whispers, and I know it's the truth.

"Will you help me with Daniel? I need him to be okay with this, too," I can't help but beg. I love Daniel in my life, and I don't want anything to strain our friendship ever.

"I'll work on Daniel. And if I have to distract him with hot sex, so be it," he grins.

Nearly crying in relief, I whisper 'thank you', as he nods his head silently.

Turning to kiss my forehead as he pulls me tighter to him, Neil asks, "I guess I have to stop calling him Buttons now, huh?"

"Yes, please..." I grin as we silence again.

Minutes after our talk while finishing our coffee, I try to relax. "My head is still pounding, Neil. Honestly, I'm not trying to get out of jogging, but it'll kill me if I jog with this headache."

"Too bad. What's the worst that can happen?" He asks standing and walking away from me.

"An aneurism? Brain damage? Barfing in the street?" I moan.

"Oh, *pleeeeeease*. Move it, Samantha," he pushes grabbing the keys from my purse, already opening my door while standing against the doorjamb with the look of a totally insufferable asshole.

"I hate you," I mumble standing to walk toward him.

"As if. Move it, *fatass*," he smiles as he shoves me out the door smacking my ass again.

*****

Once we're 4 blocks from my apartment, finally, thankfully, my throbbing head lessens enough that I can actually jog without holding my head tightly with my hands. Catching Neil smirk at me leaves me no option but to flip him off though, until laughing he takes off at a run I can't possibly match again.

Picking up my speed, eventually rounding the next corner I see him leaning all sexy against a lamppost casually waiting for me to catch up while looking at his watch with a bored expression.

"I may die today," I gasp for breath hunched over with my hands on my knees.

"No, you won't. People like you don't die jogging. You're too sexy and too good to die jogging."

Looking at his smile, I can't help but ask, "Then how exactly *does* someone like me die?"

"In bed, of course," Neil laughs. To my own *as if* expression, he decides to elaborate. "Samantha, you're going to become a doctor, fall madly in love with an Ambassador to a European country, have one child for me and Daniel to spoil rotten, become a goodwill Ambassador yourself, and live to be 91 surrounded by all your family and friends, until you pass away gently in your sleep from old age. That's your future, darling. I know it."

"That sounds amazing Neil, but what if I turn out like-" *my mother* I don't have the chance to finish.

"Not a chance. I *know* things. And THAT my dear, is your future. Dying from jogging is *not* your way out," he grins and starts moving again. "Plus, I have a secret about Matt I was going to tell you before you dropped the Allan bomb on me," Neil teases jogging backward away from me.

"How do you even know him?"

"I met him yesterday at the gym. Samantha and Slayer... Samantha and the Suh-lay-er," he sings.

"What?" I giggle. "What are you talking about?" I beg over his chanting as he smiles and shakes his head at his secret.

"Somebody wants... to suh-*lay* you..." he sings.

Then I see it.

Just as Neil reaches the sidewalk step to the street, the car moving quickly through the intersection doesn't see Neil.
But I see them both.
Screaming and lunging forward, I just make contact with Neil's arm as I pull him and lose my balance in the sudden confusion. Falling sideways as Neil fumbles to grab me in turn, I feel the shock of pain hit my side, until rolling over the hood, I continue falling to the ground to the sound of more screeching.
And then it's over as quickly as it began.
My head bounces sideways off the pavement as I feel the crunch of my own leg under the wheels of the car.
Before I can even think though, I hear Neil screaming above me. He's yelling and screaming, and so goddamn loud my hangover head is pounding again.
When the car is moving again I know it only because the sudden agony that rips back through my leg is so stunning I can't even scream in my shock. I think the front of the car must have been *on* my leg. But I really have no idea what's happening anymore. My head feels so heavy, and almost empty or something.
And the yelling won't stop.
Moving my hand slowly sideways, Neil finally grabs for me.
"Please be quiet, Neil," I sputter kind of choking.
"*Samantha!*" He screams again. "CALL A *FUCKING* AMBULANCE!" Shit. He's gonna kill me with his yelling.
Fighting another little choke, I whisper as best as I can, "Please Neil- stop screaming. You're hurting my head." Gasping a little, I try again, "I need some quiet now."
But I still hear Neil screaming, and now I think I hear him crying out, too. Actually, I think I feel him touching me all over, but I'm so cold suddenly I want to just get warm under a comfy blanket in my bed.
"Can you hold me warm, Neil?" I barely breathe feeling my lungs actually constrict as I try to speak. That last breath of speech was very hard and it exhausted me totally.
"I can't move you, honey. I don't want to hurt you worse. Oh *god,* baby. *Please,* Samantha. Please open your eyes for me? Daniel's going to fucking *kill* me for letting you get hurt."
"You didn't... I..." but I choke again before I can finish speaking.

It's weird, but it feels like I'm choking on my own saliva which I can't seem to swallow down fast enough. Trying to think, I know this situation seems very serious, and as I start shaking uncontrollably I realize I'm really scared suddenly.

"Please hug me, Neil. I'm so... cold. Um, I need Daniel," I cry for the first time. I'm sure I'm in shock but I don't care. I want Neil and Daniel with me for this.

Trying to think of all the do's and dont's during a trauma, I realize I don't really remember them and I don't care either. I just want Neil and Daniel to hold me because I love them so much.

"I love you- and, and Daniel," I gasp again as I swallow and try to breathe.

"*SOMEBODY! PLEASE HELP US!*" Neil screams once before he silences again.

When I feel myself picked up I know he's broken every first aid rule there is, but I still don't care. I need to be held by Neil right now. I need his comfort, and I want his warmth.

Neil and Daniel slept with me side by side to keep me warm for the first horrible week after Allan cheated on me, and they held me when I had my nightmares. It was during that sad time for me that I knew I loved them each beyond all reason and hope. I'm in love with them both, and I know they're in love with me, too. We're such a strange little trio.

"I love you, Neil," I whisper. "I wish we had had a ménage together," I can't help but grin at Neil to ease the horrible tension of this situation for him. Suddenly choking again I let my eyes close for a second.

Feeling myself shaken, Neil forces my eyes back open. Leaning over my face, I think I'm across his legs in his arms on the road. I think, but I'm not really sure of anything except his lovely dark eyes staring down at me.

"When you get all better, we will, okay? Me, you, and Daniel. We'll be together, and we'll live happily ever after together, I promise. Okay, Sam? *O-kay?*" Neil begs shaking me again.

I'm so tired and cold, and I'm not even sore anymore, though I think I must be. I think I even hear more people around the two of us, but everything is suddenly fading away fairly quickly for me.

"Samantha! Don't do this to me. Oh *fuck*. Honey, please stay awake. Daniel will miss you so much- you'll break him with this, baby. Please stay awake for us, okay?" Neil cries to me desperately. "HOW LONG?"

"I don't know..." I moan realizing I actually don't know how much longer I have.

"*Fuck!* Not you, honey," Neil says shaking and moving me painfully closer to his chest. "How long till they get here?" He asks again, and I think he means Daniel and my girlfriends.

"Are they coming, Neil? Will Danny be here soon?"

"The ambulance is ten minutes away, Sam. Just ten minutes, okay?" He says again shaking me. "Come on, Sam. Hold on for us until the ambulance gets here. I'm going to fucking *kill* you if you try to take her from me one more time!" Neil growls as I feel his leg kick out beneath me. But the confusion and noise around me is so overwhelming, I can only close my eyes and try to painlessly snuggle into his warmth.

"Samantha. We have to wait only a few minutes, and then they'll be here and they'll take you to the hospital and everything will be fine. *You'll* be fine. Just hold on for a few more minutes, baby."

"Can I talk to Daniel?"

"How?" He cries desperate sounding. "Here. Just a sec. Just hold on, Sam. I'm calling him for you."

As I'm jostled painfully, I hear Neil tell someone to fuck off again, but I'm sure he doesn't mean me this time. And then I hear real, true panic in his voice for the first time.

"Daniel! *Danny!* Wake up. Sam's been in an accident and she needs to talk to you. No! Just talk to her for a minute. *Now*, Daniel."

When I'm moved slightly again I hear Daniel panic and yell. "SAM! What's *wrong!?*"

Opening my heavy eyes again, I realize I'm lying across Neil staring up at his face as he cries on me. Feeling his pain all around us is breaking my heart for him. God, I never wanted Neil to suffer like this.

Nodding, Neil pushes me to talk even as I keep hearing Daniel yell at me in the darkness that surrounds me.

"I love you, Daniel."

"*WHAT?* What's *happening*?" Daniel begs loudly as I shake my head slightly to say all I can in this moment.

Grinning up at Neil, I whisper, "I love you. And-" But I choke again. Trying to pull in a painful breath, I whisper my final words to Daniel I think. "Neil says we can have- a ménage to- gether... if I stay." When Neil smiles down at me so beautifully, I feel my first real heavy tears fall.

"I have to go now, Daniel. Please love Neil forever. For me..." I whisper because I really have nothing more to say anymore.

If I move I hurt. If I inhale I hurt. If I cry I hurt. So my silent stillness is the best thing for me right now.

"Samantha. I need you to-" I hear Daniel, but I can't hold my head against the phone anymore, and slowly with a nod of understanding Neil pulls his phone from me to talk to Daniel as the sound of Neil's voice slowly fades away from me completely.

Fading, I have a strange moment of clarity and suddenly realize the truth of my situation which is pretty damn funny. I mean really- death by *jogging?* Who the hell could've dreamt this shit up? With a little cough-laugh, I shake in Neil's arms, and say all I can to my dearest friend.

"I guess you don't know... *everything*. I didn't make it... to 91."

Sadly, that one sentence took the last of my breath. Though it was whispered and barely heard I think, that little effort seemed to have stolen the last of the air from my lungs as I gasp and struggle uncomfortably.

"Samantha! Stay with us! Stay! Fight hard, Sam. Oh, come *on*," Neil begs. "I can't live without you, Sam. I can't! It's you and me against the world, remember? We've been together for over 5 years and we need so many more years together," Neil cries shaking me again.

"*SAMANTHA!* Choose. To. Stay. Look at me. Come on baby, *STAY*!!" Neil yells against my face as he kisses my lips again and again.

I really want to stay but I feel myself being pulled away.

Opening my eyes again, everything is so dark and cloudy except Neil's eyes that shine brightly on me as I suddenly panic.

"How... do I stay?" I beg on a gasp, but I can't hear Neil's answer.

Oh, *god*... I can actually feel myself slipping away.

How do I stay? What do I do? I want to stay but I don't know what to do, and I'm so afraid of leaving.

I didn't know dying felt like this. I thought it was just you and then not you. I didn't know you could actually feel your body dying away as you die away. I never would've thought death was so clear as it happened.

I wish I could see the future, and I wish I could figure out what will happen now. I wish I knew what to do.

Suddenly, I realize I don't know my reality anymore. Whether Neil is still speaking or not, I can't hear. Whether Neil is still shaking me or not, I can't feel. Whether Neil forgives me or not, I don't know.

I do know Neil and Daniel will always be the best love I have ever known.

"Choose. To. Stay. Samantha! Make the choice to stay."

I hear Neil but I think it's too late for me. And I still don't know what to do.

Oh... it's all fading to darkness for me now. And I really don't want to go.

Choices...

CHAPTER 4

Slowly waking again, I try to take in my surroundings. I've done this slightly awake trip a few times I think because I kind of know things, but I could never quite hold on long enough until now to *really* know things.

I do know I'm in a hospital though, and I know I'm alive which is good because honestly I kinda thought I wasn't before. Plus, I have pain everywhere which again confirms I must be alive, because nobody ever says we still have pain when we're dead.

Looking down my body, I see first my raised leg in traction, looking post-surgery wrapped and swollen but I don't remember why. What the hell did I do? I know I was jogging with Neil this morning, but that's about it. I must've fallen jogging. Goddamnit, he'll never let me live this one down, and neither will Heather.

Trying to move to pull the forced oxygen tube from my nose, I'm stunned still again. My chest is *killing* me. Oh my GOD! On a gasp and wince, I stop moving my arms immediately as the pain winds me. I must have cracked ribs or something. Jesus, talk about a fall. So, I've hurt my ribs and screwed up my leg. Trying to assess my body I realize everything else hurts and is throbbing painfully as well.

"Samantha?" *Really?* Oh, this sucks. Where the hell is Neil when I need him?

Turning my head slowly, I see first my mother, then my dad holding her shoulder from behind. What the hell is she doing here? I have no idea, and I find I can't even really speak to ask.

"Samantha, you're in the hospital," she whispers stating the obvious.

"I can see that," I reply deadpan as my throats screams and my lungs ache. Though somewhat rude, I'm hoping the whole hurt ribs thing lets me get away with not speaking to her much.

"Welcome back, Samantha," my dad says with a huge smile. "I'm going to tell the nurses you're awake again." Moving to my side, my dad takes my left hand and squeezes my fingers gently.

"Okay," I moan then gasp.

Jesus! My *everything* hurts, so that's all I'm saying. I don't care that my mom is looking at me expectantly, I'm not talking to her. It hurts too much, *and* I can't stand her. So here's my perfect excuse to just ignore the nightmare of my mother sitting anxiously beside me.

"I chose to get clean, Samantha. It's been 8 days..." my mom suddenly says quietly in my hospital room.

Like I care. What the hell is 8 days to her? Nothing. 8 days is a 'Shit! I can't find any pills!' Or a 'My doctor won't give me another prescription for all my imaginary pain for a few weeks'. Sadly, it can even be just an 'I can't find a good dealer on the nice streets in the city'. *Whatever.*

8 days is nothing so I don't acknowledge her statement. 8 days is nothing but words at this point because we've experienced 8 days hundreds of times in the last 15 years. Plus, a few days ago, my dad already told me she'd been clean for weeks which means she lied again. Big surprise there.

Before I can ignore her statement for longer, which really is just hanging in the air of my bright hospital room, my dad returns with a nurse.

"Hello, Samantha. I'm Christina, and I'll be your nurse on duty this evening. How are you feeling?" She asks gently while typing all my vitals and stats on a tablet.

"Horrible," I whisper then flinch again. Flinching hurts as much as breathing and talking does, so I'm kind of screwed.

"I'll administer more pain meds and a sedative for you. Right now, sleeping is the best medicine," she says moving around my room to the pain control machine. "These are measured doses of morphine, so you can't take too much. And here is the handheld button so you can take more as you need it," she says kindly placing a little device beside my hand with Velcro attached to the sheet.

It's funny, my whole body is in agony, and all I can think about is my junkie mother. She's so close to a machine filled with vials of morphine that I swear to god if she knew which tube in my body actually had the straight line to the drugs she'd rip it from my body and stab herself with the needle to get a fix. I can't help almost laughing at how fucked up this situation seems. Wow. This must be so hard for her.

"Samantha? I'm Doctor Danieli," the doctor I didn't notice entering says trying to get my attention. Oh, sorry, Doc. I was too focused on thinking of my junkie mother. "You had quite a fall 8 days ago." Huh. 8 days? Superb timing, mommy. It totally makes sense though. My mother always did get clean for a few days during or after a big drama. It's usually when the drama fades that things get really interesting with her.

"Samantha?" The doctor says again in my face with a penlight suddenly shining in my eyes. "Can you hear me, Samantha?" He asks again, as I try to focus on him for a minute.

"Sorry, I'm having..." gasp "... a hard time concentrating," I whisper with a groan. Talking fucking *hurts!*

"Okay. Then let me break it all down for you. I know you're pre-Med so I'm sure you want just the facts. Right?" Yes, I nod. I don't need drama, I just want to know what's going on with me and how I get better.

"You had an accident last Sunday morning, and it's now the following Monday evening. You had a collapsed lung from impact, a broken tibia and open fracture, and a severe concussion with a small fracture on the left side of your skull, near the frontal lobe. Amazingly, you've experienced no brain swelling, though we've preformed 2 Cat Scans and an MRI anyway to be sure. Your ribs are cracked with one actually broken, so taped up, and your lung is re-inflated, though the cracked ribs are going to make you feel like you can't breathe or even move comfortably, which you won't for at least a few weeks. Still with me, Samantha?" Dr. Danieli smiles, so I nod again.

"Will she be okay?" My mother suddenly asks, and I hate her. Glaring as best as I can, my mother slumps back into her chair a little further from me and stops speaking.

"Please go on," I moan.

"There's nothing we can do about the small skull fracture, which seems to be knitting well on its own. You did however have surgery last Friday on your broken leg, once your lung was finally stabilized. The Ortho team used Intramedullary nailing on the tibia, one upper and one center, near the actual fraction, but not close enough to the open fracture to cause further swelling or potential infection. Any questions so far?"

Looking at him, I already feel confused and totally overwhelmed. What I need is a list. Lists always make me feel better.

"Ummmm... Would you mind just..." gasp "...listing the injuries? I need to hear each one singularly..." small breath "... so I grasp the potential effect and recovery."

"Very methodical. I get it. Okay... You have a slight fracture in your skull which is healing. You have 4 cracked ribs, and one break straight through which are taped and slowly mending. You had a collapsed lung, a pneumothorax with the removal of the excess air through a needle and suction tube. Your lung, though inflated, will be monitored closely for infection, and forced oxygen will remain for at least another day, maybe 2. Your leg was broken right in the center of the tibia and nails have been inserted to hold it in place for at least the next 4-6 months. You have an open fracture on the front of your leg, but it's been disinfected and stitched up, along with the surgical entry and exit points." When the doctor takes a much needed breath, I nod my head at him in understanding.

"Samantha, you're a very lucky woman. And you're already healing at a rapid pace. But this recovery could be very long for you- much longer than I think you realize. Though saying that, you also have youth on your side, so bones heal faster and knit better before 30 years old. Plus, I understand you don't smoke or do recreational drugs, which is also a bonus for healing quickly. But you will have an enormous amount of pain for the next few weeks while the open fractures and the skull fracture heals. And your lungs and chest will feel very tight and extremely painful for at least a month. Do you understand everything so far?"

"Yes, thank you. Is there anything else?" I kind of whisper. "When can I leave the hospital?"

"Minimum 5 more days. 2 days on oxygen, then at least 3 days without to make sure your lung stays inflated and functioning at optimal level. You're to stay on fluids through an IV line and feeding tube which will help provide nutrition, prevent dehydration, and improve the blood flow to your lung. I'm sure you know the right balance is needed to ensure that your lung doesn't fill with fluid so blood and oxygen can reach all your body's other organs. When you're released you will have an open cloth cast with stabilizing pins, and you need to start Physiotherapy immediately."

"My skull?"

"Will hurt," he grins, and I almost laugh. But thankfully, I hold my side and smile instead. Laughing right now would kill me I'm sure.

"What do I do now?" I ask trying to move a little without adding pain to the absolutely everything that already hurts.

"You rest. Sleep all you can and take the pain meds as frequently as the machine allows. While at the hospital, you have an endless supply of pain reliever to help you sleep past the initial trauma. Of course, when you leave you'll have a prescription for anti-inflammatories, a heavy treatment of antibiotics for infection, and a pain reliever, probably Demerol with an anti-nausea mixed with it. You'll be given a diuretic to help avoid fluid buildup, and an inhaled bronchodilator to open the air passages. Plus, depending on the symptoms, I may issue single injection morphine for the first week you're home- long enough to keep you comfortable, but not long enough to make you dependent or addicted. What else can I answer for you?"

There are so many things I want to know, but I'm already exhausted. I can't handle all this pain everywhere, and I really don't want to think about all the negatives facing me. I have an uphill battle for sure, which will interfere with my summer job and potential schooling in September.

"Nothing right now."

Looking over at the morphine machine, I realize I desperately need a hit, so I take it. Squeezing the little handheld button, I immediately see the green light change to red with a slow decrease of cc's along the side of the machine. I'm getting a dose, and I think I'll feel great- okay *minimally* better in about 2 minutes.

"I'm just going to sleep for a bit," I mumble.

Smiling, he seems to understand where I'm at. "Of course. I'll be back to check up on you a little later."

"Thank you," I groan trying to shimmy down my bed a little. I know I'm raised on my back on purpose, but I can't sleep like this. I need to be on my side to sleep which doesn't seem possible with my leg in traction or with my chest taped and heavy. I know I need to move, but I don't think-

"How can I help you?" My mother asks softly, and I instantly cringe.

"You can't."

"Samantha, please. I'm just trying to help you."

"Where's Neil?" I ask instead of listening to her pretend attempt to parent for the thousandth time since I was a kid.

"The *gay* friend?" And there it is. My mother's horrible, homophobic tone.

Coming from a junkie, I can't believe she has the nerve to discriminate against gay people, or against *anyone* for that matter.

Feeling angry, in pain, frustrated, and so over this moment, I answer all I can. "Neil. My best friend, and my *family*," I give her a little dig.

"He's been here, Samantha," my dad jumps in running interference as usual.

Suddenly feeling totally stoned, and really, fairly emotional as my tears well up I realize I want nothing more than to see Neil and Daniel. Desperately.
   "Can you get him for me, daddy?" Pulling out the daddy card is pathetic, but I need it to work and I don't care how pathetic I sound right now. I'll just blame the meds later.
   "You're in the ICU, Sam. So only immediate family is allowed," my mother tries to sway me.
   "They *are* my family," I say with obvious slurring to my mother again. Turning my head to look right at my dad as the weight of the meds kick in heavily, I beg again. "Please, dad? Please put Neil and Daniel on the list as my brothers or something. I need them. Okay?"
   As my eyes start clouding over, I know I've won because my dad is already nodding at me with sympathy. Knowing he understands, and wanting the comfort of my boys, I exhale slowly. Feeling physical and mental relief, I finally let go as the drug haze takes me.

*****

   Slowly waking again, I try to reason where exactly all the pain is coming from until I realize it's still everywhere. All over. Everything I am and have ever been is drowning in pain. I'd almost laugh at my melodrama if I could, but I think even laughing would kill me right about now. Christ, how long since I took a hit of painkillers?
   "Samantha?" *Oh!*
   Opening my eyes, I see Neil and he's all I need- well, almost all I need. Trying to hold it in, I can't. On a gasp, a sob breaks free as I moan his name.
   "Oh, baby... I'm here. You don't have to cry, Sam," Neil says as he moves right up to my face to stare at my eyes. "I'm right here, honey."
   Still crying, I stare at his beautiful brown eyes and watch as they slowly tear up as well. Forever, we stay staring at each other, until Neil leans over, snaps a tissue free and gently wipes my nose under the breathing tube.
   I feel so emotionally horrible all of a sudden. Physically I'm in agony,

but my heart hurts for some reason.

"I think I'm really sad, Neil," I whisper as a tear rolls down his cheek.

Leaning in to kiss my forehead, Neil breathes deeply and stays still against my face. Feeling like he's guarding me safe from anyone seeing me breakdown, I finally just bawl my eyes out. I cry a good, long, cathartic, pain-filled, sad cry, with Neil keeping me hidden from the room around us.

I cry for the pain, and I cry for the ugly circumstances I suddenly find myself in.

When my crying slows, and my breathing feels horribly labored, Neil finally pulls away and gently calms me until I slow down.

Whispering soothing words, Neil begs me to breathe slower and easier so I don't hurt myself, and slowly, I calm myself down enough to pull in a deeper, painful breath before I panic at the loss of air in my lungs.

"Good?" He asks quietly a few minutes later.

"Marginally," I smile. Pausing again, Neil finally breaks our silence by asking how the pain is. "Brutal. Who would have thought jogging could cause such injuries," I wheeze sarcastically.

Smirking, Neil replies, "If it was just the jogging, I'd give you your excuse to never jog again. But I'm thinking the car was probably the culprit in all this."

And that's when I realize, I don't actually know how I got hurt. I remember hearing I was in an accident, but I don't think I was awake long enough over the past few days to actually get the whole story from my dad.

"I was hit by a car?" I ask Neil feeling totally confused. "Because I only remember jogging with you." And breathing as best as I can I continue, "Oh, and you running away from me when I was gasping for breath," I moan gasping for breath again with a grin at the irony.

Shaking his head, Neil releases his own breath before he speaks. His behavior suggests he's having a hard time speaking which again is so rare for Neil its making me a little nervous.

"What happened?" I push.

"Oh, Sam... You were hit by a car pulling me out of the way," he says choking up which only confuses me more. That's a good thing, isn't it?

"Then why are you so sad?" I ask confused.

"What do you mean why am I sad? Look at you. You're hurt, and banged up, and broken all over. I thought you were going to... but then you fought back and you're here, and I begged you to stay over and over again, and you did. I was so sure you weren't going to be okay because you looked so bad on the street, but you're alive. And you saved me from getting hit, so of course I'm sad. If I could trade places with you, I would in a second," Neil cries to me.

"Well, I wouldn't. This super sucks, but I'm glad you're okay. Can you even imagine Daniel if *you* were hurt like this?" I ask wheezing again, but Neil doesn't engage my joking.

Shaking his head again, Neil whispers, "Daniel would be as fucked up over me as he is over you right now. He loves you so much, Samantha. And he's been devastated over this. Once your dad put us on the family list late last night, Daniel pushed right past your mother, and threw open the door to see you. He's been here for the last 11 hours straight waiting for you to wake up again. The only reason Daniel isn't here at the moment is because he's talking to one of the Doctors to figure out what you'll need, what he can do, and what we'll all do to help you recover."

"Oh... But Daniel-"

"Blames me for letting you get hurt. And he's kind of pissed at you for getting hurt, so he's been in a super pissy mood since last Sunday. And I'm telling you I'm either going to bitch slap him soon, or fuck him against a wall to get him out of his mood," Neil says with a sad smile.

"But-"

"Samantha, Daniel is freaked right out about you being hurt, *not* that I blame him, I've been sick over this too. But he's just so fucking angry right now. He ripped a piece out of your mother when he heard her whining and crying about her *precious daughter* and her injuries to some woman, and he never acts like that. You know that."

And I do. Daniel is always calm, beautiful, and intelligent. He sees the good in everyone, or finds the reason for the bad in someone.

"What do I do?" I ask nervously.

When Neil visibly flinches at my question, he practically yells, "Nothing. You did enough. Now you just rest and get better, and you let me take this heat from Daniel."

"I don't understand why he's angry. Daniel is-" When the door opens to Daniel, I stop speaking immediately.

Standing for a moment in the doorway, he glares at Neil, then turns to me with a smile. In an obviously strained voice, Daniel asks Neil why he didn't get him as soon as I woke up.

Quickly looking between them as he speaks, I can see the hurt on Neil's face, and the anger radiating from Daniel. I can see and feel the tension between them, and it isn't right.

"Danny?" I whisper as he immediately walks to me, nearly pushing Neil out of the way to take my hand.

"Hi, honey. God, you scared me, Sam. *Please* don't ever do anything like that again," he begs.

Okay, I can see I have to fix this quickly. "Don't do what? Save my best friend from getting hurt? Because-"

"Sam-"

Shaking my head, I cut him off and continue. "Because I would've done the same for you, just like you would've done it for me or Neil and Neil would've done it for either of us," I rasp. Pulling in another deep breath, I try again. "Please don't be mad at Neil. I don't even remember the accident, but I know I would save him again from getting hurt if I could."

"Then you're an idiot," Daniel snaps making me feel like *I* got bitch slapped. "Oh, god... I'm so sorry," Daniel moans leaning his head against my thigh. "I didn't mean that at all. I've just been so stressed out and worried, and I needed to be mad at someone for your accident. I'm very sorry," Daniel chokes up.

Looking at Neil, I see a stream of tears falling down his face, Daniel is nearly crying, and I want to cry. God, this is so awful, I'm desperate to fix it.

"This isn't very hot, guys. You're losing all your hot gay points, quickly," I try again to lighten the mood. And though Daniel huffs a smirk, he's not quite over it. "I'm going to be fine. I have a long recovery, and my leg is pooched for a long time so jogging is out- *yay*. But I'm going to get better. And as long as I don't move, or breathe deeply, or like move any part of my body, I'll be okay," I smile again as Daniel releases a much needed breath.

"Fuck, I was scared," he admits. "After Neil called me, I met you both at the hospital and seeing all the blood around your mouth and body freaked me right out. You just looked so mangled, and horrible, Sam. And you wouldn't wake up for me," he moans.

"Well, I'm awake now. Okay?" I say softly, squeezing his hand to pull him back to the present with me. "Daniel. I'm awake now."

"Okay..." He exhales. And I can sense I almost have him back.

Smiling, I squeeze his hand again. "You look awful. Like unshowered, unkempt, and totally un-gay, my dear. I'm horribly disappointed in you," I grin as Daniel looks at my face and smiles.

"It's hard to look put together when you're scared shitless, Sam. And *really?* Like you look any better?"

"But I'm not gay. Or uncharacteristically gorgeous. *And* I've been hit by a car. So suck it," I grin.

"I wish…" Neil mumbles behind us, and I can't help but laugh, then flinch, then scream, then grab for my own chest again as Daniel jumps forward to help somehow.

"Sorry, baby," Neil moans stepping forward around Daniel to kiss my forehead in apology.

"*Pleeeeeease*, don't make me laugh, Neil. Not for a week at least, okay? This hurts. *Badly,*" I moan as he nods.

Feeling horrible, pain-filled, and exhausted again, I look over at my meds machine and need another hit.

"Can I get you anything?" Neil begs as I shake my head no. "A magazine? Your t.v. is hooked up if you want to watch it. Do you need a drink or anything?"

Shaking my head again, the pain is becoming overwhelming. "I need to take some medication so I can sleep for a bit I think. Did the doctors tell you everything?"

Talking quickly, Daniel gives me the highlights. Wheelchair for first 4 weeks because of my ribs, maybe longer. My leg looks good and is stabilized but it'll be months before I'm stable enough to use it without a cast of some kind. My head looks good, considering. My lung is taking to the oxygen well. Essentially, for being smoked by a car only 9 days before, I'm doing really well- the pain notwithstanding.

"What happened with my mother?" I ask Daniel who looks a little shocked that I know. Glaring at Neil, he simply shrugs off Daniel's look.

Turning back toward me, Daniel exhales his visible anger and confesses. "She was being a dramatic bitch, and she blocked us from the room. So when I heard her talking about her *precious* daughter who she doesn't give a shit about, I lost it on her. I caused quite a scene myself, and Neil had to physically pull me away when your mother started crying. I'm sorry, but she just pushed my buttons too far crying about you to another mother in the waiting room. I didn't mean to, but I told her off. I didn't mean-"

"It's okay, Daniel. My mother is famous for her dramatics. Right, Neil?"

I smile as Neil laughs a little.

"Yes, Samantha. Remember the time she called me out for being gay?" He shakes his head as I smile.

"Yup. I believe she even used the f-word that time."

"Yes, that's right. 'A useless Fag- corrupting her impressionable daughter,' or something like that."

"Setting me up to go to hell with you."

"Because a fag is going to hell, and all the *good* people will be laughing at us when God punishes us," Neil finishes our sentences with an eye roll and a dramatic sigh.

"So please, Daniel, don't feel bad about telling her off. My mother is a walking contradiction. A lying, cheating, stealing junkie who believes somehow *she's* going to heaven, while a *useless* gay is going to be punished," I say with a dramatic sigh, gasp for breath, and an eye roll of my own.

"Okay. I feel way better about telling your mother off now," Daniel laughs as Neil moves to hug his side.

"We good?" I ask.

"We're getting there," Daniel replies softly. "What do you need, Sam?"

"Nothing right now. I'm really tired again, and the pain is brutal, so I want to push this magic button," I say looking at the Velcro'd button beside my hand. "Then I'd like to sleep. Can you both please go home and clean up? This is not the visual of my beautiful boys I want when I wake up again. Please?" I grin, and I know things are getting back to normal when Neil bends at the waist then curtsies.

Pushing the button, I always find it almost soothing watching the waiting green light change to red as the dose line slowly decreases. It's methodical and exacting. And if this was what being a junkie was like, I could almost see the attraction. But it isn't almost like being a junkie, so I haven't warmed to my nasty mother in my pain-filled haze. I really do hate her.

"Go to sleep, honey. I'll see you later this afternoon," Daniel whispers against my forehead as he kisses me again.

"What time is it?" I'm suddenly curious.

"Around quarter to 8, I think. They let us stay all night after we were given permission to be here because Neil flirted with the only gay he could find in the ICU wing," Daniel grins with a huff as I smile back.

"A boys gotta do, what a boys gotta do," Neil pipes up as I feel the world slowly fade around me.

My body is already growing heavy, and my mind is fighting to stay awake for them. My eyes are fluttering opened then closed again, and I think I'm almost out when I hear a faint whisper.

"Let go, Sammy. Stop fighting it..."

CHAPTER 5

Waking again, I see Allan's head resting on my bed. Hunched in the chair beside me, he can't possibly be comfortable in his sleep, but I don't want to wake him if he actually can sleep like that.

I was wondering when he would show up, and here he is. I wonder what he felt when he heard about my accident, and I wonder what he felt when he realized I was too hurt to meet him for dinner Sunday night.

Looking at his head, I see his hairline receding slightly which I've never noticed before. Grinning, I touch the thinning hair and wonder if he'll be a bald older man. I don't know what his grandfather on his mom's side looked like, so I'll have to ask him one day. Something tells me though that even balding, Allan will be an attractive older man, which I kind of look forward to.

I like the thought of growing old with Allan by my side. I like imagining our beautiful children, and maybe even our perfect grandchildren in the far future. Smiling, I can almost imagine the kind of house he'll build us, and about the neighbourhood our children will grow up in.

I know I'll probably spend less time with our kids than a typical mother would because of my career choice, which does worry me some. But I also know I'll try to make them feel as much love from me as I possibly can whenever I *am* with them.

I'm actually quite comfortable with the fact that Allan will have to be a major player in raising our children when I'm a doctor. And I don't think Allan is the type to ever resent me for it, or not want to do it. Over the years we've often spoken of our little future family with happiness, and Allan has always been excited about being a dad in our future, which excites me, too.

I've always wanted children, well, at least one child, but two preferably. Knowing from my own experience as an only child, things can be quite lonely, if not devastating when you're forced to be an adult before you should. There is no one to grow up with but your parents, and if they suck like my mother did, your childhood kind of sucks too.

Anyway, after our rather quick and dramatic breakup, I truly believe Allan has changed, and I believe he'll always support me emotionally through my schooling and afterward. I believe he'll always work hard at our relationship from now forward, just like he's promised he would if I ever took him back.

Allan hurt me terribly 6 months ago, but in a way, I can almost understand why he did it. Okay, that's not exactly true. I don't understand *why* he did it, but I believe *he* believes the reasons behind why he did it, which truly helps me understand his choices a little better. Eventually, I even started believing the story he told me because it really did ring true of the circumstances we were in at the time.

Basically, he was scared and a little bored, which though hard to hear, made sense too. We started dating young and we spend almost 4 years together. We were very comfortable with each other, and though there wasn't really a spark anymore, there was still love between us.

Allan admitted he wanted to propose to me before he cheated. He admitted he was going to propose before I started Med School, but then he became a little scared of committing himself to me forever. He watched his friends screwing randoms at bars, and he panicked a little more, until the opportunity struck one night to experience something more before he committed to me fully, and sadly he took it.

He admitted she was hot, unknown, and all over him. Naturally, hearing that made me want to scream in pain, but I kept it together long enough to hear him out.

I didn't excuse his actions, but somehow I understood why he did it a little better. It was almost an itch he wanted to scratch before he settled into forever with me. It was something he needed to do before he committed to me fully so he was sure he *could* commit to me forever.

But again, I didn't allow him to excuse his behavior, I just listened to the *why* of it.

After that rather exhausting phone conversation, when I finally learned the answer to his cheating, I remember thinking, why didn't he just break up with me, see what else was out there, and then decide if I was what he wanted in life, instead of hurting me so badly. I thought it and then I asked it out loud to his stunned silence.

After forever, Allan finally said, 'I've always loved you, Samantha. And I didn't want to hurt you by breaking up with you. But honestly, I didn't think I'd get caught. Then I just didn't know what to do after Neil caught me and threatened me and told me to stay away from you. So I did stay away, until I realized it *was* you I wanted, and would always want for the rest of my life.' And it was that honest confession from Allan, which was the turning point in my hatred for him.

I started understanding a little more, but certainly not forgetting. And now we're here. I'm in the hospital, and he's sleeping next to me with his hand on my thigh as he rests.

Brushing his hair again gently with my fingers, he finally wakes up on a gasp as he sits up too quickly and looks around the room all confused and panicky.

"Shhhh..." I whisper as he acclimates. He has always woken up strangely confused and dramatically fast, almost like he was freaked out, or preparing to fight for me or something. It was usually funny and almost comforting to me when we were together, but now it just seems a little sadly nostalgic.

"You're awake. I just heard, Samantha. Neil only called me last night when I was allowed in the ICU, that's why I wasn't here sooner. I promise that's why," Allan says all anxious.

"It's okay. Neil and Daniel were only let in last night too I think, or maybe yesterday." Grinning, I'm feeling a little confused myself. "Whenever. It doesn't matter. You're here now," I reply breathless still.

"I'm here," he moans. "How are you? I mean, I know you're hurt, but how are you? Can I get you anything?" He asks again still fidgeting like he doesn't know what to do for me.

"I'm okay, and I don't need anything right now. How are you?"

"I'm good. I'm so glad you're awake. Neil freaked me out when he told me what happened. He made you sound so bad, like I was going to walk into your room and see you dying or near death or something," he shakes his head like he's relieved.

"You do remember how dramatic Neil can be, right?" I grin as he nods. "Then you should have known I wasn't on death's door if he was even speaking."

When Allan doesn't reply, I know there's something more. I know he's freaked out, because he's never this quiet with me. Allan and I have a very heathy, verbal relationship, and silence has rarely been a part of us, unless we were in a fight of course.

"I'm going to be okay, Allan."

"Are Neil and Daniel going to take you home? Are they taking care of you when you get out?"

"I assume so. I thought you and I would discuss it before I was released though," I say a little hesitantly as I try to pull in a full breath.

"When are you getting out of here?"

"A few days, at least. Allan, I'm okay. I probably look much worse than I am. What's wrong?"

"I wish I knew about this sooner," he moans as I take his hand again.

Smiling, I try to soothe him as best as I can. "I'm sure Neil was just waiting until he had something to tell you. Plus, you couldn't visit anyway."

"I wish I'd known sooner though..." Allan whispers again as I start to feel panic growing inside.

"Look, if I hadn't been in the accident I would've been having dinner with you Sunday night and we would've been okay. This is just a little setback, but we'll work through it," I try to reason with him. Allan is being much more reserved and distant with me than usual.

"You were meeting me Sunday then?" He asks quietly staring at our joined hands.

I can actually feel the tension in his body by the way he's holding my hand tighter than necessary. I can feel the tension growing, and I can feel my own upset starting to mimic his.

"What's wrong? Just tell me," I breathe quietly.

I think I know what's wrong. Though honestly if he tells me what I think is wrong is actually what's wrong I'm going to fucking kill him.

Lifting his head and looking at my face super dramatically he inhales deeply before he finally spills. "I didn't knew you were in an accident on Sunday."

"*Allan...*" I almost growl.

Inhaling sharply again, Allan spews his guts all over me. "I slept with Monica Sunday night because I was pissed off that you didn't show up. I didn't mean-"

Exhaling a hard breath and reaching for my own chest which feels like its suffocating, I moan all I can. "Get out of here."

Attempting to turn over and away from him I can't move which makes me feel like an idiot, and helpless, and fairly annoyed with my own inability to move, my situation, and with my own stupidity.

"Get out of here. Now," I groan.

"Just listen, please."

"No."

"*Please*!" He begs again.

"No," I shake my head as the pain in my body increases.

"Samantha, please. I didn't know you were hurt."

"Get out."

Walking around the bed, Allan tries to face me, but I turn my head away again. It's a little childish, but seeing as I can't fucking stab him, or beat the shit out of him, or like even raise my voice because I still have oxygen being forced into my body, all I can do is turn my head away from him again.

"I thought you blew me off. I thought we were finally getting back together and then you didn't show up and I felt depressed. So I-"

"*Fucked* someone else."

"No! Not like that. I was upset and Monica-"

"Stop talking, Allan. *Please*..."

Cringing at his attempt to explain, I wish I could scream. I wish Neil was here so he could scream for me. I wish I could scream every disappointment of every single thing this man who claims I'm the love of his life has done to me this year. I wish I could make him understand what he's done to what was once us. But I doubt he'd understand anyway.

"If I had known you were coming, I wouldn't have gone to Monica's."

"Oh, *god*... Please, Allan. Stop talking. It's done. You went to Monica when you thought I didn't come to you. You poor little baby. You felt slighted by the woman YOU slighted so you went to someone else within minutes. Did it even cross your mind to call me? Did you even think there may be another explanation? Somehow I doubt it." Gasping for breath, I need to finish this nightmare. "I was meeting you for *dinner*, Allan. That's all you said you wanted. That's what you said. Dinner with me so you could see me again, because you *missed* me. It wasn't a make or break it. It was just dinner. But I was going to use that dinner to surprise you by agreeing to give us another chance. It was just *dinner*," I wheeze again struggling to breathe.

"But you weren't there," he tries to justify his actions again.

"The fact that you feel bad proves you're a scumbag, and that you know you were wrong. Otherwise you wouldn't be here defending yourself, and you wouldn't be trying to pathetically justify any of this."

Finishing that little tirade almost did me in. The last words were wheezy and nearly whispered, but still effective I think. Allan isn't moving or even trying to move while I try desperately to pull much needed air back into my lungs as all the pain in my body suddenly screams again.

"You did this. You made a choice. You chose to sleep with someone else when you thought I wasn't coming back to you for *dinner*."

"I was upset-"

"There's nothing else to say. So get out."

"No, I want you to understand how I felt when you didn't show up for dinner."

"When I was hit by a car and fucking *DYING*!" I scream once and stop. That's it. I'm not risking my health for this piece of shit. I'm not doing this ever again. I never should've believed him in the first place. Once a cheater, always a cheater. I'm the fucking idiot here. He's just the asshole.

"Get out, Allan."

"Samantha... just listen. I was only with her because I thought you didn't want me anymore. I promise, Sam. I love *you*, not her."

"Oh, god. Shut up," I can't help moan. "I'm going to call the nurses and have them make you leave. Your name will be removed from the family list, and I never want to see you again. We're done here."

"No, we're not!" He yells close to my face, honestly surprising me with the anger directed at me.

Taking in his demeanor, I can't believe he actually thinks he's the wronged person here. I can't believe he has the nerve to stand there arguing with me. Actually, I can't believe he's still here at all. It's over and he's lost me forever.

"Go back to Monica. She actually wants you for whatever reason, so you may as well take her."

"I don't want Monica. I want *you*," he whines.

"Imagine I died in the accident and take your comfort from her. Because I died to you last Sunday as far as I'm concerned. You may as well pretend I'm dead. You made your choice. And now you can move on with Monica. Without me."

"Look, I'll come back tomorrow and we'll talk things over," he continues like there's actually a hope in hell of me ever speaking to him again.

Exhaling, I realize I'm not even sad about this. I'm resigned. Allan and Samantha are over. Forever. And really, I don't even care anymore.

"Goodbye, Allan." Somehow those words held the strength of finality behind them though they were words merely whispered.

Waiting, neither speaks, and after what feels like hours, Allan finally walks around my bed toward the door.

"I just wanted to be happy again..." he says so quietly he sounds pathetic.

Laughing at his back I want to throw up. "Then go be happy with Monica, Allan. She'll take you."

"We're not done yet," he says holding onto the punch bar of the door.

Laughing again, I say a very sarcastic, "Okay, Allan. Whatever you say," as he pushes the door open with a loud bang.

Still laughing at his arrogant denial of our obvious end, I turn for my morphine and decide on a little pain relief. Physically or emotionally, who gives a shit after the day I've had?

Thinking back to when I was awake and asleep, I think I know I didn't even ask for Allan once when I was hurt. No one has told me I did, and he wasn't informed sooner about the accident, which means I probably didn't ask for him. Even Daniel would've respected my wishes and called Allan sooner if I had asked for him. But I'm pretty sure I never did.

I know I needed Neil and Daniel with me. And I know I wanted Heather and Livi around. But until I saw him sleeping on my bed, I don't think I really thought about Allan through all this trauma, whether I was asleep or barely awake.

I guess both Alan and I made a choice that Sunday.

CHAPTER 6

Okay. I've had enough. I'm out of the ICU, and I'm finally free to leave this afternoon. Though everyone has been very kind to me, I'm going stir crazy and I want nothing more than to go home. I *need* my comfy clothes, my uncomfy couch and my own television while I recover.

My friends have come off and on every day for the last 3 days I've been in the normal ward to try to entertain me as best as they can. But I'm exhausted from being here and desperate to get home. It's like I'm on an endless vacation without any sex, sand, sun, or booze.

Preparing for home I've been sponge bathed and dressed, but my hair is disgusting. I can actually scratch my filthy head beneath the greasy, dirty hair and cringe. I'm breathing much better as well, yet my ribs hurt so badly no matter what I do, I find it hard to do just about anything. And though my skull barely hurts now, I think that's more of an in-comparison to all the other bigger pains I'm suffering.

Unbelievably, I've been in the hospital for 15 days, and I'm getting out today.

During my freedom from the ICU, my girlfriends came by to give me outside world updates whenever they could. I was told Olivia decided to work it out with Matt, and Heather is still looking for someone to love, though she would never say anything so sad or telling.

I've learned Allan has sent me dozens of flowers, a teddy bear, and has called frequently. He even came by a few times to see me after our awful showdown but was somehow blocked by either my boys, or by Heather.

Actually, I heard he was even stopped once by a very pissed off Olivia. For being a tiny little thing, Olivia can be verbally kickass if need be, which apparently shocked the shit out of Allan. So Allan relented but still calls way too frequently, forcing me to hang up on him just as frequently.

Anyway, when I finally told my friends what happened between Allan and I, they freaked on me. Daniel and Olivia were shocked I ever thought of going back to him, and Heather was surprised that he actually thought I would *still* go back to him after what he did a second time with Monica.

  Even I'm surprised he still thinks he has a chance with me if he's patient, because I thought I made it pretty clear he doesn't have a chance in hell. Just the fact that he's still screwing Monica, which he doesn't know I know shows me his insincerity and desperation before and after my accident.

  I've come to realize Allan doesn't want to be alone. Period. I think Monica probably isn't meeting his emotional needs like I did, but she IS a warm body. So he's doing her while trying to get me back. But again, he doesn't know I know he's still screwing her, or that it wasn't just the one time when he was 'depressed' because I didn't show up for our reunion dinner like he implied it was.

  Amazingly, before I could even tell my friends what had taken place between me and Allan, Neil ran into Monica the very next day and she sheepishly admitted she and Allan were a couple.

  So there you have it.

  My ex-friend stayed in camp Allan, and now she's doing my ex-boyfriend, while said ex-boyfriend begs me to give him another chance behind current girlfriend's back.

  Christ. They deserve each other

  My dad and mother have been by almost every day as well, though those visits are sad and awful. Honestly, my friends lighten my mood when they visit, but sadly, my parents depress me while they sit here uncomfortably.

  I even (almost) felt bad once for my mother. Heather was telling me and Daniel another one of her stupidly hilarious stories while I tried not to laugh or move while the two of them were dying laughing, until the door suddenly opened to my mother- then whooooosh. The laughter stopped, and the humor fled right through the opened door with her arrival.

  Pausing, we all stopped everything, and I almost felt bad for her standing there, totally insecure, knowing she was the cause of the sudden atmosphere change. In the momentary silence as I looked at her I realized she looked so sad, she made me feel sad for her. But then she glared at my *gay* Daniel and my momentary *almost* sympathy disappeared as quickly as it arrived.

Even with the accident, nothing has changed between us, except for the fact that every time she sees me she gives a one sentence update. 'I've been clean for 10 days now... I've been clean for 12 days now...' etc. I can't wait to hear her say it today on the 15th day while I still give her no reaction.

I honestly don't care how many days she's been clean, no matter how often she says it, or how much she actually believes she'll stay clean this time. She won't stay clean, because she can't.

My mother isn't just a junkie, she also has severe mental health issues without the official diagnosis- though one day I'll get it. My dad won't be able to protect her, and I'll be a doctor, so I'll have someone officially diagnose her, which she needs desperately. Then maybe, once she's treated properly I'll entertain her. Until then however I need to keep my distance for my own self-preservation. I *need* to hate her, so I don't feel anything for her. I need to hate her so she can't hurt me ever again.

Honestly, I don't hate her because she's sick though. And really, I'm not the bad person here. I hate her because of what she's done when she's sick- which could sound like an excuse for her, but it isn't.

She chooses to not stay in rehab, just like she chooses to be a horrible person when she's high. She also chooses to forget I'm her daughter, and not a bank or a whore when she needs a fix. And *that* is something I will NEVER forgive her for.

Attempting to whore out her 18 year old virgin daughter to a disgusting, fat, old man who suddenly showed up in my bedroom so she could get a weeks' worth of whatever she was on that week is my absolute unforgivable with my mother.

Luckily, nothing happened to me that day though, but not because she intervened or changed her mind. Nothing happened because I saved myself- my mother did NOT save me that horrible day.

Once I saw the man enter my room and begin closing my door to the jangle of his belt buckle being loosened, I screamed bloody murder.

I screamed loud, blood-curdling screams, one after another. I screamed *rape*, and *fire*, and *help* so loudly, the man panicked, threw my door back open and knocked my mother to the ground outside my door. But I still screamed.

As my mother sat on her knees in the hallway holding her right cheek, I screamed until I saw her crying which prompted me to gasp a breath as I stopped screaming as suddenly as I began.

In an absolutely surreal moment, I was crushed by the silence after my screams while my mother cried quietly in the hallway on her knees.

And in that silent moment, I did feel bad for her- for one split second. I almost went to her until she whispered sadly, 'Now what am I going to do?' And that absolute stunning reality that she wasn't crying for me smacked me in the face like a 2x4 across the head.

My mother was crying because she didn't get her drugs. She was NOT crying because a strange, fat, smelly old man wanted to rape her 18 year old daughter in her own childhood bedroom so she could get high.

So after the 2x4 awakening, I did what any 18 year old girl would do- I screamed at the top of my lungs, "I FUCKING *HATE* YOU!" And her reply? 'I know. But don't tell your dad what happened, okay? He'll be really hurt by it because he loves you, Samantha.'

God, I remember after she spoke those words shaking my head to clear it. I actually physically shook my head back and forth like they do in cartoons, because I just couldn't believe what I was hearing. Eventually though, I shook my head clear of the drama, and she died to me in that exact moment.

She didn't say she loved me, and she didn't say she was sorry. She didn't even attempt to lie or make up an excuse for what had happened in my bedroom.

My mother understood I hated her with no emotion whatsoever, and then she said my *dad* loved me. She couldn't even say she loved me herself, or that it made a difference if I loved her back.

I remember wiping away a single tear sliding down my cheek and deciding I would never again cry over the horrible woman who was my mother. I realized she didn't deserve my tears, my sadness, or my love anymore, so I wasn't going to give her the feeling that she was still cared for or loved by her only child. She didn't love me enough to keep me safe, so I was never again going to try to keep *her* safe.

Sadly, she died to me that day. I've just been waiting for her to finally die in real life ever since.

When I finally realized the sad reality between us, walking past her in the hallway outside my childhood home, I remember feeling the urge to kick her. Actually, I *really* wanted to kick her. But thankfully, I didn't stoop to her level, nor did I act out all my fantasy rages on my mother.

I simply walked past her with nothing but shock and disgust and I called my dad from the kitchen phone as calmly as I could to beg him to pull strings at the University to get me into a dorm. And after my dad's initial surprise he asked what happened, so I told him the partial truth.

I remember exhaling a hard breath before I said, 'Mom did something unforgivable, and I hate her. But she's asked me not to tell you what she did to me because *you'll* be hurt by her. So I'm done. Ask her or don't. I really don't care anymore. But get me out of this house before I kill her, daddy. Because I will.'

Amazingly, after my words and the brief pause following my statement, my dad said he'd make it happen, and he did just that.

My dad is a high school biology teacher and he's friends with the vice chairman at the University, so I guess he pulled whatever strings he could while I waited. I slept at Heather's house for the 4 days needed until I was allowed to move into the dorm on a Monday morning, midway through my first semester in University.

After that day, I returned to her home just once to quickly pack up my old room with Heather and Heather's mom, Linda, while my dad kept my mother away. I moved the extra stuff I couldn't take with me to the dorm to Heather's basement. And I packed all my clothes and necessities for my new home in Scarlet Dorm. I moved out that very day and I've never been back to my childhood home since.

I left all my music, and books, and trinkets, and everything else I thought as a teenager was important, and I took only what I felt I truly needed in my new life away from the douchebag that was my mother.

Incidentally, I've had every Christmas, Thanksgiving, and Easter dinner with Neil in our dorm, and then at our apartments as we grew up. I've celebrated my birthdays with my dad and Neil in restaurants without her, and I've visited my dad at his school if I wanted to see him. As I said, I've never been back to my mother's house for even a moment to visit my dad, and I never will.

My childhood home died with my mother the day she tried to sell me for a fix.

But the best part of that horrible story- the irony of all ironies- because of what my mother did, I moved into the dorm mid-semester, and I met the beloved Dorm Leader, Neil Hastings.

I met the only man allowed in the all-female dorm after the 10:00 curfew, who was totally gay, loved by everyone, and really, my life saver. Because of my pathetic, homophobic, junkie mother, I met Neil, one of very few people who have ever truly loved me unconditionally my entire life. Because of my mother, I was given the *fag* who I would love forever. And that irony alone is too funny not to remind her of whenever I have the chance.

Bitch.

*****

Waiting for Daniel, Neil has already packed up my room, boxed all the flowers and gifts, and helped me get dressed in a pair of walking shorts over the open cloth cast, metal, and bandaging. Dressing, I realized my one leg looks pretty gnarly with all the screws, bruises, and bandages, but funny enough, it was my other, gross, hairy leg Neil had a *major* problem with.

Cringing as he touched my hairy leg, he mumbled he was going to have to watch a video on shaving lady parts, as I burst out laughing, then screamed a little in pain to grab my aching ribs again.

The laughing thing around my very funny friends and my boys is becoming a real problem for me. But at least they've kept me entertained and reasonably sane in the hospital until I can finally leave, if Daniel ever gets here.

"Where the hell is he?" I whine.

"Any second, Sam. He already called when he left your place, so he'll be here any minute. Be patient. What the hell else can you do?" He smirks at me. "The nurse isn't here with the wheelchair rental anyway, so just chill. You sound like a little bitch," he laughs as I swat his arm.

"Sorry... I just want to get home."

"Soon, honey. Then we'll get you all set up, and you can relax while 2 hot men take care of your every need and desire," he wiggles his eyebrows as I raise my own.

"*Every* desire?"

"Maybe..." He grins as I swoon.

"You're such a vagina-tease, Neil. Seriously."

Laughing, he smiles his sexy Neil smile. "I know. I have the whole dicktease/vaginatease thing down pretty good, don't I? I'm thinking of giving-"

Gasping, "Oh, god. *No...*" I interrupt Neil totally stunned as Daniel and Olivia walk into my room.

Pushing a wheelchair covered in pink velvet or something, there's a pink horn attached to one arm, fringes hanging from both arms, and a red glittery, like platform or something where the feet should go. I can't even speak until Daniel swings it around and shows off the back of the chair. 'PRINCESS by day...' in huge black letters screams against the soft pink material.

"... *Slut by night,*" Neil adds as I sit there with my mouth hanging open.

Choking, "I can't," is all it takes for them to love my horror in this moment. Olivia jumps up and down clapping, as Neil jumps up to do the same with her beside my bed.

When Daniel grins at me he admits, "It was all them, but I tried to help, Sam. I really did. I was totally out bitched with this one though." All I can do is nod at Daniel shocked.

"Ummm..." I've got nothing. I can't even believe what I'm looking it. This is like a hidden camera episode. What will she do? Give in, or have a full-out hissy fit? *Shit.*

"Don't you love it? I called you Princess, but Neil added the 'by day'. It's friggin' adorable isn't it? Come on. Get in!" Olivia laughs at my still stunned expression, but I start to rise anyway as Neil turns to help me.

"Just go with it, Sam. This is way too much fun for the rest of us. You know, we've been stuck waiting for you to get out of the hospital forever, so we need this," he says like an ass.

Leaning into Neil, he helps me slide my bad leg forward slowly as my ribs threaten to crack again from the strain of rising.

Honestly, I just need one of the pains to lessen a little. I need to focus on healing one thing, not two. But I guess I'll just have to get used to it all as I struggle from one day to the next.

Parking the chair behind me Daniel holds it still, and wraps his hands around my waist as Neil gently helps me sit. The thought of crashing down in the wheelchair is enough to give me the sweats, but thankfully, I'm lowered slowly and gently into the softest wheelchair ever.

"Okay. This is the most comfy chair ever, but still, *Princess by day*?

Don't you think there are other people out there besides you sexual freaks who know that expression?"

"We hope there are," Olivia giggles. Smiling back, I'll admit this *is* kind of funny, though I really wish it was to one of them instead of me.

"Alright. Let's go," I give in. Accepting my fate, I know there's no point fighting them. I'll never win.

Once outside I realize no one can really see the *Princess by day* with Daniel pushing me from behind so I feel a little less paranoid. But then I panic thinking about Neil's jeep as we make our way outside to the front patient loading zone. I don't know how I can possibly handle getting in, never mind handle all the bumps and banging his jeep is notorious for.

"Um, Neil? I don't think I can get in your jeep," I say nervously as Neil lifts the back hatch and places all my gifts and flowers into the trunk.

"We'll help, honey. Don't worry. And I promise I'll drive slowly to avoid every pothole on the road. It's only 6 blocks. Okay?"

"Okay..." But I'm still nervous of all the pain coming.

Waiting at the side, Daniel walks to the other side of the jeep and gets in while Neil helps me slowly stand.

"Turn sideways so Daniel can slide you in," Neil says as Olivia nods.

"Come on, Sam, lean back and let me help you," Daniel whispers in my ear giving me a shiver as Neil laughs at my reaction. Wrapping his arms around my waist, I'm lifted and slid until I'm in. Slowly being slid across the seat as Neil lifts my bad leg gently, I'm up against Daniel with my leg extended across the backseat. The pain is brutal in my chest at first, but when I lay back a little more against Daniel, the tightness lessens slightly as I relax. Exhaling softly, I'm sure I can do this.

"Just breathe, Sammy. I've got you," Daniel whispers again as Neil closes the door, fights putting my ridiculous wheelchair in the trunk, and runs around to the driver's side as Olivia hops in the front.

"Daniel Zakkary Reeves... You have GOT TO stop breathing in my ear," I whisper feeling him shake with a little laugh against my back.

Suddenly homebound, the drive is slow, and Neil is amazing like he promised. We make it back and the jeep exit is essentially the same but backward. Neil holds me from the front this time, as Daniel slides me backward out until my good foot touches the ground and though almost doing the splits in the air, slowly, my bad leg is lowered again as I'm gently placed in the waiting wheelchair Olivia holds steady.

By the time we get to my apartment doorway though I'm totally exhausted. Waiting for my door to be unlocked I know it's time for pain meds and more sleep.

*****

  Opening the door to look in my apartment I'm struck with the weirdness of everything. I've only been away for 15 1/2 days, but I feel so strange opening my apartment remembering the last time I left it.
  I remember Neil swatting my ass to get me moving for our jog. I remember jogging, and complaining, and I remember my hangover headache. And then all I know is pain.
  I have no actual memory of the accident, but it has been explained to me in detail from Neil, so I kind of feel like I remember it.
  Neil told me the accident was a slow motion, everything stops in a millisecond trip through hell for him. He explained seeing me spinning him out of the way, getting hit in the side of my ribs to watch me fall sideways off the hood. He remembers seeing the car bump over my leg because the driver was too shocked to actually stop her car. Then he too remembers almost nothing of the next few minutes.
  Neil says his memories become clear again when he was telling me to stay awake. He doesn't know how long it took for the ambulance to arrive, and he barely remembers the driver of the car, who incidentally wasn't charged because Neil admitted he crossed the street without looking.
  Neil even blocked out all the blood surrounding us, but he clearly remembers asking me to stay with him. He remembers begging me to stay and swears he'll never forget that moment between us for as long as he lives. Neil remembers begging me to stay for him and Daniel, but that's all he says he remembers, which is okay.
  I don't remember anything about the accident itself, and I don't want Neil to have to suffer with the horrible memories of it alone.

  Once we enter, again, I'm overcome with the weirdness of everything I see and feel.
  My apartment looks bizarre. All the furniture is against walls and clustered together, creating no gaps between furniture, or pathways

against carpets. My apartment is suddenly a weird open space with every single piece of furniture pushed up against every available wall surface.

"We moved everything around so your wheelchair would fit," Olivia says helpfully.

"Thank you. It just looks so cluttered and weird, doesn't it?" I ask looking around at my chaotic looking apartment.

"Yeah. But you can get to the couch and right through to the kitchen in your wheelchair with the table moved."

"I guess... Daniel would you mind pushing me to my bedroom. I'd like to lie down for a while," I practically moan. "Oh, and I need my purse and a glass of water too, please."

"No problem, honey. The hot Doc said you'd get tired quickly," Daniel nods moving me slowly to my bedroom.

Making the corner is slow because with my leg extended there isn't much room to navigate around the hallway, but eventually we make it to my room safely.

Once in my bedroom, I tell Daniel I need to get out of the chair by myself. Struggling to lift my body hurts my ribs terribly, but I need to practice. So slowly, painfully, I manage to stand and slide myself across my bed just as Neil and Olivia arrive with my purse and a glass of ice water.

Looking at my 3 friends as I gently lie on my bed, I'm overwhelmed with the emotion and exhaustion of my situation. Fighting tears, I choke up a little and thank them for all their help, even as they brush off my gratitude.

"I'm staying for the day and night," Olivia says sitting gently beside me as she goes through my purse and takes out the meds I need. "And those 2 are trading off for the rest of the week."

"But you have work."

Shaking his head, "Nah. We both took time off work this week to help you settle in," Neil speaks before Daniel, and their kindness does me in totally.

Crying as gently as I can, I find my face buried in my hands, as Olivia soothes and comforts me as best as she can.

Feeling embarrassed by my crying, I mumble, "I'm just tired. Sorry..." to Olivia's, 'Of course you are, Sam,' until I eventually stop crying beside her.

Wiping my wet cheeks with my fingers, I take one last look at my friends, drink down the meds, and settle back into my bed slowly. I really am exhausted from just this little physical movement, and I desperately want to rest again.

"Thank you for being here," I whisper to Olivia's shining eyes, and Neil's beautiful smile. Bending to me Daniel kisses my lips gently and tells me to sleep, which I do, almost immediately.

*****

Waking in the dark, I really have to pee. I mean I knew I'd have to go eventually, but just the thought of getting back up, getting to the bathroom and using the toilet makes me want to cry again like a wuss.

So after a long, annoyingly painful, exhausting journey, I finally find myself in the bathroom and again I want to cry when I turn on the light and see the gross that is me.

Jesus *Christ*. I smell, my hair is a greasy, nasty train wreck, and I'm pale and tired looking.

When there's a knock on the hallway outside my slightly opened bathroom door, I say come in as Olivia enters looking like she desperately wants to help.

"Um I have to pee, and I have to shower, and, um, do you mind seeing me naked?" I blush as she laughs.

"Nope. I'd *loooooove* to see you naked," she responds with a cheeky grin. "The nurse we spoke to before you left told us how to wrap up your leg for a shower. Wait here, okay?" Nodding a duh as Olivia takes off, there's nowhere I could possibly go.

10 minutes later I'm garbage bagged and duck taped from ankle to upper thigh leaning against the wall with Olivia's hand against my hip. Slipping my shorts down my legs, Olivia fake shudders at my hairy good leg, then proceeds to get a pair of shorts and t-shirt to change into for our shower.

Alone, I turn to collapse on the toilet with a little scream of chest pain, until I finally pee while she waits outside for me to finish. Somehow being naked and showered by Olivia seems less embarrassing than peeing in front of her, and thankfully she totally gets it.

   Once we slowly get in the warm shower together after I finish using the toilet, Olivia is awesome. She makes little jokes about showering with me, and she is helpful and attentive while I try to stand in the shower. Stripping off my long t-shirt and bra last neither of us acknowledge all the bruising and scars on my chest, though Olivia does dramatically pause staring at my boobs with a smile until I swat her away.

  "Just help me, ya perv," I say as she laughs at my pitiful swat. "How's Matt?" I question needing to ease my naked embarrassment.

  "Good. We're trying to have a real relationship, and he's been better about all his guys' nights this past week. So, I've decided nobody's perfect, except for Daniel- If only he didn't *prefer* the dick," she smiles. "Anyway, I'm just going to ignore the little annoying things about him. For now."

  "Are you happy, Livi?" I whisper.

  "Pretty much," she nods. So I let it go.

  Olivia would talk to me of there was a problem, so I have to assume Matt is really trying for her.

   Holding my hips and back against her front she gives me the opportunity to wash my nastiness away. Eventually, she even reaches over and hands me the hand held shower head so I can clean myself better.

  "Let me wash your hair for you. Can you stand alone for a minute?"

  "Yes, please," I beg holding the tiled wall and balancing as best as I can on my good leg.

   Olivia proceeds to wash and rinse my long hair twice, and extra conditions it because the knots and tangles were hard to work through with her fingers. Being extra gentle at the front of my scalp to avoid the stiches, Olivia rinses me clean again, and I could just about kiss her for helping me. I feel so much better, less gross, and less everything else once I'm clean.

  "Just so you know, Daniel wouldn't allow anyone else to be here last night but me," Olivia suddenly says above the sound of the water.

   Amazingly, she's answering a question I wouldn't dare ask for fear of sounding bratty or self-centered. But honestly, I did wonder why Heather wasn't here and why my boys left me so quickly.

  "I won because I had a few days off and I convinced him I could be here

24/7 while you got readjusted. Neil threw a fit of course, and Heather was sad, but Daniel insisted they leave you alone for a few days. That's also why the boys left last night so you didn't feel overwhelmed, or like you had to entertain the bunch of us. I just thought you'd like to know. Oh, and Allan was denied *all* access to you which he's pissed about, the dickhead. Um, Neil also told your parents under no uncertain terms that they were NOT to come over unannounced because they wouldn't be allowed in. So there you have it. We all wanted to be here when you returned, but Daniel pulled rank, and set up your visitation schedule," she laughs.

"Thanks for letting me know. Maybe I'll pull rank over him and invite everyone over tomorrow for a little I'm home party."

"He'll kill you. You know how protective he is, especially with you. Are you almost done, Sam?" She asks. Nodding, I'd love to stay in the shower forever, but honestly my good leg is starting to struggle holding up all my weight.

After helping me slowly step out of the tub, Olivia dries and clothes me in my hideous pink pajama dress I love. Helping me walk slowly to my room after she removed the garbage bag from my leg, I don't even attempt sitting back in the wheelchair just to have to rise again in seconds.

When I make it to my bed, Olivia gently brushes out my hair, and strips herself of her wet clothes to put on a pair of my comfy sweats.

"Do you need anything else?" She smiles sweetly as she squeezes my hand.

"Thank you so much, Olivia. You're been so good to me, I can't-" but I almost start crying again so she stops me.

"You would do this kind of stuff for any of us. You *have* done this stuff for us. Remember when you dealt with that asshole for me, or when you took care of Neil after he was beat up 3 years ago?" Ugh. I almost flinch, but just catch myself in time. That is so not a memory of a broken Neil I want to relive right now.

"Please... I get it. I'm just saying thank you. It's not every day a girl gets to shower with her girlfriend naked," I grin to fight my tears.

"Maybe not for you..." Olivia says with another smile. "Okay. What now?"

"I'm exhausted again. I just want to sleep if you don't mind?" Looking at the clock I see its 2:47am which explains my complete exhaustion.

"Go to sleep, Sam. No thank you's and no apologies. The boys said they'll be here by 9, so you have a few more hours of peace and quiet. Your hair's all wet though, do you want me to wrap it up or dry it for you?"

"No, it's okay. I figure it can't look worse than it did before it was washed. Thanks, Olivia." Holding her hand I move my leg over with her help and lay back down to sleep again. I wish I could take another pill, but I know it's too soon for me.

With a final smile and a sweet kiss on my forehead, Olivia makes her way out of my room, closes the door, and within seconds I feel sleep bearing down on me again.

Exhaling before I feel myself pass out, I'm impressed I made it through my first night home without losing my mind from the constant pain and struggle. Fading, I'm more than ready for this nightmare to be over though. Quickly.

CHAPTER 7

Waking to a soft touch and bright light all around me, I fight being awake as hard as I can.

"You have to wake up, Sam. I know you're tired, but it's been 3 weeks since you got home. You've done nothing but sleep for 3 weeks and it's time for you to get back into life now," Daniel says softly.

Opening my eyes, I blink Daniel clear and see he has Neil with him as backup like he threatened to do some time ago. An hour ago? A few hours ago? I really don't have any idea when, or really what time it is anyway.

"I'm sore..." I moan trying to turn to my other side while Daniel sits next to me and helps push me gently to my side.

"I know you are. But you're going to continue being sore if you don't get out of this bed. You've already missed 4 Physio appointments, and I don't think they'll hold your spot much longer. Come on, honey. It's time to get up," Daniel says again trying to pull the covers off me, until grabbing for them quickly, *unbelievably* I forget for a second that my chest hurts and as I move I'm bombarded with all the goddamn pain again.

"*Fuck!* I'm so tired of this shit," I cry out furiously. I'm not a whiner in life- I'm a doer. I get things done and I succeed. But his little trip through a pain-filled hell has just sucked the life right out of me.

"Daniel, I don't want to get up yet. I will though. I promise." I try begging again even though I'm fairly sure I won't win this time.

"Sorry, Sammy. You're getting up this time." Shit. I knew it.

Huffing my frustration, I try one more time. "Can I be a total bitch for a minute?"

"Of course you can," Daniel smirks at me. "But remember Neils right here, and he can out bitch anyone. Are you sure you have the strength for it?" Daniel asks, and again, I know he's right. But I just don't care anymore.

"Look... I know you're both trying to help, but you can't help me. And I'm tired of thanking you for all the help you do give me. I'm tired of sleeping, but I'm too tired to get up. And I'm tired of feeling shitty, but I *feel* shitty. I want to get up, but I'm not ready. So *please* fuck off.

Nodding, Daniel actually grins at me. "That was pretty good, Sam. But Neil is *way* better. Neil?" Even as I brace for it, I know this is going to be brutal.

"Samantha. *Darling…*" He drawls out. "You smell like shit. You look like shit. And you're an ugly, bruised, nastyass mess. Basically, I can't be friends with you anymore if you continue looking and *smelling* like this. So, get off your fucking ass, get your shit together, and get the *fuck* in the shower. Daniel will hold you up if you want while I hose away all the nastiness, or you can have a little pride and do it yourself. But either way darling lamb- in the next 3 minutes you're going to be hideously, odorously naked in the goddamn shower. Understood?" Odorously? *Really?*

"Neil, fuck *off*. You don't get to tell me what to do."

"Choose, Samantha. We do it, or you do. You have 3 minutes to get yourself in the fucking shower one way or the other. Do NOT try to out bitch me, lovely. You have never won before and you won't win this time. Get. The. *Fuck*. Out of bed."

Feeling like I'm going to cry again, I reach for Daniel and try one last time. "Danny, please… Just a few more days. I'm so tired and I need-"

"To get out of bed, Sam. I'm sorry, honey, but Neil's right. You have to start moving again so you heal a little better. You need-"

"*Please?*" I cry desperately.

Leaning forward, Daniel half hugs me and lowers his voice to reason with me, I can tell. "This isn't you, Sam. You're a tough cookie. I know you still hurt but you have to find the strength to get up. It's been 5 weeks since the accident, and you've done little more than sleep and take pain meds. And I'm nervous, baby. I think you're becoming a little too dependent on the pills and-"

"You really think that?" I gasp shocked.

Nodding yes to me, I'm stunned. I'm not a junkie. I'm nothing like my mother. I don't get addicted to things, and I would never take too much of anything. I am NOT like my mother.

"I only take what's prescribed. I don't take any more than that."

"You were allowed to take double doses the first 5 days you were home. You were given instructions which included the double doses 3 times for 5 days to be lowered to a single dose 3 times a day as needed. But you're still taking the double doses *every* day, and you're not even trying to slow down."

"I am. I just needed... I thought I was still taking the right amount. Honestly." But even as I say it I think I know I'm lying.

Part of me seems to remember thinking I should ease up on the pills a while ago. I think I remember when Heather renewed my prescription for me I knew it was way too soon, but... *shit*.

"Um, I think maybe I am taking too many. But it's not on purpose. I just need them for the pain still," I explain desperately so they understand.

"Sammy, that's what everyone says who becomes dependent on pain medication. Think about it. You *know* this. You've even studied this. The person starts justifying the usage until they don't even remember why they shouldn't be taking as many as they do as they take them. Think about your mother for a second. She-"

Suddenly feeling angry at such a disgusting comparison, I can't stand hearing any more of all this shit. "Stop. I get it, Daniel. Okay, I'll cut back and watch it. But it doesn't change anything. I'm still just as sore as I was the first few days."

"But you're also as inactive as you were the first few days. You do nothing Sam, and it's starting to show. Your legs are losing muscle mass, and you're getting very thin. I know you're weaker than you used to be, and it's obvious you're not recovering well."

"I'm trying," I whisper but before Daniel can speak Neil jumps in.

"You're not trying anything, honey. And I get it- you're sore and it's easy to give into the pain, but as Daniel said this isn't you. You don't give in or give up. No. Look at me," Neil says as I turn away. "Samantha. Look at me," he growls until I do. "I love you to death, baby. And I'm very sorry this happened to you, but it's time to get better now. You have to. You start school again in less than 3 months and you have to be up and at least walking around on crutches by then. But you don't have enough strength yet to even hold them, never mind use them. You have to start stretching out your chest muscles again. You've been lying down so afraid of the pain from your ribs, you're actually making your chest tighten up worse. You're going to hurt for so much longer by not dealing with the hurt now."

"Neil..." I try to get his attention.

"I know this has been hard. And quite frankly it's obvious you're also dealing with depression either from just the meds, or from a combination of the meds and the horrible pain you're in, but you have to try now, honey. Do you understand what I'm saying? I talked to your doctor and Daniel looked up-"

Exhaling hard, I've had enough of this lecture. They have NO fucking clue what this feels like, but I'm pretty tired of it all myself. This has been a pain I think I need to get out of. It's time to get out of this painful purgatory now, I think.

"Okay. Done. Can you both get out of here and let me get up on my own. I'll take a shower and I'll move around a little, okay? But please no more tag-teaming, and no more lectures. I know you're trying to be helpful which I guess worked, but I don't really want to hear it anymore."

"Okay. Do you need any-"

"No. Leave me alone. I'll meet you in the living room when I'm done."

"What about wrapping your leg? I could help you," Daniel offers but I shake my head no.

Sitting up slowly, I shake my head again. "I'll do it. It's fine. Could you both just go away now," I plead totally exhausted by everything.

Leaning over me, Neil kisses my forehead and whispers 'I love you,' as I nod against him. I know he does, and I know Daniel does. But right now I just don't care. This weird painful trip through hell has been beyond annoying, and to be honest I'm a little annoyed with myself as well.

They are totally right though. I should've been moving by now, and I should've been trying to get around. I know that. But it's hard to do something when you feel like shit, even if you know you should be doing it anyway. I just didn't have the strength to get up and do what I should've been doing, but I'll find it.

Once I'm garbage bagged, and the water is running, I finally take a look at myself in the mirror and I *am* gross- embarrassingly so. I look pale and stringy, and pretty hairy actually. Looking, I laugh a little at my hairy everything which I let go to shit when I couldn't be bothered to move or function. Ugh... I'm like a skinnier looking version of Chewbacca. Well, maybe not that bad, but still, I'm pretty bad.

Turning the water back off, I slide my shitty leg kind of behind me so I can reach slowly and painfully under the sink for the bottle of men's hair remover cream Neil left here. I've never used it, preferring to shave, but under the circumstances strong hair removal cream makes more sense to start with than a dozen razors does.

When I hear the knock, I feel almost pissed again. Reining it in though, I open the door a crack, hiding my naked body to Neil asking what's wrong.

"I heard the water stop."

"Don't worry Neil I'm still going to shower," I answer a little bitchily. "Can you get me a magazine?" With nothing further, and no bitchy comeback, Neil leaves to return seconds later with 2 magazines as I close the door on him.

And then I get to work. My good leg, the top of my bad leg, my bikini line and lady parts, and even my nasty underarms. I am a gigantic white, stinking mess, with the horrible hair remover egg-Sulphur stench all around me. But eventually I sit on the closed toilet, grab a magazine and wait the required 10 minutes before scrubbing myself female again.

In the shower, I scrub away everything, and though a few parts are still a little hairy, mostly I'm good enough that a little reach with the razor is all I need. Washing my hair is quite painful because moving my arms up and over my head still kills my ribs, but slowly I manage.

And honestly, I feel a little bit human and more like my old self when I'm done. I even feel a little better emotionally though I'm somewhat dizzy either from standing for so long, or from the meds, I'm not sure.

When my good leg's toe nails are cut, and I'm wrapped in a big towel, I finally call out for Daniel.

"Yes?" He answers immediately. Shaking my head, I realize he must've been leaning against the damn door the whole time. "Are you okay?"

Smiling, I open the door a little as all the steam leaves the room to see both Neil and Daniel standing there with their arms crossed leaning against the wall looking anxious but annoyingly gorgeous as usual.

"2 things- one kind of gross and one easy."

"Hit me," Daniel says with a smile.

"I need my toe nails cut on my bad leg, and I need clothes and the new robe Neil bought me before the accident."

Before I can even finish, Neil has bolted from the wall and he's already in my room as Daniel laughs and enters the bathroom beside me. When I slowly sit back down on the toilet, Daniel is already squatting on the floor to lift my leg against his thigh. Without any acknowledgement Daniel removes the garbage bag, ignores my still hairy warped leg, and takes my toes in his hands to begin cutting the nails I can't reach because of the cast.

"Thank you," I whisper as Daniel gives me his beautiful smile with a nod.

"You look so much better, honey. I'm sorry we were so hard on you."

"Don't be. I'm sorry I was so awful. I've never been hurt like this before, and *clearly* I don't handle pain well," I admit just as Neil places my new robe and clothes on the counter with a *thank god* before he leaves us alone again.

"There was more than pain, Sam. Your mother coming around, and what Allan did, and all the phone calls you kept having to avoid from him. Plus the accident which would've freaked anyone out. I think it all just became a little too much for you. But I know you can do this. You're Sam. And I need you back, okay?" Daniels exhales slowly looking at my face.

Staring back in the quiet between us, I feel almost a sadness coming from him. "What's wrong?" I ask touching his cheek, actually feeling his upset all of a sudden.

Looking at his beautiful blue eyes and his handsome face, I don't know if the sadness was always there and I was too upset myself to see it, or if maybe he hid it from me as I recovered. Whatever the reason, I see it now. "Tell me," I push.

Finishing my toes, Daniel seems to shake his head before looking back up at me. Relaxing on his shins, I can tell he's sad from his posture alone. Oh my god. What *is* it?

"Are you sure? This time is about you right now," he whispers.

Quickly nodding, "Yes, I'm sure. I'm sick of me, and I'm already feeling a little better. I want to know what's wrong. You can trust me," I nearly beg.

"I know I can trust you, Sam. Okay…" he says again before another little pause until he looks back at me and begins. "Things are just a little strained between me and Neil right now. It's not anything specific, but we're just not quite the same. We love each other, and we still go home to each other, but we're different somehow. There's something between us, and I think it's coming from me, though I don't know what it is," he exhales again. Waiting, I don't speak but rather hold my breath as he collects his thoughts.

"We're not cheating, or fighting, or anything really. But there's a tension or something, and I know Neil hates it as much as I do, but I don't know how to fix it. I don't know if it *can* be fixed."

"Of course you can fix it," I can't help interrupt. "You love each other so much," I gasp. I am so upset by this sudden shock I can barely hold in my tears. "Oh, Daniel... when did this start? Nothing happened?" I ask again in total disbelief.

"Not really." But I can see there's something.

"Tell me, Daniel. Tell me so we can fix it. Then you and Neil will be perfect again and everything will be perfect again. So we can all be perfect again," I almost cry.

Standing up and leaning against the wall away from me, Daniel seems to be struggling with what to say. Watching him, my heart is pounding. I've never seen Daniel this shaken, or struggle like this before.

Taking a deep breath, Daniel looks hard at me as he continues. "Honestly, I don't know what it is. If I did I'd try to fix it but I *don't* know, and I know Neil doesn't either. We've talked about it, and we're not breaking up, we just don't know what the issue is."

"When did it start?" I whisper.

"Your accident. But don't freak out," he soothes immediately. "Not because of your accident. It was at that time that I realized Neil and I were more different than I thought. He was so calm and relaxed about you being hurt, whereas I was completely freaking out. Not that he wasn't freaked, but he just acted so calm I wanted to scream at him to be as out of control as I felt."

Thinking quickly, I need to find an explanation to soothe Daniel. "Maybe he was holding it together so *you* could freak out?"

Smiling, Daniel nods. "That's exactly what Neil said he was doing when I asked. He said he knew he couldn't be the Queen at the hospital because I was," Daniel laughs. "God, you're so similar. No wonder I love you both," he exhales and then just stops as we each try to figure out what's going on.

"What can I do to help? Do you want to talk to Neil with me there to run interference or something?"

"No. Like I said there isn't an actual thing to work past. We're not fighting, and we're not mad at each other. It's hard to fix nothing, even though there *is* something going on. I don't know, Sam," he shakes his head a little. "Maybe once everything is better with you, and our schedules are back to normal in September, Neil and I will fall back into place. I hope so," he smiles sadly.

"Me too. I want you to be okay. Actually, I *need* you to be okay. Um, do you want me to talk to Neil?"

Quickly shaking his head again, Daniel says no. "Maybe later if we can't figure it out, but not yet. He and I have to figure this shit out together, okay?"

"Okay. But I'm here if you need anything," I whisper leaning toward him as close as my extended leg will allow.

Taking my hands, Daniel leans down and kisses my forehead before whispering, "That goes both ways, Sam. *Anything,* honey." And I know he means it. Nodding against his lips, I know Daniel would do anything for me.

"Let me give you a minute to put your clothes on," he smiles turning for the door.

Suddenly grinning with a little laugh I feel totally embarrassed. "Ah, thanks for cutting my toe nails," I giggle mortified. "I'm sure that was pretty gross for you."

"Nah, it's all good," Daniel says. "I have *some* experience with women," he smirks referring to his past with women before he accepted he was gay. "I'll help you with all girlie things, because if you ever ask Neil to help you with lady parts he'll freak right out," he laughs as I nod.

Taking my hands and slowly helping me stand off the toilet I've been sitting on for what feels like hours based on my leg and chest pains, I groan but laugh at the thought of Neil and 'lady parts'.

"Deal."

When Daniel finally opens the door to leave me to dress myself, he asks our question. "Good?"

"Good," I reply, feeling instant relief at something normal in my life.

Leaving the bathroom a few minutes later in the t-shirt and boxer shorts Neil provided under my soft beautiful La Senza housecoat, I limp slowly toward my bedroom to the hushed, angry sounding voices of Neil and Daniel. Pausing in the doorway, I wait only a second or two until Daniel spots me and stops speaking immediately.

"What are you doing?" I ask them both.

"I changed your sheets and was just making the bed for you," Neil fake smiles to cover their tension. "Do you need anything else? We're ordering takeout shortly, and the girls are coming over for dinner."

"Why? Isn't it Sunday?"

"We were planning to have an intervention tonight, but I got you out of bed way easier than I thought I would. So now it's a late birthday dinner," Neil laughs at my grin.

"An intervention?"

"Yup. We couldn't stand to see you like that anymore. Good?"

"Good," I exhale. "Can I lie down for a little while though? My ribs are hurting again, and I feel pretty dizzy and tired from all the movement."

"Sure, Sammy," Daniel chimes in with a strained look at Neil as I make my way to my freshly clean bed. Not even bothering with my still wet medusa hair, I ease down on the mattress and lift my bad leg with Neil's help.

"Come here," I say tugging Neil's shirt so he gently climbs over me. "You too, Danny. Get in here with me," I beg as he nods and helps me move over to the middle so he can climb in beside me.

Finally relaxing on my pillows, Neil settles into my side and puts his bent arm under my head lifting it higher as he tugs the comforter over us.

"Do you remember when we met?" I ask Neil feeling horribly nostalgic suddenly and wanting the three of us to just be the three of us again. I feel like we need to reconnect so we can get back to being normal.

"Of course I do," he says seriously.

"Remind me," I beg as he kisses my lips softly before he begins talking.

"Let's see. I was the fabulous 22 year old Dorm Leader in Scarlet Dorm- aptly named by the way. I've always been very Scarlet O'Hara with my-"

"*Focus*, Neil," I say sternly as both Neil and Daniel laugh.

"Sorry. I met you when you moved unexpectedly into my dorm in late October which was totally weird, and quite frankly, unheard of. So naturally, I needed the scoop. I figured you were some hardass trouble maker who was booted from a different dorm, and I wanted to know what I'd be dealing with."

"But?" I cut in.

"But instead I found a very young girl who looked a little shell-shocked standing in her new room alone. And when I asked your name and you spoke with a kind of monotone, clipped anger that wasn't aimed at me in particular, I felt a weird protective pull toward you instantly."

"And then what happened?"

This is my favorite part. I've heard this story hundreds of times over the last 5 1/2 years and this is the part that gives me chills *and* a warm feeling deep inside my chest.

"And... I asked you why you seemed so pissed and you looked at me with your beautiful blue sad eyes, huffed, pulled your hair back into a sloppy ponytail and said so deadpan my heart actually stopped as you spoke, 'I'm a little pissed off because my junkie mother tried to have me raped in my bedroom by a fat, smelly old man so she could get her next fix, and that's why I'm suddenly here- to get away from her. So you'll have to forgive my anger'. And before I could say anything or even reply, you stared hard at me and said, 'Oh, and if you *ever* repeat that to anyone else, I'll fucking kill you. Understood?' And that's when I knew I was going to love you."

Smiling, I look at Daniel for a second as he nods me and Neil home.

"And then what did you say to me, Neil?"

"Ummm... I said, 'Wow, Darling, you have just met your soulmate. And I would cut a bitch for you'," Neil whispers hugging me gently to his side.

"And with tears in my eyes, I nodded and whispered thank you as I fought to hold in the upset and shock that was still heavy in my chest. I fought crying so hard until you sat down on my new bed, in my new dorm, in my new life, tugged on my arm and said, 'Go ahead. Cry it out. Or *I* will. Then we'll get out of here and have a drink to celebrate your move,' which I did. I released all the upset and tension I'd been holding for 5 days and I bawled like a baby beside you as you held my hand. When I finally pulled my shit together after fifteen minutes, you took me to the campus bar and we had *many* drinks together."

"And that was that, as they say..." Neil tapers off.

"That was that," I agree.

After a minute or 2 of silence I look to Neil and then at Daniel and all three of us are smiling looking toward the ceiling lost in our own thoughts and memories of our past.

"And how did we meet?" I ask Daniel who chuckles and asks *really* as I nod yes.

"Let's see. I showed up at your old apartment, greeted Allan, couldn't figure out if I had the right apartment until you came barreling out at me yelling, 'Who the fuck are you?'"

"And?" I grin at Daniel as Neil buries his face in my neck.

"And then I introduced myself and asked if you knew where I could find Neil Hastings, who I never would've thought was actually there at the time, but amazingly was," Daniel answers a little breathy as we all pause and remember the scene.

"You were so beautiful standing in the doorway looking at Sam begging to know where I was. I remember my heart sped up as I leaned hidden against the wall watching you speak to her," Neil says softly. "You looked like a beautiful blonde angel standing in Sam's doorway while she glared up at you trying to figure out if you were a good guy or a bad guy."

Smiling, Daniel adds, "I felt the same way when I saw you leaning against that wall. You were so dark and handsome hiding there. But then little Sammy here suddenly shoved my chest and screamed at me to stop when I attempted to walk to you," Daniel laughs again smiling sweetly at me. "You were quite fierce that day."

"I was," I nod. "Someone had just tried to break my Neil 2 days before," I say with a moan as both snuggle in a little closer to me. "I was reeling, and though you were totally gorgeous and you looked so sweet standing there, I would've killed you if you were there to hurt Neil, with or without Allan's help."

"Believe me, I could tell," Daniel whispers. "Thankfully though, Neil stepped forward and told you it was okay, and I remember staring at Neil but seeing your head whip between the two of us before you finally moved aside and allowed me to enter your apartment. So the first time we met, I was afraid of you because you looked like you would kill me if I so much as said the wrong thing to Neil. But I didn't care how angry you looked- I wanted to make sure Neil was okay. And I *really* wanted to see him again," Daniel says a little sadly.

"And that was that, as they say..." Neil again ends our little trip down memory lane.

Slowly turning toward Daniel, I wrap my arm around his chest pushing my bad leg against his side and snuggle in as I feel his hand go over my side to Neil.

I don't know what part of Neil he's touching, but Neil snuggles in closer to me and soon I'm spooned by Neil and held tucked into Daniel's side while they look at each other. And truthfully, even with the slight tension that still surrounds them, I'm in heaven.

This is my absolute favorite place to be in the world. This is my happy place, and I need them to stay in love together so we can all keep our happy place.

I love them. And I need their love around me always.

*****

Waking a short time later, I feel Heather and Olivia crawling over me on my bed. Looking, I can't help but laugh as Heather mouths *lucky bitch* at me. Being moved slightly, Heather lies down in Neil's arm and Olivia scooches in closer to Daniel leaving me in the middle.

"Have you ordered yet?"

"Yeah... So we have about 15 minutes to really get it on," Neil says wiggling his eyebrows as Olivia sits up.

"Um, I have a question first. Does it count as cheating if it's with a gay guy?" Olivia asks too seriously for the situation we're all in.

"Nope," Neil and Heather answer at the same time as I giggle.

Lying back down Olivia says, 'good to know,' as Daniel pulls her closer from the edge.

Though a Queen-sized bed, 5 adults lying side by side is super tight, and warm, and just kind of sweet. Almost like an old school Friends episode without all the outside drama or fake humor.

Twenty minutes later when the food arrives, we all sit on my bed eating. I'm still in the middle but propped up with my 4 friends sitting in various crossed legged arrangements around my bad leg as we eat our Chinese food happily together.

And as I watch everyone laughing and eating, I know I will never forget this night as long as I live.

It's the night I know I would do anything to keep my boys happily together. And the night I want to see my girlfriends happy while they look for their own lives to fulfill them.

Thinking about my life and my surroundings, I *know* when I woke up and chose to live again I made the right choice.

CHAPTER 8

Waiting for my friends to arrive, I'm dressed, make-upped, and ready. Tonight is our last big night out before I start Med School on Monday, and though nervous as hell, I'm also ready to finally start school after my shitty summer.

God, the summer was long, painful, and pretty damn hard actually. Yet at the same time, I can't believe how quickly it seemed to pass. Almost like a dream, I woke up this morning to find myself at the end of the summer, ready to start my new life in Med School. I feel like I just woke up and the summer is over. I feel like I'm starting a new chapter of my life in the quick blink of an eye.

The struggle to move past all the pain, and quite frankly the pain *medication* was brutal, but after the day Neil and Daniel forced me to wake up, I *woke* up. Slowly, I cut back on the pills and I moved my body. I took less everything, and I moved more constantly, but it was hard. I remember each day thinking I wasn't going to survive the constant pain, exhaustion, or even pep-talks, for that matter. But I did. And thankfully, my memories of that struggle are distant and nearly forgotten.

I barely even remember starting back to work 9 weeks ago and now I'm suddenly finished for the summer. All I do remember is attempting to bank as much money as I could, which really wasn't as much as I had hoped before the accident because of my reduced hours, and all the doctor's appointments and Physio appointments I also had to go to throughout the summer.

One amazing surprise this summer that helped immensely though was Neil finding a University loophole, which meant insurance covered 80% of my living expenses and any accident incidentals over the summer. I had finished my exams a few days before the accident, but the school term wasn't officially over until a week later, so I qualified for the medical coverage Daniel insists I pay for each term, just in case.

Luckily, my accident qualified for the 'just in case', and I was helped over the summer with all my living expenses, thank god. The money I made working at the lab part time didn't net enough to lessen my insurance payments, so again, thanks to my boys and their homework, I was able to keep anything I made over the summer, which should help with the living expenses my student loans won't cover during the school year, at least minimally.

  Today was my last day at the lab, and tonight is the last time for quite a while that I can just let loose and have fun with my friends- well, as much fun as a cast and crutches will allow.

  After the initial 5 *Bad* weeks as they're called, when I woke up from my pain-filled slumber in hell, I've spent the last few months getting myself better. My lungs and chest don't hurt at all anymore, or at least not enough to acknowledge, and my leg is setting properly in a plaster cast. I should even be ready for a walking cast in a few days which will help considerably.

  I hate crutches, and though I've become a pro at them, they are seriously annoying and constantly in the way. But I guess they beat the alternative; a wheelchair still, or even worse as Neil pointed out like an asshole- no leg at all, every time I complained about the appointments, tripping over my crutches, or the constant annoying aches and pains I still have each and every day of my life.

  Looking at myself in the mirror, I'm pleased to look healthy again. I've gained back a little of the weight I lost in the first month after the accident, but not all of it, which is good. My hair is thick and healthy looking, and I even managed to get a little sun on my face and arms sitting on my balcony after my shifts at the lab when I'd chill over the summer.

  Tonight, I'm wearing a long flowy peasant looking, empire-waist dress in a soft cream color. My dress naturally makes me look more tanned than I really am, but amazingly, my arms are super toned now from these damn crutches, and they look great uncovered. Just my pale pink toenails and one cream colored flat sandal are visible below my dress. Actually, even as I turn and look, the girth from my cast is barely noticeable within the flow of my long dress.

  Looking closely at myself, I feel pretty. With my upper chest and arms showing beneath the spaghetti straps, and my hair pulled back in a sloppy looking ponytail which actually took me an hour to perfect, I really do feel attractive again- something that has been hard to feel this summer with my constant Chewbacca leg and crutches limp.

But Regardless of what I think, Neil will definitely let me know if I'm delusional when he arrives, so I have to wait to see if I pass his attractive standards.

Though loving and as supportive and sweet as ever, Neil never holds back a WTF are you thinking comment. So pouring my first drink of the night, casually waiting for both Neil and Daniel to arrive with my 2 girlfriends, I have to wait out the final approval of my clothing, hair, and make-up choices by Neil before I can call myself officially attractive-looking tonight.

No matter what Neil says though, it's okay. I'm excited about us all together tonight, and I'm looking forward to being with my friends again as a whole group- something we haven't done much of this summer.

Heather even promised to be on her best behavior tonight when we spoke on the phone earlier, forcing me to question, 'what exactly *is* your best behavior?' Laughing, Heather eventually admitted she wasn't entirely sure.

*****

"Why, don't you look slutastic," Neil smiles from my bedroom doorway as I turn to him.

"And don't you sound like the total cliché gay best friend," I grin back.

Walking into my room and dramatically jumping on my bed, he replies, "Of course I do. I'm gorgeous enough to be a model. I'm gay. AND I'm your best friend," he says all duh. "Plus, you love me. You would do me in a second," he says as I smirk at him through the mirror. "Admit it. I'm sexy as hell, awesome, super cool, and totally doable," Neil gloats with another smug smile as he leans back in a sexy pose to prove his point.

"Yes, darling," I sigh dramatically. "If only you weren't totally gay, and madly in love with someone else, I would do you in a second. Good?"

"Good. But your sarcasm doesn't hide the fact that you want me. Badly," he grins again.

Turning to Neil, I want to deny him but I can't. Sitting on my bed beside him I give in as usual. "You're right. You are still my ideal, Neil. Except for the whole YOU ARE GAY thing. Um, do you realize we have this exact conversation every single time we all go out?"

"Yes, I do. It's so I get you all hot and bothered over who you can't have, so you go and do someone you can have."

"Really? So this isn't about your constant need to be told how gorgeous you are? This is all for me?"

Laughing, Neil kisses my cheek. "Yes, this is all for you, Samantha. I swear I don't even care that you want to do me. It doesn't affect me one way or the other. I don't-"

"I call bullshit. You love all us girls wanting you. And it's sad really, why do you care if-"

"Because he's a whore," Daniel suddenly says behind me in the doorway as I cringe. Whipping my head to Daniel I feel the sudden thick, uncomfortable silence between us, and again, I don't know how to fix it.

I hate the hurt in the air, and I dread this pain for them.

Standing slowly, I limp over to Daniel as he hugs me tightly. Whispering in my ear, 'I'm sorry', I know he is. I also know he's hurt, and confused, and sad, and just angry all the time.

"*Daniel...*" Neil exhales, but Daniel shakes his head no to Neil as we pull apart, and again the tension in my room is so tangible it threatens to choke us all.

"Not now," Daniel says coldly to Neil as he takes in my outfit from head to toe. "Sorry for that, honey. You look beautiful tonight. *Really* beautiful. I love this color on you," he says kissing my forehead as he tries to ease the tension around us.

"Are we ready?" I *need* to get out of here before we destroy the celebratory mood I had planned for the rest of the night.

"Olivia texted me. She and Heather will be here in 10 minutes, give or take. Have you talked to Livi today?"

"Yup," I grin. "She's pissed at Matt, so she's going *all* out tonight she said. All out, like in Heather style apparently," I laugh.

"Well, that'll be interesting. Watching Heather and Olivia dual over *walking* dicks should be entertaining for the rest of us," Daniel grins before turning to walk out of my room. "I'll go get us some drinks while you two finish up," he says not even looking at, or acknowledging Neil.

"Okay," I breathe sadly as he leaves my room and closes the door behind him.

Turning back to Neil, I want to smack him, and scream at him, and hurt him, but I can't. Neil is in pain and he has tortured himself for a month now. He needs me to be his rock, even though I feel like bludgeoning him with a rock.

"I know..." Neil exhales. And as I wait he continues. "He won't leave me, but he won't love me either. He walks around in a fog and speaks to me in monosyllables. I've tried everything, even earlier today, but he just walks away when I try to speak or apologize."

Sitting back on my bed, I take Neil's hand and try for the thousandth time. "I don't know what to say, or how to help you. *You* screwed up, so you have to wait it out. There's nothing else you can do, unless you walk away from him. Do you want to leave him? Do you want to break up?"

Shaking his head, Neil looks at me so defeated, I suddenly want to bludgeon Daniel for hurting Neil, too. Christ, this sucks.

"I love him so much, Samantha. You know I do. But I fucked up royally, and I can't fix it, and I can't make him forgive me, and I can't do anything but wait."

"So you wait longer. Or you leave him for good. Daniel hasn't left you, which says how much he loves you, but I just don't know if he can ever move past this."

"I know, but-"

"There's no but, Neil. YOU made a bad choice. You chose to be a cheating asshole to the love of your life, so you either wait it out and see if Daniel can move past it, or you make the other choice- You end your relationship," I whisper to the love of *my* life.

"But I can't keep waiting for him to love me again."

"Then make a choice. You screwed up, so Daniel can react however he wants, for as long as he needs. You, however, can choose to not wait him out. That's it. Those are your only 2 options here. Wait Daniel out, and hope he can move past this. Or leave him, and move past it yourself. That's all there is, honey."

Waiting, the silence after my words is so heavy, I feel like bursting into tears, but I can't. Neil needs me, and so does Daniel. I have to be here for them, like they're always here for me. From Allan cheating on me, to the accident, my boys have always been there for me, so I have to give them my love and attention back. They need me. And I need to fix them, which I'm working on.

"I miss him..." Neil whispers and that's my undoing. Feeling the pressure nearly explode from my chest, the sob I feel is so quick I barely hold it in as Neil reaches for me. Hugging each other tightly, I know he's crying gently, while I try to hold my own tears and sadness in for him.

"I'm so fucking *mad* at you," I whisper in Neil's ear as he nods against me.

"I know, baby. I'm so sorry I fucked everything up," Neil moans in my arms. "I know what you went through when Allan cheated, and I know how angry I was. I didn't mean to do it to Daniel. I just... fucked up," he says again, and my heart breaks for him.

Neil and I have been together for almost 6 years now, and we've lived with each other throughout everything. From my start and end with Allan, to Neil and Daniel's start and hopefully NOT end, we have been together. And we always will. But this one is really hard.

We can finish each other's sentences, and speak to each other without saying a word. We are the same person now, in male and female form, and we get it. We know what's at stake this time.

Daniel is our happily ever after.

Daniel is the shining white Knight neither of us believed in until we met him. Daniel is everything we could have ever hoped for each other, but now he's fading away, and it's killing us.

From the moment he walked into Allan and my apartment after Neil was beat up badly 3 ½ years ago, I've dreamed of Daniel in our lives always.

Daniel is the dream for us both. Daniel is a blonde haired, blue eyed beauty wrapped in depth, devotion, love, and intelligence. He is a dream come true for me and Neil, and he's fading away from us.

I can honestly say losing Daniel as the other love of my life (tied only with Neil) hurts worse than any of my other loses in life. My mother doesn't even register, and my own ending with Allan doesn't come close to this pain now.

Losing Daniel is breaking my heart in a way I don't think I will ever recover from. And losing Daniel is going to destroy Neil for the rest of our lives.

"Please hold onto him," I beg.

"I'm trying," Neil moans, and there is nothing else we can say.

"You need more mascara to make your beautiful blues pop, Samantha," Neil says standing at my dresser to get us out of our funk.

Nodding, I do as I'm told, which is way easier than fighting Neil. So after more mascara, and a quick lipstick redo, Neil and I finally get our shit together enough to join the others.

"Did you *finally* get laid?" Heather screams across the living room making me laugh. When Neil responds, 'she wishes' with a smile, I see it's a fake, strained smile.

Neil is going to play off the upset to act fabulous for the others, but I know he's bleeding inside. I know his mistake is taking a toll on not just Daniel, but on himself as well.

Turning to Daniel, I pick up his drink, take a huge gulp and choke, "What the hell is this?"

Shrugging, Daniel doesn't even smile. "Whiskey. I needed something strong tonight," he replies with a finality that ends any further comments... *Except* from Heather, of course.

"But you're gay!" She laughs. "You're supposed to drink something fruity and girly. Have one of Sam's cranberry and Vodkas, at least."

Laughing at her stupid comment, Daniel seems to thaw a little. "Even the gays like a stiff... um, *drink*, from time to time." And as he finishes his statement, the pause he added was so intentionally dramatic, we all laugh at his playfulness.

"We all need something, um, *stiff*... tonight," Olivia chimes in, and as Neil laughs at Olivia's attempted sexual innuendo, I watch Daniel's body language collapse again. He is struggling to be happy, and I hate it.

Looking between them, I see Neil watch him too, and the sadness that fills Neil's eyes hurts me as much as Daniel's pain does.

I wish my girls knew what happened so they'd stop teasing, but they don't have a clue. They think Neil and Daniel are still blissfully in love. And though Heather and Olivia have seen the obvious changes in demeanor and speech between my boys, they haven't questioned me about it too intensely.

I've been asked once or twice if everything is okay, so I've lied and said absolutely, like both Neil and Daniel asked me to. This is *their* private matter, and other than me knowing what's really going on, they want to keep it private.

Pulling at Daniel suddenly to take the sad look from his eyes, I teeter on my crutches and ask him to join me in the kitchen. Waiting, Daniel seems to decide if he wants to be with me or not which kind of hurts, but finally, he nods as he stands with me.

Limping past Neil who collapses heavily in a chair, Daniel and I enter my kitchen, only 20 steps away, but as he turns to me I see clearly his sadness and hurt and anger all at once.

"I'm so sorry, Daniel," I whisper, as he shakes his head at me to stop.

"It's all good, honey. I'll be fine," he lies for the thousandth time.

"It's not good, and you're not fine. Please tell me what I can do. Tell me what Neil can do. Tell me something so we can make this better," I beg desperately absolutely hating this situation.

"There's nothing you can do."

"There's something. Please, tell me," I push.

Though I know I'm being completely illogical, I can't see to help it. I just need a thing to work with. I need a list. I need *something*, so I can do it, or say it, or make it happen. I need to fix this for the three of us.

"Samantha," Daniel exhales. And as I hear my full name I know this is going to be hard to hear. "There is nothing *you* can do. You know that. I don't even think there's anything Neil can do at this point, because he's already done it. *I* don't even know what to do, so you can't help me. I know you want to but-"

"*Please*?" I beg again.

"There's nothing," Daniel sighs and I'm done.

When my eyes fill with tears, he takes me in his arms as a crutch slides from against the counter to the floor with a clang, and I know we've been seen. Without looking, I can hear the silence from my living room as my girls look, and I can almost feel Neil watching us sadly.

Neil wants me to figure out how to fix this because he can't. He has never said as much, but that's what we do. I fix Neil, and he fixes me.

"I love you so much, Daniel," I cry in his ear as he squeezes me tighter than he has since the accident. "Please don't break up with us."

"I'm trying not to. I don't want to. But I can't keep feeling like this," he apologizes as I pull away to look at him.

"You won't always feel this way. Neil is so sorry. He knows he screwed up, and I *swear* he'll never do it again." But even as I say it, I'm sad to admit I can't really swear to that. Neil is Neil. And Neil always screws up his relationships with sex.

"Sam, I love you, but you can't fix this. No matter how much you want to. Maybe I just need some more time, I don't know. It's only been a month since he... But I'm not ready to let it go yet. I'm really hurt-"

"I know you are. But-"

"No, Sam. I'm *really* hurt. Think about how you felt when Allan cheated." When I visibly flinch, he continues. "Neil and I made something amazing together. And now he's destroyed it."

"He didn't!" I gasp.

"Sam."

"No! He didn't *destroy* it," I yell. "He damaged it. That's all. He hurt it and maybe broke it a little, but he didn't *destroy* it!"

Still yelling, I'm desperate for Daniel to understand. I know everyone can hear me over the quiet music, but I can't stop myself. I'm reeling from all this upset.

"*Please?* Neil didn't destroy you, so you can still be fixed, I promise. Just give us time. Give us a chance to make it better. Give us some time to make you love us again!"

I know I'm losing my shit. Fuck, I *know* it. But I can't stop it even as it's happening. I have honestly never felt this out of control in my life.

"It's not an *us*, Sam. It's a me and Neil. *Us* is fine," he moans.

"No, we're not! You're going to leave us forever, and we won't have you, and then we're alone, and sad, and I can't live like-"

"Samantha!" Neil gasps beside me suddenly as he tries to tug me away from Daniel.

"No! This is *not* destroyed," I yell pointing back and forth between them. "You are *not* destroyed. Oh, *please*..." I moan.

Feeling myself moved, Daniel tightens his grip on me as he bends low into my face so I can see him better through my tears and hysteria.

"Okay, Sam. We're not destroyed. We're just a little broken. Okay?" Daniel begs as I nod and try to exhale.

I don't know what's come over me, but I can feel reality slipping away. I feel the loss of us and myself, and just everything so clearly I feel like I'm dying inside.

"You can't be destroyed," I cry again. "We need you, Daniel. You're everything," I moan as I feel my body moved.

Being lifted by my waist in Daniel's arms, I see the look of shock on Neil's face the further we travel from him, but he doesn't intervene. I see Olivia's stunned face for a split second, and Heather's tears as I'm carried around the corner to my room by Daniel.

Pushing open my door wide with his foot, I'm gently seated on my bed before Daniel collapses beside me with a bounce. Stunned, I don't move or speak. I'm too afraid to do anything.

I've never been manhandled before, and in another life, or under different circumstances, this may have been a turn on. But right now it's just so sad and desperate, I feel nothing but Daniel's pain.

"I'm sorry," I whisper. When he exhales slowly and looks at me, I pull my shit together as best as I can. "I don't know why I freaked out like that. I didn't mean to."

"I've never seen you act like this before. This isn't you, Sam, and you have got to stop making this *your* pain," Daniel says as I flinch again. "What I mean is, *you* didn't hurt me. Nothing with you and me has changed."

"But it has. Neil fucked up and-"

"*Neil* fucked up. You didn't. You're still my girl, and I love you just as much as I always have."

"But they're the same thing," I try to argue.

"They aren't the same thing," Daniel argues back. "You and Neil are a packaged deal, I know that. *Everyone* knows that. But you are not the same person as Neil. He is awesome and amazing, and *not* so loyal to me, Neil. But you are awesome, and amazing, and totally loyal to me, Sam. You are not one person, and I can love *and* hate one without the other. I do love and hate you both."

"Please don't hate, Neil," I beg for the thousandth time. "I don't know why it's really important that you stay together, or why it's so important that you love each other. I wish I could explain what's happening but I can't. There's just something more I'm supposed to know or figure out, and it's *important,* Daniel. So please don't hate him," I exhale softly and wait.

And then I see it. Daniel's complete collapse around me. He has been trying to hate Neil, but he doesn't. He doesn't hate Neil, and I feel hope for their relationship for the first time in a month.

Exhaling, Daniel looks so sad, I truly wish he did hate Neil in this moment though, just so he didn't hurt so much. But only in this one moment.

"You know I don't hate him. I love him, Sam. I've loved him from the moment we met. Lying on a sidewalk, beaten up and throwing up, I loved him. When he tried to be tough and sexy as I knelt on the sidewalk beside him, I loved him. When he smiled, all bloody and nasty, and teased that I was a sight for sore *everything,* I loved him. When he asked me to leave him alone because he was embarrassed before the ambulance arrived, I loved him. And when he smiled at me 2 days later in your apartment, all bruised and sore, leaning against that wall hiding, I loved him," Daniel chokes up.

Waiting for him to finish, I find I'm holding my breath.

"I love him, but right now I feel so betrayed and sad, I honestly don't want to love him anymore. But that's not you, Sam. I still love you as much as I always have, and I promise I always will. So you have to stop making this pain yours. I know you want to help, but you can't. I know you want to fix us, but you can't. I know you always fix everything for all of us, but this time you need to let this play itself out. You need to be the amazing woman you are for both of us until we either break completely or slowly heal."

Taking my hand, Daniel continues softly. "You are my amazing, better, female version of Neil, and I need you to stay that way. I need you to love me like you always have, and I need you to be as strong as you always have been for us. But you have to stop making this pain yours Sammy, because it isn't yours to suffer. Okay?"

"It's not that easy. I love you both so much, and I'm so mad at Neil, and I'm devastated for you, and I just don't know what to do, which is a first for me. I always know what to do."

"I know you do. But not this time. This time, you have to watch from the sidelines. You're starting Med School in 2 days, and your life is going to change totally. So focus on you, and let me and Neil work our shit out. You have to make a choice, Sam. You have to choose to accept that Neil and I will either fix this or fuck it up totally," Daniel tries to ease all our tension away.

"I'll try."

"You and I will never change, I promise. Even if Neil and I can't move past this, I will *never* break up with you," he grins as I exhale a laugh. "You *are* my girl, Sam. Forever. And I choose to keep you in my life forever- with or without Neil," he says wiping my tears away with his thumbs.

"With, I hope."

"Me too," he confesses as I hug him tightly to me.

After his words, there is only our silence, as I pull myself back together again in Daniel's arms.

"Are you ready to party?" Daniel asks me with a genuine smile.

"Yes. Are you?"

"Yup. Maybe we can both pick up tonight, then I'll really screw things up with Neil- give him a taste of his own medicine," he laughs as I hit him.

"Not funny," I chastise.

"I know," he says defeated again. "But maybe I'd feel better for half an hour."

"You wouldn't."

"I know…" Daniel admits as he takes my hand and slowly lifts me from my bed. Checking myself in my mirror as he watches, we each give little tentative smiles as I quickly redo my mascara.

Looking closely at myself, I realize I don't feel attractive anymore. I feel like I look drawn and kind of pale with sadness. I look like a person mourning but who is trying to pretend everything is okay.

Once finished, leaning into his arms, Daniel helps me hop to the living room without my crutches. Plopping down on the couch I see Neil and the girls pretending everything is fine. Sitting beside them, we all pretend no drama occurred just minutes earlier.

But we all know the reality now, the choices made, and the consequences suffered.

CHAPTER 9

Entering the club, I'm helped by Neil in front blocking people from me, and Heather behind me with her hands on my hips. Struggling to walk carefully, as soon as I'm assaulted with the music, I release any residual tension I felt inside me to just breathe in the atmosphere of noise, alcohol, hot bodies, and fun.

God, I need this night. I need it as my last night in a long time, and I need it to wash away all the upset we've had for months.

"You need to work those crutches, girl, so some chivalrous bastard gives us his table," Heather yells in my ear.

And it works. Before the five of us are even near the bar, a gorgeous guy- *holy shit*, its Slayer- walks toward us pointing backward to an empty table with multiple chairs waiting for us beside the dancefloor railing. Yay, Slayer!

Watching Matt hug Neil and shake Daniel's hand pleases me. He doesn't seem homophobic in the least, so he gets points with me immediately. Plus, the waiting table was a nice touch.

Turning to us girls, Matt leans into me first to give a little hello hug, but it's awkward- not just with my crutches, or because I don't really know him, but also because Heather still talks about *her* slayer from time to time. Shit. He hugged me first which has girlfriend drama written all over it.

"Thank you for the table," I yell moving out of his quick hug to place myself beside Heather and Olivia. Jesus, it takes only a millisecond for Heather to literally throw herself into Matt's arms for an intense, way too long hug as Matt looks over her shoulder at me with an awkward-looking smile.

"Thanks, for coming! I knew you would. I haven't stopped thinking about you for months," Heather giggles all over Matt who I can see honestly tries to pull away from her death grip.

Eventually, Matt succeeds and pulls from Heather to hug a sympathetic looking Olivia hello, as we all turn to land at the table he held for us, almost like he knew we were coming.

Oh, *shit*. He knew we were coming. Looking hard at Neil, he answers my unspoken question with a little nod and smirk.

Before anyone can even say anything to each other, Daniel hops back up and offers to buy the first round with Olivia already standing to join him. Giving me a sympathetic look because of my inability to join them, Olivia kisses my cheek and whispers, "I'll get you an extra drink, cuz you're crippled and trapped with the impending show." Laughing, I appreciate her understanding and loyalty.

This is gonna suck. Heather was already hammered before we even left my apartment, and now she has a reason to get more drunk, and act like a desperate ass all over Matt *all* friggin' night.

Looking around the club, I try to take in the atmosphere. The music is great so far, and I wish for nothing more than to dance with my friends, or alone, or just anything. I miss the freedom of dancing so much, I would kill to let loose without my shitty leg and crutches.

"Matt has a *fucking* girlfriend!" Heather practically screams in my ear as I jump.

"He does?" I ask as she nods. Christ that was quick. I didn't realize he even had time to tell her, but I guess he needed to get it out of the way fast. Especially since Heather was already in his lap when we all sat down.

Pouting, Heather nods. "Gay or taken. The standard. I always miss my chance, and I *really* liked him. I feel shitty, and I don't want to hang out with you guys anymore," she adds as I turn to her in question. "Nope. I want to fuck gorgeous Neil and I can't. I want to fuck super-hot Daniel and I can't. You're sexy as hell but you won't even throw me a pity fuck," she pouts as I laugh again. "So that's it. I'm joining a singles, horny club, and I'm not hanging out with you guys anymore."

Taking her hand, "If it helps, I won't be partying again until after my December midterms, so consider this your last chance for months to get one of us hammered enough so you can take advantage of us. Let me see what you've really got," I tease as Heather sits up straighter and grins at me.

"Sweetheart. You couldn't handle me or my moves," Heather shimmies as I laugh.

Nodding, "I think you're right. With your *vast* experience, you'd be too much for me. Maybe even for Neil, as well," I tease as Heather launches herself into my arms.

"I love you, Sam," she says in my ear as I shiver. "Wish me luck. I'm going to go dance my ass off, and I am NOT leaving tonight without a *walking* dick," she adds standing from the table with a kiss blown to Neil as he looks over at us from his conversation with Matt.

Watching Heather leave, I feel a little 3rd wheel-like sitting here with my leg extended, and my drinking hand empty while Neil and Matt talk to each other.

"I don't have a girlfriend," Matt suddenly says in my ear making me jump *and* shiver again. "I didn't want to hurt Heather's feelings, so I told a little white lie," Matt smiles. But I'm not feeling it. I don't like lies period, but this one seems a little too manipulative.

"Good to know," I nod. I don't think I like Matt suddenly. Then again, I understand why he would lie to Heather to get her to back off of her hot pursuit.

"I'm a good guy, I swear. I was feeling awkward around Heather, and telling her I wasn't interested had drunk girl drama written all over it. So sadly, I took the cowardly route and pulled out the fake girlfriend card," Matt continues as I turn away and look for Daniel and Olivia. Seriously. What the hell is taking them so long? My buzz is fading way too fast here.

"I was sorry to hear about your accident. I called Neil to ask about you a few days after we met and Daniel told me what happened."

Turning back to Matt, I'm intrigued. He called to ask about me before he knew I was hurt. Interesting. But still. *Heather*. Gah.

"Are you okay?"

Really looking at Matt, it's undeniable- He's gorgeous. I think his eyes are maybe dark like Neil's, but his body is totally different than Neil's. Whereas Neil is tall, dark, and subtlety ripped, Matt is tall, with light brown hair. He's also fairly muscular- which though not usually my thing except with Daniel, suddenly seems to be totally my thing. He has a lovely smile, white, perfect, I suffered through braces teeth, and one dimple in his right cheek. He's a hottie for sure.

"Samantha?" He smiles with a little head tilt.

Exhaling, I feel like an ass. "Yes, I'm fine. Thank you."

Leaning into me, Matt smiles again and asks, "What are you thinking about right now? I'm curious."

"Life..." I respond like an idiot.

Still trying to engage me, Matt asks, "I hear you're starting Med School on Monday. That's quite an accomplishment. What kind of doctor do you plan on being? A GP? Specialized?"

Turning back to face Matt when I finally see Olivia and Daniel walking toward us, I digest his easy question and demeanor and just answer.

"Psychiatry."

"Really? So you want to mess with the minds of others? That's interesting," he says looking at me closely. "Is there any specific reason for your career choice?"

Taking in the atmosphere again, and feeling strange in this moment- almost like I'm doing something wrong, or being tempted into something bad, I go for drama to end the conversation. I'm not usually so dramatic, but I think I'm suffering a kind of mental snap of sorts tonight.

Waiting seconds for Olivia to place my drink in front of me, I blurt out, "My mother is a bi-polar junkie who is also borderline insane I believe. So I'd like to have the medical credentials to either lock her sorry ass up, or at the very least medicate her into submission."

Okay. *Wow*. That was dramatic even by Neil standards. Shit. Waiting for some ridiculous response, I don't get one. Turning back to Matt, we make eye contact again, and I suddenly know exactly why he's the Slayer. My panties just combusted by his sexy gaze alone.

"Parental revenge? There are less intensive, faster, and even cheaper avenues to attain it. Over 10 years of post-secondary, and well over a hundred thousand in debt? I must say, I respect your commitment." Responding so seriously, I pause until I see his smile start and finally, thankfully, I release my breath and burst out laughing.

"Thank you for your understanding," I laugh again as Olivia sits beside me with my drink and an extra shot on an actual bar tray.

"I stole it from the bar," she grins doling out everyone's drinks from the tray.

"Good thinking," I agree before choking back my Jäger shot with a near gag.

After our drinks I don't have the opportunity to talk to Matt again for at least 20 minutes, a few good songs I long to dance to, Olivia checking out and bashing all the men in the club, Neil and Daniel sitting with Matt in between them pretending to still be a happy couple, and Heather *still* on the dance floor shaking her ass.

Watching Heather closely, I see she's within a group of 4 men who are grinding up against her, tugging at her, copping multiple feels, and moving her in between them all suggestively. Shit. This looks really bad.

"I'm getting ready to intervene," Daniel acknowledges my unspoken as we both watch Heather.

"Could you now? She's a little too drunk for that scene I think, and it looks like it's getting ugly."

"I've got this," Daniel says rising as Olivia looks at me sadly. Before I can say anything else, I see Matt also rise to follow Daniel and I'm impressed he's willing to get involved with my friends and their drama.

"He's really fucking hot, Sam. I would love to hook up with him," Olivia says as we watch the potential dance floor drama begin.

"Hands off, Livi. He has the hots for Samantha," Neil adds as both Olivia and I turn to him.

"He does? Well, good for you, honey. But how-"

"I'm not. Heather likes him. He lied and said he has a girlfriend, and really, what's the point? I'm starting school on Monday and I don't need any distractions."

"Fuck the distractions. Just screw him tonight!" Olivia yells with Neil leaning across the table for an Olivia fist bump.

"I agree with the lovely Olivia. Go get suh-layyyed, Samantha," Neil says smiling as I'm struck with an intense sense of déjà vu trapped in this moment.

Thinking of what I'm trying to remember, and watching Daniel take Heather into his arms, as Matt stands slightly to the side, I'm mesmerized. Daniel is beautiful, and Matt is hot as hell, and watching them try to reason with a drunk Heather makes me want them both.

"He's so beautiful..." Neil whispers as I turn to him but Olivia takes his hand across the table before I can.

"I don't know what you did, Neil, but I can imagine. You stupid fucking idiot," she says so calmly I choke on my drink and try not to laugh as Neil winces.

"I agree with the lovely, Olivia," I can't help add as Neil mouths *fuck off* to me.

"Can you fix it?" Olivia asks a sad looking I want to hug him and kill him at the same time, Neil.

"I'm trying to," he moans.

"Good. Fix it. You and Daniel are amazing, and I need you to be good with each other," Olivia admits sadly.

"I agree..." I say just as I see the first hard swing hit Daniel right in the face. *Fuck!* Before I even understand what's happened, Olivia has tipped our drinks as she stood knocking the table back, and Neil is gone. Practically hopping over the table, Neil is on the dance floor so quickly I don't even have time to panic.

But it's over before it even really started.

Matt has the puncher in a weird choke-like hold or something, and he's walking off the dance floor with the guy to a waiting bouncer. Neil is already touching Daniel's face, and drunkass Heather is crying in the middle of the dance floor as people move away to stare at her.

"Fucking *drama*..." Olivia breathes beside me as I lean to the left and right of walking people to try to see what's happening.

"*Sorry!* Sorry, I didn't mean to cause that," Heather cries as she makes it back to our table.

Matt is still talking to a different bouncer, and Neil and Daniel are making their way to the bar, I think.

"I *said* I was sorry!" Heather cries, and I want to scream at her to shut the hell up, but I hold it in. Barely.

"Stop being such a fucking drama queen, Heather. You sound like an idiot. What the fuck did you do?" Olivia yells.

I know I'm going to have to diffuse this one quickly as Heather leans into Olivia's snarling face.

"Sit down, Heather. Now," I bark, and she does.

"I just wanted to keep dancing, so I told Daniel to leave me alone."

"You told Daniel to leave you alone?"

"I may have yelled it, and the one guy thought Daniel was harassing me so-"

"So you acted like an idiot, causing Daniel to get punched in the face when he was trying to get you out of the stupid situation *you* caused?" I can't help the anger from seeping through. "Did you even see those guys, Heather? They were laughing at you, and grinding against you, and almost using you for a fucktoy between them. What the hell were you going to do, go home with all 4 of them?" Shit, I'm pissed.

"No. Sorry," she whines as she gulps her drink still crying pathetically.

"I really wish you could dance," Olivia complains and I agree. I need to get away from Heather for a minute. She's pissed me off, and she's being all drunk girl crier, which I hate.

"I need to get up for a minute to see Daniel. *Don't* move, Heather," I glare so she knows I'm serious. All I need is for drunkass Heather to stumble out of the bar right into one of those idiots arms.

Walking a few tables away from Heather, I hear Matt suddenly ask behind me, "Where are you going?" Turning to him he has such a beautiful smile, I feel the desire to kiss him almost instantly. "Stop looking at my mouth that way, or I'll kiss you," he whispers in my ear making me blush and shiver. Jesus Christ, this guy is hot. "Where are you going? Do you need any help?"

"She's fine," Olivia shoves between us. "Sam just needs a breather from all the drama, and she needs to see Daniel. So since she can't dance, we're going for a little walk."

"Do you like to dance?"

"Yes..." I'm feeling heated and kind of aroused standing this closely to Matt as I wobble on my crutches.

"May I?" He asks before pulling my crutches from my hands. Shocked, I barely even protest, and neither does a grinning Olivia when he hands them to her. "Hold on," he says as I finally protest.

"Don't. I'm too heavy, and I need to check on Daniel," I fight.

"Um, you're about 5 foot 5 to my 6'2, and I outweigh you by at least a hundred pounds. I also bench press more than you weigh, I guarantee it. So stop fighting me," he smiles. "Neil is busy nursing Daniel's pride more than anything else. And the asshole and his friends have been removed from the bar. Everything is fine now, so please stop fighting my arms," he grins again looking me straight in the eyes until I stop. But only because I'm thrown off balance by his words, oh, and by my bad leg as I fight standing.

Being scooped up into his arms around the waist and held under my knees I find my own arms naturally go around his neck. Though our faces are merely inches from each other, I choose to look all around me pretending to look for Daniel. I can't possibly stare into his eyes this closely. There is no way to look at his face as he carries me to the dance floor without swooning, or blushing, or sweating, or just, *yeah*... I'm totally screwed.

"This is my second time being manhandled tonight, and I'm not a fan," I try to say angrily, but as he smiles I know he doesn't believe me, or even care.

"Put your right foot on my boot, and let your left leg dangle. We're dancing, Samantha," he says ignoring me completely while he pushes through people to the middle of the dance floor.

Moving down his body, I do exactly as he says, and it's amazing for me. Dancing, our moves are a little too grindy for my liking, but I know it's only because he's holding me up against him. Smiling, and trying to enjoy myself, I turn my head away from his intense stare as often as possible, but I'm always drawn back in by his eyes.

"You have moves," I grin.

Laughing, Matt agrees, "You have *no* idea." When his innuendo settles into my lower belly, I envision his moves in and around me and fight a moan.

"I have a treat for you," Neil yells at us, shocking me as he suddenly stands beside us.

"Do you know what he's talking about?" Matt asks, and I really don't when Neil waves goodbye as quickly as he arrived. With Neil, it could be anything though which makes me nervous while we continue dancing.

"Um, not a clue. But it could be-"

Oh...

On a gasp, I want to kill and kiss Neil at once as the next song begins. Here it is. My song. 'Fuck You' by Virtual Embrace.

Jesus, I'm blushing just from the song choice, and I can't look at Matt for even a second. He seems like he'll know I'm turned on, fighting every urge I have to move to my song.

"I take it you like this song." Before I can come up with a totally reserved answer, he breathes in my ear, "*Move,* Samantha. Let me see it. I've got you."

Feeling Matt's erection against my stomach, and feeling his heat, and loving this song, and envisioning dirty, dirty things becomes too much for me.

Suddenly, I want to be like Heather and not give a shit what people think. I want to be like Olivia and give only a little shit what people think. I want to be anyone but me in this moment... So I move.

Keeping one hand around Matt's neck, my other arm raises as the thrill of the beat takes me over. Leaning into Matt's hands behind my back I close my eyes and just move. As sexy as I can on one foot, and as fluid as the tight space allows, I move.

Instantly everything disappears for me; my friends, my family, my future, and my reality.

Everything fades away as I move to the heavy bass and electronic sounds that fill my soul. I feel alive and whole. I feel awake and in a dream. I feel like I'm making an important, life-altering decision, and I want to choose this moment.

Here I don't picture Daniel's heartache, or Neil's sadness. I don't know Olivia's abusive past, or Heather's desperation. I don't know Allan's betrayal, my mother's madness, or my father's denial.

I am Samantha, and I choose to live in this moment forever.

But my song eventually ends and reality surfaces far too quickly.

Opening my eyes, I realize I'm plastered against Matt's chest grinding against his thigh between my legs. I am wanton and dirty, and I feel sexy as I look up at Matt's gleaming eyes.

"Are you ready to be manhandled again?" He breathes in my ear as I nod. Surprising myself, I actually nod a sexy surrender to the Slayer.

Being moved back off the dance floor in his arms again, I'm embarrassed, but not quite enough to stop whatever may happen. I don't want to stop it. I want something deep, and dark, and completely unlike myself. If I'm really honest with myself, I want to just screw a random and be young and single and normal and...

"Get your purse," he says as we near our table to only Neil and Olivia.

"Where are Daniel and Heather?"

"He's putting her in a cab," Neil beams. "Here's your purse, darling. Sam lives closest, so get going Matt before she changes her mind and actually *becomes* a virgin again," Neil adds like a smug asshole.

"Walk behind me," Matt almost demands as Olivia hands me my crutches with the biggest smile I've ever seen on her face.

"Just do it," she whispers as I give a tiny nod. And then I'm doing it.

Matt walks with smooth strides in front of me as everyone moves out of his way. He is walking with a purpose and people seem to understand not to mess with him. He is parting the Red Sea for me, and I'm almost giddy with my nervous excitement.

This is potentially my first one night stand. And Matt is only the third man I've ever slept with. Mark twice before Allan, Allan, and now probably Matt, if I don't come to my senses soon, which I probably should. Even though I don't really want to.

Suddenly pressed against the darkened hallway wall before the exit, Matt is bending low in my face.

"Don't change your mind, Samantha. And *please* don't overthink. You don't strike me as the one night stand type, so I'm sure you're trying to reason your way out of this. But trust me, I want this and I want you. I've thought of you way too often since we met a few months ago, and I'm not an asshole. You set the tone. You tell me to stop. And you tell me when I leave. That's it. Okay?"

Looking at Matt's eyes, he seems sincere enough, plus my Neil knows him and seems okay with it, and really, it's not like I'm the first person to ever pick up at a bar, so...

"Okay."

Being kissed suddenly by Matt is a welcomed shock. He kisses like a god, all hard and intense, and soul consuming. Moaning, I'm pressed into the wall harder as I try to climb into Matt and his kiss.

"Sam?" Gasping a breath, Matt and I both turn to Daniel watching us with a head tilt and arms crossed. "Good?"

"Good," I blush. "Oh, Danny..." I reach out to him. "Your face looks sore. What can I-"

"I'll call you in the morning, honey," Daniel cuts me off.

Looking at Matt for a silent second almost like a warning, Matt nods and extends his hand as they shake again, but not in *way to go* kind of way, more like in an acknowledgement of me and my safety sort of way.

"Can we go please? I have to hurry before reality sets in and I talk myself out of this," I smile as Matt looks back at me and Daniel kisses me on the cheek to leave us in the hallway.

Quickly readjusting my crutches with Matt's help, we're out the door, and getting into a waiting cab within seconds.

CHAPTER 10

Honestly, I don't know how people do this. I keep blushing and giggling a little because of my nervousness. How the hell do women pick up at bars without looking stupid with all the little giggles and awkward movements? I feel like I look like a total moron right now, which is not sexy in the least.

Finally opening my door, I drop my keys and purse on the kitchen counter and turn to a calm, cool Matt slowly walking in behind me with a sexy smile.

"Um, I just need a minute, okay? Help yourself to anything," and as he nods without speaking, I hobble to my bathroom for a quick redo- of everything.

Peeing as quickly as I can, washing my hands, and brushing my teeth, I finally finish with a quick facecloth wash of my girly parts. Reapplying my deodorant after a quick armpit dry shave, I take a look at my faded makeup, wipe the smudges, rip the elastic out of my hair quickly, and finally decide I'm ready.

Christ, I'm nervous. I'm not sure what I do when I open the door, or how this even starts. But as I inhale deeply and pull open the door, Matt is standing in the hallway with a big smile and an extended hand.

"Which is your bedroom?" He asks looking at identical doors, until I motion with my head the end door. And then we're moving. Me on crutches and Matt walking slowly behind me until he enters my room- and there the slowness stops.

Dropping my crutches, I'm pushed against the wall again and my hair is grabbed in a tight fist at my neck as he kisses my mouth hard. *Fuck,* this is hot!

I can barely breathe as we kiss. My neck is wretched to the side by my fisted hair, and I can't really move while I feel him inch up my dress quickly. Moaning loudly, envisioning my fantasy wall sex, I gasp when I feel a finger slip under my panties to slowly enter me while his thumb presses down on my clit.

Moaning into his mouth, I'm on fire. My body is so sensitive, and my good leg is shaking so badly, I know I can't hold myself much longer. But before I collapse down the wall Matt seems to understand.

Moving me gently to my bed, my dress is lifted overhead before I can attempt to settle, and my panties are torn from my body as I gasp and moan at the sexy brutality of his actions when he slayed my panties.

And then I laugh.

Honest to god, I can't hold it in. I burst out laughing at the thought *I've been slayed!* Holy shit, I'm losing my mind. Neil immediately pops into my head as I imagine telling him in the morning I was slayed, which is a major buzz kill for sure.

"Something funny?" Matt asks while climbing up my body to lean over me on his forearms.

Still giggling, I try desperately to stop. "I'm sorry. I'm just nervous which makes me laugh like an idiot."

"Is that why you'd spontaneously laugh in the cab? Because you were nervous?" Matt asks with a grin.

"No. I spontaneously laughed in the cab because I'm an idiot," I say so deadpan we both burst out laughing. "I'm so sorry. I'm totally embarrassed by this," I admit with another stupid laugh I can't suppress.

Holding my face with his hands, Matt breathes against my cheek. "Just an FYI, Samantha. Laughing at a man who's trying to please you can be very damaging to his ego, which may even cause performance anxiety, which will ultimately stress the poor bastard out until he leaves limp and shaking, to eventually get hammered alone in his apartment, until he wakes up hungover and horny as hell but is afraid to try to pick up again for fear of more performance anxiety and laughter in the future." Matt says all of this so seriously, I pay close attention until I finally see him smile at the end. "I, however, am not affected by your laughter like that," he grins taking my hand and rubbing it against his jean covered erection.

Rubbing my hand against him, the laughter I had fades quickly. I think Matt is either very large, or maybe even average, which seems way larger than Allan's button on a bag. So essentially the same thing for me and my sexual experience.

"My ex-boyfriend had a tiny penis." *Seriously?* Yup, I just said that.

"That sucks for him. I'm only a slightly longer length, Samantha, though I'm quite girthy which women seem to like. Would you like to see how much *girth* I have?" He teases.

"Yes..." I answer mesmerized again by Matt's eyes, and his smile, and his body, and his presence all around me. He is so much, and actually so clothed to my leg cast, bra, and nothing else.

"Can you take off your clothes?" I ask shyly.

"I will. Do you have all the laughter out?"

"Yes."

"Good," he says suddenly moving away from me.

Oh! *Jesus,* he just face planted in my crotch. Striking hard and fast, my body bows before I even know what to do. I can barely breathe, but this time I love struggling for breath.

Moving my good leg over his shoulder, I'm spread wider by his hands, as my bad leg rests flat on my bed. Lifting me from underneath I feel myself brought into his mouth deeper, and it's amazing.

This feels so dirty and sexy, and just wild. I hear Matt moaning against me, and I hear the sounds of my body coming to life by his tongue. I'm enjoying everything, every touch, every- *oh!*

Gasping again, I'm climbing high very fast. I mean this was Allan's thing for me, but I thought it was just going to be Allan who could get me to- *ahhhh* Matt is so good.

Digging my heel into his back, I need harder, and faster, and maybe deeper. I need just a little more. I need whatever Matt's doing with just a little bit more.

"Um, harder, Matt," I beg and he does.

Impaling me harder and deeper with his fingers as his tongue tortures me, my climax builds quickly as I moan and move all over his face.

Pulling at my headboard, and struggling to maintain my position, my body is jerking and bowing on its own. I'm breathless and my heart is pounding in my chest. I'm so close. I'm closer quicker than Allan ever brought me, and I'm closer than I thought I would ever get with someone else.

"Oh! *God...*" Groaning and grunting my climax, it's so sudden, and painful, and pleasurable, I'm not even sure what he did, but I think he may have nipped me with his goddamn teeth. Whatever. It was amazing, but he keeps going until I'm too sensitive, and I have to stop him.

"Please stop. You have to stop now. Come here and kiss me, Matt," I nearly whine in my post orgasmic state until he rises up my body to kiss me deeply.

"No laughter?" He grins against my lips.

Exhaling hard enough to move my hair from my face, I shake my head no against the pillows. He is amazing, and perfect, and special, and just wow. He's like a dream. He's a sex god- A dirty, sexy, funny sex god.

"My turn," he whispers before kissing me hard again.

After kissing forever, I manage to lift his shirt up and over his back with my hands pulling him closer to me. Inching my hands between us, I tug at his belt and finally release his jeans button as he moans.

God, I want him naked with me and he quickly understands. Rolling onto his back away from me, I rip my bra off and watch as Matt slides his jeans and underwear off with his socks before lying back down beside me for another kiss.

Touching his arm and shoulder, he is so smooth and muscular, and just so comfortable next to me, I feel nothing but attraction to him in this moment.

When Matt stops kissing and touching me to raise up on his knees, I want him. Staring, I realize I absolutely love his body. Matt is muscular and toned, and he seems fairly hairless on this chest, but tanned and beautiful. I can't even stop myself as my fingers trail down his chest and abs, through his treasure trail to join his hand on his cock. His big, beautiful, long, thick cock.

This is either going to hurt, or be amazing. I can't really see any other option and I *really* want to experience either one with him.

Sitting up, I look at a raised Matt and lean into him. Licking his stomach ridges, I moan as the feel of his muscles and taste of his skin bursts on my tongue. Olivia was totally right about this.

Quickly taking him in my mouth, we both moan when I lick and rub the underside of his cock before taking him in further.

"You are so beautiful, Samantha," Matt says quietly as he gently wraps my hair in his fist away from my face. Holding my hair, he doesn't use it to force me to take him deeper or harder. And based on his moans he seems okay with letting me try to do this to him my own way.

I'm nervous though. I don't know how to please *all* of Matt's size, and he's right about the girth thing. I've only ever done this with Allan, who compared to Matt was like a pathetic little tootsie roll.

Oh *shit!* Laughing again, I can't hold it in which forces Matt to pull out of my mouth.

"I'm sorry! *Shit!* Sorry... I swear its not you," I say giggling still but trying to pull him back into my mouth by the backs of his thighs.

Smiling down on me, thank god, Matt asks, "What's it about then?"

Still giggling a little looking up at Matt I try to keep it together but blush when I confess, "You're only the second man I've ever done this with, and I had a quick *unwanted* visual of my ex's tootsie roll sized penis compared to your huge one. I'm so sorry."

Laughing suddenly in a quick burst, Matt replies, "You're forgiven. But only because I was the *huge* one in your visual and not the tootsie roll."

"You are," I exhale, watching Matt begin stroking himself with a tight fist as my laughter fades quickly.

He is so sexy and confident and strong. He looks like he could have anyone, but as he watches me watching him I realize with a sense of amazement that it's me he wants in this moment. Groaning as he strokes himself, I take in his body and imagine being tempted to do anything with this man.

When he starts to pull on a condom, I want him desperately.

"Lie down, Samantha," he moans my name like a dirty word and I lay back instantly.

Leaning down over me Matt gives me a soft, sweet kiss that I feel right inside my chest.

Entering me as we kiss, Matt moves slowly- *too* slowly actually. He's being almost sweet and romantic about it. But I don't want romantic. I want hard. I crave hard with this man, but I'm a little shy asking for it. I don't want him to get the wrong idea about me. Then again, I did take him to bed the first time we've ever really spoken, so how much worse can his impression of me be?

"Where are you, Samantha?" Opening my eyes I see the concern on his face, which I don't want either. I want *Slayer* Matt.

Smiling, I try for sexy. "I'm right here, enjoying your girth," I grin to his laugh. "But would you mind harder and faster?" And even as I blush, I see his smile fade to pure, molten desire in an instant. *God*, he's hot.

Without speaking Matt groans and moves. Hard and fast he picks up the pace, until moving again, he leans up on his knees as he takes my good leg and places my foot on his chest.

Spreading my legs wide, almost scissoring my body, I use my own foot as counter thrust against his chest, and it's amazing. My bad leg is still lying flat beneath us, but with this new open position, I don't give a shit about my leg. I'm being hammered into, and it feels amazing.

Joining Matt's grunts as I push against his chest and raise my pelvis to him deeper and deeper, I feel him start working my clit and I almost jump off the damn bed.

If I actually orgasm during penetration, I'm going to- Oh my *god*... I'm going to have another orgasm soon.

Closing my eyes, and moving as best as I can, I envision the song 'Fuck You' with all my dirty fantasies, and suddenly I'm so ramped up, I barely even care that Matt's with me. Well, I do care, but I just don't.

He's amazing, but this moment, right here, hard, heavy, and breathless is making my mind blank, and my body writhe with the pleasure.

Grabbing my own nipples, I pull and twist and moan loudly, waiting for the climb I'm feeling to take me away from everything, and everyone.

I am alone, suffering a pleasurable hell in heaven. This moment is slowly taking me from everything I've known into all I want to know with this man.

And then I'm suddenly done.

Blanking out, I know I screamed way too loudly for my neighbors, but I couldn't stop it. The internal assault was so intense, I felt nothing but the release of all the pressure I've felt for a lifetime.

Panting, and opening my lazy eyes I look up and gasp stunned.
Matt is *hideous!*

All skeletal and black, Matt is a monster like demon thing on top of me. Fucking me hard with gnashed, sharp teeth and a long black bloody tongue dripping from his mouth, he grunts. Screaming, I close my eyes again and feel the life drain from my body with the terror of my sight.

Being fucked by the demon I feel it's scales between my legs and it's claws digging into my foot on it's chest.

When I try to push it away it fucks me harder. Shoving at its head growling over my face, it fucks faster. Screaming in my desperation to get away from it, it fucks me louder.

Crying out, I'm so terrified I suddenly stop all movement and wait for the demon to stop fucking me.

"Holy *shit*, Samantha. That was amazing," Matt suddenly exhales, and though totally petrified I open my eyes quickly to gorgeous Matt as he's always been smiling over me.

Shaking my head to clear it, I'm still stunned.

What the fuck was that?

Oh my *god*... I just suffered a quick delusion I think. I suffered a hallucination. I suffered something. Freaking out inside I'm desperately trying to come back from it as he waits for me.

Matt is right here. Matt isn't a hideous demon. Matt is right here with me, in all his sexy, male hotness.

Moving very slowly out of me with a wince and a hard exhale, Matt must have orgasmed during or shortly after my own orgasm. Sadly, I didn't see it though, or even hear him because of my quick horror.

Moving my leg slowly back to the bed, I feel a hip cramp almost immediately. Arching, I try to take the pressure off my hip as I slide my bad leg further to my side away from Matt. Shit, my hip hurts, but it's the fear that's killing me.

"Are you okay?" He asks with a very satisfied grin I try to return even though my hip is killing me and my mind is racing in fear.

"I'm out of shape," I huff. "My hip is killing me and I have to move. Can you shove me to my side," I pretend to laugh as he does.

"This is definitely a first for me, Samantha. Your post-coital talk is sexy as hell."

"I can imagine."

"The leg cast? Also a first for me," he grins.

"Me too," I admit, still scared and shaken, trying to move away from him a little without him noticing my physical retreat

"Seriously though, are you okay? Are you sore at all? I didn't think you'd want me to be so hard with you.'

Smiling, I'm slightly embarrassed by my sexual demands but I really don't care. I'm trying to forget the image of the monster, and I'm trying to look content in this moment so it doesn't come back for me.

As far as I'm concerned, Matt and hard sex are amazing, though quite frankly I'm scared to death to do it again in case I see what I saw again.

"Are you sore?" He again asks with concern.

Exhaling the last images of the horrible demon, I look at his face and smile for him. "Other than a good sore in the right place, I'm fine. But I do need to use the washroom," I mumble trying to move to the side of my bed.

"Do you need any help?" Grinning, he quickly amends, "Getting to the washroom- not *using* it."

Laughing, I say no, as I reach for my robe and tie it tight. Thank god, Neil bought me this robe to wear. I feel much better clothed. And sexily clothed is even better.

Reaching, I just make it to my crutches when Matt takes my arm and I flinch. Damn it. I'm trying to be so calm, but flinching doesn't help anything. Turning to Matt, I know I have to pretend harder.

"What's wrong? *Did* I hurt you?"

"Not at all. I'll be right back," I fake smile and kiss him quickly on the lips. But even as he tries to deepen the kiss, I almost fall off my bed pulling away from him. Christ, I just need a minute alone to think.

Grabbing my crutches from the floor, I leave my room, and make it to the washroom fast. Turning and nearly slamming the door, I lock it, flick on the light and just pause.

I am NOT crazy like my mother. My mother doesn't even suffer from delusions I don't think- or at least I don't know that she does. Fuck, I hope she doesn't, otherwise, I have a whole new diagnosis to give, and more personal paranoia to suffer in my future.

Okay. Be rational. Maybe in the throes of a second orgasm, I spaced out or something. It's not like I ever had multiples with Allan. And never during actual sex. Usually, I had one early on, then he'd pump his tiny penis into me forever, I'd fake one, then he'd release his own real one minutes later.

Maybe 2 orgasms was too much for me? Okay, that's the theory I'm going to go with to explain away whatever the hell just happened in my bedroom.

Matt is not a black, skeletal demon monster, and he doesn't have a long, freaky bloody tongue dripping and hanging from his mouth.

He's sexy as hell, nice, funny, and he showed me a good time. Neil knows him, and Daniel seems to trust him. He is not a demon, and I am not delusional. I just suffered a weird moment. Okay. Done.

When I finish using the toilet, I clean myself up and brush my teeth again. After a few calm *rational* moments alone, I'm ready to face Matt and all his amazing sexiness.

Walking back into my room, he doesn't disappoint either. Lying with the sheets pulled up to just his waist, Matt looks delicious in my bed.

"Am I staying the night?"

Oh. One night stand etiquette. Um... "If you'd like?" I mumble embarrassed.

"I'd like. I'm going to use the washroom, and get us some water. Would you like anything else?"

"I can get it."

"Nope. I think you've worked your uninjured leg enough for one night. Crawl into bed, Samantha. I'll be right back," he says already standing gloriously naked in front of me, passing me with a quick little kiss as I turn to watch his ass leave.

Walking back into my room minutes later, I can't believe how good looking Matt is. It's unnatural really. I think he's even better looking than Neil and Daniel, which is saying a lot.

Wherever we go, men and women stare at my boys, because undeniably, they are both stunning in their own way.

Neil is the dark to Daniel's light. Neil is dark, classically handsome, and Daniel is light cherub-like beautiful.

Looking, I realize Matt seems to fit in the middle somehow. Strangely, when I really take him in, he actually *is* the fantasy combination of both Neil and Daniel for me.

Matt is not as tall as Neil, but he's taller than Daniel. He's less muscular than Daniel but more ripped than Neil. His hair is medium length brown to Daniel's short blonde and Neil's longer black. And he has green eyes I see, to Neil's rich brown and Daniel's light blue.

"You're the combination of both," I mumble out loud before I can stop myself.

Grinning with a head tilt, Matt sits on the side of my bed to hand me a glass of water and asks, "Of what?"

Thinking quickly, I lie as convincingly as possible. "Sexy and funny."

"The combination of sexy and funny? That sounds like a good thing."

Nodding, I whisper *it is* before sipping my water and reaching for the nightstand.

"Are you ready to sleep?"

Not trusting myself to be remain rational if I start thinking again, I simply nod and smile as he crawls back into my bed beside me.

"How do you sleep? Which side?" He pauses holding the covers.

"It doesn't matter. My ex slept on the left, but both Daniel and Neil sleep on the right. So I'm easy," I grin at the unintentional innuendo.

"Clearly," he laughs. "Do you sleep with Neil and Daniel often?" Matt looks curious, not judgmental, so I decide to answer honestly.

"I don't know. Sometimes. We go through phases. Plus my couch is really uncomfortable to sleep on. But it's nothing sexual," I defend quickly. When Matt gives me his own *no shit* face I move on. "Whatever. If they crash here, they crash with me. That's all."

"That's all," he smiles before settling in beside me to sleep.

Waiting for me to get comfortable, I'm *not* comfortable actually. I'm feeling awkward still, but eventually I settle as best as I can.

Moving my cast over farther to the right, I'm suddenly spooned by Matt and his warmth. Not even attempting to be casual, Matt surrounds me in his warm body, whispers good night and tugs me in closer to his chest.

Amazingly, I feel myself fall asleep within seconds, I think.

CHAPTER 11

"Samantha! *Sam!* Wake *up!*"

Oh *shit!* I hear her before I can even think. Turning over quickly into Matt I nearly push him from the bed in my scramble to adjust my leg as I sit up.

Throwing all my hair back from my face, I can't believe I'm staring at an angry looking Heather standing in my goddamn bedroom. What time is it anyway?

Looking quickly I see its only 6:15, and besides being a totally absurd time for Heather to be at my house, I can't believe she had the nerve to enter my apartment and my goddamn bedroom unannounced. Who the hell does she think she is? *Neil?*

"I can't believe you?!" She yells again. *Me?* Before I can even respond though she yells, "Nice tits, Sam! You look like a whore," prompting me to quickly close the front of my Neil robe in a panic. What the hell is happening here?

Turning to Matt who slowly sits up against the headboard and pillows with the sheets pulled to his waist, he honestly looks like he doesn't know what the hell to say or do, which makes two of us.

"I told you how I felt about him! I told you I liked Matt, and you *fucked* him? He was supposed to be mine. What kind of friend are you?"

Feeling Matt move to speak, I place my hand on his thigh to stop him. Whatever he may or may not say is just going to set her off more, so it's best if I deal with her.

"Heather, can we do this later? Or in the living room?" She's acting like a bit of a psycho with all the yelling so I'm not really in the mood to deal with her like this.

"*Later?* Like after you *fuck* him again? He. Was. *Mine!*" Wow. *She's* lost her fucking mind.

"Um, excuse me, Heather, but I was never yours. And what Samantha and I may have done together is none of your business."

"How could you do this, Sam?" She asks me ignoring Matt completely. "I came over here to apologize for last night. I actually felt bad about ruining your last big night out. But you turned around and *fucked* him?"

"Heather, please. Can we talk about this later?"

"I don't think so. What's there to talk about? I told you I liked him, and you didn't care. You waited for me to leave so you could fuck him." Moaning, "You're such a bitch now. You knew he was mine to love," she says so pathetically that after the initial shock of her words, I just catch myself before I laugh. *Mine to love?* Holy shit. Heather is totally delusional, too.

"Okay. I'm done. Samantha, would you like to finish this, or can I?" Matt asks with barely veiled anger as I squeeze his leg again. He'll only make things worse if he engages her.

"I thought you had a *girlfriend*. Where is she? Is she hiding somewhere?" Heather looks around my room and under my bed crazily. "We all know how well Sam gets along with the gays. Is your girlfriend gay, too?" Heather asks laughing at me when she stands back up.

"Heather! That's enough. You sound like a total idiot," I snap shutting her up quickly. "Matt didn't want to hurt your feelings by turning you down, so he lied about a girlfriend. *Obviously.* Otherwise he wouldn't be here. And I didn't wait for you to leave, or conspire against you at all. Matt and I just seemed to hit it off, and before I knew it I had decided to go home with him. That's it. We're two adults who hooked up. There was no conspiracy against you. I promise," I say gently to ease the end of my rant.

I know she's being an idiot, but she's been my good friend for a decade, and I love her- even this shitty side of her.

Nodding, I think Heather has finally calmed down enough to understand what I'm saying. She looks calm, but anything could set her off again.

"You had a choice, Sam. You could've left him alone because you knew I liked him, or you could've fucked him because YOU wanted to. You had a choice, and you chose to be a backstabbing whore."

Suddenly laughing, I can't stop it. "A whore? *Really?* Because Matt is only the third man I've ever slept with versus the what? 100 plus *you've* nailed since you were 17? Give me a fucking break," I laugh at her absurdity. I'm feeling pretty pissed now actually.

"Heather... I don't know you or even like you for that matter." Matt suddenly jumps in. But when I squeeze his thigh harder and look behind at him he shakes his head no to me. "Nope. I tried to stay quiet. But she's being ignorant and insulting, and pretty fucked up actually. I would never get together with someone like you, Heather. You-"

As Heather gasps, I try to get his attention, but he continues on.

"*Never*, Heather. I don't like desperate, and I *hate* needy. And sadly, you are both. Within like a minute of meeting me you had claimed me, kissed me, practically fucked me in the bar, and declared me yours without even asking me if I was interested. So here's the truth for you. I would never be with you, Heather. *Ever*. And whether Samantha and I had hooked up or not, that wouldn't have changed. That's why I avoided you, and that's why I lied to you about a girlfriend. That was *my* choice."

Suffocating in the sudden silence after Matt's explosion, I'm desperately trying to think of a way to calm them both down. I love Heather, but even for her this behavior feels a little extreme. She never talks to me like this, or acts so messed up with me. I'm always the calm to her slightly erratic, but this... I don't even know this Heather.

"Can we go talk in the living room?" I ask gently.

Exhaling, I see the tears in her eyes threatening to fall, but amazingly they don't land on her cheeks. Slowly shaking her head, Heather seems to collect herself, and I hope the crazy has finally passed.

"There's nothing to talk about, Sam. You had a choice and you made it. You-"

"Heather-"

"You made it, Sam. And I'll never forgive you. After everything I've done for you, I never would've thought you'd stoop so low."

"What are you talking about?" I beg confused. What has she done for me?

"I was always there for you in high school, especially when your mother was a fucking mess. And it was me and *my* mom who helped you when you were raped."

Gasping, I'm momentarily stunned... until I explode. "What the *fuck* are you talking about?!"

Suddenly jumping out of the bed totally naked, Matt grabs for his jeans before pushing his legs through them roughly as he turns on Heather.

"You are so fucked up, you know that? I don't need to hear this shit, and Samantha shouldn't have to explain something like that to me because her *friend* told me. You're a real bitch Heather, and I don't know why you'd hurt her like that, especially when I am *nothing* to you!"

"You were EVERYTHING to me! Fuck *her*! I'll show you a real woman!" Heather screams, and I swear Matt's going to hit her as he leans down and gets right in her face.

Fighting the covers I move as quickly as I can to get off my bed but it's too late. Matt has essentially forced Heather against the wall with his hands bracketing her between his arms. Growling in her face as Heather smirks at him, almost like a dare to kiss her, he finishes this nightmare.

"You are a desperate *loser*, Heather. I wouldn't fuck you if I was paid, and you need to understand something else-"

"Matt!" I scream to stop him but he ignores me completely.

"I choose, Samantha. Any day. In every *way* over you. You are a psychotic bitch, a total nobody, and a real shitty friend."

"No, I'm not! I took care of her after her mother had her raped!"

Screaming, I can't even hold in my rage anymore. There is no friendship left. There is nothing but Heather and her crazy lies in my room. Heather is a liar and a psychopath.

"Shut up, Heather! Shut the *fuck* up! I swear to god, if you say that one more time, I'll kill you! Get the fuck out of my apartment. *Now!*"

As I struggle to stand, and breathe, and really, just see beyond the tunnel of darkness I seem to be standing in, I notice Matt has moved away from Heather with his hand outstretched like he wants to either help me stand or hold me back from hitting her. He's looking at me almost like he can't bare to touch me now or something. I don't know, but he looks like he's stuck in one spot as I struggle to stay standing.

I don't know what to do now and Heather is still just standing there.

"Are you choosing him over me, Samantha?" Heather asks bawling her eyes out in front of me. "Is he your choice? Not me?"

Fighting the weird darkness that's closing in on me, I don't understand her question, and I can't really talk to her anymore. I'm tired, and I need to go back to bed.

"Please leave, Heather."

"Is that your choice?" She asks quietly like she's in total disbelief. "A man you fucked once over your best friend of 11 years?"

"Heather, go home. I can't talk to you right now. I'm too pissed."

"No. I want you to say it. I'm not leaving until you say it!" She screams again.

"*Fuck,* Heather. Can't you just leave her alone?" Matt tries until Heather turns on him.

"Oh, I already know *your* choice, *Slayer*. But I want to hear her make her choice. What's it gonna be, Sam? I leave, or he leaves?"

Is she kidding me with this shit? She's actually giving me an ultimatum after all she's said and done this morning? In my own bedroom?

"Samantha, I can go," Matt says as I shake my head staring at Heather.

Whispering with tears still pouring down her face, she begs again. "Your choice, Samantha? Me or him?"

Leaning against the wall, I hold myself up barely as I stare at my old friend. Thinking of all the years we've been together, all the fights and funnies we've shared, I can't believe she is actually forcing this. I can't believe she thinks she *can* force this. Who the hell does she-

"*NOW*, Samantha! Make your fucking choice." Fucking *bitch!*

"Fine! Get out, Heather. *Happy?*" I spit at her because I'm beyond pissed and totally done with this whole scene.

Inhaling sharply, Heather is *all* drama. Acting wounded, actually grabbing at her chest, she moans, "You made the wrong choice, Sam," as she backs out of my room. "Good bye, Samantha. I loved you," she whispers.

And then she's banging down the little hallway into my dining room table I hear as the glass rattles, until I finally wince as the door slams shut through my kitchen.

Sitting down hard on my bed again, I can't even comprehend what just happened. There are no words for the depth of that kind of drama. There is nothing I can say or do to fix that kind of madness.

Heather has completely lost her mind.

"Samantha?"

"I'm really sorry you had to see all that. I'm not sure what happened, or why she acted like that, or why she said what she said, or why she made me make a choice, or why-"

"It's okay, Sam. You don't have to explain anything to me."

"Can you please leave? Please?"

"Do you want to have breakfast with me?" He asks so kindly, I'm honestly tempted. But then I'm not. I want to think about everything Heather just said and did. I need a list of the crazy, so I can try to understand it better.

Begging, my mind is racing. "Please, Matt. I appreciate it, but I can't look at you right now. I'm embarrassed by Heather's behavior, and by her lies and delusions, and just *please*... I'm so tired now," I practically whine. Matt may be amazing and sexy as hell, but I really need to be alone now.

"Okay, Sam. No problem. Can I call you later?"

Pausing, I know I'm supposed to want to give him my number. I'm supposed to want the one night stand to be more. I know I'm supposed to feel something, but I don't feel anything right now.

"Ah, why don't you let me call you?"

"*Will* you call me?" He asks sitting beside me on the bed again. "I'd really like to see you again." Taking my hand, he tries to tilt my face up to him with his other hand, but I don't want to see him. All I can think about is getting him the hell out of here.

"Of course I will. Here let me walk you out."

"I'm good. I'll let myself out," he says with a big exhale.

Standing, he smiles a beautiful smile as I look up at him. God, he's attractive, but I'm not feeling it right now. When he leans down for a kiss, I instantly turn my head so he kisses my cheek, and though I see his surprise and maybe even embarrassment from the gesture, he doesn't acknowledge it.

Looking around my room as I sit silently, Matt grabs all his clothes, even tugging his boxers into his jeans pocket while he slips into his t-shirt and socks looking at me constantly, I can feel.

"Have a good day, Samantha. I had an amazing time with you last night. Please call me," he says before walking from my room with a little goodbye smile.

"I'm sorry..." I whisper to my suddenly empty bedroom.

The darkness that threatened me when Heather was here is gone, but so is the happiness I felt around Matt.

Instead, I find myself in grey, and I don't want to face it yet. All I want is to crawl into my bed, heavy under my covers until I can think clearly about all the choices I have to make.

Holding my breath as Matt walks away, I only release the pressure when I finally hear my front door open and close again signaling the end of my last night out before my life changes again completely in little more than 25 hours.

*****

"Hi, Neil," I whisper feeling him slide in next to me before I even open my eyes.

"Why, don't you look slutastic," he says tugging my Neil robe closed before he takes me in his arms and kisses my head. Snuggling into Neil, I exhale a huge breath and long to stay here forever.

The last time I looked at my clock it was 10:00ish, and though totally exhausted, I was never able to actually fall asleep after Heather and Matt left.

For the last 3 hours my mind won't stop racing, and though frequently the case with me, all the techniques I usually try aren't working this morning. There is no meditation, lists, or breathing exercises strong enough to fight the insanity going through my head over and over again.

"Matt called me," he whispers as I flinch.

God, I know I'm not ready to do this yet. I don't know what to say about Heather, and I really can't understand what the hell happened with Matt.

"I'm pretty tired and I haven't been able to fall back asleep. Can you just stay here and let me sleep before we talk about Heather and Matt?"

"Sure, honey. Go to sleep," Neil tugs me closer to him while resting his chin on my head. Almost immediately, I feel the cool calm Neil washes over me until I fall asleep in his arms.

*****

Waking, I hear raised voices and anger. I know one voice is Neil, but I can't place... Oh! For Christ's sake! *Really?* Not her again. *Please*, not her.

When my bedroom door is thrown open, I see first my mother crying with an angry flush, then Neil smirking against the wall without a shirt on looking just fucked and yummy. He may not have been just fucked by me, but he looks like it, which I'm sure is reason enough for my mother to fly into my room mental.

Waiting for something from my mother I slowly sit up as Neil quickly motions to my chest grinning. Looking down I see my breasts are out again on full display. Okay, Neil must've planned this robe on purpose. Suddenly laughing at the bizarre situation I'm in, I quickly cover up.

"Did you buy me this friggin' robe because it never stays closed?" And as he laughs behind my mother we both ignore her completely. "You did, didn't you? You little shit," I giggle tying it tighter around my waist.

"Samantha? Oh, *no*... what have you done?" My mother moans as I cringe.

Her voices is whispery soft which I know is definitely short term. My mother is a yeller, and wispy sounding conversations aren't really her thing. Then again, my mother isn't really my thing either, so I need to end this visit quickly.

"What have I done? I've slept with the gay, of course," I smile staring right at her as Neil tries to smother his laughter.

Turning to Neil, my mother asks politely, "May I have a minute alone with Samantha?" But even as she speaks, both Neil and I are shaking our heads no.

"I don't think so, Mrs. Newman. See her over there?" Neil points at me. "Well, she and I are a packaged deal. We have been together for almost 6 years now, and we will be together for many, many more. I realize you don't want to accept this but I love her to death, and she loves me just as much. So go ahead and discuss the *fag*. He's standing right here with her where he belongs, but he promises not to interrupt you."

Finished speaking, Neil dramatically exhales and crosses his arms across his smooth, sexy, naked chest as he settles in against the wall. Looking like a beautiful weapon for me, I prepare for my mother, and smile at my Neil. God, I love him.

Turning her head back to me with a nod of defeat or maybe even acceptance I notice my mother holding a crucifix at her chest with a shaking hand.

Oh, *Jesus*. She's really found Jesus, I laugh again staring at her. This scene is already playing out like something Neil and I will reminisce about fondly for years to come.

"Samantha, I've been clean for 142 days now. I made a choice to get clean for you, and I did it. I prayed to God you would be okay, and when you were saved, I knew I had to keep my promise to Him, and I have."

"Good for you," I interrupt.

"It IS good for me. *And* it's good for you. I'm your mommy, Samantha..." My *mommy*? "... And I'm here to save you from bad choices like I should've been doing all along."

"When you were high?"

Nodding, she continues no matter how much I try to piss her off. "Yes, especially when I was using substances I shouldn't have been using to maintain the sanctity of my body."

"The *sanctity of your body*? Oh my... You *have* found religion," I smirk.

Looking back at Neil he seems to be completely entranced by my mother. He isn't laughing or grinning like I am. He doesn't even have a smirk on his face. He looks almost like he's studying her, maybe wondering when she's going to snap like I am.

"Samantha, the Lord has been very clear about sins and sinners. And also about forgiveness. So I'm begging for your forgiveness again. I know I wasn't an ideal parent to you when I should have been, but I've changed. I know I hurt you and betrayed you, but I'm a better person now. I'm a much better person now, and *you* can be a better person too," she smiles holding her cross, looking and dressing like a mother for the first time in my life.

Nodding like I actually care what she says, I ask, "How exactly do I become a better person?" I can't wait for this one.

"Well, for starters, you need to open up your heart and soul to forgiveness."

"Because it'll benefit you."

"No. Because it will benefit *you*. How else can you make room for the spirit of our Lord if you have a soul filled with anger and hatred?"

Speaking as seriously as she is, I figure I may as well go for it and ask the question she's dying to answer. "I'm not ready to forgive you mother. So what else can I do to become a better person? Drop the damned homosexual? Free myself from the sins of the gay?"

"Samantha!" She snaps. "I didn't make the rules, I just abide by them. And you should too. I want you to be able to get into Heaven," she finishes much calmer.

"*Heaven?*" I ask pausing in disbelief. "What? Like I can't get into Heaven because my best friend is gay? Why wouldn't I be allowed into Heaven?" I ask stunned. "I've never hurt anyone, and I've been a good friend to everyone I know. I *love,* mother. And I'm a good person. I've done nothing wrong, but loved people unconditionally. Isn't that what God wants? Aren't we supposed to love unconditionally? Aren't we supposed to be good people to *everyone*?"

"Yes, but-"

"I help people mother, and I'm going to be a doctor helping *all* people like God wants. I'll even help the gays, who *God* created." Ha! I know I've got her when she doesn't respond right away.

Waiting for more, I've truly had enough. I can't stand this day, and I really can't stand her. A person can only take so much crazy before losing their shit. And I've reached my limit today.

"We're done, mother. YOU are leaving. He is not. *Neil* is staying forever. So get out of my apartment, and stay the hell out of my life. I have no pills left, and I have no money to give you. The sanctity of my body has recently been used in a *very* sinful manner, and I doubt you'd want it anymore anyway. It's tainted with many, many sins. Isn't it, *mommy*?" I glare the unspoken.

"Samantha-"

"Suddenly finding religion doesn't make you an expert on life or living. And it sure as hell doesn't make you an expert on what I should or shouldn't do."

Exhaling my irritation, I would pay Neil to literally pick her sorry ass up and walk her to the door, but I know he wouldn't dare. Neil is too respectful and kind, and way better than I am.

"You know what?" I ask feeling totally pissed looking at her still trying to find an argument that works for her. "Neil is a much better person than I am- the gay thing notwithstanding of course," I add sarcastically, as Neil finally jolts against the wall to laugh with me. Christ, I thought he was in a catatonic trance for a while there.

"Your friend can-"

"Neil Darren Hastings is an amazing person, and you would know that if you hadn't spent the last 6 years I've known him a total junkie, or the last, what is it? 142 days being a temporarily reformed junkie who ignores him."

"I don't ignore him, but I do disapprove of his choices," she says simply, almost like it matters what she thinks.

Shaking my head, I need her to get it. "Your disapproval doesn't matter to me. *You* don't matter to me anymore. But Neil does. Neil loved me and cared for me when I was alone. He helped me get past everything you put me through. *Neil* made me believe I wasn't going to become a piece of shit like you when I was messed up and confused. He loved and supported me, when honestly, I was scared every goddamn day back then that I'd end up a useless junkie like you were."

"I wasn't-"

"*What?* A junkie? Useless? Yes, you were. But it doesn't matter to me anymore. And this new religiously clean you matters even less to me than the junkie you did. The time for you to be a parent faded the day I left your house when I was 18. You're not a recovering addict, you're-"

"A woman trying to make amends with her daughter!" She screams in my doorway.

God, I *need* to end this. "Nope. You're still a junkie, but with a new drug. You need help, mother. You always have. You're sick and you need *proper* medication. But you never do what's proper. You find a new drug to aid you temporarily, and then you get addicted to it until you have to find another one to give you the beginners high again. Look at you now."

"I see me quite clearly, Samantha," she says almost vibrating with her anger.

Struggling to sit back against the headboard, I find myself shaking my head again as I take her in. "Do you really? Well, if you did see yourself clearly, you'd see what I do. A junkie currently off actual drugs *maybe*, who instead is using religion, or Jesus, or whatever the hell as your new drug."

"I'm not using drugs!" She screams as she moves closer to my bed.

"Fine, maybe not *actual* drugs, but you're using God now as a drug instead. And I'm really not interested. Get professional help. Get a diagnosis. Get a life, for Christ's sake. But stay the hell away from me while you get it."

"I'm your mother," she actually pleads like it should matter.

"By blood yes," I exhale. "But that's all there is between us- *blood*. As far as I understand from everyone else I have ever met, a mother doesn't steal, lie, cheat, and sell their daughter. But you do, and did, and probably will try again at some point. But it really doesn't matter to me anymore. I've moved on, and you should probably do the same thing."

Pleading as she leans into me, I can't stand our proximity. I want her out of my bedroom, and out of my life.

"Samantha... You're my *daughter*."

"Please stop. There's nothing here for you. I want you to take your crucifix and get out. I have a big day ahead of me with my *real* family, and I'd like to start it now. We're done."

"We're not done, Samantha," she tries again. But I'm completely and utterly done.

"Yes, we are. Get out. I'd like to talk to my favorite sinner some more and I don't need you here while I do it. Seriously, mother, get out of my apartment before I physically have you thrown out."

Gasping, she has the audacity to look shocked. "You would never hurt your mother like that!"

"*Physically?* I don't know. But emotionally, I absolutely could. Though I've held back this time, don't think I don't know what will break you. Because I know. I just choose to be a better person than you. That's the choice *I've* made. So unless you want me to really hurt you, you better get out," I finally exhale and just stare at her.

I need her to get it. And I need her to walk away. For some strange reason I think tears are close, and I would kill myself, or her, before I ever let her see me cry again over her.

But it's getting close.

Shit.

"Leave! Jesus *Christ!* Honestly, I don't want to be mean, but-"

"Samantha," Neil finally jumps in to stop my anger. But it's too late.

"*Fuck.* Just go. I won't say every mean thing I've ever wanted to say to you, but you better leave now, because my last shred of self-control is dying out, and I'd like to hurt you a little, Mother, like you've hurt me. So get *out!*" I demand until she finally moves.

What the hell did I need to say to her? How much clearer could I make this? She's as dense as she always was.

Watching her walk out of my room, she sidesteps around Neil widely in my little hallway, almost like she could possibly catch his gay or something.

Laughing at her retreat, Neil follows her out and honestly, if I was him I'd grab her from behind and wipe all my gay on her. But luckily for her Neil isn't me. Besides, Neil would never be so mean or childish. Though right now I kind of wish he would just once with her.

Moving from my bed, I slide my cast forward and try to stand. I need to pee, brush my teeth, and shower.

Really, I just want to get all these layers of filth off me. From sex with Matt, and Heather's crazy, to my mother's religiously pathetic attempts, I feel filthy and disgusting.

"Do you need to cry?" Neil asks with his typical concern.

"Oh, probably. This has been a brutal day for me. So I'm hopping in the shower to hide," I say as he nods before leaving my room again.

"I'll make lunch while you shower. I love you a million times, Samantha," he whispers with a Neil eyes crinkling smile, and my heart melts.

"I know," I whisper back as the first tear falls. And then we're done.

I have a few hours until Olivia, hopefully NOT Heather, and Daniel arrive for dinner before I start another new chapter in my life.

CHAPTER 12

   Waking at 7:00, I dress quickly to start my first day of Med School. I'm scared and nervous, but really excited, too. I've worked toward this for the last 3 years of my life.

   Though probably 2 years older than my fellow students, I'm not going to let that bother me. My delay in University to choose my major, deciding 2 years in that I wanted to be a Doctor, has given me an advantage, I hope.

   As Daniel pointed out, I'm much more settled and I've lived a little, before the inevitable NO life I'm about to endure for the next 3, maybe 4 years before starting my residency.

   Plus Allan, though still constantly on the fringes of my life, begging still, and calling way too frequently, allowed me to make my choices without fear of failure. I had hoped I could do this, and Allan told me I could.

   He was amazing when I made this decision, and he helped me prepare for it emotionally. I was supported and loved, and it helped me prepare for my new life.

   But again, nothing has changed between us. What he doesn't understand, or is unwilling to accept is he and I are over. Even when he called last night to wish me luck while I had dinner with Daniel, Neil and Olivia, I still felt nothing for him. Eventually, after a very one-sided conversation, he finally just wished me good luck, but added he missed me before I hung up.

   In one last desperate attempt, he even said he missed my friends, too. Pathetically, he wanted to know if he could call Neil or Daniel to catch up, but I asked him not to. Selfishly, I don't want any of my current friends in camp Allan, and I doubt they'd join it anyway.

   My friends are mine, and I trust them to stay mine. Though after Heather's ultimatum and performance yesterday morning, there is some question as to our future friendship, but I know Olivia, Neil, and Daniel love me as much as I love them.

After an awkward pause when Allan again asked if he and I could meet for dinner, I said no, wished him well, and asked him not to call me again while my friends listened to each and every word I said. Blatantly.

Not even pretending to give me privacy, Neil sat beside me on the couch listening, Daniel stared at me the whole time, and Olivia gave me a thumbs up when I refused to have dinner with Allan again, for the hundredth time.

After the call, as I rejoined my friends at my dining room table, we didn't even discuss the Allan call. Instead, Olivia begged for the dirt on Matt and I caved. Typically, not a kiss and tell kind of girl, I told them all the sexy details anyway.

When I announced I was *slayed*, Olivia moaned with jealousy, Neil clapped, and Daniel grinned at me. I told them about the initial wall intensity and hair fisting, the humor, the hot sex, and about Matt's *extreme* attention to detail. I ended with the spooning, and the request to hear from me again which they were all pleased with and approved of.

I gave them a brief recap on Heather and her behavior, explained I did feel badly about sleeping with a guy she liked, but admitted I didn't feel bad enough to forgive her words, lies or ultimatums. And thankfully, my friends agreed with me totally.

After the what the fucks, wow's, and *seriouslys?* Daniel offered to talk to Heather and find out what the real issue was, so I agreed. Olivia said she was staying out of it because she and Heather always clash anyway, so she wouldn't be any help to me. And Neil said he was too pissed to talk to her which would potentially make things worse if he approached her right now. In the end, Neil decided he too was staying out of it, which I understood.

Quite frankly, I don't want to talk to her, and she better have a damn good explanation for lying, belittling and accusing me of the things she did, especially in front of Matt which was totally humiliating.

After discussing Heather, when we all made our way back to a sex conversation, I neglected to mention the horrific demon monster vision I had in the middle of the sex. I don't want my friends to have to question why I had the visual, and I certainly don't want them to visualize Matt and sex like that. *I* don't even want to think about it. But sadly I do. Frequently.

No matter how many times I try to forget it, I see the black skeletal demon Matt when I least expect it and I cringe. The rational part of my brain says to forget it, blaming the orgasmic intensity, or maybe even the alcohol I drank for the vision. But my irrational side isn't listening to me at all.

Again, when I least expect it the monster creeps back into my memory, and the image of the long black, bloody dripping tongue assaults me all over again.

It's become like the shower curtain scenario. We all *know* there's no one behind the shower curtain. We know that rationally. Yet at some point, sometime, everyone walks slowly into their bathroom, stares at the curtain for a few seconds then in a desperately wild attempt to stop the fear and uncertainty, we violently rip open the curtain... to nothing.

That is Matt and the demon for me. There is nothing behind the shower curtain, I know, but until I somehow rip it wide open I'm going to keep thinking about it with fear.

At this point I'm thinking I should just experience the Matt sex trip one more time to see if the stupid vision returns again so I can let the irrational side of my brain finally rest.

Plus, I want to see him again. And I *really* want to have sex with him again.

Finishing my coffee before I leave for school, I'm as prepared as I can be. My books and notes are packed in my gorgeous leather over the shoulder Prada satchel Daniel bought me as a special, *way* too expensive back to school gift which he wouldn't let me refuse, and I'm ready to dive in.

Looking at an incoming text from Neil, I read,

-**You're a smart, sexy, awesome bitch. You'll do great.** ♥ xo

Daniel's text should be coming soon, and though not in Neil's style, I'm sure it'll say basically the same thing.

Med School- here I come.

*****

Finishing my first day of tutorials, I'm absolutely exhausted. I have brain overload, and I'm totally overwhelmed. I have a test on Anatomy this Friday, and a test next Monday on the Lymphatic system. I have 2 tests in less than a week, and something tells me these tests will set the tone for the rest of the semester for me.

   Walking into my apartment building at 4:30 I'm hungry and exhausted. Tomorrow is going to be a longer day for me, and all I want right now is to eat, crawl in bed, and read my notes until I pass out.
   Tomorrow is my intro to Biology, and probably my least favorite subject, which is funny itself considering it's the subject my dad has taught for over 25 years. But it's crucial, required, and pretty damn important for a doctor to understand biology, so I'll prepare for it and study it until I'm a biology genius whether I like it or not.
   Opening my door, I hear my name before I've even stepped through and I can't help my exhausted sigh. I really didn't feel like company tonight.
   "Unless you're naked and ready to fulfill all of my dirtiest fantasies, I'm going to kill you for being here," I announce before dropping my satchel on the kitchen counter with my keys.
   Turning, I wait for Neil's comeback, but instead see Neil and Daniel sitting on the couch together.
   Inhaling slowly, I can sense the darkness all around them. "What?" I breathe not really wanting to know. If they are officially breaking up because Neil's an idiot who made a huge mistake, I'm going to lose it on both of them.
   Walking into my living room with my crutches, I place them slowly on the floor beside me to buy time before I slump in a chair.
   "Just say it."
   Watching Neil take Daniel's hand I'm both happy to see it and totally afraid. I know they're not back to the touching phase, and I know Daniel is still too hurt to forgive Neil, so this must be a big one.
   Whispering *please* again, I wait just seconds before Daniel lifts his bruised face courtesy of Heather's dancefloor antics to stare at me.
   Crying out suddenly like he's in agony, Daniel moans, "Heather killed herself, honey. Sometime yesterday morning, but I don't know when."
What?
   I feel sucker punch winded, mixed with shock, horror, and an inability to move or breathe.
   "*What?*" I eventually wheeze.

"Samantha. This isn't your fault, baby. Please don't take this as your fault, because it isn't," Neil says quickly as he moves for me.

Reaching past the coffee table, Neil takes my hands and gets right in my face. "Samantha. Look at me. Look!"

When I try to focus my eyes on Neil, I see Daniel's head lower again as he cries silently. I don't know what to say, or do, or think, or, "I think I'm going to throw up," I gag in my hand.

Jumping, Neil runs to my kitchen quickly to a cupboard. But the sounds of the metal bowls clanging against each other is so loud my hands cover my ears quickly as I breathe through the nausea.

"Samantha. Here's a bowl. Come on honey, take your hands away from your ears." I can still hear through my covered ears but I don't want to move. What the hell happened?

"Daniel... do you hate me?" I beg because though completely irrational, I need to know if I've lost Daniel as well as Heather.

Lifting his face to me, Daniel cries, "Never, Sam," and I feel a slight momentary relief.

"I don't understand what happened," I cry to a kneeling Neil in front of me and a destroyed looking Daniel 2 feet from me.

"We don't either," Neil whispers. "Daniel tried to call her a few times today until her mom finally answered. She was hysterical but eventually she was able to tell Daniel what happened."

"How did she find her?"

"Heather sent her mom a weird, cryptic sounding text yesterday morning around 7:30, but Linda didn't read it until noon. Um, Linda went over to see her, and that's when she found her," Neil fills in the facts they do know.

Looking over at Daniel again I ask, "How did she do it?" *Really?* That's my question.

"Linda thinks an overdose, but they have to do a Tox screen to be sure because there were no pill bottles around her, and nothing was obvious to the police."

Oh god. *Linda.* She's going to lose her mind. She and Heather are so close.

Looking around my apartment, I have an unreal thought. I know it's in pretty bad taste, but once in a while Neil can be very tacky if he's bored, so...

"Is this a joke?"

Visibly jolting, Neil and Daniel both say no together, and I know it isn't. I guess that was wishful thinking on my part.

"Okay. Sorry. I'm not sure why I asked that. This is just so unbelievable. I mean I saw her yesterday and she was fine. Well, not fine, but still fine, ya know? Or I guess alive and not dead. She was just being an asshole, but she was going to call me in a few days and I was going to yell at her for being an asshole, and then she'd come over and we'd eat popcorn and watch Survivor together because she still has that weird thing for Jeff Probst-"

"Samantha."

"And then we'd be good again. But I'm not sure she'll see any more Survivor will she? So... *Oh!* Should I call Linda? What do I do now? Should I go to her parents' house? I'm not sure if Linda wants to see me, but she loves me too, or she did, so maybe I can. What do you do when someone dies? I have to bring some food over I think. Don't I, Neil? Aren't I supposed to bring a lasagna or something so the family remembers to eat but they don't have to cook it themselves because I know Heather hates cooking and-"

"Sammy."

"But Heather won't have to cook anymore will she? Lucky *bitch*." I laugh, then realize I laughed and cover my mouth in shock and then I just stop everything.

This is bad.

Am I a murderer?

What the hell happens now?

I still have the blue sweater I borrowed that Heather said matched my eyes perfectly. Actually she still has a bunch of my clothes, and all my childhood things in her basement. I guess they're gone now, too. Like Heather.

Suddenly standing as Neil quickly leans backward away from me, I know what I have to do.

"I'll be in the shower. I'm sorry for your loss. I know you both love- *loved*- Heather. And this is bad."

Stumbling for my bathroom, I leave the crutches where they lay and just force a limp hop to my bathroom as quickly as possible.

I know I have to garbage bag my leg, but I don't really care. What's the worst that can happen? It starts to unravel? What exactly *does* happen to plaster that gets wet? Everyone knows not to get casts wet only because we're told not to. But does anyone actually know what happens if they *do* get wet? I was having this one removed on Thursday night anyway for a new walking cast so maybe I'll just risk it.

"Sam. Stop," Daniel says in front of me as I try to close the door. "We need to talk. You're in shock I think, and we need to talk about this. Come sit with me," Daniel says softly while taking my hand away from the doorknob.

Shaking my head, I make sure not to look at him. If I look at Daniel right now I'll lose it for sure. He is so beautiful and his eyes are almost see-through blue because he's been crying, and I just don't want to look at him like that. It hurts too much to see him this sad. And he's been so sad lately because of Neil and now because of Heather.

"I'm so sorry, Daniel. I promise I didn't know. She was just acting a little crazy, but I didn't think even for a minute that she would do something like this. I would've helped her no matter how pissed off she made me. I would have helped her if I'd known."

"Sam, come here, baby," Daniel tries again but I just can't. I have to freak out a little by myself.

"I can't. Just let me have a shower then I'll come out and we'll talk all you need to."

"We *all* need to talk. Neil's calling Olivia right now, so I'm sure she'll be on her way over soon. Can you give me a hug, Sam?"

I know I should. I know it's a tiny request from my mourning friend, but I just can't. I'm almost positive I'll lose it if I hug Daniel right now, so I need to get away from him.

Slowly closing the door on Daniel in the hallway, I make it to the toilet before the tears start, and I start the water and undress before the pain starts. I wrap up my stupid leg before the anxiety starts, and I even make it into the shower before the insanity starts.

Sitting against the side of the shower, I think about Heather and I want to scream.

Heather was so sweet and dumb, and lovely and bitchy, and kind of innocent but whorey at the same time. She was just like 18 years old always, though actually 24. I guess she'll always be like an 18 year old now.

I can't believe this has happened.

I can't believe I pushed my friend to suicide, and I can't believe I made the choice to send her away Sunday morning. I can't believe she left my apartment and killed herself.
I can't believe this was her choice.

My heart is broken and bleeding, I think. The pain is unbearable, and I don't know how to stop the agony from shredding my heart. I really don't know what to do this time. I don't know how to fix this, and I don't know how to fix Heather. I don't know what to do now that she's already gone.

Crying myself stupid, I allow the water to heat the coldness inside me and I allow the water to wash away the tears I promised never to shed again after I left my mother's house. But here I am- crying again. Crying for the 10th time in less than a year.
Allan, the bastard, started my tears when he cheated on me, and now I've cried at least 10 times since the day I found out about it.

Without eating, or studying, or drying my hair even, at only 6 something in the evening I'm going to bed. I know the boys will probably try to wake me, or feed me, or just talk to me, but I can't talk yet.
I feel terrible, and I'm absolutely devastated over Heather though I can't even really feel it yet. I'm numb, and I don't want to talk about what hasn't hit me fully.
Plus, I'm much better at being a rock for everyone else. So that's what I'll be for them to help fix this nightmare. Tomorrow.

*****

Waking to Daniel beside me, I kiss his shoulder softly and prepare to go to class. I can't do anything today for Heather or Linda anyway, so I may as well go to school until the viewing Wednesday night.
"How are you, honey?" Daniel asks with his sexy morning voice and I can't help but smile, which I'm sure is wrong under the circumstances.
"I'm good. Look, I know you thought I needed you here so you stayed and sent Neil home last night with Olivia, but I'm okay. Please go home

when I'm at school. I don't need any help, and honestly, I don't know how to help you guys yet. So maybe you can help each other?"

"We really should talk about Heather," he says as I flinch. "Sam, one of your closest friends just killed herself."

"I'm well aware of that, Daniel," I breathe nearly silently. "I know what she did, but I'm not ready to deal with it yet. And I really don't need you here to comfort me. I'm okay. What can I do to help you though?"

"Sam. I stayed because I needed *your* comfort, and I didn't want to be alone-"

"But Neil is-"

"Neil," he exhales deeply. "I'm sorry. But I'm just not in the mood to deal with his shit right now. I don't want to pretend, or fake it, or even lean on him just because I'm upset and desperate. Nothing has changed between us simply because there is something horrible going on around us."

Sitting back down beside Daniel, I take his hand and try one last time. "Maybe you can help each other and then you won't feel so badly about what he did to you? I don't know what to say except he's really sorry and he swears he won't do it again. He was an asshole, but he hates being without you so much, I think he's learned his lesson."

Turning to stare at me, Daniel looks almost angry suddenly before he speaks. "Samantha, *please.* You know as well as I do that's bullshit. Neil cheats. It's what he does. It's what he did before me and even with me in the beginning. He isn't going to stop ever."

"No, this was just a mistake. One mistake. But he won't do it again."

"I know about the others, Sam." *What?* "I know when we first started dating he was still screwing anyone he could. I know while I was thinking of a long term relationship with the funny, sexy, wonderful man I instantly loved, he was off screwing anyone he could. I also know it was you that stopped him," he says with a sad smile.

Feeling totally put on the spot, I don't know what to say. I can't lie to Daniel, but I don't want to admit Neil was still cheating in the beginning either. "Ummm, he was..."

"A whore. I know. But I thought he would change for me. And I know you threatened him and actually slapped him once when you caught him with someone else. He told me all about it, like a year later. Why else do you think I love you so much?" He asks with his beautiful smile to my stunned silence.

"You're my sweet, sweet Sammy, and I adore you. I love you for being Neil's conscience. And I love you for loving me enough to bitch slap your best friend and soulmate when he wasn't smart enough to see what he had with me in the beginning. But things have changed. Neil stopped cheating and we made a wonderful life together. We were doing so well, and we were so happy. But as soon as things turned a little sour between us he ran off and slept with someone else. He says just once-"
"It was."
"Fine," he huffs. "Just once. But still, one time is enough for me. Neil got drunk and slept with someone when he lives with me, says he loves me, and says he wants a future with me."
"He does want all that with you, I swear."
"But I don't think I want it with *him* anymore." Looking at Daniel struggle, the pain in his voice causes me to stop and really listen. "That's the difference now. We were having a hard time after your accident, so he went and ruined our relationship totally. Instead of waiting out the hard time with me, or working on it together, he bailed."
"But he loves you."
Exhaling loudly, Daniel cuts me off. "I keep saying the same thing, but neither of you will understand or let me go. Well, *you* I don't want to let go of ever," he says with another hand squeeze. "But I think I want to let go of Neil now. I'm *tired,* Sam."
"Please, Daniel. Just try a little longer. I know it's wrong and selfish of me to ask. And I know I didn't try with Allan, but we were different. We loved each other, but you guys love *love* each other."
"We did," he agrees.
"You do. Otherwise you would've left as soon as he told you he cheated the next morning. Which quite frankly for Neil was fairly impressive. The old Neil-"
"Never would've told me. I know," he exhales again shaking his head. "Neil pulled that same rationalization out when I didn't want to talk to him. Whatever, Sam. I think I'm pretty much done. This last month and a bit has been awful for me. I love him, hate him, want him, and can't stand him. And living with him is brutal because he flaunts his body nonstop, like I'll just jump him and everything will go back to normal."
Smiling, I can't help it. Neil always uses sex and his body to get what he wants. Even with me. "He loves you so much, he wants to tempt you into forgiving him," I grin.

"Believe me, I know. And I've *been* tempted, trust me. But then the hurt returns and I look at him and feel such anger I wish I could make *him* hurt as much as I do, but that isn't me, Sam. I don't hurt people. When I'm around Neil though, I suddenly feel like causing him pain, and that makes me feel worse about everything. So I'm stuck in this thing that I hate with the person that I love. And I'm tired of it," he admits looking totally exhausted suddenly.

"Just a little bit longer? *Please?* Wait until next week, then make a decision. You can stay here forever, or until you're ready to make a move with or without Neil, and I promise I'll stop bugging you about it. It's just so hard for me. I'm like related to Neil at this point, but I can't let you go either. And I know you two are amazing together, I've *seen* it. So I want you to wait before you leave him, just a little bit longer. *Please?*"

Laughing, Daniel hugs me and nods. "You don't use sex on me, but you're just as persuasive as Neil is when you want something."

"I know. He taught me," I laugh. "I'm so sorry, but I have to go now. I'm going to be late for class and I can't miss the first lectures. Come back here after you're done tonight if you want to get away from him, and we'll talk all night if you need to. I should be home by 5:30ish, and we can make dinner together."

"Sounds good. Have a great day, and stop thinking about me and Neil. There are so many other important things to think about right now."

"I know. I just don't want to deal with one of them. Dealing with you guys is way easier, and I'm good at it," I grin again before kissing his forehead goodbye as I leave for school.

Choices...

CHAPTER 13

Screaming at the screen, I see the whole auditorium of students jump and turn to stare at me in my peripheral. *Whatever.* I don't care. I'm losing my mind. Or I've lost my mind. Or, holy *SHIT!* I'm completely fucking mental.

Peeking through my shaking fingers covering my face, Heather is still talking to me from the screens across the whole auditorium. 3 screens, center, left and right are filled with her all around us, and I can't make her go away. Can anyone else see her?

Talking, she's lying naked, dissected and partially sown back up again. Her brain is on the scale, and her heart is beating on the table beside her body.

"You didn't make the right choice, Sam. You didn't choose right. And this is all your fault," she says loudly again.

Oh *god. Help* me! Begging her to stop, I can't help but look at her again on the screen.

I know people are talking to me, and I think there's a TA next to me talking. But I can't hear what he's saying. I'm mesmerized by Heather's moving lips talking to the ceiling.

"You didn't make the right choice, and now look what's happened."

Begging, I don't know what else to do. *"Please,* Heather. I'm so sorry. I always chose you, just not then. You were acting crazy, and I was pissed off, but it wasn't forever. I just needed you to leave that morning. Not *forever!"* I scream so she understands.

When her head turns to look right at me, I can't help another scream from escaping my chest. With dark sockets and eyeless voids, she is staring at me sightless. Where are her eyes?

"You didn't make the right choice, Samantha. You made the wrong choice Sunday morning, and now look at me. What's left of me?"

"Heather, please?" I cry to her broken body.

Standing and pushing past the person holding my arm, I stumble in my cast, pushing against people, using the backs of seats and shoulders to get to the bottom of the stairs. 4 million stairs later, I'm standing tiny and exhausted in the middle of the 3 huge screens with Heather all around me.

"I'm so sorry. I choose you, Heather. I do. I'm so, *so* sorry," I cry again. Shaking, I can barely hold myself up, but I don't care. I need her to come back, and I need her to know I choose her.

"*Heather?*"

"Samantha, I need to go away now."

"No! Heather, please listen to me. I'm sorry, honey. I'm sorry I slept with Matt, and I'm sorry I made you leave. I didn't mean forever though. I *never* meant forever."

"You didn't make the right choice, and now look what you've done."

"I didn't!" I plead. "I wouldn't. I love you, Heather. Since we were 14 and freshmen."

"Samantha. You didn't make the right choice, and now look what's happened."

"No! Come back, Heather. I'm sorry. I'm so sorry," I sob to my sweet, sad Heather.

Begging, and pleading, and trying, and crying, I don't know what else to do. Collapsing beside the center podium, I stare at Heather on the table, and beg one last time. "Please, Heather. I choose you. I promise I do."

"Oh, Sam. It's too late for that, isn't it? I mean, I don't even have a heart anymore." And as she tsks the obvious, I can't help but laugh at her stupid humor. "And where the *fuck* are my eyes?"

When she suddenly smiles, I think I'm forgiven. I think we'll move past this. I think maybe everything will be okay between us again, until she speaks.

"You made the wrong choice, Samantha," she says fading away. "Good bye, Sam. I loved you," she whispers, and I know she's really gone.

"I'm so sorry, Heather." Whispering, I wish she believed me, and I wish she understood. "I would do anything to go back to Sunday morning, but I can't. I wish I could make a different choice, but I can't. Heather? Please come back..." I beg her still silent body.

Staring at her in our sudden silence Heather looks asleep, but mangled, and dissected, and destroyed on the table. She looks heavier than usual like she's bloated, and her hair is darker like its dirty, and she seems taller like she grew, and...

Focussing on Heather as I slowly find myself sitting back in the auditorium surrounded by bright light all around me, my eyes eventually adjust to the woman on the table. She's in her fifties maybe, and dead, and dissected, and *not* Heather.

She is someone's mother or daughter or friend. But she's not *my* friend. She is a woman who is *not* my Heather.

"Oh, thank *god*..." I suddenly giggle exhaling.

Laughing, I turn to use the podium to stand but I'm surrounded by people. There are people everywhere. Some closer and some farther, but they're still there. All around me, everywhere. Staring back at all the faces I don't know I'm totally embarrassed suddenly.

"Um, it's okay. I thought it was my friend up there. But it's not Heather," I say thumbing the screens behind me. "Wow. That was fucked up, huh?" I laugh self-consciously. "Sorry for all this," I mumble feeling unbearably uncomfortable, and pretty mortified actually. I need to get the hell out of here.

"Ms. Newman we have someone coming to talk to you," my new Professor says, and I think he must think I'm crazy, which given the circumstances I probably would think, too.

"Really, Professor -" ummm...?

"Neilly."

"Really?"

"Really."

"Neilly? Holy *shit!* We sound like a Dr. Seuss book," I burst out laughing again. Jesus Christ, this gets better and better by the second.

"... have to evaluate you before-"

Shaking my head I try to understand him. "Excuse me?" What did he say? "Look, I'm fine. I freaked out a little but not because of the class. And *not* because I can't handle this lecture. This wasn't about school at all," I try. But Professor Neilly is already shaking his head at me with disbelief and maybe even concern as I try to explain.

"I swear to god, I'm not crazy. I just thought I saw someone I know on your screens. But I *don't* know that woman, so I'm fine now. I am *so* sorry I interrupted your lecture. It will NOT happen again, I assure you."

When another teacher and an actual lab coat wearing doctor appear beside me, I bite the bullet and decide a fight about my sanity will look worse for my sanity, so I need to stay calm.

"Where should we go to talk?" I huff my defeat. "I really am fine. I thought the autopsy woman was my friend Heather who died," I explain.

Then it happens.

A sob bursts from my chest before I even know it's there and can stop it. Sudden and violent, I can't stop it, and I can't control it.

Crying my eyes out, I try to walk away from all the people watching me, but I'm immediately taken by the arm and helped up the steps back to my seat, and satchel, and crutches, and jacket.

Wow. I can *not* stop crying.

I'm snotty and sniffly, and shirt sleeve wiping my face and nose, but the tears won't stop. If I could, I'd kill Heather for this embarrassment alone. Oh *god!* Laughing at my bad joke, I want to hit my head against a desk. That's a tacky Neil joke, not a Samantha joke. And it's so wrong, but still, I'm laugh-crying nonstop.

"Sorry, my oldest friend just killed herself, and I may be handling it poorly," I laugh again at the absurdity of my *under*statement.

"I'm very sorry to hear that," lab coat Doc says gently.

"I'm okay. I was in shock when I found out last night so I didn't really deal with it at all. Um, I think it just kind of hit me today that she's really gone and I panicked or hallucinated or something because I didn't talk about it when I found out like I maybe should've. But honestly, I'm already feeling much better."

Lifting my satchel flap, Lab Coat puts my 2 books inside, and throws it over his shoulder as he lifts my crutches to my arms smiling at me.

He's doing the calm doctor, passive observer thing to help ease my hysteria. Wow, I actually know these tricks. I've played them myself with my mother, and with Heather ironically. And look at that, it's working. His calm smile is making me feel calmer.

"Where are we going?"

"Well, we can talk in the hall, or in my office, or in Emerg if you'd like..." He says lifting his head to look over my shoulder at someone behind me on the steps. "... Miss. Newman."

Wiping my nose again on my sleeve, I try for casual. But the damn crutches are in the way as usual, and I look like a total loser trying to hobble up the steps. Plus, I'm exhausted and pretty much done with this whole drama.

"The hallway will be fine."

"Wherever you're most comfortable."

Quietly walking up the rest of the steps to the doors, he sweeps in and opens them wide for me as I look behind me to the nearly empty auditorium. There are maybe a dozen people left but they are *all* watching my departure. This is going to follow me for years to come, I think.

"Does this go on my permanent school record?" I ask sounding desperate as I slump on the bench outside the auditorium doors.

"Yes," he nods sitting down beside me. Not even attempting to lie to me, I appreciate his honesty even though I wish he was lying.

"So this incident is going to follow me when I apply for my residency in a few years?"

"Yes. Though I'm sure the event will be noted and explained by Professor Neilly, and even by myself. But yes, it will stay on your permanent school record," he agrees calmly.

"So because I freaked out on my second day of school, not about school at all, I'm probably screwed for life?"

"I wouldn't say *screwed* for life, but you will certainly have to explain it during the residency interview process. You'll also have to have an exemplary record moving forward to show no history of mental imbalance if you choose to continue in Med School. But otherwise, you can move forward today if you choose to. You can leave this behind you until such time as it is questioned down the road."

Nodding, I totally understand. I've screwed myself, though not entirely, pretty damn good. From here on out I have to keep my shit together, have amazing grades, participate in all extras, and form a bond with my future Profs and TA's so my future isn't completely jeopardized.

"Do you want to tell me what happened today?"

"There's really nothing to tell. I was in class and somehow either I fell asleep or I just zoned out, which is *not* something I typically do, I promise. Anyway, I thought I saw my friend on the screens being autopsied, and I needed to apologize to her."

"I see..."

Turning to look at Lab Coat, I doubt he sees at all. "I'm actually very stable, though you probably don't believe me under the circumstances. I just couldn't accept yesterday that my friend Heather killed herself because I pushed her away the day before. So I was a little freaked out. Heather was always like a pain in the ass little sister to me. She was funny and dumb, and silly, but loyal to a fault. And I loved her even though I wanted to kill her sometimes."

"That *does* sound like a little sister," he smiles. "I have 2 of them myself."

"So you know?" I ask as he nods. "I'm just reeling from the choice she made. I don't understand it, and I can't really accept it."

"It's hard to accept something so sudden and shocking. Most people would be *reeling*, as you put it. Was there any history of emotional or mental imbalance before? Did you see this coming?"

"No," I exhale. But I did, didn't I? "Well, the suicide I didn't see coming, but Heather wasn't the most stable at times. She just hid it for the most part." But I don't know if that's true either. "Maybe she didn't hide it very well, but we all just overlooked it. Or thought it was just her. Or maybe wanted to believe she'd get better, or, I'm not sure anymore. I *never* thought she would do something like this, because I would've helped her, I promise. I'm usually good at spotting mental health issues- I've been around them my whole life with my crazy mother, so I know things. But I honestly didn't see this coming."

"Even trained professionals can sometimes miss the signs, so you shouldn't feel bad."

But I do feel bad. I also don't feel like talking to this guy about my friend anymore. I need to figure this shit out for myself.

"Look, I don't mean to be rude, honestly I don't. But how much longer do we have to talk before I've convinced you I'm okay? Do we need to go to your office? Or fill out a report? I'm sorry, but there is a very rational reason for my very irrational behavior. So I'd like to move on now if it's possible."

"We could talk a little while longer in my office if you'd like."

"Please... I'm okay. I want to call my best friend and go home. I have Heather's visitation tomorrow night plus a full day of classes tomorrow, and I'm exhausted. I'll set up an appointment with a grief counsellor if it'll help speed things along. I just want to go home, and I *really* need to email my Professor to apologize for disrupting his class."

"I can't force you to stay, and I can't force you to talk to me."

"So I can go," I exhale relieved. "Thank you very much for trying to help. This was a totally messed up day for me, but it will *never* happen again."

"I understand. Can I at least request you call me once tomorrow? Just one time. We'll finish my report of the incident, and you'll put my mind at ease," he smiles his middle-aged, formerly handsome, now has a big belly and graying hair smile.

Pulling out his business card, I see he's the Dean of Medicine, and I want to bash my head on a desk again. The *Dean?*

"Don't be intimidated," he grins. "I was a first year Med School student once myself. And unbelievably, back then the sight of blood made me nauseous. Try explaining that to your professors," he smiles warmly at me.

"Thank you very much for everything. I promise to call tomorrow," I say as I stand and collect my crutches and bag from the bench.

"Have a good day, Samantha. I look forward to your call tomorrow," he offers his hand and I take it.

I need Neil and I need to get the hell out of here. This has been a long, horrific day, and if I'm not careful I may cry again before I even get home.

"Where are you? Neil's not answering."

"At your place. You said we'd cook dinner together," Daniel says like I've confused him.

"Right. I forgot. I'll see you soon then. I'm leaving campus now and I need a drink when I get home. Like a really good, heavy on the vodka drink. Could you please have it waiting for me when I walk in the door?"

"Sure."

"Naked?"

"Done," he laughs. "Good?"

"Almost," I whisper and hang up.

*****

"What's going on? Spill it, Sam," Daniel demands stripping me of my satchel and keys, and handing me a large vodka and cranberry right at the door.

Making it to the couch with Daniel hot on my heels, I slump down and take a huge gulp of Vodka before I can even begin to explain what happened.

"What's wrong? You look terrible," he pushes again.

"Um, I freaked right out in a lecture today, and I've kind of screwed myself for life with this one. It's going to follow me forever to humiliate and embarrass the shit out of me. I'm going to have to always explain what happened and *why* it happened. So I'm totally pissed at myself for my freak out, but I'm really freaked out by my freak out. And I'm glad you're here," I burst out laughing at my manic sounding confession as he scooches in beside me.

  Lying upright against the end of the couch, Daniel pulls me by my waist right up his chest, until I get comfy between his legs and finally exhale all my tension in his arms.
  Waiting a second to collect my thoughts, I breathe a sad, "I really lost it today."
  "What happened? You never lose it so it must've been-"
  "Bad. Very, *very* bad."
  Gulping down half the large horribly strong drink, I lean back into him for a Danny snuggle, before finally spilling all of it.
  Repeating the story in my rational mind makes things seem so much worse. I can't even imagine what my fellow students thought, or saw, or believed was actually happening to me. Realistically, I was a complete psycho, having a very public meltdown wrapped in a hallucinatory-like episode.
  It's so hard for me now to remember what happened, because in my rational mind, I see clearly how delusional and fucked up I was behaving. And yet at the time I know there was nothing rational about me.
  I could have sworn on my life that what I was experiencing was actually happening. I would have bet my life on the fact that Heather was having a final talk to me. Not really saying goodbye, but more blaming me.
  "She blames me," I choke.
  "Sam."
  "She does. Daniel, listen to me," I beg turning to look at his eyes. "Heather told me over and over again that I made the wrong choice Sunday morning. She told me I made the wrong choice, and because of that she's dead. She actually said, 'Look what happened. Look what you caused', and she meant it. She really does think I did this to her."
  "Sam... I want you to stop for a second and rethink everything you just told me. You just described what happened as an intense hallucination, but now you're talking about seeing Heather like it was real again. You know you weren't really seeing Heather, therefore, you know you didn't actually hear her say those things to you."
  "I know but-"
  "There isn't a but here, Sam. Heather didn't say those things to you

because she wasn't really there. You *know* that. I think maybe you're just sad, and feeling guilty, and in shock still, so you freaked out imagining Heather having an autopsy. And something made it all feel really real to you. But it wasn't real, was it?" Thinking again, I know he's right. She *wasn't* there. I KNOW that, but it felt so real.

"I know. But god, did it ever feel real when it was happening."

"Most hallucinations do. Otherwise, people wouldn't freak out, right?" Nodding my head as we stare at each other, I know he's right.

I'm not irrational, or delusional anymore. And I get it, in theory. But it really did feel like Heather was talking to me. I know she wasn't though- I just have to keep telling myself that until I actually believe it.

"I feel so strange right now, Daniel. Like I know something but I don't. Or like déjà vu or coincidence are going to strike again soon. I have a weird kind of an emotional, like displaced feeling or something. Jesus, I can't even explain what I mean other than my heart and my mind don't feel like they're working together right now."

"I think you're struggling with what she did, and you're feeling guilty, but you don't have to. If you really think about it you know there was clearly more going on with Heather than her simply killing herself over a fight you two had. We've all fought with her before, loudly, and terribly, and sometimes in a way we didn't think we could move past. But we always did move past it, almost effortlessly."

"I know, but it's hard not feeling guilty. I had a fight with her, and an hour later she kills herself? How could I not?"

"Okay. Well, I told her off Saturday night for starting that fight with her drunken drama. Even after she apologized, I didn't let her off the hook for getting me punched, or for looking like a slut among 4 drunken idiots. I really hurt her feelings, but I was pissed at the time. So should I feel guilty because she killed herself the next morning?" Daniel asks so seriously, I want to hug him close to me. Daniel would never hurt anyone, especially intentionally.

"No, you shouldn't. Heather loved you very much. She even told me once when she was drunk that she kind of created dramas with others because she knew you would step in and save her. She actually told me she hated that you were gay," I admit laughing as he looks at me a little stunned.

"Heather said if you didn't *prefer* the dick, she'd make you her boyfriend forever." Remembering how serious she was, I burst out laughing as I tell him the last part of Heather's drunken confession while Daniel waits behind me. "She actually said she'd wear a strap-on if she had to to get you into bed."

Laughing my ass off, Daniel pushes me away laughing and shudders with a shocked look on his face. "A strap on to be with me? I'm flattered, I think," he laughs a little uncomfortably.

"You know, it's so sad now because I didn't know how lonely she must have really felt. She used to tell me she wanted to fuck Neil senseless because she thought of him as like a slutty equal of sorts, but she wanted *you* to be her boyfriend because you were always taking care of her and looking out for her. She thought of you as the best boyfriend ever. She was even jealous of the relationship I have with you and Neil- together and separately. But not enough to resent me I didn't think. Well, I don't know anymore." I stop rambling as we silence together.

I can't, and don't want to speak for Heather. I'll never know what she really felt, and I'll never really know who she was, which feels like the worst part of all this. I knew her for 10 years, but did I really know her? 2 days ago, I would have said I knew her inside and out. Now? I don't have any idea what was going on with her, or why she made such a horrible choice.

After we sit forever in silence, Daniel moves me gently to his side as he swings his leg over my head to stand. "Let me make us some dinner."
"Pasta? It's quick and easy."
"Perfect. Do you want to take a shower before dinner?" Which is actually Neil and Daniel code for, 'Hey, Sam. Do you need to cry in private?' Which I don't yet. Shaking my head, I raise my glass to finish the last of my nearly straight vodka, and settle in on my couch.

When we've finished dinner and lie on the couch again watching some useless television, I decide studying is out for the night. I don't have the brain capacity for it, and I'm not really in the mood anyway.
"Are you staying here tonight?"
"Yeah. It's nice not having to fake a lack of attraction to my sexy bed partner," he says laughing at my insulted face. "You know what I mean," he grins.
"I know *exactly* what you mean. I do it every time you sleep with me in

my bed," I wink before walking to the bathroom to get ready for bed. "Do you need to call Neil to let him know you're sleeping with your unattractive, not sexually attracted to her in the least, *unsexy* bed partner?"

"I wouldn't go *that* far, Sam," he smiles. "I'll call Neil, and I'll crawl in soon. Good night, honey."

"Good?" I ask hoping he is.

"Good," Daniel nods as I leave the room.

CHAPTER 14

Walking right up to Linda, I'm scared to death of her reaction to me. She could slaughter me as I stand or... "Oh, *Samantha*," she cries pulling me into a tight, sad, horribly emotional hug as I cling to her to hide my own pain and upset. At this rate I'll be crying in 2 minutes.

"I'm so sorry, Linda," I whisper in her ear as she hugs me tighter. "I can't believe this happened."

"Me either," she moans. Pulling away, Linda looks closely at me, brushes my hair from my face to tuck it behind my ears, and smiles. "Heather always wanted to look like you, you know?"

"*Why?* Heather was beautiful. She was a no makeup natural blonde beauty, who looked stunning when made up, too. Everyone thought so," I say a little uncomfortable. I'm not sure how many times I can say Heather's name before Linda starts crying again.

"She loved that you're a blue-eyed brunette. She once told me that was a pretty rare combination, and that all the most beautiful famous actresses had the same look as you. I even had to convince her not to dye her hair dark when you girls were teenagers because she wanted to look like you so badly," she laughs a little huff. "There was just something about you that Heather always wanted to be like. Well, except good in school, and a doctor, and settled..." Linda tapers off. This is getting too sad to acknowledge, and truly awful to hear.

Feeling desperate to make her feel better, I beg, "Can I get you anything? A drink of water, or something to eat?" But she's shaking her head as she takes my hand.

"Your mother and father were here before the visitation began. She looked good, Sam. She gave me a bible and told me she was praying for me and for Heather's soul. I think she may have been judging what Heather did..." Flinching, I hope my dad stopped her from being an ass. "...But your father steered her away and asked me to ask you to call him. Thank you for coming," she says so sadly, I can't understand why she would possibly thank me for being here.

"Of course. She was my best friend for years."

Tilting her head to the side a little, Linda gives me a funny look, almost like a smirk. "Well, maybe not your *best* friend, because everyone knows Neil, and now Daniel are your best friends. I know even Olivia rates higher than Heather did. And Monica was also your best friend until she left you for Allan. So really, Heather wasn't your *best* friend, Samantha," Linda says with the first signs of anger toward me.

"I'm close with all my friends, and Heather was no exception, I promise. She was like a sister to me."

Waiting for a comeback, Linda just nods. She doesn't look convinced, but she nods anyway and squeezes my hand again. Waiting, I think we're okay.

"She texted me before she did it. It was an 11 page text I had to scroll through forever, but it was enlightening. Did you know she hated her name? She actually wrote that. She said her name couldn't have a nickname like the rest of you have. And she actually listed them," she laughs. "From Sam and Sammy to Liv and Livi, she wrote about Danny, too. Though she did say no one could call him that but you."

"Neil doesn't have a nickname," I choke, grasping for anything to make sense right now.

"That's true..."

Staring at my eyes, Linda pauses then continues speaking when I can think of nothing else to say to her.

"It appears Heather also knew I preferred you as a daughter. She said Neil would always be yours, Daniel loved you more, Olivia confided in you most, and there was a Matt, too. Whoever he is, she knew he wanted you and not her. Did you know that? Did you know everyone in Heather's life preferred you over her?"

"That's not true," I stammer. I don't know what to say here. Linda doesn't look mad as much as resigned or something. Exhaling, I watch her eyes fill with tears again, and wait for something bad to be said. When nothing comes for a minute or two, I jump into the strained silence between us desperately.

"I loved her very much, Linda. Heather and I have been friends for almost half my life, and I loved her very much. I'm not sure what to say or do, but I'm-"

"Struggling to understand?" She interrupts as I nod. "I guess she just wanted you to choose something. She said that in the text. She said you didn't make the right choice. She said you had the opportunity to choose, and you chose wrong. She said 'look what's happened. Look what she did', and I didn't know what she meant, but then she mentioned a Matt, so I figured you must have chosen him over her somehow. I guess that was one time and one person too many for Heather. I don't know..."

I really don't know what to say anymore. If Heather really thought and felt like that, then I feel so much worse for her. I never wanted her to feel like she wasn't loved as much as everyone else was. And I never thought I did anything *to* make her feel that way. I was always good to Heather, and I always made time for her, I think.

After a minute of silence between us while Linda smiles and nods at someone else, she suddenly continues talking to me.

"I was so proud of you when you were accepted into Med School. Remember when I took you girls out for dinner?" Smiling, I remember. Both Heather and Linda were so drunk they were hysterical together. We had such a great time that night.

"I may have told her too many times I was proud of you over the years. Maybe I shouldn't have talked so much about how wonderful you were. Maybe she didn't think I thought she was wonderful, too. I don't know what she thought because she didn't tell me she felt so unloved until that morning." Choking up, I reach for Linda again but she steps away from me suddenly and holds her hands together in front of her body.

Waiting for me to reply, I honestly don't know what to say. What could I possibly say to make her feel better? I'll sound like a bitch if I say Heather did this because she was clearly unstable. Or I'll sound like a liar if I deny knowing what she was talking about with Matt. I don't know how to fix this.

"There are many people here waiting for me to talk to them, Samantha. Everyone wants to talk about how sweet, and silly, and pretty my daughter was. And I'd like to listen to that today. I'd like for Heather to be the center of attention just once in her life. So, would you mind leaving? I don't really care to know what you did or didn't do. And I'm not interested in explaining to everyone that you were *Heather's* best friend, even though she wasn't really yours."

Crying out, I can't help it. "But she was. I loved her. I just didn't-"

"Make the right choice," she whispers and again I feel like I've been punched in the stomach. All the air has escaped my lungs and the world has started spinning around me. I need to get out of here, because she's right. I shouldn't be here if I caused this.

"I'm so sorry, Linda. Honestly, I loved her," I plead one last time.

"Please, Samantha. Looking at you hurts me, and I don't need any more pain right now. My daughter is dead, okay?" Nodding, I have to get out of here myself.

"I'm very sorry," I whisper before turning quickly to find the fastest way out.

Not even looking for my friends, I need air really fucking fast. I can barely breathe, and I feel tears and darkness trying to swallow me. I hate this feeling, and it comes way too frequently now.

Ever since my accident, I've had multiple times of this near darkness trying to take me but I can't let it today. It can't have me right now and certainly not here. This is Heather's day. And I need to give Heather her day.

Stepping out of the funeral parlor around the smokers and all the people talking in soft voices outside, I tear apart my purse for my phone to text Neil.

   -I'm ok. please stay with the others. I need some alone time.
   I'll call you later.

And within a second there's a reply.

   -What can I do?
   -Nothing. I'll call later. Make sure Livi and Daniel are ok. Take
    care of them. I ♥ you.
   -Luv u 2. D and Livi are standing with me and all is ok. Go
    home. I'll b there later. Don't argue. I'll see you at home
    later. Good?
   -Trying
   -xo

Turning to head for a cab I'm immediately stunned by Matt walking up the steps in front of me. Catching my breath and leaning into my crutches, I can't believe we're 3 feet from each other suddenly. I didn't think I'd ever see him again, and I'm not sure I ever want to.

I didn't return his 2 calls on Monday or Tuesday, and I've avoided calling him because I just can't deal with anything else right now. I don't want to talk to a constantly calling Allan, a calling Matt, or my other 3 friends thinking I'm going to lose it at some point again. Heather's funeral and school are about all I *can* handle right now.

"Hi," he says quietly like he's unsure of what my reaction to him will be.

"Hi," I try to smile back but can't.

"I'm not sure if this is appropriate or not, but I wanted to pay my respects to Heather. And I wanted to make sure you were okay."

As he walks closer to me, I almost step backward. I'm not sure why he makes me feel uncomfortable suddenly, other than he was the fucking demon I remember too often. But looking at Matt just steps from me makes me feel weird and off-center again.

"I don't know if you *should* be here. Linda, Heather's mom, knows about a Matt." What else do I say? He chose me, I chose him, and Heather chose death? "How did you hear about her?"

"Neil." Of course. "You didn't return my calls, so I called him yesterday to see if you were okay."

"Because we *slept* together?" I ask with an obnoxious huff. "I'm fine."

"Not because we slept together," he answers quickly. "Because you were pretty freaked out when I left Sunday morning, and I hated leaving you like that."

"Why?" This is too much. I'm nothing to him, and he is certainly nothing to me.

"Look, can we sit for a minute?" Matt motions to the little bus stop bench on the sidewalk.

God, I really don't want to do this now. I don't want to deal with Matt, or this, or anything else. I want to go home. I have too many lectures tomorrow and tests coming up. Plus after Heather's funeral I'm getting this piece of shit cast removed tomorrow afternoon for a walking cast, finally. I just need all the shit to end for a while.

"Please, Samantha?" He asks still keeping 2 steps between us. He looks almost sad or something, which is weird considering he didn't even know Heather. Not really.

Nodding, I hobble my ass down the steps to the bench, and with a tragically graceless slump, I fall into the bench with a loud exhale.

"Can I give you a hug?" Matt asks gently as I freeze.

Looking at Matt quickly, I don't know how to respond, so I just stare at him panicking. He doesn't seem to understand what a big mistake that would be. If a girl is on the edge and you're nice to her, or hug her, she cries. Everyone knows that.

Whenever I've been on the brink since the day I met Neil, he snaps at me and calls me a name, or insults me in a funny way if I'm almost losing it. Neil knows the rule: Don't be nice. Be a prick and Sam can keep the upset away. Be nice to her and she'll lose it.

"Please don't hug me, Matt. I'll probably cry if you do. Can't you call me a bitch or something?" I ask grinning at his *what the fuck* expression. "Honestly. Be mean to me so I don't lose it here."

Shaking his head, he grins back. "Can't do it. *Won't* do it. Sorry, Samantha."

Looking around the street, I realize I hate this part of town. It's super loud, always busy, and the traffic never stops. I wish people understood there was a dead girl in there who deserves to rest peacefully. It would be nice if they stopped honking at each other while speeding down the street to pay some goddamn respect to Heather.

"I'm sorry for your loss," he whispers breaking up my thoughts on traffic, and I almost break down.

"It *was* a loss." Leaning forward, hunching over my own body, I look at the sidewalk and say the things I wish I could've said to Linda. "Heather was so sweet. She was the kindest person I've ever known."

"Tell me," he whispers softly.

"Um, I came home once and there was a cute little porcelain trinket on my kitchen counter. It was a blue-eyed blonde little girl hugging a blue-eyed brunette little girl and under the girls on a silver plaque it read, 'I'll always choose you. Best friends.'

Oh *shit!* I'll always choose you. I'll always... Hold it in. Hold. It. In! My heart hurts so badly right now I feel like it's going to explode on the sidewalk.

"Heather bought you that?"

Gasping, I fight the sob stuck in my chest. "Yes, just because. That's all the note said. 'Just because', and it was so cute. It wasn't really my thing, and I certainly don't collect porcelain, but it was so sweet I kept it on my living room table for a while. But I'm not sure where it is now." When did I move it? Where did I put it?

"What else," Matt asks gently, and I can't help telling him about her.

"I remember going to her apartment 3 years ago when Allan and I had a fight." When Matt looks at me in question, I explain. "Allan was the boyfriend I mentioned of almost 4 years, but we broke up 9 months ago." Nodding, Matt waits for me to continue. "Anyway, I went to Heather's to rant and she was eating tuna out of the can for dinner, which she hates. So I thought maybe she was dieting or something. Not that she ever needed to- she had an *amazing* body. Anyway, I teased her about dieting until she told me it was all the food she had, which I didn't believe. But when I opened her cupboard to pull something else out for her, there was nothing. I looked in her nearly empty cupboard with only half a bag of rice, another can of tuna, a sloppy joe can, a half eaten sleeve of crackers, and some spices. I remember looking at her strangely because she and I had just gone grocery shopping not even a week before together." Trying to breathe, I remember that day so clearly.

"When I asked where all the groceries were she told me she gave them to a mother and kid in her building. Like *all* her food. She said she packed up everything unopened and frozen and carted it down the 2 flights to leave it outside the woman's door. I knew Heather must've been starving because we were both broke students, though I had Allan if things got too dire when I was in school. But Heather was alone, working at a dry cleaners so she didn't have much of anything after rent and tuition."

I remember what it was like for us then. My dad gave me a little money each month, but he made too much as my parent to entitle me to full loans, but not enough to help me all that much. Plus I didn't want my parents' money because of my mother. So I worked and went to school, and I lived with Allan, but things were still always tight. I can't even imagine how tight it would've been for Heather who lived alone but paid for everything herself because her parents couldn't help her out much.

Wanting to finish my story, I smile at Matt for a second and feel okay about sharing this part of Heather with him.

"Naturally, I asked why she gave away all her food until she eventually told me when I promised not to tell anyone else. Um, I guess the mother and Heather started talking casually in the laundry room of their building until her son quietly asked for something to eat. Apparently, the mother told him soon, but Heather saw her actually look kind of distressed as she whispered soon to her son. She told me she watched the little boy nod like he was starving but understood, and he stopped asking immediately to just sit silently on the orange chair beside him Mom. Heather said the little boy smiled at his mom sweetly but didn't say another word about food the whole time they waited for their clothes to dry for over an hour."

Okay, so I'm not actually crying, but tears *are* sliding down my cheeks. God, I need to finish this so Matt understands the Heather I knew. I don't want Matt to only know that awful drunk Heather he met at the club or the scary psycho Heather from Sunday morning.

"Anyway, the mother looked away from Heather embarrassed and mumbled, 'things were just really tight right now', and Heather nodded like she understood and didn't say anything else about it. But later that day she called me to go grocery shopping because I had a car- well Allan had a car. Anyway, we went shopping, and I remember mocking her for some of her food choices," I laugh shaking my head.

"The cereal she had got a laugh from me because it was the most sugary kids brand available. And I think she had 4 bags of cookies which I thought was way too many. She also had like 5 bags of chips in her cart as well. I remember even asking if she was having a party without me and she replied with a smirky *maybe*, as she continued filling her cart with every food staple and treat you could think of. She spent close to $200 dollars which was a fortune for us. But at the time I had no idea she was shopping for them, or treating the little boy to all the yummy things his mom probably couldn't afford to buy. And you know what?" I ask as Matt says 'what?'

"When I stood in Heather's kitchen looking at her like she was crazy to have spent all her money on someone else, I couldn't help but ask, 'Does she know what you did for her?' I asked her that because I was only 21 and still immature enough to want acknowledgement for doing something so amazing. But Heather didn't. She actually said, 'God, no. I wouldn't want to embarrass her. I just wanted to help her.' And she did help her," I smile sadly to a silent Matt.

"Heather actually shamed me in that moment. I felt embarrassed that I wouldn't have done something like that, or even thought about it really. But she did. Heather was standing there eating tuna from a can which she hated with nothing else in her apartment to eat until probably her next pay day, and I was ashamed of myself, which was also not her intention."

Remembering that day, I can't help but smile. Heather was just so kind to everyone. *Always*.

"What did you do after that?" Matt asks taking my hand to rub my knuckles gently.

"I convinced her I felt like pizza, ordered one, and ate only one slice so she had the rest to eat the next morning for breakfast. Then I went home and asked Allan for a hundred dollars."

"You did?" Matt smiles, as I nod. "For what?"

"The next day I went grocery shopping and lugged everything up Heather's stairs and placed the bags outside her door about 5 minutes before she was getting home from work so they weren't stolen by her neighbors before she arrived. I even waited in the stairwell, peeking my head through the little window to make sure no one stole her food," I admit laughing. Smiling back at me, Matt asks what happened.

"Nothing. Heather found all the food, smiled and shook her head which made me feel really good for a second. Then the little shit picked up all 8 bags of goddamn groceries and walked back down the opposite flight of stairs to her neighbor's apartment again."

"She *did*?" Matt asks incredulously as I nod.

"She did. I actually ran down the opposite stairs and looked through the windows until I saw which floor she stopped at to watch her leave the groceries in front of another door. And you know what's funny? I was pissed off at first because she didn't acknowledge the food I bought her and keep it, then I was humored while I stairwell stalked her. Then I was happy when I saw her leave the food for someone else. But I'll admit I was dying to know who got my food. I wanted to know if it was the same mother and son, but I couldn't ask, could I? That would've defeated the purpose of doing Heather a kindness if I brought to her attention the fact that I was the one who did it, which obviously she would've known was me anyway. But still, it's not like I could've asked her, so I had to let it go."

Pausing for a moment smiling, Matt asks, "Did she ever talk to you about it?"

"Yes. Maybe 2 weeks later Heather casually mentioned her neighbor's son who she loved hanging out with, and then she turned to me with tear-filled eyes and said quietly, 'She's sick, too,' which made me feel horrible. I was so sad and humbled, and just shocked by everything in that moment, I had to excuse myself while I got my shit together in my bedroom alone. So that's it."

Pausing for another moment in thought, Matt finally asks what I didn't want to have to answer. "Do you know what happened to them?"

"Yeah... She died last year from breast cancer which is absolutely brutal," I choke out. "Like she didn't have enough shit going on in her life. I remember when she died Heather was so sad, crying in my kitchen as she confided in me everything they went through. So I took her to the funeral and I held her hand the whole time while we sat beside the little boy, Ethan. I was absolutely heartbroken for Heather, and for Carey, who I had never met but felt somehow connected to."

"And the son? Ethan?" Matt whispers seemingly as entrenched in my story as I am in the memory of the story.

"He went to live with his dad after the funeral. God, Heather was so devastated to see him go, but she promised to visit him so they could play video games together," I can't help cry. "I guess it was a bad breakup, but while Carey was sick the dad came around a lot and even helped out. So by the end Carey and her ex-husband were friends again, and he became close with his son again until..." *she died.*

Wiping my tears away, I feel just horrible inside. I feel horrible for everything and everyone suddenly. Heather, Carey, Ethan, Linda, my friends, and even myself.

"I need to go home now. Thank you for listening to me, Matt."

"Samantha, I-"

"Please not now. I feel so awful, and Linda hates me, and I'm really sad. I just need to go home," I say rising.

Looking at me as he quickly stands too, Matt hands me my crutches and purse, looking really sad himself. Why? He didn't even really know Heather.

"What's wrong?" I whisper.

"Can I give you that hug now? Just a hug because *I* need one now." Looking at Matt, I find myself slowly nodding because I really want a hug, too. If my friends were with me I'd hug them, but they're not. So stepping into Matt, I try to hold in my agony as he pulls me tightly into his arms.

Matt is so warm, and he smells amazing, and he's comfortable to hug, the awkward sadness of the situation notwithstanding. Leaning into him, my cheek just reaches his chest, and I feel a little better for a moment.

"*Samantha?* Are you okay, baby?" Allan suddenly asks. Exhaling a *fuck* into Matt's chest, I tense right back up before turning to Allan.

Pulling away, I notice Matt keeps his hand on my back as I look toward Allan... and Monica. Oh, for Christ's sake. Then again, Monica had known Heather for years as well, so I guess its okay. But really?

Watching Monica quickly snatch Allan's hand, I almost laugh at the possessive gesture.

"Samantha, are you okay, sweetie?" Allan asks again with so much emotion and concern Matt actually shuffles behind me, while Monica looks at him with shock.

"I'm fine, Allan. Everyone's inside," I try to dismiss him. But he doesn't nod, or move, or do anything but stare at me, which is totally uncomfortable. Forever it seems the silent staring continues until it's just so awkward Matt jumps in.

"Well, *we* were just leaving," Matt says with obvious implication in his tone, as I groan inside.

I know Matt's intention was to help me, and I appreciate it, but Allan is not easily deterred and Matt probably just made things worse for me.

Looking at Matt closely, Allan smirks before speaking. "*I'll* take you home, Samantha."

"I'm fine, Allan. Please go see Linda."

"I'd rather see *you*," he says quietly and in my peripheral I actually see Monica flinch beside him.

"Allan. I'm not doing this right now. Or ever. I've told you every single time you call me that I don't want to talk to you anymore."

"You still *CALL* her?!" Monica yells grabbing his shirt sleeve.

Ooops. I didn't mean to open that up. I just wanted him to go away. Allan doesn't even look at Monica, though. He just stares at me.

God, I would die of embarrassment if I was her, and I actually feel bad for her right now. She really doesn't deserve my pity, but I still kind of feel it.

Whispering, I'm emotionally spent. "Please leave me alone. I don't want to do this right now. I'm trying to keep the drama out of today because this is about Heather. Remember, *Heather*? My friend who died?" I say to try to get Allan's attention.

"Of course. I'm sorry. I'll just take you home and come back to pay my respects to her family afterward."

Staring at Allan I'm stunned. Seriously. I'm so over Allan and his pushy shit all the time. We are over, but he just doesn't get it.

"We're done, Allan. We've been done since you slept with that woman from a bar. We've been over for 10 months now. *10*. And we're not getting back together, and I don't want you to call me anymore, and I don't want you to take me home. Matt, honey, let's go," I smile reaching for Matt's hand desperately.

"*Honey*?" Allan sneers leaning in closer to me. "You don't use pet names, Samantha, except with your *boys,* so I know you're lying. You and this guy aren't together," Allan actually laughs at me.

"I didn't with you," I whine. "But with Matty I do." Oh my god. *Matty?* My sudden desperation is making me sound like an idiot.

"Let's go, Sammy," Matt tries, and though I appreciate it, in a completely ridiculous bout of insanity I want to yell at him, too. No one calls me Sammy, but Daniel. Wow. Okay. I'm losing it.

Bursting out laughing, I take in Monica's silence and humiliation, Matt's calm posture as he tries to help, and Allan's obnoxious smirk. He knows I'm full of shit, and I know he knows it. But I just don't care anymore.

"I don't want you anymore, Allan. No matter how many times a week you beg, and no matter what you say or promise me, that is never going to change. We're done. Take Monica with you and have a good life without me. You had your chance, and you made a choice. And me and you apart is the consequence of that choice."

"No, it isn't."

"That's all there is now," I say with a finality Allan can't possibly argue. But he does anyway.

"So you're choosing this loser over me?" Allan asks with another goddamn smirk.

"*Loser?*" I bark. "You know nothing about Matt. He isn't a loser. *You* sound like a jealous idiot though. Go away! Go screw Monica. Go screw all the others! Do whatever you want. But stay the fuck away from me!" Stumbling on my crutches, Matt rights me as he helps me dramatically attempt to storm away.

"You're such a *BITCH!*" Monica suddenly screams breaking up Allan and my drama, and I can't help but laugh again. I don't want to be in this drama, I really don't. I'm better than this, but there's only so much pushing a person can take.

"*I'm* a bitch?" I ask as she nods. "You were my friend for years, Monica. We did everything together. You, me, Olivia, and Heather," I choke. "We were a close set of friends and I didn't think you could possibly hurt me like you did. But you left me when my boyfriend of almost 4 years cheated on me and within a month of that, you were chasing him? And *I'm* a bitch? You made a choice, Monica. You chose to sleep with the ex-boyfriend of your good friend. *You* did that! I was just left picking up my life, post Allan, and post Monica."

"It wasn't like that!"

"*Really?* Then what was it like?" I ask dumbfounded.

"He tried to get you back but you wouldn't have him. After your accident especially. Allan tried everything. And I knew all about it. He didn't lie to me. He told me he was trying to win you back. He even told me he asked you to marry him. He told me he tried to help you, and that he wanted to be the person who took care of you after the accident, but you wouldn't let him. You didn't choose him. So I did."

"And that doesn't sound pathetic to you?"

"No! You didn't want him. You thought you were too good for him!"

"He cheated on me, then ran and screwed YOU for Christ's sake!" I scream right back.

"So!" Monica screams louder on the busy street around us. "He did cheat, and he was sorry. But *YOU* wouldn't take him back. You thought you were too *special* to be with him! You wouldn't even let him apologize. So, fuck you! I took him instead and we've been together and happy ever since!" She yells with a triumphant smile.

"Did you?" I can't help but sneer because I've had enough. "Well, if you took him and have him, then why the hell does he still call and beg me to come back to him? Why the fuck does he say you're awful in bed, an idiot, and an emotional void. Isn't that what you said Allan? She's just someone to fuck? Yeah, I think that's it. So be careful Monica."

"Samantha," Matt tugs at my waist to get my attention, but I can't stop. I'm beyond furious, and so fucking fed up with Allan and his bullshit all the time

"What?" I scream at Matt. "Don't tell her she's pathetic? Don't tell her she's a joke to Allan? Don't tell her she's the fucking loser here? Look at you, Monica!" I yell turning back to her. "Look closely. Allan is standing beside you still begging *me*, even though you think you're both *happily* together. He's not even denying what I just said, *or* defending you. Doesn't that make you feel like shit? Because it should."

In the silence around us as Monica looks at me with wide eyes and tears streaming down her face I know I should stop, but I just can't. I've never wanted to hurt anyone so badly in my life.

"Monica," I exhale. "If you had stayed away and not acted like you were better than me because you had Allan, I never would've said anything. But you kept pushing me."

"Whatever, Sam. You're a total bitch now."

"Maybe. But you're the pathetic loser here. I'm doing fine, and I've moved on. And Allan has someone to screw while he waits for me to *never* take him back. But you're just standing there taking in insult after insult, and Allan's obvious rejection each time he admits he wants me back. Even now, he's trying to be with me in front of you, and you're still just standing there holding his sleeve. And it's really pathetic, Monica," I laugh.

"It never should've been Heather. It should've been *YOU!*" Monica screams as she suddenly punches my face.

Falling to my side, the explosion was so quick I couldn't even prepare for it, not that I would've known how to. I'm a girl, and I'm not used to being hit. I've never been hit actually. I've never been in a bar fight, or had someone dislike me enough to hit me. This is so bizarre, I can't help but laugh my ass off as the pain bursts in my face.

Slamming onto the ground and Matt's leg at the same time, both he and Allan grab for me, but I fucking hate everyone.

Laughing on the sidewalk, with Matt hunched in my face talking to me, I again reach for my phone to text Neil. Ignoring Allan and Matt completely, they keep talking to me and trying to help me stand back up, but I'm not having it. Screaming and growling at them, I need everyone to get the fuck away from me before I freak the fuck out.

911- out front. That's all I text. That'll be enough to have Neil come running. I just need to wait out all the sounds of everyone around me.

I don't want to look at anyone and I don't care what they're saying because I'm too busy just trying to see clearly. My eyes are pouring pain tears and my laughter is making me lightheaded. My leg is actually hurting as Matt helps adjust me on the sidewalk with Allan touching me still even as I push his hands away from me.

This is just so funny.

I've been hit by the woman who betrayed our friendship. I've been hit by the woman who loves the man who betrayed our relationship. I've been hit by a crazy ass bitch who doesn't know the shitstorm that's coming for her when Neil gets here. She's *so* fucked. And so I laugh all over again.

*****

"*Samantha!* You *hit* her?!" Daniel yells at either Matt, or Allan, or Monica, I'm not sure. And I don't really care.

Looking at Daniel leaning in my face, I just want to go home. That's all I want in this moment- the quiet of my home.

"Can you drive me home? Please, Daniel?" I ask with more tears as he touches my sore, already swelling face gently with a look of anger I've never seen from him before.

Reining in his anger, he whispers, "Of course, honey."

Taking my hand, and leaning into my side, Daniel helps lift me, and as my bad leg suddenly drops down straight when I stand I feel it right in my hip. Looking at Daniel, I don't understand what's going on around us, which is okay. I don't want to hear any more from anyone tonight.

Neil is yelling and I hear Olivia's voice practically screaming. Matt has moved to the side I see as Daniel and I walk away from Allan still yelling along with Neil and Olivia. I don't hear Monica though. Interesting. But then again, I don't really care. She's a bitch. And I've finally said goodbye to my old friendship with her. I have my closure finally.

"Monica is over for me," I say to an intense Daniel. "She said I should be dead, not Heather, and she has justified everything she's done to me and our friendship. So I can finally let her go now," I cry as Daniel nods.

Walking away slowly from the drama, Neil runs up to us to hand Daniel his keys, and without even looking at me he says angrily, 'you and me. Later,' which almost sounds like a threat, but I know it's not directed at me. And even if it was, who cares?

Today was supposed to be about Heather and somehow it became about me. Again. But I didn't mean to.

"I tried to pay my respects, and I was just going to leave so Linda had some peace."

Tugging me tighter to him as I hobble, Daniel breathes, "I know."

"I swear I didn't mean to do any of this, and I really don't think this was my fault because I tried to walk away. But Allan and Monica just wouldn't stop going at me."

"I know."

"I really didn't mean for any of this to happen. Monica attacked me first, and I tried to walk away. Matt even pretended to be my boyfriend, but they just wouldn't stop."

"I know, Sam."

"Honestly, Daniel. Linda told me it's always about me, and I didn't mean to make it about me tonight. I tried to walk away from all the drama," I cry louder as we round the corner to the parking lot.

"Stop, Sam. Look at me. I know you didn't. I know you *wouldn't*."

Looking at my beautiful cherub, I beg, "Is it me? Please tell me the truth."

"No, it isn't you," he says angrily.

"Daniel, I need to know. I thought I was good and strong and stable. I've always tried to be an awesome friend and a good person. I thought I was-"

"You are, honey. You're a very good friend," Daniel stops to look at me.

"But Heather?"

"Did a horrible thing. I don't know why, but you weren't the cause. You were very supportive of her, even when you told her off," he grins. But I'm not feeling the humor right now.

"And Monica?"

"Is a bitch. Plain and simple. She chose to be with Allan, and now she's paying the price for it. Things haven't worked out the way she wanted, so she has only herself to blame, not you."

"But she *does* blame me," I insist.

Unlocking Neil's doors, Daniel helps me climb inside the jeep, but before closing the door he hugs me tightly only to pull away to kiss my sore cheek gently.

"Of course she blames you. What's she going to say? 'I know I betrayed you, and I know I walked away from our friendship, but hey, I've totally fucked myself over by hooking up with your piece of shit ex-boyfriend? My bad?' So she's blaming you because it's easier."

"And Linda?"

"Is devastated, and needs someone to be mad at. So who else, but her daughter's best friend?"

Holding my stomach tight, I cry, "I feel a little like a whipping post right now," pathetically as he nods before closing my door.

In the silent drive back home, I can't help but think of everyone I saw tonight. Shy of my mother, I saw everyone I know, love, and hate. Yet, I ended up being driven home by someone who loves me.

"You love me," I breathe in the dark silence of the jeep.

"I do. Very much," Daniel agrees taking my hand.

"So I guess I'm not as bad as I think I am if the person everyone loves,

loves me. Right?"

"People love you, Samantha. I promise," he whispers squeezing my hand. "We all need you and love you very much. You're the center of our little group, and you keep us all together."

But I didn't, did I? Heather is gone. Monica is gone. Allan is gone. All that are left are Olivia, Neil, and Daniel. And even they are breaking away.

"We used to be a tight group of 7, but we're dying away," I say sadly then realize what I said. "Oh! I didn't mean it like that!" I choke before silencing. I'm not speaking anymore tonight.

"I know you didn't mean it that way. You need to relax, Sam."

Opening my door, Daniel doesn't even wait for me to decide what I want to do. Walking to my bedroom, I follow in a kind of numbed out darkness and exhaustion that makes me feel nothing anymore.

"Let me help you," he says gently.

Sitting me on my bed, Daniel unzips and pulls my dress overhead while helping me pull on my big hideous pink nightgown Neil hates. Without acknowledging my body at all he even took off my bra without looking at my chest.

"Come here, Sammy. It's time to sleep," he says toeing off his shoes as he settles into the middle of my bed.

"I get this cast off tomorrow after the funeral, and I'll finally be able to walk somewhat normally." That's all I have to say under the circumstances because my brain is fried, and my emotions are all over the place.

"That's good. We'll finally be able to dance together again," he smiles sweetly as I snuggle in.

Exhaling, I really need all this punishment to stop. "I can't wait to dance again. It feels like forever since you and I danced together."

Since I was normal, and happy, and alive, and just Samantha. Since the accident when everything changed for me. Since that Sunday morning when I went for a jog with a hangover and my best friend.

"Relax, baby," Daniel says kissing my head. "You're a good person," he whispers as I cringe inside.

"But all my choices?"

"You've made the right choices," Daniel says with a conviction I don't feel at all.

CHAPTER 15

I'm done my first semester of Med School. I'm totally done, and I did well. In the blink of an eye, everything came together and I finished my term without drama or further incident. I survived the late night studying, the lack of social life, and the constant speed in which Med School requires and flew by.

Amazingly, I'm suddenly here. I'm finished for almost an entire month before my next term begins, and I honestly can't even remember how it all went down.

I was starting school, Heather died, and now I'm finished for the semester. It was like a hazy trip through excitement and fatigue that I successfully came out of on the other side somehow, but can't remember.

Tonight I'm finally going out with my friends, and I can't wait to just exhale. I'm going to party and dance a cast-less dance of happiness.

I'm healed and whole and ready to let my hair down for a night of fun. I have a drink. I'm dressed up. I'm relaxed and ready. My friends should be arriving soon, and I can't wait to see them though it may be a little hard, all things considered.

Neil and Daniel have split up. Officially. Neil and Daniel have promised to play nice tonight though, especially after I offered to see them individually instead of as a group. They both insisted however, they were grown-ups and could be in the same room with each other without causing a scene for one night to celebrate my momentary freedom.

Daniel is staying at his parents' house until his new apartment is available on January first, and Neil kept their old place, miserably alone.

Sadly, they just couldn't come back to each other no matter how much they loved each other, though they tried to for months. Neil tried each and every single day to convince Daniel he'd never cheat again, but Daniel couldn't believe him. And Daniel said he tried to see past Neil's cheating every day, but couldn't.

Daniel even admitted to feeling a little psychotic by the end of their failing relationship. He said he felt anxious and nervous, and paranoid every time Neil left the apartment, came home even 10 minutes late, spent time at the gym, or just spent time with his coworkers after hours for a quick drink or a bite to eat.

It didn't matter to Daniel the logical reason Neil wasn't around, he instantly imagined Neil sleeping with someone else and he eventually became quite mental over it.

The fights started soon after and then the insecurity took over completely. Daniel started working out more, obsessing over his appearance, while watching Neil obsessively. No matter what reason or explanation, Daniel started doubting even the simplest of things Neil said, until they were just so tired of arguing they barely spoke.

Daniel even admitted to following Neil once after he left his office to see what Neil was *really* up to. And horribly, when Neil saw Daniel stalking him through a coffee shop window, the humiliation was complete for Daniel. And the end was obvious.

Neil approached Daniel outside with concern until Daniel admitted he was simply following him. In an unbearably sad moment between them, Daniel admitted he followed Neil, didn't trust him at all anymore, and sadly, Daniel walked home alone when Neil said he couldn't keep saying he was sorry.

Both Daniel and Neil were tired, and embarrassed, and just so sad after the coffee shop incident, Daniel moved back to his parents house that very night before Neil even returned. And that was their end.

Neil wishes he could do anything to have Daniel back, and Daniel wishes Neil never cheated so they could go back to the way they were.

As for me, I still talk to both every few days. I *love* them both. And thankfully both want me in the other's life still. Neil is still my gorgeous, funny, sexy best friend. And Daniel remains my beautiful, stable, loving cherub. So nothing has really changed for me, except for the closeness we three shared together.

But honestly, my heart is broken over this break up. For them especially, but selfishly for myself as well.

I loved having Neil and Daniel by my side. I loved the flirty, easy comfort they provided me in life. I lived for the knowledge that they were mine to love and adore always. And though each swears nothing will change between us, it already has. They are coming over separately, and they will both try to act normal with each other as to not disrupt the harmony we used to share. But it'll be fake and forced.

Neil won't joke about some hot guy, followed by Daniel pulling Neil's hair into a stunning kiss after a teasing growl. There won't be any playful relaxed love between them, and I know I'm going to miss it.

I wish so many things could go back to the way they were before my accident. I wish we all still danced and teased and loved each other easily. I wish I was still the odd man out of the beautiful love affair I envied and worshipped every day of my life.

But sadly, I know we can't go back, no matter how much it hurts.

*****

"Why, don't you look slutastic," Neil smiles from my bedroom doorway as I turn to him.

"And don't you sound like the total cliché gay best friend," I grin back.

Walking into my room and dramatically jumping on my bed, Neil replies, "Of course I do. I'm gorgeous enough to be a model. I'm gay. AND I'm your best friend," he says all duh. "Plus, you love me, and would do me in a second if I let you." Shaking my head and grinning at him through the mirror he continues. "Admit it. I'm sexy as hell, awesome, super cool, and totally doable," Neil says with another smug smile as he leans back in a sexy pose to prove his point once again.

"Yes, darling," I sigh dramatically. "If only you weren't totally gay, and you actually offered me the opportunity to rock your world I would do you in a second. Good?"

"Good. But your sarcasm doesn't hide the fact that you want me. Badly," he grins again.

Turning to Neil, I want to deny him but I can't. Sitting on my bed beside him I give in as usual. "You're right. You will always be my ideal, Neil. Except for the whole YOU'RE GAY thing. Um, do you realize we have this exact conversation every single time we all go out?"

"Yes, I do. It's so I get you all hot and bothered over who you can't have, so you go and do Matt again," he grins.

"Really? So this is all for me?"

Laughing, Neil kisses my cheek. "Yes, this is all for you, Samantha. I swear I don't even care that you want to do me. It doesn't affect me one way or the other. I don't-"

"I miss you," I whisper and Neil stops teasing immediately.

Looking at me for a few seconds, he leans in to rest my head on his shoulder as we hug. "I'm always here, Samantha."

Nodding against him, I know he is. But everything just feels so different now. "I know, but you're sad Neil. And I don't know how to help you."

Pulling away, Neil kisses my lips gently. "It's not for you to fix. It's for me to move past. I did this, and I'm suffering the consequences. I made a choice, honey. A piss poor, drunken, slutty choice, and I've lost one of 2 people I love. So I'm sad. But it's not your sad, and you can't fix it. Daniel can't-"

"What?" Daniel asks leaning against my bedroom door.

Why the hell do I never hear people enter my apartment? Oh, because of the music, and because they all have keys. But still...

Exhaling, Neil looks at Daniel and smiles sadly. "You can't forgive me, and I can't say sorry anymore."

"I forgive you- I always did. I just couldn't move past it. But I tried, Neil," Daniel says almost begging Neil to understand, which he does I can tell. Neil isn't confrontational, he's quiet, which means there is nothing for him to argue about.

Sitting between them again, I watch with sadness the life they shared together dead and buried. And once again I don't know how to help or what to do.

In a moment of desperation, I ask Daniel, "Can we still do the nasty when you decide to have children?" And as Neil almost jumps on the bed beside me, Daniel can't stop the slow smile from spreading across his face.

Breathing, "Absolutely. You're the only woman I *could* sleep with," I grin at his smirk and laugh at Neil's expression.

"Gross..." Neil mumbles which makes me laugh harder.

"Do you want a drink?" Daniel asks looking desperate to leave my room, and Neil. So nodding, I give him his release as I watch Neil watching him leave.

"This is so hard," he breathes. And I can see and feel how hard it is, just from his expression alone.

"I know," I hold his hand. "But it won't always be. Look at me. I'm over Allan now so completely, I can't even stand the sound of his voice anymore. NOT that I want you and Daniel to get to that particular place, but maybe just a little less love for a little more friendship would be nice. Maybe if you two can get to the friends stage it won't hurt as much."

Looking at me like I'm mental, Neil whispers, "That *would* be nice, if not totally naïve, Sam. I can't stand the thought of being without him, so I sure as hell won't be able to handle him moving on. Fuck, if he hooks up tonight, I'm going to throw up," Neil whines.

"Well, I doubt he'll move on any time soon, so stop worrying. Tonight is supposed to be fun, and I seriously doubt Daniel would hook up so soon after you, or in front of you for that matter. He's too classy for that."

"I know... Okay. Enough of all this shit. Let's get you fab so we can hit the bar. I need the biggest fucking drink they have," Neil laughs pulling me up by my hands. "And you're changing," he says with a grimace.

Laughing, Neil seems back to normal. "No, I'm not. I love this dress. You told me I look slutastic, so I'm keeping it on."

"But it's cream-colored in winter. Fine," Neil pouts when I shake my head no to changing. I swear half the time he just likes dressing me up. "Then let's go, Slutty."

"Have you spoken to your mother lately?" Daniel asks when we join him in the living room. He's already made me and Neil drinks. Yay.

Shaking my head, Neil looks over at me with a classic Neil smirk. He knows what's going on with her. Sadly, he was the subject of another one of my mother's freaky holier than thou rants only 2 weeks before.

"Um, not really. She did *surprise* us on Thanksgiving when we came back here to meet my dad for a visit- which he lied about and said was going to be *just* him. Anyway, she was horribly rude as usual," I say as Daniel turns to look at a nodding, smiling Neil. "But now instead of using being strung out as an excuse for all her drama, she uses religion. She's gone totally extreme. Like scary extreme, right?" I ask Neil.

"She is. You should see her, Daniel," Neil laughs. "She's wearing like flowy dresses, and a giant crucifix that she holds in her hand all the time when she speaks, and she's even got a bible with her in her purse at all times, and she-"

"Acts demented," I can't help add. "Seriously. She makes weird cryptic little comments, followed by verses from the bible that are numbered and everything. And she sometimes gets all loud and dramatic, then instantly stops speaking and starts mumbling to make us strain to hear something she's saying that we can't even understand. She talks about sins, and sinners, and lumps all variety of sins in together. Like doctors who perform abortions, homosexuals, thieves, and even murderers. Everyone who she considers a sinner is in the same category as the next one."

"It's very uncomfortable," Neil adds seriously. "I can't stand strung out mommy, but this one seems way creepier. She's almost scary now. On Thanksgiving, and even last week when I saw her in front of Sam's apartment she told me both times how she prayed Sam would live, so now she has to pay back her debt to The Lord by saving all sinners from damnation. She actually said that to me last week. Then she offered to help me redeem my soul before I quickly walked into Sam's building with my key and tugged the door closed behind me so she couldn't get in," he shudders laughing. "It's really messed up," he cringes again as I nod emphatically.

Thinking about the way she acts and speaks now, I feel almost afraid of her potential. I'm afraid she's going to do something extreme or maybe even violent and blame it on religion somehow. I don't know, but I get an anxious, nervous feeling around her now, as opposed to the simple repulsion I used to feel when she was near me.

"I can't stand it. And the constant reminder that she made a deal with God so I would live is a little too much for me to handle," I exhale.

"Wow. Have you talked to your dad about it?" Daniel asks with a very concerned expression.

"Yup, but what's he really going to say? 'Yes, your mother is batshit crazy-*er*, but at least she's not a junkie anymore?' Honestly, I think he's probably just so tired and worn out from dealing with her for so many years, he simply goes with the crazy now. I mean really, why fight it? She's messed up as usual, and she's never going to change. The only thing that ever surprises me is the fact that he doesn't leave her because I honestly can't understand why he stays. They don't sleep together I don't think, she mumbles about bible passages all day long, and she's friggin scary now. Why the hell does he stay with her?" I ask more to myself than either of my boys.

"He loves her," Daniel breathes deeply. "Some people can put up with a lot from the person they love."

Though nothing more is said, I can almost feel Neil wanting to beg Daniel to put up with him for their love. Even as my chest constricts with my own sadness, neither Neil or Daniel speak for seconds in our awful uncomfortable silence, until Daniel stands and mumbles he's making another drink.

Watching Daniel walk away, Neil doesn't make eye contact with me, and Daniel doesn't stop to offer me another drink. The collective discomfort is so sad, I can do nothing but rise myself to change the music.

When Unkle Bob's 'Swans' begins, followed by Bright Eyes 'Lua' I sit silently drinking beside Neil. I know there's nothing I can do to change what's happened, but the soothing sounds of my favorite playlist can at least take me away from the little bubble of darkness that suddenly surrounds the three of us.

2 drinks later, Olivia finally joins the little semi-uncomfortable party of Neil, Daniel and me, and I'm stunned. Walking right in, she makes a beeline for me with a giant hug, momentarily shocking me with her appearance.

Olivia looks terrible. I mean she looks lovely still, but really, she looks just awful. She is *way* too skinny, and everything about her seems kind of dull or something. I can't explain it. Her hair is the same but shorter, her face is the same but gaunt like, her clothes are the same but too loose on her already tiny frame. And she looks terrible.

"What are you staring at?" She laughs awkwardly. "I know it's been a few months, but you couldn't have forgotten me already?" She grins, which I return awkwardly.

Hugging her tighter to me again, I actually feel Olivia's bones through the cute little dress she's wearing, and I'm sick with my shock. "Of course I haven't forgotten you. I saw you a few weeks ago. It's just-" When I suddenly see Daniel shake his head behind Olivia I stop talking immediately. There's something going on. There's something huge I can tell. But I have no idea what it is.

"It's what?"

"Nothing. I'm just decompressing from school, so everything feels weird right now. How's Matt?" I smile to reassure her that we're fine.

"Can I make a drink?"

"Of course you can. I cut up your Caesar celery," I say noticing she blew off my Matt question.

I'll have to try again later. If there's something going on with Matt, something that explains the way she looks, I'm gonna kill him. Trying to recover from the shock of Olivia's appearance, I take her to my kitchen arm in arm.

"Have you heard from dickhead lately?"

"Yes... Every friggin' day," I huff. Allan is an annoying daily constant who will not move on or leave me alone.

"Have you told him to just fuck off?"

"Of course. In every way possible, but he still doesn't get it. I mean we split up over a year ago now, and we haven't really spoken since my accident. But he still thinks I'll eventually give in and take him back, no matter how many times I say otherwise. Now I just ignore his constant calls whenever I can. But it's super irritating," I admit as Olivia continues mixing her drink.

"Men are idiots," she laughs turning to look at me with her drink.

Striking a pose, I ask, "Notice anything fabulous about me?"

"You're fatter?" Olivia barks a laugh as I swat her tiny, frail little arm.

"No! You asshole. No cast."

"I noticed. And I can't wait to dance with you. It's been a while since I've had a little girl on girl tango action on the dance floor with drooling boys watching. Will you still drool, boys?" She yells through my kitchen to the boys as both Neil and Daniel nod yes. "Good. I haven't gone dancing since the last time we all did in September..." she finishes lamely.

Waiting, everything stops as her sentence does. Here we go. I was afraid of this, and I was waiting for this. I didn't know how or when, but I knew someone would hit the Heather button and we'd all fumble. I didn't think it would happen this soon, but I knew it *would* happen.

"I'm sorry." Shit. Both Olivia and I say it at the same time, and we both freeze again staring at each other. Waiting for her to speak she doesn't, or maybe can't, so I jump in.

"How have you been with everything? I haven't really spoken to you much because of school, but I always wanted to."

"I know you did, Sam. It's okay," she says smiling as she leans against the counter looking at me. "It was hard at first, but I'm okay now. I'm actually a little pissed at what she did. I mean, come *on*- she has a fight with you so she kills herself? *Oh!*" As I instantly gasp at the accusation, she seems to catch herself. "I didn't mean it like that. I swear I didn't. I just meant, like, we all fought with Heather at least once a month, and that time with you was the time she did it. Well, I'm just kind of pissed at her, and I know I shouldn't be, but I am."

Choices...

"I-" Cutting me off again, Olivia seems to need to talk this one out, so I let her.

"I was pretty upset at first, like we all were, I know," she says taking my hand. "But then I got over it, and now I'm just kind of like *whatever*. I mean, life is short, right? So to end it sooner by choice is such a waste, and the way she did it, and the text to her mom, and kind of blaming you..."

Thankfully, Olivia slowly stops her ramble as I try desperately to hold in the need to defend myself. I never wanted this for Heather, even for a second. I never wanted it or imagined it.

"I didn't know that one fight would be THE fight, Livi. I really didn't," I moan almost begging her forgiveness.

"I know. But it's hard. Sometimes I can't help but wonder if you told us everything that happened that morning." *What?*

Gasping, "What do you mean? I told you guys everything that was said." But Olivia just nods like she doesn't believe me. "Matt was there. You can ask him!" I nearly panic. "Olivia, there was nothing else. I told you all the truth, and I don't know why she would go to such an extreme, or why she felt she had to, or why she did it."

Grabbing my hand again, Olivia exhales a hard breath. "It's okay, Sam. I didn't mean to sound like that. Honestly, I just have a hard time understanding why she did it, so I look for answers somewhere. I'm not accusing you though."

But she really *is* accusing me. To say what she's said, I know she doesn't believe me entirely, and I can't stand it. I've never lied to my friends before, and I wouldn't lie about this- no matter how bad it made me look or feel. I told them the truth of that awful morning, and if Olivia doesn't believe me I don't know what I can do to convince her.

"Please don't cry, Sam," Olivia whispers as she hugs me. And again, I'm kind of shocked by my tears. I haven't cried since the funeral. Not once. Ever. And I didn't even realize I was crying, which seems worse somehow.

"I'll be right back," I pull from her hug even when she tries to hug me a little tighter. Nope, I'm not doing this. I was just starting to feel less guilty about Heather, and Olivia made all the guilt rise back up to smack me in the face.

I made it through Heather's funeral the day after the Allan/Monica showdown, sitting in the back with Daniel, while Neil held Olivia tightly in the second row. I stayed far enough back so Linda wouldn't have to deal with seeing me. And I sat far enough back to pay my respects to Heather without hurting anyone else.

I never wanted this for Heather, and I hate that she did this to herself. But I don't cry anymore at night, and it does hurt a little less now. Well, until I'm reminded of everything that happened. Like I just was by my last girlfriend Olivia.

"You still love me, right?" I ask my beautiful cherub standing in my doorway. When he smiles and nods I feel remarkably better. "Good. Because you're kind of the model by which I know if I suck or not. You're my white knight, and everyone loves you. So if you love me, then I must be good still," I say as Daniel shakes his head grinning.

"I'm not a white knight, honey. I'm actually just a guy who thinks you're pretty amazing, no matter what shit is thrown at you."

Exhaling, as I put down my eyeliner, I whisper a thanks as Daniel leans into my back and hugs me.

"You're good, Sammy," he sighs before kissing the back of my head.

Exhaling the last of the tension and upset I felt with Olivia, I beg Daniel, "Will you dance with me at the club?"

"I can't wait to dance with you at the club," he smiles.

"Thank you, Danny."

"You're welcome, Sammy," Daniel whispers waiting for me to finish my makeup touch up before tugging my hand back to the kitchen for another drink.

Sitting on my couch awkwardly waiting for Olivia and Neil to stop arguing over the merits of dirty reggae and sexy electronica to have sex to, I can't help but smile. I couldn't imagine having sex to either type of music, but seeing as Neil's a pro at sex, I'm going to have to take his side, just for his experience alone.

"I'm sorry I upset you," Olivia whispers in my ear, causing me to shiver before she hugs me tightly. "You just never talked about what happened, so it felt like you didn't care as much as the rest of us did, which is totally unfair, I know."

"Liv... I had to get back to school, and I needed to move on because it hurt to think about Heather like that, and I don't really talk about bad stuff anyway. I usually just keep it all in," I speak quietly to her as Neil and Daniel pretend to ignore us.

"I know that. Sorry, Sam. I know you do. Shit... You always listen to us vent, and I rarely hear you vent back. I guess I just took it as you didn't care as much as you should've," she admits which is awful to hear.

Looking at her eyes for a second, I say as seriously as I can, "I cared very much about Heather. And I can't believe what she did. But I never want to talk about it because it hurts too much. You can though, and I'll always listen."

After my words, we're silent again while Olivia nods and looks down at the drink in her hands like there's nothing else to say. And really, what else *is* there to say?

"We're all getting hammered tonight. Period," Neil announces to both Olivia and I agreeing. Livi even throws in an, 'Amen, sister' with a giggle.

CHAPTER 16

Bypassing the line because Daniel knows the new doorman, Olivia and I are practically bouncing with our excitement. The music is so loud, even outside, the cold December air seems to hum with bass beats and vibration.

Like morons, Olivia and I didn't wear winter coats to carry around the club all night- instead jumping from the cab, each being held tightly by Neil and Daniel to keep us warm as we pass the freezing people who actually have to wait in line like we used to.

"I love you for knowing him," I giggle as we pass the bouncer who let us in.

"I SUPER love you for knowing him," Olivia says to trump me.

Pausing for a moment with an adorable smile and eyebrow wiggle, Neil says, "Do I even need to tell you how much I love you, Daniel?" Thankfully, Daniel just goes with the moment and doesn't take the teasing seriously though.

"Nah... I know exactly how YOU feel," Daniel smiles back with his own eyebrow wiggle, thank god.

Moving inside, past the people who have to leave their drinks against a wall between the 2 different clubs, we make our way into the smaller club section for the alternative music, then stop for a moment to get our bearings.

The flashing lights and loud music are always disorienting for us when we first enter. It's almost like we need to take it all in before we can make our way through, which we always do with more excitement.

"Drinks first?" Neil asks as we nod.

At the bar, Neil orders our usual, plus a shot of Jäger each to start us off. Clinking shot glasses, Neil and Daniel seem almost normal, or like they're trying really hard to be normal with each other.

Typically, they never had overt displays of affection in public anyway, with the exception of their one nightly dirty dance, and maybe a quick kiss here or there. So other than that, they seem almost the same with each other, so much so that I find myself watching their every move together with desperate hope.

"Stop staring," Neil suddenly says jarring me from my thoughts.

"I'm not," I argue, but we both know I'm full of shit. I can't help it though. I want them to fall back in love with each other so badly, I'm almost obsessed with the idea. I NEED them back together. For them, and for me.

Walking to the handrail against the dance floor, we're all still looking for a table to perch at while watching the dancers shake their asses. I'm jonesing to get down there. It's been forever since I danced, and I need it. I need to lose myself in the music for a little while.

"Have you spoken to Matt recently?" Olivia yells in my ear as I shake my head no.

"Just three times. He called the day of the funeral to see how I was after the Allan/Monica thing, and he invited me to a Halloween party, but I had an exam the next day so I couldn't go. Oh, and he called to ask me to dinner on Black Friday, but I was still reeling from my mother's impromptu visit the day before, so I turned him down again."

"She showed up at your place?" Olivia asks a little shocked.

"Yup. It was brutal. She is officially a batshit crazy, bi-polar, ex-junkie, extremist bible-thumper. Ask Neil about it. He was scared shitless," I laugh as she shakes her head.

"I can imagine. A bible thumper and a homosexual? Sounds like a match made in hell," she laughs.

"How's *your* Matt?" I ask to get the scoop I'm concerned about.

Turning away for a second, I can tell she's about to lie by the fake smile and wide eyes she suddenly sporting. "He's really good."

"Really?"

"Yes, *why*?" When she seems defensive, I know to tread lightly. Olivia usually clams up when she's defensive.

"I was just asking. We haven't spoken much since September, so I don't know how things are going," I try to appear casual.

"We're good. Just normal, ya know? Some days are better than others. But we're good, Sam. I promise," she says before turning to look at the dance floor again.

She's lying- totally and completely lying to me. I've known Olivia way too long, and way too well, to not know when she's lying to me. And honestly, it scares the hell out of me. I don't want another friend going through something I can't help her with. I don't want to be in the dark with another friend who's struggling.

   Pulling her closer, so we're not yelling over the music, I speak right in her ear. "You know you can talk to me about anything, Olivia. You always have before. And I'm good for it, I promise."

   Exhaling and nodding her head against my own she replies, "I know you are, Sam. But I promise there's nothing to tell. Matt and I are great, and everything is good. We're even meeting up later at my place," she fake smiles again.

   Looking at Olivia, I fake smile back and feel nothing but sadness for her. I don't know what's going in, but between her appearance and her lying to me, I know there is way more than she's saying. All I can hope is to get it out of her during the next 3 ½ weeks I have free from school.

   "Neil found a table," Daniel says beside us, like he was waiting silently for us to finish talking. I didn't even notice Neil left us when I was focusing on figuring out what's going on with Olivia.

   "Awesome. Let's go," she says grabbing my hand.

   At the table, Neil and Daniel grill me about Med School. Daniel wants to know what the lectures were like, and Neil wants to know about all the gross things. Its funny yell/talking in the club because everything feels exactly the same. Daniel is the calm, cool, angel, and Neil is the dramatic, hyper little devil among us.

   "Yay!" Neil claps suddenly right in the middle of Olivia describing her new boss who she can't stand.

   "Hello ladies... And Daniel," Matt says behind me as I feel a warm shiver race up my spine. A *warm* shiver, I swear to god.

   "Hello, Matthew. What brings you here?" Neil asks very seriously.

   "*Daniel,* of course. You told me exactly when he'd be here, and what I could expect once I arrived. And he doesn't disappoint," Matt replies just as seriously. "So it's good to see you again, Daniel," he continues his little game at my expense.

   "Hi Matt. You're looking as drop dead gorgeous as usual," Olivia beams. "Do you remember our dear friend, Samantha? I'm not sure if you remember her, but you met once or twice before." Ha! She's going to play Neil's game, too. Well, screw them.

   Turning, I look right at Matt and extend my hand. "Hello Matthew. I do believe we've been intimately involved once against a wall, *and* in my bed," I say seriously to Neil barking a laugh and Daniel tipping his head at my victory.

"Hi, Sam. It's good to see you again," Matt smiles warmly, dropping all the teasing. "Can I get you all a drink?"

"I'll help," I offer because clearly Matt and I need to talk a little.

Walking toward the bar with Matt holding my hand through the large crowd, he keeps walking to the end of the bar against a dark wall. Looking at one of the bar bouncers he gets a nod and I don't know what's happening until he pushes past a few people and lifts the end of the bar, still tugging my hand.

Moving to the side of one of the huge beer fridges, Matt opens a bright neon door and the music fades almost completely as I pause just inside the door.

"How are you, Samantha?" Matt asks as I look around the storage room filled with booze. This seems like a serious breach of the law or something having someone surrounded by all these opened bottles of alcohol.

"I'm good," I whisper nervously. "Why are we in here? And why are you *allowed* in here?"

"I used to be a bouncer here, so they know me. And I wanted to talk without having to scream in your ear all night," he grins.

Looking around, the room suddenly feels a little too enclosed for me. I'm against the door, so I feel like I can open it and get out if I need to, but it's still fairly tight in the room and I could really use a drink, actually.

"Vodka and cranberry?" He grins like he read my mind.

"Please..." I smile and wait.

As Matt lifts a few large container lids, he pulls out a red plastic bar cup and grabs a bottle of vodka from the clearly marked Vodka shelf. Looking around for the cranberry juice, I spot it first and point as he reaches for the jug of juice.

"How strong?"

Giggling, I respond, "That depends on what you want to talk about."

When he laughs, I relax a little more. "So, straight Vodka then with a drop of cranberry for color? Got it."

Mixing my drink, he actually does make it properly as I watch him with a weird tingly feeling of what the hell is going to happen here. The heavy bass can still be felt in the storage room, but the music isn't blasting around us. Strangely, this feels almost more intimate then when Matt and I were alone in my apartment together.

   Handing me my drink, and grabbing a beer for himself from another huge fridge at the back of the room, he smiles before taking a gulp almost like he's as nervous as I am.

   "Thank you." Taking the drink from him I have a sip, and it's pretty good. Though warm without ice, the taste is delicious, and exactly what I need.

   "How are you, Samantha?"

   "I'm good, Matt. I already said that," I blush. "How are you?"

   "I'm good. How was school?"

   "Good. Exhausting, but really good."

   "That's good," he repeats and smiles again while shaking his head. "This is so weird for me. I'm nervous around you," he laughs self-consciously.

   "Me, too," I reply before gulping down half my slightly stronger than usual drink.

   "I want to kiss you, Samantha," he whispers, and just the sound of his voice is like a caress on my skin. I'm nervous, but I feel sexual excitement growing as I stare at him. I want him to kiss me suddenly. *"Can* I kiss you, Samantha?" He says my name again almost like a dirty word.

   "Yes..." I whisper and then wait.

   The awkward build up to this kiss has made us each too nervous though I think. I don't know how to move, and Matt seems to be thinking too much as well. Placing his beer beside him on a rack filled with lemons and veggies, the bottle just touches the edge but tips as he pulls away.

   "Shit!" He barks as the beer bottle smashes beside his boots, and as I jump forward to help we actually bang heads together like total losers.

   Bursting out laughing, Matt leans over my head, and palms my skull with this hands as he continues to laugh above me. Kissing my head, he pulls away and says quite fiercely, "I'm usually much smoother than this," which of course makes me laugh again.

   "You'd have to be," I giggle, and the awkward moment is over.

   "Um, why don't I kiss you later?" Matt grins.

   "Sounds good. We should get everyone's drinks now anyway. Olivia is already imaging very dirty things, and Daniel is probably starting a search party."

   "And Neil?"

"Um, he's pissed because we're *not* doing very dirty things in here."

"How would he know?"

Shaking my head, I smile thinking of Neil. "Trust me, he knows. Neil knows dirty things and can sense them within a 15 mile radius. He's already shaking his head at us in disappointment."

"Huh. Well, hopefully we'll get his approval later," Matt says with sexy smirk as he takes my hand and opens the door.

"The beer bottle?"

"I'll tell Kevin at the bar."

Arriving back at the table with our drinks, I notice way more empty glasses than should be there.

"We bought our own drinks while waiting for you to do whatever you two were doing!" Olivia smiles. "I'm hammered, Sam. Let's dance!" She screams already tugging my hand back away from the table.

Turning to my boys, plus Matt, they're all smiling, and Matt looks like we have a sexy little secret between us that he isn't going to share.

"Did you just have *bar* sex?" Olivia asks me like its completely unheard of, which it is actually.

Pouting, I shake my head no. "I did get smashed in the head by his head though. But at least he made me a drink first."

"You're pathetic," she laughs as we step down onto the dancefloor. "Dance with me, baby. I *need* this," she says and her words seem like so much more suddenly than just wanting to dance with her girlfriend.

Without saying anything, and without telling me what's wrong, Olivia seems to be begging me for more, so I give it.

I dance my ass off with her, forgetting all the sadness we've had, and forgetting the life that's waiting for us. I dance like my leg is completely healed, and I dance like Olivia is healthy.

We dance together; fun, spinning, grinding and laughing with each other. We dance until all we know is the thrill of the music, and the depth of our friendship surrounding us.

After a few songs, Olivia starts whining about having to get another drink until we turn for the dancefloor exit. When I'm suddenly taken into Daniel's arms he hands Olivia a fresh drink and asks, "Trade ya?" Smiling, she takes the drink and kisses him goodbye. "My turn," he breathes in my ear and I'm done.

Dancing with Daniel is amazing. It's always easy and beautiful, with no stepped upon feet, or awkward movements as the music changes and shifts rhythms. He moves effortlessly, and takes me along for the ride.
"I miss you," I suddenly moan in his ear as he turns me so my back is to his front.
"I'm always right here, honey. *Always...*" He moans himself before spinning me quickly and raising my left leg over his thigh. Holding my back tightly, I'm moved against him so suggestively to Nine Inch Nails 'The Only Time', my back bows backward until I burst out laughing when I'm lifted back into his arms just as he grunts the infamous sexy Trent Reznor grunt in the song.
Singing and dancing to Trent, I realize *'this is the only time I really feel alive'* is my anthem. Dancing with Daniel is when I'm happiest, and when I feel truly alive.
"You're making quite a show of this dance, aren't you?"
"Absolutely. I need to punish Neil somehow," he says before moving me again right against his chest to grind against me with laughter. "And you're the only one I *could* do this with without him freaking out, so it's fun," he laughs to me shaking my head.
Dancing to another song, I look around us and suddenly see Allan. Jesus Christ, *really?*
Quickly stumbling, Daniel rights me as I whisper, "Don't look, but Allan's watching us. God, he just won't go away," I groan.
"Where?" Looking around anyway, I know when Daniel spots Allan because our bodies are less fluid while we move. Daniel actually tenses a little holding me.
"Wow. He's *glaring* at me," Daniel seems a little surprised I think. "How often does he still call you?"
Trying to avoid eye contact with Allan I pretend to ignore him. "Every single day. If I don't answer he leaves long messages begging me to give him another chance, and when I do answer he starts begging immediately until I hang up. He *never* stops calling me," I huff as our dancing slows to a completely ridiculous slow dance among loud, sexy, fast-paced music. We look weird I'm sure, but the thrill of our dance seems to have faded with the presence of Allan.
Pulling me in tighter, Daniel says quite angrily, "It's time for you to make a report about this, Sam. Period. I'll take you tomorrow, and if you argue about it I'll tell Neil he's still bothering you," he practically growls

knowing me well enough to know I would argue the embarrassment of going to the Police. He also knows I hate dealing with a pissed off, ever-protective Neil, so he's essentially tied my hands, which I hate.

Attempting to pull away from him, Daniel pulls me closer. "Don't, Daniel. It's fine. I don't need to go to the police. Allan is just intense. That's all."

"To what end?" He asks as I pause to stare at him. "Honey, this is how all bad post-relationship situations start. One person can't let go and eventually they make the life of the other person hell."

"It's just annoying calls," I plead.

"Until it isn't Sam. And I think telling him to leave you alone every goddamn day for over 8 months since your accident is long enough for him to have moved on. If you don't want me to tell Neil I won't. But you and I are going to go make a report tomorrow at the very least. Okay? Please, Sam. Just say okay for me, and we'll enjoy the rest of our night."

Looking at the love and concern in Daniel's eyes, I give in. "Okay..." I nod because I know he's right, and because I simply can't say no to him ever. Honestly, I know Allan is being too obsessive and weird, but I haven't wanted to deal with it in case he became worse.

When Daniel and I leave the dancefloor I make a point of NOT looking to the railing Allan was watching us from. I want to enjoy myself, and I'm not in the mood for Allan and his shit tonight. God, this night with my friends keeps going up and down hourly it seems and I'm a little tired of all the drama.

Smiling at Neil as we approach, he pulls me to his side and begs, "What happened out there? You and Daniel looked like you were fighting."

"We weren't. When have Daniel and I ever fought?" I laugh at his absurd question.

"You haven't. But *something* happened," he pushes until I hug him tighter and think of a quick cover so he doesn't start looking for Allan.

"We were just talking about my stupid ex," which is enough of the truth to not be a lie, but cryptic enough to not announce Allan's presence at the club he would most likely never go to if not to watch me. Allan hates alternative music, preferring instead the other attached top 10 pop music dance side of the joint club.

When Olivia and Daniel leave Neil, Matt and I to get drinks, I try to be normal. I don't want to feel self-conscious with Allan in the club, and I don't want to ruin my night with another mood change. And luckily I'm saved almost immediately by the music.

Weezer's, 'Sweater Song' starts and like the hundreds of other people in the club, Matt, Neil and I start singing the song while belting out and laughing to the '*woah, woah, woahhh*' chorus like everyone else does.

"I wish I had a sweater for you to unravel so I'd soon be naked," Matt sings in my ear making me shove him away laughing.

Looking for a moment to my left I see Allan staring at me again, and I'm instantly uncomfortable. He really is glaring like Daniel said. I guess I didn't notice it before because I looked away too fast when I saw him. But right now, as he glares at me from maybe 15 feet away, I'm mesmerized by his face.

Listening as the Pixie's 'Where is my mind?' fades away in the background, the irony isn't lost on me. I don't know what's happening, and I don't know where I am. My mind is blank, but for the intense eyes holding me captive.

Waiting for something to happen, everything fades away but Allan. Even as people walk between us, my focus never wavers, and neither does his. I'm stuck in an intense staring contest, but I feel so afraid of Allan in this moment I can't move out of the trance I'm trapped in.

I'm sure my face has changed from playful with Neil and Matt to *what the hell* as we stare, but Allan doesn't change at all. Not moving, or even breathing it seems, Allan's face remains screwed up tight with his lips slightly parted as I watch. His eyes hold me still with their anger and intensity while he glares at me, almost like he's willing me harm.

I'm shocked by his look of hatred toward me, and I'm scared to death of Allan's eyes suddenly.

"What the hell is going on?" Neil breaks up the moment between me and Allan as I'm tugged closer to him by my arm. "What the fuck is *he* doing here?" Neil continues, but I have no words as the lights and music quickly return to me.

I've never seen anyone look at me like that before. I haven't felt fear like that since I was 18 years old in my bedroom with the strange man I was given to. And I haven't known fear like that since I was with Matt's monster in my bedroom.

Moving in closer to Neil, I find my own voice soft and quiet as I whisper, "I have to go."

"Fuck *that!* I've had enough."

When Neil starts to move, I quickly grab his sleeve to pull him back to me safely. When he bends to my face, I hear myself moaning as he listens with wide eyes. "There's something *wrong,* Neil."

"What did he do, Sam?" He pleads.

"I have to go. But *please* don't talk to him."

"Samantha, I'm not afraid of that piece of shit," Neil says angrily as he crowds me protectively. Trying to see past him, I have to make sure Allan hasn't moved toward us so Neil and Matt are safe.

"Samantha?" Matt questions. Without words, I shake my head no to his question. Matt shouldn't have to get involved in this shit. It's bad enough Neil wants to.

"I have to go. I'm not feeling well," I lie. Kind of. I actually don't feel well anymore, but it's more mental sickness than anything else. Shaking, I remember how evil Allan looked as he stared at me.

"Samantha, let me take you home," Matt offers as I jolt again. "*Just* to take you home. I promise," Matt smiles down at me with Neil nodding beside him.

"Neil, promise me you won't talk to him. Promise!" I scream suddenly panicked.

"I won't," he exhales but he's full of shit. The second I leave, Neil's going to approach Allan.

Pulling his shirt closer, I plead so he'll pay attention. "Listen to me. Daniel's taking me tomorrow to fill out a police report, so you can't do anything tonight." I'll confess anything right now to convince him to stay away from scary Allan. "He's just being weird, but I don't want you to get in the middle of anything, just in case. I don't want you to do anything Allan can use against me if the police talk to him. Okay?"

Nodding, Neil is actually silenced, which would be funny if I wasn't worried he'd ignore me to talk to Allan the second I leave the club anyway.

"*Promise* me, Neil. You can't lie to me, and I'll be hurt if you do anything to get involved this time. Please, Neil. There's something else going on here, but Daniel and I are going to fix it tomorrow, okay?" Begging Neil to keep him safe from scary Allan, I turn right into his arms with Matt standing close to my side waiting out the drama.

"Okay, honey," Neil exhales. "But I don't like this." Shit, I don't like any of this either. "I'm going to call you later, Sam, so you better answer. And we're going jogging again tomorrow, so I'll see you in the morning," he says just fiercely enough that I know I'm not getting out of jogging anymore. Damn.

"Fine." Turning back to Matt I try one last time. "I can just grab a cab, Matt. I'll be-" But the look I get is so male, I almost laugh.

"Not likely, Samantha. Daniel and Olivia are on their way over. Let's say good bye, then I'll get you home," he says with a finality I don't even want to argue with from the man I barely know, but have slept with.

When Olivia plops down and spills the 2 drinks she carried, she seems to take in the mood before I can even speak.

"*What?*" She looks so scared. "Is Matt here?" She asks a little too panicky. Watching her, I'm stunned by her reaction to her boyfriend maybe being here.

Grabbing her hand, I pull her 2 feet away from the boys and whip her around to look at me as she actually cowers a little like I'd hurt her. Freezing me in place with her sudden fear, my heart breaks instantly.

"Oh, *god*, Olivia. What *is* it?" I practically cry. "Why are you afraid of Matt, and why can't you talk to me about it?" But she doesn't speak. She just looks at me with her huge dark brown eyes that seem way too big for her gaunt little face.

"Please, Livi. I promise I won't tell anyone anything. *Talk* to me. I can see it all over your face. I *know* there's something going on, and I can see how afraid you are. Please tell me," I beg just before I feel my tears threaten to fall.

"Samantha, let's go," Matt suddenly says behind me and I want to rip his face off. Olivia was about to speak but Matt's presence just made her clam right back up.

"In a minute, Matt," I snap, and thankfully he seems to understand I need him to back off as he leaves quickly.

"You're leaving?" Olivia nearly cries and I can't help but pull her into a hug.

"Let's have coffee tomorrow, just like old times. I'll buy every goddamn cookie I can find tomorrow morning, and we'll have a coffee/cookie date like we used to. *Please,* Olivia?" I beg as she wraps her arms around me to hug me tighter. She is obviously deciding if she can talk to me or not.

"Okay..." She moans and I know I have her.

Pulling away to smile down at her, I kiss her quickly and hug her once more. "I'm not feeling up to staying, but I will if you want me to."

"Are Neil and Daniel staying?"

"With you? Of course," I grin. "Now you get the boys all to yourself."

"Yay!" She yells, pulling herself together, looking a little more Livi-like. "Is Matt taking you home?" She asks suggestively, almost completely recovered from her upset.

"Yes. *Just* taking me home. He may even come back after."

Smirking, she says, 'yeah, right' and I can't help smile back.

Turning back to our table, all three men are watching us so intensely I almost laugh. Even Matt who barely knows Olivia is watching the 2 of us like he knows there's something heavy going on. He wants to get involved somehow like Neil and Daniel clearly do, I can tell.

"Promise me. A coffee/cookie date tomorrow around 11:00," I push one more time to make sure she agrees.

"I promise. Now go get a piece of his fine ass," she breathes in my ear making me shiver like she obviously intended by her grin.

"Take care of her," I look at Neil and Daniel, and naturally, both seem totally offended by the suggestion though they each nod anyway.

I know damn well Olivia will be taken care of, just as I know they would never leave me or my girlfriends alone in a club. But I needed to say it. I'm feeling sadly protective of Olivia right now, and I need to know what's happening to her so I can help her.

"Are you ready?" Matt asks handing my small purse over as I nod. Stepping into Daniel, I tell him I'll see him tomorrow for our police date as he hugs me tightly in approval, followed by Neil telling me he loves me like he always does when we part ways.

"Okay, let's go. Thank you," I whisper to a nodding Matt who takes my hand to lead me out of the club we love, on the night I'm starting to hate.

Leaving with Matt, I don't see Allan again, but I can actually feel him all over me.

CHAPTER 17

"What the hell was that all about, Samantha?" Matt asks as soon as the cab doors close.

"Nothing," I say until he turns right around on the seat to stare at me. "Fine. Allan was there staring at me like a psycho, and I just needed to get out of there," I huff.

"He's still bothering you? Even after the situation at the wake?"

Looking out the window I just nod. I honestly didn't think it was a problem until Daniel showed me it was. I didn't see it was a problem until I actually watched Allan watching me. Now I *know* it's a problem.

Allan looked like he absolutely hated me, which is such a strange feeling considering I have another goddamn message from him just hours ago saying how much he still loves me.

"It's being dealt with tomorrow by Daniel and I," I sigh as Matt takes my hand.

After a few minutes of silence between us, when we're only a block from my apartment, Matt finally speaks. "Not to sound like a caveman or anything, but I want to beat the shit out of him for upsetting you still. It really pisses me off that *tootsie roll* won't back the fuck off," he says so seriously, I can't help but laugh at the tootsie roll comment.

He sounds exactly like a caveman, and it doesn't impress me. I'm sure it should, but that kind of testosterone show has never impressed me in a man. I can take care of myself. I have since I was 18.

"I'm coming up to make sure you're okay," Matt says like he doesn't want an argument, and honestly, I'm too tired to argue with Matt's little demand.

"I'm sorry I didn't return any of your calls. You're pretty great Matt, but I wasn't then so I couldn't talk to you," I whisper as he takes my hand. Exhaling, I wait out the last of our drive silently.

When we open my apartment, I stand awkwardly in the kitchen close to the door, not really allowing Matt to enter my apartment all the way.

"Um, I'm not good company tonight."

"Let's talk, Samantha," Matt pushes, walking right around me to my living room as I roll my eyes. He's like another Neil- sexy, pushy, and strangely kind of endearing for it.

"Would you like anything?"

"Nope. I just want to talk for a bit before I leave."

"Okay," I mumble walking to my living room to join him.

Sitting opposite of Matt with the coffee table between us, he seems humored by where I sit. I don't give a shit if he finds me funny though. I'm tired and strung out.

"Scared of me, Samantha?" He teases, making me ease up a little.

"No. I'm sorry, I'm just exhausted. Tonight didn't really go as planned."

Tilting his head to the right, Matt asks, "And what did you have planned?"

"Fun," I reply stupidly. "Reconnecting with my friends. Enjoying my life a little after an intense school semester I barely remember. I don't know. I didn't expect Allan to be around, and I didn't expect Olivia to look terrible without telling me why. So tonight nothing was really as I hoped it would be." Exhaling, I find myself confessing to Matt in a way I never do. "Things just keep changing around me, and not really in a good way."

"I've noticed. You don't seem as happy as you did the first time we met," he says gently leaning across the table to put his hand on my knee.

He looks so kind right now, I'd love to talk to him. But I don't know him, and I don't know what to say. The reality is, I'm *not* as happy as I used to be, but he shouldn't know that. He shouldn't know anything about me at all.

Matt said this wasn't a booty call situation, but I can't help feeling like it probably is. I mean why else would a man I barely know, whom I've slept with once before bring me home, settle in, and try to appear all caring and interested? *Sex.* That's why.

Looking at Matt, I need to make a choice here. I can either wallow in my confusion and upset over tonight, or I can enjoy the hot sexiness of Matt. I can choose to give into the temptation for a little while before I sink back into my darkened life tomorrow first with Olivia, then with Daniel and the police afterward.

Choices...

I have a decision to make. And I need to make a choice.

Quickly deciding on Matt, I stand and smile before I walk away. "I'll be right back. Make yourself comfortable."

In my bathroom, I prepare once again for sex. Pee, armpit dry shave, deodorant, lady parts facecloth wash, hands and teeth, and makeup check. I even pull my hair down and brush it once upside down so it looks full and long before making my way back to Matt for some hot, hard, dirty sex to lighten my darkened mood.

"Matt?" I call standing in my living room hallway when he's nowhere to be found.

"In here," he teases as I turn around to see him sitting up in my bed, naked at least from the waist up under the covers, though I assume the waist down as well. "You said to make myself comfortable, so I did," he grins as I lean against my bedroom doorway with a dorky grin myself.

"Come here, Samantha," he says with a voice like silk, and I immediately move to him. "Take off your dress for me. I need to see you," he moans. Standing there mesmorized, I feel myself shiver from just his voice alone.

Building up my courage for a few seconds, I thank god for all the sexy underwear Neil always buys me. Lifting my long dress over my head, I pull my head and hair out and shake myself free until I'm standing in just my white lacy bra and panties.

"You're so beautiful, Samantha," he says turning his legs from my bed to plant them on the floor. Taking my waist, Matt pulls me closer to him to rest his head against my stomach with his hands on my ass.

"Thank you," I whisper as he looks up at me. I am very average- height and body. I also have scars all over my body now which I'm self-conscious about. But against Matt, with all his muscles and height, I suddenly feel almost petite and attractive beside him, especially when he stands up naked in front of me with a look that screams sexy.

Smiling down at me, he breathes softly, "I'm finally going to kiss you now."

Staring back at his dark green eyes, I feel myself sink a little into the moment. I want to kiss him, and I really want him to kiss me. I suddenly want to just enjoy myself with this sexy man who likes me still, for whatever reason.

"Well, what are you waiting for?" I ask as he bends to me.

Fisting my long hair and tugging my head back a little, Matt takes my jaw in his hand like a possession and kisses me so softly I'm shocked by the gentleness of his kiss. I expected hard and forceful, but this kiss is so sweet, I almost don't like it. This feels too intimate, or too emotional somehow. I can't explain it, but I don't want it.

Pulling Matt closer to me with my hands behind his back, standing on my tiptoes I change the kiss to faster and harder until he growls in my mouth as his tongue enters me to suck and nip at.

I'm playing harder and he's catching up.

Releasing my jaw, Matt slides his hand around my back and as I feel his fingers against me, my bra is released. Waiting, I pull away slightly and slip my own arms from the straps as our hard kiss continues.

Moving me, I'm lowered onto my bed with Matt bending over me to try to maintain the kiss. Eventually though, I pull away gasping for air. I'm drowning in his mouth. My heart is racing and my chest is pounding, and I suddenly feel desperate with my need.

"I can't wait to taste you, Samantha," Matt says staring down at me as I blush. "I've missed you."

Looking back at Matt I say nothing. I have nothing *to* say. I miss him in *this* moment, too. But I'll be too busy when school starts again to really miss him.

"You are so delicious," I whisper as he smiles down at me.

"I think that's my line," he grins before kissing me softly on the lips until I pull away.

"But you are Matt. I get the whole muscular, manly thing, but you're really beautiful to me."

Ducking his head into my neck, he says a thank you, and everything feels very strange suddenly. I think I somehow killed the mood, or made him think too much, or just changed the atmosphere around us. I changed us, but I didn't mean to.

I wanted sexy, dirty Matt, but I felt compelled to let him know I thought he was beautiful like my Neil and my Daniel.

Leaning back up on his forearms, Matt moves suggestively between my legs, and again the mood changes almost immediately. My mind and body are conflicted. I feel his tenderness, but I crave his intensity. I need him hard and heavy to wash away my shitty night.

"I need you, Matt. Just for tonight," I add so there's no confusion or misunderstanding between us. I can't give him anything more than right now. And I don't want him to want more than that from me.

"Just tonight?" He asks simply as I nod.

"I'm sorry, but I have nothing more to give you right now besides spontaneous moments like tonight. I can't make any promises, and I don't know what each day will look like when I'm back in school. Some days felt like eternity, and other days whipped by. Honestly, I barely even remember the last 3 months of my life."

"Okay. Tonight then. I guess I better make it count," he smiles before moving his hand to hold my face again in his palm.

Kissing me, Matt goes with hard and deep which I love. His kiss drags the breath from my lungs and an arch from my spine. Wrapping a leg around his back I pull him in harder to me to grind against each other, as I kiss him back with everything I can give him. Tonight.

Feeling Matt slide my panties from my body, I use his back to lift myself before he just tears them from me anyway. And again, the quick thought *I've been slayed!* is nearly too much, but Matt takes that moment to slide his fingers inside me slow and deep as I arch into his hand.

Feeling him move his hand for a different angle, I'm suddenly jolted with feeling. He found my sweet spot almost immediately, and my moaning reaction is obvious. Pulling him harder to my mouth as I writhe against him, I suddenly want to devour him.

When Matt pulls away from me with a smirk to my groan, he makes his way to my chest. Nipping me and kissing his way down my body, with his fingers still working me, I'm desperate for him to take me. I need this. And I want Matt.

Waiting, almost with bated breath, I watch his slow dissent and arch whenever I can to make him go where I need him to go. Shy of pushing his head down, I wait holding his hair as he adjusts his wide shoulders between my legs and raises my left thigh bent against my own chest with his hand hard against the back of my thigh.

Looking up at me as I pant, Matt takes one long, slow lick with his tongue pressed firmly against me, and we each moan at the same time. Oh *god*... I want him so badly, I'm shaking with anticipation.

Watching, Matt opens his eyes again and stares at me as his tongue starts working my clit. Fast and hard, he puts enough pressure on me to make me groan with the pleasure. He is wicked and amazing, forcing me to climb quickly within my arousal.

"I love the taste of you, Samantha," he whispers against my wet flesh as I shiver and moan at the sensation. "I've missed you," he breathes then lowers his head again as I close my eyes to the sensations building within my body.

All around, there is a charge in the air. I feel the intensity, and the depth of his caring. I even feel my own emotions growing toward him.

I said tonight, but I wish for so much more. Matt is my in between fantasy man. He is both my Neil and my Daniel. He's my funny Neil, and my strong protective Daniel. He is both my loves combined and I enjoy him.

I picture being happy when I'm with him for as long as that is.

Gasping quickly, I feel Matt penetrate me deep with his fingers as his tongue continues to torture me. I'm on the precipice. I'm on the edge of release. I'm ready, but I just need a little more.

Grabbing Matt's head I force him deeper into me as my hips rock and my body tightens on him. I can't control my reaction to him. And I don't *want* to control myself with him.

Matt makes me sexy, and dirty, and *alive* when I'm with him.

Panting, I'm almost there. "Please, Matt. *Please*, harder. I just need a little more," I moan as he growls inside me and takes me deeper.

Oh *god!* Turning my head into the pillow I scream my quick sudden release as my breath leaves me on a rush and my mind blanks.

But again he doesn't stop.

Trying to ride out my orgasm, he continues using his tongue and fingers on me, but the pleasure quickly turns to pain as it always does for me after an orgasm.

Still deep inside my body, I open my eyes to the demon lapping up my body with his long, black spiked tongue dripping in blood all over me.

Pausing in my sudden horror I watch for moments until he looks up at me with black soulless eyes. Panicking, I finally find the breath to scream.

Pushing at its head, my left foot makes contact with its shoulder and face over and over again until I'm grabbed by the ankle and twisted to my back.

Screaming to get it off me, I fight as hard as I can. Tugging and pulling myself away from it across my bed, I'm suddenly flattened by its hard body pushing me into the mattress as I continue screaming for help.

When my mouth is covered I try to bite it. When my hands are twisted

behind my back, I try to dislocate my own shoulder to get away.
 I don't fucking want this!
 Oh, *god*... '*HELP* me!' I scream behind the claw covering my mouth as I fight for my life again.

 "Samantha! *Stop!* Please baby, stop! Holy *SHIT!* What's wrong with you?!" It screams in my ear as its scales shift against my back.
 With my cheek pressed hard into the mattress, I move my neck as far as I can to try to see what it's going to do to me.
 Matt.
 Holy *fuck!* It's Matt.
 The quick reality change is so intense, my body simply bows against itself as a sob bursts from my chest. When I feel my hands and mouth released, I curl around myself in my bed and sob endlessly.
 I don't know what's wrong with me. I don't know anything anymore. I don't know how to stop this fear and the horrific nonreality from strangling me. I'm struggling to breathe, and to think, and to live with this.
 What's *wrong* with me?
 Where is my mind? I wanted to sing at the club.

 "Samantha," Matt speaks quietly against my side as I cry in deep shuddering breaths. "What happened? Why did you freak out? Did I hurt you?" He asks quietly as I shake my head no.
 I can't speak, and I don't want to. If I understood anything I'd be embarrassed by my freak out, but I don't understand anything anymore.
 "Why did you lash out at me? Did I hurt you?" Matt presses quietly, and I want to scream.
 "I'm sorry," I hiccup crying.
 "It's okay, Sam. But what's wrong. You're really freaking me out here," he says close to tears I think. His voice is hoarse and kind of shaky.
 Oh *no*... I've totally fucking lost it.
 Jesus Christ, he was so clearly a monster. A big, black skeletal, scaly demon with his spiked tongue ripping my... Shivering, my teeth start chattering as I try to forget the image of the bloody spikes I saw tearing me open.
 Reaching down between my own legs, I wipe my hand through the moisture and with shaking fingers raise them to my face to see... *nothing*.

There's just moisture from his tongue, or from me, or from whatever. But there's no blood so the spikes didn't tear me apart. I thought I was bleeding, I *saw* I was bleeding. But I wasn't bleeding. I was just losing my mind, thank god.

Wrapping me in a blanket, he begs, "Please tell me what happened?"

I know I owe him something- some explanation that explains something about whatever the hell just happened to me. I owe him something, but *I* can't even understand what happened, so there's no way he'll understand, no matter what I say.

"I'm so sorry, Matt. I didn't mean to freak out," I gasp as another sob tears through my body.

"Can I call Neil or Daniel for you? Do you need someone else? I don't know what to do for you," he cries in the darkness around us.

"I'm okay. Can you please leave, Matt?"

"Samantha... you shouldn't be alone right now," he whispers leaning against my back as I pull away from his touch. Dammit, I didn't mean to do that, but I don't want him touching me. He's so freaky when he turns into that.

Shit. He doesn't turn into anything. I imagine he turns into something. But it's so real, I can't believe he didn't turn into that thing to do what he did to my body.

"What did I turn into? What did I do?" He asks shaking my arm as I pull further away.

I'm talking out loud now and have no idea as I do it. I'm a crying, sobbing mess whose talking out loud when I think I'm still in my head. Oh *god*... I'm losing it totally.

"I just need silence for a minute so I can think," I beg as he nods again.

Waiting for minutes, or hours, I don't know, nothing comes to me. There is nothing I can tell him. There is nothing I understand myself.

After forever in silence, I finally speak to a desperate looking Matt. "I can't tell you what happened, but I wish-"

When we hear loud knocking on my front door, we both freeze. Waiting for a second the knocks come harder and longer until I don't know what to do. Waiting as my mind spins Matt suddenly stands and tugs on his jeans before I can even think.

"Stay here. I'll see who it is," he says already leaving my bedroom.

What's *happening* to me?

"Um, Samantha, can you come out here for a minute? The police need to speak with you," Matt says in my doorway with an police officer beside him.

Gasping, I grab for my comforter and try to cover my naked body better as the officer and Matt walk away after closing my door.

What the hell do I do? Trying to stand, I'm so disoriented, my head spins and my hand has to catch my body against the wall before I fall. I feel physically drunk, but mentally sober. I'm a fucking mess.

The police are here, and with a sense of impending panic, all I can think is *who died?*

Did my mother finally OD? Did my dad kill her because she's crazy? What the hell is going on?

Please don't let it be Neil, or Daniel, or Olivia. Please not my three people left. Please be okay. I'll lose my mind if one of my remaining three people are hurt, or fucked up, or dead.

Feeling my tears build in fear of the bad news I'm about to receive I pull on a pair of sweats from my bottom drawer while looking for a hoodie to wear. When an officer knocks on my bedroom door and calls out 'Miss Newman?' I gasp in fear.

Am I in trouble? Who died? Panicking, I don't know why they're here, and I don't know what's wrong.

"Miss Newman, are you okay? I need you to come out here please. I need to speak with you," the officer says again knocking on my door.

"I'm coming. Just a second," I cry as I throw on a hoodie and rush to open my bedroom door.

"Where's Matt?" I ask way too loudly. I can hear the panic in my voice, and I know I sound a little delirious. I'm not acting right, but I can't stop myself. Why the fuck are the police here?

"Can you follow me to the kitchen, Miss Newman? Officer Ehler is standing in the hallway with Mr. Potito so we can speak privately."

"What's wrong?" I ask leaning against my kitchen counter wrapping my arms around myself. "Who died? Do you want coffee or anything?" I ask shaking my head at myself. 'Who died, want coffee?' I sound like a psycho.

"No, thank you. I'm Officer Ringler, Miss Newman."

"Samantha," I interrupt, as he nods.

"We received a call from one of your neighbors about a probable sexual assault taking place."

"By who?" I yell. "Who was sexually assaulted?" Who called what in? But like a slow moving train I eventually clue into the obvious as the lights start flashing around me.

"Oh! *I* wasn't sexually assaulted, I swear! And Matt wasn't either."

Almost crying, I suddenly burst out laughing at the thought of me sexually assaulting Matt. He's so muscular and tall I'd have to drug him first, I laugh again. *Fuck*, I probably shouldn't say that to the cops.

Waiting for my laughter to slow down, the cop finally continues. "Samantha, Officer Ehler is speaking with Mr. Potito, and we have reason to believe there was a sexual assault that took place this evening based on the physical evidence, and also from the caller's description of the events he heard."

"What evidence? I wasn't. And Matt wasn't either! I swear no one was sexually assaulted here," I giggle again. "I'm sorry, I'm just so embarrassed. Nothing bad happened. Matt and I *were* together, but it was one hundred percent consensual, I promise."

"Can you tell me what happened? Mr. Potito has a cut on his face and bruises forming on his cheek and shoulder," Officer Ringler says so seriously, my embarrassment laughter fades at the thought of what I must've done to Matt when I freaked out.

"Like the *graphic* details?" I choke humiliated.

"Yes, please. If you'd feel more comfortable, I could call a female officer?"

"No. Um, Matt and I know each other and have mutual friends, and we've been, ah, *intimate* before, together," I mumble embarrassed. "Um, he brought me home tonight after I saw my ex-boyfriend who I need to talk to you guys about tomorrow actually. Anyway," I shake my head to focus. "Then Matt and I were making out," I say totally embarrassed.

Making out? What am I, *twelve?* Jesus Christ, this is like an urban legend or something. The cops breaking up hot sex thinking the guy is hurting her, but she's the one begging for more. Although I wasn't asking for more when the monster arrived, Matt stopped then I think, so *Matt* didn't hurt me. Just the demon did. But I'm not tore open and bleeding, so I guess that thing didn't hurt me either. But...

"Samantha, are you okay? Mr. Potito can't get to you again, and you can tell me the truth. I promise you'll be protected. Even if the night started out consensually, once you said no, all events should have stopped. Is that what happened?" Officer Ringler is looking at me so sadly, I can only shake my head and cry *no*.

Inhaling deeply, I push past my embarrassment and tell him the truth. "Matt was performing oral sex on me, and it was really good, and my orgasm was very, very intense, so I freaked out a little. I didn't realize I had hurt him, and he certainly didn't hurt me. If I was screaming, it was during the orgasm, I promise. Everything was just really intense, and as soon as I orgasmed, when I realized I was losing it a little, Matt stopped immediately and tried to talk me back down."

Huffing my medusa hair from my face, I look at the officer and tell almost the whole truth.

"Matt was pleasuring me like I wanted. But I freaked out when I had an orgasm. I didn't know I was screaming loud enough to bother my neighbors. And I certainly didn't know I hurt Matt when I was coming- Oh! Having an *orgasm*," I choke.

My humiliation is so complete, I actually feel like a child in front of this nodding police officer. With no reaction, but just a head nod as he listens to me recount most of the truth of what happened, I'm totally mortified.

"Look, I'm 24, pre-Med, and perfectly capable of telling you if I was being assaulted or not. And I wasn't. I may have to move though," I grin to his slight smile, thank god. "But otherwise, absolutely NO sexual assault happened here tonight. I'll swear to it and sign anything you want me to sign."

Pausing for a moment and watching my face closely which gives nothing away, he eventually nods like he's convinced.

"Okay, I'm going to go talk with my partner and Mr. Potito to confirm his version of events. It shouldn't take much longer. Could you please go take a seat on the couch while I slip out to the hallway?"

Nodding, I move away from him as he opens and closes the door quickly. The door was quick, but I did catch the sight of Matt leaning against the wall outside with his arms crossed wearing nothing but his jeans.

Slumping on the couch, I don't know how to fix this, and *I* did this. I chose to be with Matt again, and I've screwed up royally. I thought he was the shower curtain. I thought if I slept with him again nothing bad would happen and then I'd know I was just being mental for whatever reason the first time we slept together.

This was my choice, and I know we'll never be able to come back from it.

When the door opens ten minutes later, Matt walks in looking slightly pissed off but resigned. The 2 officers following him seem completely at ease, however, which I think is a good sign for us.

"Miss Newman... After speaking with both of you individually, we believe the events are as described. Both your version of events coincide, and other than Mr. Potito saying you freaked out *on* him after your orgasm..." deep blush "... And your version of not knowing what you did to him after your orgasm, everything else seems fairly consistent. We have asked Mr. Potito to leave for the rest of the night which he has agreed to, but you are free to speak with him again whenever you choose. Typically, we have found with some victims of assault, given time away from the perpetrator, they may change or recount the events when the fear has been removed. Often, the victim sees or remembers the events as they actually took place over time," he says so seriously I can't help jump in.

"My story won't change! Matt didn't hurt me at all. Everything was just super intense, and I'm fine. I'll be fine," I practically yell as Matt stays quietly standing away from me. "I'm sorry for this, Matt," I moan as I feel tears starting up again.

"I'll call you tomorrow, okay?" He says quietly as I nod. Looking at Officer Ehler, Matt asks if he can collect his things from my bedroom, and then I'm asked if I mind like Matt *is* a criminal.

"Of course. I'm so sorry, Matt. I'm sorry for all of this," I finally just cry as he gives me a sad little smile.

When Matt leaves the living room, Officer Ringler hands me his business card and tells me to call him anytime if I would like to change my statement, or if I need to talk about what happened- like something *did* happen, which it didn't. As far as they need to know anyway.

When I'm asked to read over the report to sign, after adding any information that was missed, I finally just collapse within myself back on my couch.

Jesus *Christ*. What a fucking mess.

Something did happen, but no one knows that. And I sure as hell won't ever tell anyone what I really think happened. Matt's already pissed at me, and the tale of the skeletal, bloody-tongued demon monster can't possibly help this shitty situation we're in.

In the silence around me, I feel like I'm suffocating again. Both Police officers are standing still with only the hum of their radios interrupting the chaos spinning in my head.

"I'm done," Matt says walking back through my living room clothed.

Standing, I don't know what to do. Do I apologize again? Do I go give him a hug? Do I beg his forgiveness again for being a freak?

"Call me, Samantha, when you want to talk about tonight," Matt says with a casual tone the officers couldn't understand the implication of. But I did. *Clearly.* 'Call me Sam when you want to explain why you scratched and kicked the shit out of me until I had to hold you down on your bed to calm you.'

"Thank you. I'm sorry for all this," I say to the Officers who only nod and walk out behind Matt.

Following them out, I lock my door and burst into tears again. I don't know how to fix this, and I don't know who I can tell to get the help I obviously need.

If the University finds out I lost it again, I'm screwed. But I'm smart enough to know I need help with this.

Something is happening to me, and I can't stand this feeling of being out of control. It weakens me, and makes me question everything. For the first time in my life I feel totally insecure and emotionally displaced.

I don't feel like me anymore, and the dark times are taking longer to lift each time they take me now.

CHAPTER 18

  I'm still walking around since Matt and the Police left, and I can't sleep. I can't stop thinking about what happened, and how embarrassed I am because of it. I can't stop thinking about the situation, and how I can either fix it, or explain it away so Matt and I can move past it. Not necessarily together, but at least individually I hope we can move past it.

  Maybe I can make it a joke for him. Like, '*Wow*, Matt. You're *soooo* good, the Police came running.' Or 'Holy *shit,* Matt! You made me come so loudly, people thought I was being killed.' Or... I don't know. I'm desperate for last night to be a distant memory for both of us though.

  No matter what I do or try to make me sleep, it doesn't work. I can't stop thinking about that monster vision that felt and seemed so real to me every time I try to close my eyes.

  That freaky, horrific looking demon is all I see every time I try to relax. When I close my eyes for even a second I feel it touch me. I feel my body cringe when I remember it licking me. I can't stop picturing its tongue licking my bloody body as it moaned inside me.

  Shivering at the thought of that black bloody tongue inside my body makes me want to scream.

  Jolting to the sound of my door buzzer, I'm scared to death to face anyone. I'm exhausted and I don't think I can keep it together long enough for a sufficient explanation, whatever the hell that is. I know any explanation I give certainly won't be the truth.

  God, I hope Matt didn't come back to talk me. But I hope it isn't Neil either, because he'll force me to talk to him about what happened. I wonder if Matt called him to let him know about my freak out. Somehow I think he probably did because he seemed more concerned about me, than simply pissed off when he left.

  Looking at the clock it's only 6:05, which is too early for even Neil and his jogs, so it must be Matt coming back to try again.

  I don't want to do this, no matter how much of an explanation he deserves. I owe him something though, no matter how messed up it is. I mean really, who can describe a delusion to the person causing it? He'll think I'm insane, and I can't even blame him at this point. Christ, I *feel* insane.

Then again, if I do explain what really happened, maybe he'll just leave for good and I won't have to deal with any more drama in my life right now.

I need to help Olivia and I need to deal with the Allan thing before I go back to school in a few weeks. My plate is full as Daniel would say, and I honestly don't feel like I *can* deal with any more shit right now.

I made a mistake last night. I should have forced Matt to leave when he brought me home. Or better yet, I should have taken myself home alone. I made a choice though, and it looks like I'm going to have to deal with it this morning whether I want to or not.

Standing up slowly from the couch, my head feels fuzzy, sleep-deprived and slightly hungover. Holding onto myself tightly to give me extra strength, I have to remind myself that after I talk to Matt I can try to sleep all bloody day if I want. I can sleep soon until I'm less freaked out. I *need* to keep myself moving toward the door to make this end.

Opening the door with a big inhale, I'm prepared to face Matt. Opening the door, I am *not* prepared for Allan however.

Looking, we each pause as I try to slow my thundering heart. My hands are shaking instantly, and my body feels such fear again, my adrenaline spikes immediately as I try to slam the door in his face. Struggling, the bastard already put his foot in between as he pushes the door opened against me, knocking me backward as I stumble.

Shit! Getting one loud scream in, Allan quickly subdues me against the wall.

Was my scream enough? Will my neighbors call the police? Would the police even come back? Oh my *god*... Maybe they won't return because I'm the whore who cried wolf.

Almost laughing at my own insanity, I wait for Allan to make a move against me. His hand is covering my mouth, and he's leaning hard into my chest.

Staring at me, Allan looks stoned, I think. His eyes are dilated, and he has a weird grin on his face like this is kind of funny to him.

"I waited to see if your boyfriend would come back," he growls next to my ear before blowing in it to make me shiver as he laughs.

Moaning against his hand, I push as hard as I can to get him off me but he barely moves. Pushing me harder into the wall, Allan digs his knees into my thighs, and as I cry out he smiles again.

"We need to talk, Samantha. Are you going to talk to me?" He asks almost like a dare.

I think he *wants* me to fight him. He actually looks excited about the prospect of a physical fight between us. Watching his intense eyes, and his weird tight smile preparing to fight I think, naturally I cave to protect myself right now. Nodding as best as I can with his hand over my mouth I stare at his eyes while he decides what to do next.

Pulling away slightly, and moving from my pinned thighs, he exhales, "Good. But no more screaming, okay? We're just going to talk," he says softly like he's trying to soothe me.

Taking his hand away from my mouth slowly, Allan watches me closely as I inhale deeply but don't scream.

Nodding once at me, Allan grabs my hand and forces me to walk to the couch until he actually throws me on it. "Sit there," he barks as I adjust myself to a sitting position with my feet firmly planted on the floor in case I can make a run for the door at some point.

Waiting for Allan, he paces a few times before falling into the chair across from me. The table is between us, but as he leans forward, I find myself pushing back against the couch to get further away from his intensity.

"So what's your boyfriend like?" He asks conversationally making me instantly more afraid.

How do I answer this? Anything might set him off. *Is* Matt my boyfriend or isn't he to Allan? What will piss him off less? Deciding for not, I try to be casual as well.

"He's not my boyfriend," I whisper and wait as he nods.

"So you're just fucking him?" He asks again casually.

"Only once," I admit hoping that'll make him happy. "And it was a long time ago. He's just my friend now, Allan."

Tilting his head at me, Allan doesn't speak forever. Watching a slow smile spread across his face he seems happy with my answer though, so I was right to choose honesty I think.

"You've never lied to me, Samantha. I know that. Why did you fuck him only once? Was he a shitty in bed?" He asks with excitement, so I nod yes.

I don't trust my voice right now, and I'm afraid of setting him off with the wrong answers. I've never known Allan like this. Ever. Allan was always calm, cool, and sweet. He was wonderful and supportive, and everyone loved him, until we didn't.

Nearly crying, I wish I knew what happened to that Allan.

"Do you miss me?" Before I can answer though he continues. "Because I miss *you*. Everyday. I'm sorry I cheated on you, but I already told you that. But it was just that one woman." And *Monica* I'd love to remind him but keep my mouth tightly closed. "She meant nothing to me I told you that a thousand times, but you didn't forgive me did you?"

"I did," I choke.

Shaking his head, Allan huffs a little before speaking. "You *said* you forgave me, but you really didn't. We were supposed to get back together. You were supposed to meet me for dinner so we could get back together, but you didn't show up. I was sitting there for an hour, Samantha. A fucking *hour*. Like a pathetic loser I had flowers and your favorite chocolate cheesecake pre-ordered, and I was going to propose to you, and you STOOD ME UP!" He yells suddenly jumping over the table and slapping me across the face so hard my head whips to the right as I scream just once in shock before silencing again.

Shaking as I hold my face I don't know what to do, so I just wait for more. When Allan slowly leans back and sits right on the table with his hands folded between his spread knees, I sneak a quick look at him and he's smiling again.

Well, that's twice. 2 times I've been hit in my life, and both of them somehow about or *from* Allan.

I wish I could hit him back so badly, my hands are shaking with the need. But I know he'd win if we fought, and I know I'd hurt so much worse than just this pounding pulse in my face and lip once he was done with me. I know it's not worth it, no matter how badly I want to hit him back, so again I do nothing.

"I'm sorry, Samantha. But honestly, I've wanted to hit you for months. Ever since you stood me up, I've wanted to slap you just once to humiliate you, too. Not punch you, or beat you up or anything because I don't hit women. But just a slap across the face once so you felt as hurt and embarrassed as I was when you stood me up that night."

Allan's voice is so gentle and soothing, he seems to be almost apologizing even as he's justifying hitting me.

Choices…

Keeping my head against the back of the couch I'm too scared to make eye contact in case he gets mad at me again. I don't know what to do. He's too close to run from, and he's too crazy to reason with. Starting to panic again, I realize I really don't know what to do anymore about anything in my life.

"Tell me why you stood me up," he whispers and I can't tell if it's a trick question or not. "*Samantha*... answer me."

"Um, I was hit by a car that day," I whisper back still not looking at him, which seems to make him angry again.

Grabbing my face he turns me and leans in so closely I can smell his rancid breath. "You could have called, or shown up anyway," he yells like I'm really pissing him off.

Shit, I don't know what to say. "Allan, I *was* going to meet you. I *wanted* to meet you. But I was unconscious for a few days. Remember?"

"So we were getting back together?" He asks with such hope, I know my out.

"Yes, Allan. I wanted to get back together so badly, but then I was in the accident and I couldn't get to you. Remember how happy I was when you were in my hospital room? Remember how happy I was to see you when I woke up?"

"You *were* happy. I remember that," he exhales as I smile.

I know my face is swollen on one side because I felt the pulling as I smiled, but my smile and lies seem to be working. Allan is much calmer now after my lies.

Leaning into me, I freeze as Allan kisses my sore cheek. Holding my breath I wait for him to move away, and when he does I fake smile again as best as I can for him.

"Do you know what today is?" He asks practically moaning as I shake my head no. I don't trust myself to speak right now in case he gets angry again, so I just wait to see where this goes.

"It's December 12th, Samantha. It's our 5th year anniversary."

Jolting, I don't know what to say. It is NOT our 5th anniversary because we broke up over a year ago. We split up and the anniversaries stopped. Well, they did for me anyway.

"Do you care?" He asks angrily and I quickly nod my head yes. I can tell he wants me to care, so I pretend I do. "SAY SOMETHING!" He suddenly screams making my jump again and almost cry.

My nerves are shot, and my emotions are running high. I don't know what to do or how to get out of this. Talking down Allan's crazy is totally different than talking down my mother's crazy.

"Ummm... Happy Anniversary, Allan," I whisper through my choked voice. My throat is drying up and I sound hoarse with unshed tears.

"*Oh*, you remembered. I knew you would," he smiles again. "By this time next year, we'll be married, and maybe working on those beautiful babies we want. Doesn't that sound good, Samantha?" Allan looks almost handsome and excited at the thought, and not nearly as fucking crazy as he actually is.

Nodding, I smile back as sincerely as I can. I don't trust my own voice right now, and I'm afraid he'll finally notice I'm lying if I actually speak.

"Wait. I guess we should wait for babies until after you finish Med School, right?" Talking like I'm actually participating in the conversation, he continues. "I hope they get your blue eyes and our dark hair. Especially if we have a girl. She'll be as beautiful as her mother."

Leaning into me again for a gentle kiss on my lips, he pulls away with tears in his eyes. "I always wanted a little girl with you. I love the thought of having a little daddy's girl who would hold my hand and smile sweetly when she saw me, just like you used to before you left me."

Shaking, I'm waiting for the crazy to come back. I didn't leave him. I left when he cheated on me. But I stay silent, smiling and nodding as he goes on and on.

When there's suddenly a knock on the door I jump, then freeze. Oh, god... It's my Neil. Neil's here and I can't have him hurt. I *won't* have him hurt.

"Who the hell is that?" Allan asks jumping up to glare at the door.

"It's just Neil wanting to go for a jog. If you give me a second, I'll tell him I'm too tired to go this morning. Would you let me tell him to go away? *Please* Allan?" Desperate to get Neil out of here, I already hear him singing in the hallway. "*Please?* I'll send him away and then you and I can spent the whole day together alone," I choke out trying to hide my repulsion at the thought.

Quietly thinking, Neil is knocking on my door much more frequently, and timed to that stupid farmer song I hate probably to torture me as only Neil can. Neil has a key but never uses it so he can torture me with his songs from my hallway whenever he can.

Waiting for Allan to agree, the intensity between us is killing me and making my hands sweat. Shaking, all I can do is wait for Allan to give me permission to do anything I can to save Neil.

"Just you and I, Allan. *All* day. Neil's only here for a jog, but I'll blow him off for you," I keep pushing. "I really want to spend the day alone with you," I nearly gag.

If I've ever known a moment of feeling insane, this is it. My head keeps turning from Allan back to the closed door and singing of my best friend. I need to get Neil out of here, because once he knows Allan's here, he'll never leave. And then I'll lose Neil forever.

In my soul, I know Neil will be taken from me and I may as well die beside him. Losing Neil is not something I could ever recover from.

"*Please,* Allan?" I beg as the first tear slides down my cheek.

"*Oh,* baby... Of course. I hate when you're unhappy. Go tell Neil to leave and then we'll make breakfast together, okay? I actually miss your weirdly delicious garlicky omelets," he says with a smile, choking me up further.

Allan is beyond rational at this point, and I'm scared to death of what's going to set him off again.

Standing slowly with a lovely smile aimed at Allan, I motion with my finger against my lips for him to be quiet as he nods. His eyes have actually lit up with the little conspiracy we've created so we can spend the day together. My eyes have lit up with the potential to get Neil the hell out of here. But I know it won't be easy. He's a pushy bastard and I may have to fake a fight with him to get him to leave.

Looking back at Allan, he's hiding just outside the kitchen wall, only feet from me but hidden from Neil as I begin to unlock the door to my obnoxiously singing best friend and truly, my soulmate. Breathing in deeply, I know I need to find some acting skills quickly.

Listening to Neil sing, I find my hand resting on the door as I take in a final breath and throw the door open dramatically. I need to look pissed so he'll believe me.

"*What?!*" I yell so loudly my words actually echo down the hallway.

Stunned, but quickly recovering, Neil shakes his head before asking, "*What,* what? You knew I was coming over for a jog this morning, so stop trying to get out of it," he pushes almost walking past me but I keep my arm across the doorway to block his entry.

Breathing in deep, I go for anything I can. It's fairly lame, but I can't think anymore. "Neil, go away. I need a little time to myself, and I need to think alone."

"*Really?* What the hell do you have to think about without me? *Matt?*" He growls as I flinch. Oh god, don't say Matt's name. *Please...* Neil. I wish he could read my mind right now so he wouldn't make this worse for me with Allan.

"Um, no. About us," I struggle.

"*Us?*" Neil asks again trying to push past my arm to enter. "What the hell about us?"

"Stop, Neil! I don't want you here this morning. I need a break from you, and I need to think alone. There's so much going on right now I need a little time to myself."

"Like what? What the hell's going on that you can't talk to *me* about? I know Olivia is fucked up over something, and I know Daniel's still sad which upsets you. But I'm well aware of all of that so what could possibly make you push me away. Jesus *Christ*, Sam! What's wrong with you? Are you still freaked about seeing Buttons last night?" He yells at me and my heart actually stops.

Glaring at Neil, my eyes bug out of my head as I try to get his attention. I need him to get this. Pleeeeease... *See* me, Neil.

"Is that the problem? *Buttons*? And what the hell did you do to your face?" He asks a little calmer like maybe he's slowly getting it.

Mouthing *yes*, I quickly speak out. "I don't know what the hell Buttons is, but I need some time alone from you right now. Okay?" Begging again with a contorted face and desperation in my eyes, I try for drama. "*Fuck,* Neil! Get out of here. I'm so over the *faggy* best friend drama!"

Narrowing his eyes in an obvious glare of acknowledgement I finally hit his own button of understanding. I've never said that particular f-word in my life, and I've given Neil endless amounts of shit for using it over the years.

"Fine! Be a bitch. I'm out of here. But I'll be back when you need your *fag* and his drama to save you," he yells so fiercely if I wasn't sure he understood what was happening, I'd be crying over his anger directed at me.

"*Whatever,* Neil. But you better not come back alone, otherwise, I'll kick your ass," I give one more bug-eyed stare followed by a wink as he gives me the tiniest nod before telling me to fuck off again quite loudly in the hall as he stalks away.

Exhaling, I turn around slowly after closing the door. Feeling like maybe I pulled it off, I'm suddenly spun and pushed against the door by Allan kissing me.

Oh *god*. I can actually feel my stomach twisting in nauseous knots while he thrusts his tongue in my mouth moaning. I'm going to puke in his mouth, I suddenly giggle as he pulls away from our kiss with a grin. I think he thinks my giggle was happiness for our kiss.

"That was so fucking hot, Sam. I love when you get like that with Neil. I always did. I mean I like the guy, for a *fag*," he laughs. "But he's so overbearing and possessive of you, it used to piss me right off. I hated when he tried to be your favorite, when clearly as your boyfriend I was your favorite. Right?" He asks totally unsure of himself all of a sudden.

"Of course you were my favorite," I smile as sweetly as I can trying to move away from the door and out of his reach.

Walking away from the door into my kitchen I ask Allan if he still wants an omelet. I'm desperate, and though really bizarre under the circumstances, I almost want to make an omelet to soothe *my* nerves.

Taking my hand and interlacing our fingers, Allan kisses my sore cheek again and says, "Not right now, baby. I just want to sit with you and talk for a while. I've missed you so much. And you have to tell me everything that's been going on. How's school?"

Allan is talking so casually, and so like his former self, I find the conflict between the reality of my forced interaction with him, and the gentleness of his tone, not only confusing, but truly messing with my head.

Looking at him as we sit beside each other on my couch, I find it hard not to remember Allan as he was because he seems so normal again. It's like in making the choice to force Neil to go away, Allan isn't insecure or crazy anymore. He knows I chose him, so he can relax now with me.

He seems like the man I loved for years.

Shaking my head, he smiles at me like he understands how strange this situation is between us. I'm being forced to sit here, but I almost feel like I *want* to sit here suddenly.

"It's so easy, isn't it? Falling back in love with each other? It's like nothing has changed between us."

Nodding my head again, I know enough to continue playing the role of the happy girlfriend, but just barely. I'm so confused by Allan, and by this situation, and by everything else around me, I want to snuggle in for a moment with Allan so I can stop worrying about everyone and everything all the time.

  I want to go back to this place with Allan, and I want to be my younger self with Allan talking about our days together as we snuggle on the couch and listen intently to each other.

  I want to make the choice to forgive him and move on together, and I want to know this peace again.

CHAPTER 19

   Talking with Allan on the couch I realize everything suddenly falls into place for me. I feel less lonely with him beside me, and I feel stronger than I have for a while now in his arms.

   He was so supportive when we were together. He helped me and loved me and he always held me if I needed to be held. He just always knew what I needed and gave it to me whenever he could.

   He hated my mother and kept her the hell away from me, and he like my dad and was always very respectful when they saw each other. Allan also cared for my girlfriends like a loving older brother, and he loved Neil and Daniel like they *were* my older brothers.

   Allan was always so good for me.

   Telling me about his new job as an entry level architect in an Architecture firm I've actually heard of, I feel as excited about his career as he is telling me about it. Allan's dream was to be an architect, working out of an office in our house after building us our dream home while I worked in a hospital. And amazingly, he's actually started his life like we wanted.

   Laughing at his story about a fellow employee who built a model that collapsed right in front of the partners and client, we both jump at the sound of loud knocking on my door again.

   "Who the *fuck* is that?" Allan screams again. "*Matty*?" He sneers as I slowly face the reality of our surroundings while watching him shake and fist his hands at his sides.

   Allan is enraged again, and I'm suddenly awake.

   What the *hell* was I doing? Staring at Allan suddenly standing over me, I try to shake my own head clear for the hundredth time since yesterday. I don't know what's happening to me anymore, and I can't understand all the changes around me.

   Pulling me up by my hair as I scream, he throws me toward the door again and growls, "Get rid of him. Or *I* will."

"Samantha Newman. It's the Police," we both hear through the door and freeze. "Please open the door," the officer states firmly.

But I can't move. My feet won't work and my mind is so confused after what happened before with the Police, I don't know why they're back again. Was that just last night or a few house ago? Whenever it was with Matt. I thought it was all over when they left with Matt.

"What do I do?" I whisper as Allan stands glaring at the door and me in turn.

Thinking quickly, Allan's eyes dart all over the room. "Let's hide on the balcony until they leave. Come with me, Sam," he says extending his hand.

But I know I can't. The balcony doesn't make any sense. They'll find us there for sure.

"I can't, Allan," I whisper so they can't hear us. The knocking is louder and the voices are raised, but Allan can still hear me.

"Let's go, Sam. We'll hide until they leave."

Shaking my head I'm trying to make him understand without getting angrier with me. "They won't leave, Allan. They'll look for us everywhere until they find us. I should go open the door."

"No, don't. Come on, Samantha. Come with me," he tugs my arm until I pull away from him dramatically.

Standing one foot closer to the door, we don't speak but Allan is begging me with his eyes to hide with him. He's begging me with his hand extended to go to him. He's begging me with all his soul to stay with him, I can feel it.

"I have to go let them in. They said they're going to force the door open."

Turning to the door again, listening to the yelling growing louder outside, I know I have to choose.

Looking back at Allan quickly, he cries one last time, "Come back to me..." even as I shake my head no.

Moving one step closer to the door, Allan suddenly yells as he jumps toward me, "Samantha! Make a *choice!*"

Spinning back to him again, everything stops for a second as I realize the truth of everything between us. He needs me to choose him, but I don't want to. I don't know what to do, and I don't want to make a choice.

"I can't choose, Allan," I say with such finality he doesn't argue or fight me any longer. Nodding his acceptance, Allan smiles so sweetly at me I almost feel like I made a mistake. I did love him and I wanted to choose him, but...

In a slow motion split second I watch a single tear fall down his cheek as I watch his smile fade to an unbearable sadness filling his face.

I watch the gun pulled from his jacket pocket. And then I watch him pull the trigger as he slowly turns his face away from me forever.

"*NO!*"

Jolting as Allan's brain hits my face, everything stops as quickly as he did.

Standing in the middle of my living room, I reach out slowly when his body falls to the floor as the warmth of his body cools all over my face.

The clock on the wall by the balcony says its only quarter to 8, but the world suddenly seems very dark now, even for winter.

I am covered in Allan.

Slowly lifting my shaking hand I push my warm, wet hair back from my face as it sticks to my head and hands in clumps of Allan.

Looking at Allan, I see a man bend to him and check his pulse as someone else moves me slightly.

Closing my eyes, there is no more sound. There is only a vacuum of silence spinning around me like I'm no more than dust in the room.

I am covered in Allan.

Shaking, I can't help but think of old records at my grandma's house when I was little. Like how they spun, but you could hold the record with your fingertips and make the songs warp, slower or faster depending on which speed it should normally play at. I know that sound, because I remember it. And that's how the world is coming back to me slowly.

I hear the sounds far away, getting slowly louder and faster until they start making a little more sense to me.

Gradually, the tones of the sounds and the words of the voices talking to me in my living room come back clearly like a record playing at the proper speed.

Gasping, I try to silence my spinning brain to understand what they're saying to me.

"*Seriously. I won't* touch her!"
Neil.
Gasping before I scream, I bow my head to keep the words inside me.
If I speak now, I'll cry. If I cry now, I'll sob. And if I sob now, I'll break apart completely. Then this was all for nothing.
I can't be broken.
"*Samantha?* Look at me, honey. Samantha, open your eyes and look at me."
Are my eyes still closed? If I open my eyes will I still see what I saw? If I keep my eyes closed can this all be a horrible dream?
"Samantha! It's time to open your eyes now. Can you hear me, Sam?"
"Miss Newman, I need to take some photographs of you before you can move."
"For *fuck* sakes! She's not moving. She's not even opening her eyes."
"I'm well aware of that. But before we can get her help, we need to take a few photos of her to show how close she was standing to the projection of-"
"Are you fucking *new*? She's *freaking* out!"
"I need you to step back, sir. Or I'll be forced to remove you from the room. This is only a courtesy," the man says firmly but Neil isn't going to back down. I know him.
Laughing suddenly in a quick burst, I can't help it. Neil's going to get arrested soon. Either for obstruction of justice, or assaulting a police officer, or contaminating evidence, or, or for something I think.
Leave it to Neil to get arrested while I stand here with Allan quickly cooling to a sticky disgusting mess all over my face and hair.
"Baby... Can you open your eyes for me?" Neil whispers as my laughter fades to a light whimper.
Rasping, my throat is nearly closed. I feel like I'm being strangled, but I fight the pressure to find the words. "Please take the pictures quickly, so I can wash my hair."
Did that sound weird? I know my voice did, but was that a weird request? Probably. But I need to get Allan off of me. I don't want Allan in my hair anymore.
"I don't want to open my eyes yet. I don't want to see what I just saw yet," I moan to no one.
"The ambulance is on the way. Miss Newman if you'll just stand there I'll take a few photos and then you can go with Officer Davis to remove

your clothing for evidence. I need you to be careful to not touch the clothing though, in case of any contamination."

What could I possibly contaminate? I have Allan's brain on my face and in my hair. Who else could it be? Oh my god. Bursting out laughing again, I can't stop myself. As if I'd have 2 different people blow their brains out in my hair on the same morning. What the *fuck?*

"Hold on, Samantha. *Please*?" Neil cries until I settle back down.

"I'm going to take the pictures now," the man says as more and more voices join him.

My living room is humming with activity. I hear multiple radios squawking in the background and many voices talking in hushed tones. I feel people moving around me and I hear descriptions of events being played out.

But they don't know what happened because they weren't here. They don't know what Allan said or did or wanted from me. They don't know how I felt beside him on the couch after he calmed down.

But I know. I wasn't afraid of everyone leaving me anymore when Allan was calm.

"*Daniel*..." I moan with my eyes still closed as my body starts to shake harder.

I can feel the shock hitting me from the quick cold of my body as the shivers work their way through me. I'm heavy and cold, and I'm tired of standing here. I need to have a shower.

"I need a shower, Neil," I whisper against his face. We're as close as we can be without actually touching. I can smell his heavenly cologne, and I can feel his warmth around me. "It's time for me to shower, so I can..." *cry.*

"*Soon*, Samantha. I promise. You need to be checked out first, and we need to give the police your clothes."

"Can we do it now?"

"Miss Newman, if you'd like some privacy we can go to the washroom or to another room to remove your clothing."

"Call me Samantha, please. I don't care where. Let's go," I say finally turning to try to walk toward my bedroom with my sightless vision.

"It's just her back! Fuck, there's no blood there. And I was outside with *you* guys, so who cares if I contaminate anything. I'm probably all over her clothes anyway since we do our laundry together," Neil argues.

Feeling Neil helping me walk to my room, guiding me with his hand on my back, I get to keep my eyes closed. Smiling, I realize I love him even more for understanding what I need right now.

"If you'll let me take your clothes, I'll be fast," a female says to me as I hear her snap on a pair of gloves. Nodding, I don't care. It's just a pair of sweats and an old hoodie. I wasn't even wearing anything nice to hold onto Allan with. He's forever stuck in bloody, broken pieces on my old cotton comfies.

When my hands are pressed into something powdery, I don't flinch. When my arms are raised and my sweater is removed I don't fight it. When my sweatpants are slipped down my legs I don't care that I'm naked underneath. I'm stripped and cold, and Neil is breathing beside me, but he's seen me naked before.

"No *lady parts* comments?" I ask to break up the dark silence killing me.

"Nah, not today, honey. But tomorrow I'm going to bring up that jiggly fat ass of yours," Neil says sounding totally disgusted with me as I burst out laughing again. See! Neil knows the rules. Don't be nice and Sam doesn't lose her shit. He totally gets me.

"We're done, Samantha. I just need to gather some evidence from your hair now," she says before wrapping my comforter around me tightly.

Waiting, I breathe heavily in evenly timed breaths when I feel her tugging a comb through my hair. Doesn't she know combs are bad? Nobody with hair longer than a buzz cut should ever use a comb.

Why am I thinking like this?

There's a bag moving, and more packages being ripped open, but I don't look. What's the point? Everything will just look like medical supply packages which I've seen a million times anyway.

"Just another minute, Sam," Neil whispers beside me.

"Can I sit? I'm really tired now."

"I'm done and the paramedics are waiting to check you out, Samantha," she says again in her gentle, quiet tone.

"Can I get dressed?"

"Of course. After you're assessed, you can have a shower and clean up if you'd like."

"Can I get dressed before I'm assessed?"

"Certainly. I'll be in the other room with the officers waiting for your statement."

"Can I just tell you now what happened?"

"I'd feel more comfortable if you give your statement with another officer present," she insists gently.

"Okay. Sorry..."

"Can I touch her now?" Neil begs.

Hearing his soft voice, I want to cry so badly, it's like a storm pushing through my chest. The pressure is so great, I can't stop it suddenly. Shaking, my whole body is fighting giving into the reality I don't want to face.

With no warning, Allan blew his head off all over me, and I can still feel it everywhere.

I didn't know he had a gun or I would have helped him. I didn't know he felt that sad or I would have done something more. I didn't know he was anything more than my pain in the ass ex-boyfriend, or I would have pretended to love him harder until I could've gotten him the help he needed.

I didn't know what Allan was feeling or I would have helped him, and I didn't know what Heather was feeling or I would have helped her.

I really don't think I know anyone anymore.

Shaking, I stay quiet in Neil's warm arms and let him cry for me.

Exhaling, I shut down quietly instead of dealing with reality.

*****

Walking into Neil's apartment in the afternoon, I'm only a little piece of my old self. The statements have been made, and my prescriptions for anxiety and shock were filled after we left the hospital. Neil called my dad to let him know what happened *and* to keep my mother away from me. And Daniel is waiting for us at Neil's.

Physically, I'm fine, though exhausted. But emotionally, I honestly don't know what I am anymore.

When Neil opens his door, I see only Daniel. Backlit by the bay windows, he looks like the angel I tease him about being as he stands waiting for me to go to him silently.

Feeling the weight of mourning, and the pressure of reality crash down on me, I move with a feral sounding moan deep in my throat to Daniel until he pulls me into his arms.

Daniel doesn't acknowledge all the blood and brain still on my face and in my hair. And he doesn't make a sound as I struggle with the pain lashing through me.

Letting me close down in his arms, Daniel holds me up when I don't have the strength to do it anymore for myself.

"I need to wash him off me," I moan into Daniel's chest as he nods against my head and picks me up.

Walking past Neil who doesn't speak, Daniel takes me to Neil's bathroom, keeps the lights off, places me on the counter and starts the shower.

Helping undress me, I'm stripped of another pair of sweat pants and a warm, fleece hoodie from my body in the dark by Daniel because I can't help him. My body isn't really functioning anymore.

"Please turn on the light," I beg morbidly. I don't know why, but I need to finally see myself. I wouldn't allow the hospital staff to clean me, and I slapped Neil's hand away when he brought me a wet facecloth to clean up with. But now I want to see.

"Are you sure?" He whispers to my silent nod.

Turning on the counter to look in the mirror, everything stops in this one moment.

I am a perfectly speckled ghost with dull blue eyes that are way too large for my white, hollow looking face. Everything looks so dark and dirty. My body seems so much lighter in contrast to my bloody face and hair. Looking, my dark brown hair is nearly black in places, and I want to scream.

Okay. I'm done. Looking away from the smears and chunks of blood on my face, I find the physical strength I need to jump off the counter as Daniel steps back.

Opening the shower curtain, I step into the heat and sit on the edge with the handheld.

"Does Neil have my shampoo and conditioner still?"

"Right here, honey," Daniel hands me the bottles without looking in the shower.

"I need to get that piece of brain from my hair, Daniel," I giggle. Holy *shit!* Who says that?

"Do you need any help?" He asks softly.

"Nope," I giggle again at my own stupid sounding voice.

Watching the blood drain down my body to the shower floor, I'm surprised by how red the stream of water is heading for the drain. I watch little pieces, and little clots fall away and follow the stream. I watch the color turn lighter and darker on the white basin as I move the handheld around my head.

"Bye, Allan," I laugh as my tears finally start to fall.

Laugh crying, I know I'm losing my shit, but it's okay. I was told this would happen, and I know this happens from my medical studies.

People act weird in times of severe emotional stress. People say and do things totally unlike themselves. People handle these matters so differently, and so individually, that besides the actually steps of grieving, there really is no hard and fast rule regarding the way people handle death and stress.

Besides, I'm going to suffer some severe PTSD, I know. How could I not? I'm watching Allan's blood and brain slowly fade from red to clear on the white shower floor.

Seriously, what the hell is going on with me?

Crawling into Neil's bed, wrapped tightly in a pair of his large comfy sweats, I'm warm and exhausted. My wet medusa hair is clean, and the speckled dots of Allan are cleaned away from my face.

"Can you stay with me?" I whisper as Daniel climbs right into his old bed beside me and Neil.

Without even pausing, Daniel forgets his discomfort at being back in Neil and his old bed, joins us, and pulls my back to his chest while I stare at Neil watching me from his side.

"This is my favorite place to be," I say burying my face in the pillow to muffle the awful sound of my voice. I don't want them to see me cry anymore because I know this is killing them, too.

Smiling at Neil, I touch his cheek as he turns to kiss my palm. Feeling Daniel's hand on my hip, I close my eyes and try to forget the strange, horrible reality I'm drowning in.

As I feel sleep pulling me down, I beg for the one thing I can't live through. I can deal with a lot in life. I have before, and I'm sure I will again. I'm a tough cookie like Daniel says, but I know I can *not* live without them.

"Please don't *ever* leave me or die…"

Before I get my answers though I fade away believing whole-heartedly they won't leave me ever. *If* they have a choice.

CHAPTER 20

Everything is so weird for me right now, but I love it.

Knowing I'm heavily medicated- by necessity, and by choice, I'm actually okay with it right now. I never thought I would be, but I really am fine with this fog. For the second time in less than a year, I'm stoned out of my face, and it suits me. Right *now*, anyway.

Being medicated into submission, while others care for you is awesome. You don't have to think too much, and you don't have to work too hard at anything when others take care of you.

When all the little things are taken care of by someone else, you can just try to understand what's happening to you with all the big things. When I'm fed, and dressed, and washed, and moved whenever they think I should be, it takes most of the stress out of my days. When they do everything for me, I can lie here enjoying my fog.

The big things have also been taken care of for me, so I don't have to struggle or make any life-altering decisions either. They are doing all the heavy thinking for me, which is okay.

My situation and goals and decisions are simply told to me and all I have to do is nod. The decisions I should be making in life are no longer important, and really no longer mine to make, which is a relief. I mean really, I wasn't making good choices anyway.

When you're stoned out of your face, everyone who loves you does everything for you, which is what I need right now. I do what I'm told, by whoever tells me and so far they keep loving me anyway. The only thing I *do* have to worry about is making sure they keep loving me. I have to make sure they keep loving me, so they keep doing everything for me, because if I lose their love I know I'm totally fucked.

Suddenly panicking again, I grab my phone and speed-dial Neil as the fear hits me hard.

"Samantha... *Nothing* is wrong."

"Nothing..." I moan in relief. He answered. Oh, god... He answered the phone again. He's still alive. For now.

"I'm okay, honey. I'll be home in 2 hours. But I'll call you before I leave okay?"

Crying, I whisper a thank you while I try to catch my breath. Neil's alive. And I'm okay for now. But what about... *"Daniel?"* I choke.

"I spoke to him an hour ago, and he's sitting at his desk. He's perfectly fine. He'll be over late tonight. And Olivia is at her parents' house for dinner tonight. *Remember?* She called to let you know where she'd be, and she promised to call when she was leaving her parents' house for home."

"Okay..." I gasp. "How are you feeling? Are you sad?"

"No, baby. I'm good," Neil says brightly, and I almost believe him. *Almost,* but I never know for sure what people are really feeling anymore.

Everyone hides their real feelings from me. They all say they trust me and love me, but I know they don't trust me anymore. They all hide and pretend with me, and then I can't help them, and they don't let me help them, and I hate that I thought I was good, but they think I'm not good because they never trust me to help them anymore.

"You can tell me *anything* Neil. I'll help you and love you and I'll love you forever and I'll take care of-"

"Samantha! *Listen* to me. I'm perfectly fine. I'm not sad, and I'm not going anywhere."

"But would you tell me?!" I cry into the phone. I'm getting crazy again, I can feel it. It comes so fast now I never know how to stop it from pulling me back into the darkness.

"*Breathe*, honey. I'm on my way home soon, okay? I'll be there in 2 hours. And I promise I'm fine. I tell you everything, *always*. Think of all the shit I've told you over the years. Even the gross gay sex stuff," he laughs.

He's coming home in 2 hours. He'll be home in 2 hours. He'll talk to me in 2 hours. I just have to hope he doesn't do anything bad in the next 2 hours, so I can save him.

"Do you trust me, Neil?"

"With my life, Samantha. You're my soul," he whispers so sweetly I cry a little more in relief.

"Will you tell me if you get too sad and want to die? Will you tell me when you want to die so I can help you?" Begging, my voice is thick with my desperation.

My chest is pounding and my hands are shaking so badly I can barely hold my cell. Desperately, I fight the panic strangling me to make sure I'm there for Neil if he needs me.

"Baby... *Please.* I'm not sad, and I don't want to die. But yes, I would tell you if I was. I promise."

"But you *are* sad," I argue his lies. "You miss Daniel."

"Yes, I *miss* Daniel, but I'm not sad or suicidal. And I don't want to die."

"But you will," I moan. I know it's going to happen. "You can't kill yourself Neil. You can't die, okay?"

"I won't. Listen to me, Samantha. Danny doesn't even like necrophilia, so if I'm dead I can't get back into those hot jeans of his *or* that sexy ass that I miss so much. *Right?*"

What? *Oh!* Bursting out laughing, he's right.

"*Right*, Sam?" Nodding against the phone, my hysterical laughter is so overwhelming, my head starts pounding until I have to either stop laughing or take more pills to ease the pain.

"You're right. Sorry, Neil."

"No worries. I'll see you soon okay? Just wait for me to get home and we'll make some dinner and relax in front of the t.v. for the night."

Listening hard, Neil sounds okay which is a relief. Neil doesn't sound too sad. And sad people don't make dirty jokes about necrophilia, so he should be fine until he gets home.

I'm losing it all over him again. But he loves me anyway.

"Sorry..." I say into the silence between us before hanging up, so he knows I'm okay again.

Standing, I don't even know what day it is. What day *is* it? I don't know. I don't know how long it's been since Allan did that in front of me.

Oh, looking at my cell it's Thursday. It's only been 4 days, and I have to go. Neil must've forgotten to tell me.

Walking into the bathroom, I brush my teeth and fix my hair. I look like shit, but I'm not too dirty I don't think. No, I'm not dirty. Olivia helped me shower this morning I think. I think it was this morning. She even brushed and dried my hair for me so it doesn't have that weird ugly wave it gets if it's not dried properly. It doesn't have that ugly, non-curl, stupid wave thing that looks ugly hanging down my back when I don't use a blow dryer, so it must've been today Olivia dried my hair.

Looking in the mirror, I don't have the red spots and clots smeared across my face anymore. My hair even seems clean right now with no brain in my hair, so I look much better than I did the last time I looked in the mirror.

I'm not going to freak anyone out. I'll look good and then I'll act normal. Maybe if I don't take another pill for a bit I'll even *be* normal for them. I'm going to try.

*****

Slipping into the back pew after the cab dropped me off, I ease down quietly so no one knows I'm there. I'm sure Allan's parents hate me, and I don't want to upset them today. They have enough upset to deal with without remembering how much they used to love me. They used to say I was the perfect daughter in law, and they always treated me so well when I visited. But now I think they must hate me like Linda does.

They're burying their only son today. So it's important for me to stay quiet in the back, paying my respects without anyone seeing me.

Why do people still care more about having sons? This isn't the Middle Ages. And this isn't a foreign country where women are a burden to be sold off to the highest bidding husband. Yet we're still not really equals.

Even here, in this day and age, people still say *'their only son'*, like the son is the most important thing in a family. *Why?* I don't get it.

Women are valuable now, too. We work, and care for ourselves and pay our own way, and do everything men do. Neil's an accountant, and Daniel is finishing college to be a teacher. But I'm going to be a doctor, for Christ's sake. So why are they better than me?

Why does nobody ever say they're burying their only *daughter*? Why? Am I so useless? I wonder if that's why my mother is the way she is. Maybe because she didn't have a son to make her life valuable? I don't know. But I don't think it's fair. We're special too. We shouldn't have to be bought or sold to bring value to our parents' lives. We shouldn't be sold to get a fix either.

"*Samantha?* You came..." Allan whispers in my ear as I shiver.

Jumping in my pew, I look around frantically for him but I don't see him. Where the hell is he, and why did he sound so close to me?

Staring at the first few rows, I see Allan's mom crying and I wish I could help her. I would've helped before he did what he did because she and I were very close for years. She even taught me how to cook because I didn't have a functioning mother of my own.

"Samantha! Come *here*!" Allan yells and I rise immediately. I don't want him to slap me again, and I don't want him to kill- *Oh!* He already did that, but I forgot for a second.

Looking around the chapel, I see the casket start to slowly rise and I'm mesmerized as I walk closer to it.

When a creepy looking hand reaches outside to push the lid up, I can barely breathe. I'm watching Allan reanimated. I'm seeing the resurrection of Allan. I'm watching without breathing Allan coming back to life for me. I *knew* this was going to happen again. I should tell my mother I've seen a resurrection so she'd finally think I should be allowed into Heaven with the *good* people.

I knew he'd want to talk to me like Heather did.

Holy *fuck!* It's like that movie. What was it? Nosferatu? Yes! *Nosferatu.* Allan is all white in his black suit slowly sitting up as he pushes the lid all the way back with his long, white, gnarly looking hands.

Watching as I stand silently in the aisle a few feet away from him, I'm surprised he still looks so good. He is way more pale than usual, but his-

Screaming when Allan turns his head to look at me, I'm done. There it is. Oh, *god...* the other side.

Why does it look like that? It was just a little hole. It was so little it shouldn't have done all of that to the other side of his head. There shouldn't be all that stuff hanging there. It was a little gun, but the other side is too mangled for the bullet to have caused all that. Did something *else* happen to him?

"Samantha, please?" He begs softly with his hand extended to me.

Covering my mouth so I don't scream or throw up again, I walk to him when he calls me.

Pushing past the few people who stand near me, I walk to my ex-boyfriend because he asked me to.

"Allan... I swear I didn't know," I whisper.

"I know."

"You do?" I gasp in relief. "*Really?*" I beg again as he nods.

Allan looks good. Well, all things considering. He's still handsome and lovely. Even with his dark eyes swimming in tears, his eyes look more beautiful to me then they did before he died.

Beckoning me closer, I walk to him.

When someone pulls me tightly against a chest, I fight with everything I have. They are not going to hold me back. They will not keep me from Allan this time.

"You have to hurry, Allan!" I scream past the arms holding me tighter. "Tell me what you have to say so I can help you!"

"Come here, Samantha!" He yells totally pissed off that I don't come to him. But I'm trying.

Struggling, I feel like I'm trapped in quicksand. Every step I take, seems to hold me further away from him. I'm fighting and crying out but I'm not getting any closer to him. The hands all over me are hurting me and holding me and killing me.

"Allan! *Hurry!*" I scream again still fighting the arms that want to hurt me.

"You should have chosen me, Sam," he yells past the noise and voices all around me.

"I did!"

"You didn't. You should've chosen me when I begged," he cries shaking his head.

When? At the restaurant, or when the police were knocking? What does he mean?!

"I did! I was meeting you for dinner. I chose you! I was coming for you!"

"I love you, Samantha. So much it killed me," he cries still reaching out his hand to me.

"I loved you too."

"No, you didn't."

"I did! Allan, I loved you until you cheated on me, then I hated you, then I loved you again. I *did* love you. *Remember?!*"

"You made the wrong choice, Samantha. You made the wrong choice on Sunday, and now look at what's happened," he moans.

Crying out, I can't stand all the pain. My chest is killing me and my heart is throbbing straight to my head.

Struggling to force the body off me so I can stand up, my cheek is rubbed raw on the floor as I fight. My chest is killing me, my hands are being crushed, and my mind is screaming in pain at Allan's confusion. Everything is sore and heavy, and I can't breathe anymore.
  Watching Allan slowly turn his head and lie back down, I scream his name. I need him to know I *did* choose him. I was going there, but HE chose to go to Monica instead. I need him to understand, that I did want him. And I did choose him.
  "*Allan!* I did love you!" I scream but he's fading away.
  As the casket slowly closes, I listen to his voice fade behind the wood of the lid. "You made the wrong choice, Samantha," he whispers quietly as he lays to rest finally. "And now look what's happened…" I hear faintly as he fades away completely.
  When everything stops, there is no sound, and no more fight in me.
  Exhaling, I let my body collapse around me. Feeling the cool of the floor against my skin, I say goodbye to Allan forever.
  "I'm so sorry, Allan…"

  "*Sammy…?*" I hear his whisper soft voice as the darkness begins to fade. Listening, the darkness fades more until I feel the light around me and inside me. There is a numbing taking hold of the grey I was trapped it. I hear it. I can *feel* it.
  "Daniel…" I exhale, as the last of the darkness leaves me with my breath.
  Opening my eyes, I see Daniel's beautiful blues staring back at me. See-through with his tears, he is watching me come back to him with a gentle smile.
  "Hi, baby," he says softly as I weep in relief.
  "You're alive," I cry.
  "I am. And I'm right here with you."
  "You look like an angel, Danny."
  "*Do* I?" He questions with the little twinkle in his eyes that melts my heart.
  Nodding, I feel the cold floor against my face, as I exhale all the tension from my body.
  "Will you hold my hand?" He asks so sweetly I gasp. I will always hold his hand.
  "You're my white knight, Daniel. You're mine and Neil's forever. Even if

you can't love us like you used to, I'll *always* hold your hand," I whisper without tears.

I don't have any tears left. I don't even really feel the sadness of my words anymore. There is nothing in me but the knowledge that Daniel doesn't love us the way he used to.

"I'm going to miss you when you leave."

"Sam... I'm never going to leave you. You're my girl," he says before placing a sweet kiss on my lips as I close my eyes.

Almost believing him for a moment, I take in his sweetness and exhale all the pain of the truth I know deep inside my heart. He *will* leave me, and I'll be without the angel who keeps me in the light. But in this moment, here, I have him with me.

"I think Allan blames me," I confess.

"No, he doesn't. He blames himself, honey. He told his parents and Monica that he blames himself for what he did to you, *and* to himself."

"Did he visit them too?" I ask surprised. "I thought only I saw dead people," I suddenly laugh.

What the hell was *that* movie? And why does everything I know or feel become referenced by a movie or a song? Is that weird? Do I even have a thought or memory of my own anymore?

"Did you see Allan?" Even as the question leaves my mouth, I know he didn't though. Daniel is much too sane for that.

"No. Was he here?"

"Yes..."

Looking around us I quickly realize we're both lying on the wooden floor of the chapel. There are pews behind Daniel, and feet just out of sight. There are other people around us and I feel a little embarrassed by our surroundings. I know I should probably stand up, but I'm too exhausted to do it.

"I'm very tired," I whisper as he nods his understanding.

"Let me help you, Sam," he says gently as he rolls over to stand in front of me. Looking up, I too flip to my back to the eyes of Olivia and Allan's dad. *Olivia?*

"I thought you were at your parents' house? How did you get here?" I ask confused again.

"We were here, Sam," Daniel says as he bends back down to scoop me up in his arms. Thank god he's so strong for me.

"You and Olivia came together? I don't understand."

"We came to pay our respects for you and Neil," he says so simply, I don't think I'm actually upset. I mean not *really* upset. I came to pay my respects, too. But-

"You lied to me, Daniel. The Angel *does* lie," I grin.

Smiling back, he nods yes. "Just a little white one. I didn't want to upset you, so I fibbed- just a little one so you wouldn't be upset today. I would've told you the truth later though. Okay?"

"Okay." Taking a deep breath I wrap my arms tightly around his neck. When I feel Olivia's little hand against my back, I forgive her for lying, too. Everything makes sense now. And even I would've lied if it would've helped them. I'm sure of it.

"I think I need some medication, Daniel. I think I'm going crazy. Like batshit, crazyass, totally insane crazy," I admit as Daniel walks me out of the chapel in his arms.

"I would have to agree…" He whispers with a smile as I burst out laughing against his neck.

*****

Waking in Neil's bed, I barely remember the ambulance ride I took with Daniel after the funeral. I can't remember the hospital visit I was forced to endure for 2 days afterward. I don't even remember what was said to me, or what I said in return. I don't know what I said to my mother though she showed up, and I can't remember speaking to Neil though he stayed the whole time he was allowed.

Daniel and Olivia visited, but I only know that because I was told. My dad visited too, which Neil also told me but my dad is such an inconsequential part of my life I didn't remember even seeing him.

I was then discharged and sent home with more pills and follow-up therapy appointments.

Lying in Neil's bed, I'm sane enough to know I'm losing my mind. I'm also sane enough to know I may not get it back. Most days I just wish I was already a psychiatrist so I could medicate myself, but sadly I'm not.

So I'm kinda screwed.

Diagnosing yourself is almost impossible I've heard before and now know to be true. Everything I think is wrong with me has a counter explanation from a different doctor. And everything I try to explain *is* wrong with me gets a diagnosis I think is wrong.

In my most lucid moments, which sadly is during the first moments after I take my meds but *before* I'm totally looped, I can honestly admit I'm a little disgusted and surprised by my behavior.

I never thought I would turn out like this, and I never wanted this for myself. I have hated my mother and her mental weakness for so long, I trained myself to never be weak because of her. I also hated her dependency on absolutely every substance that ever entered her body, so I forced myself to be the exact opposite of her as I grew up. I took nothing ever, and I didn't even feel the urge to.

With the exception of drinking with my friends at a club on a very specific night, for a very specific reason, I didn't ever indulge in substances. I didn't take pain relievers for cramps, and I didn't drink to deal with anything.

I was a tough cookie. Until everyone started dying around me.

Now I'm paranoid, and scared, and exhausted from everything around me. I don't trust my friends to stay alive, and I don't trust myself to keep them alive.

Now I spend my days, crying, panicking, and medicated. I either get drugged by them kindly, or I drug myself desperately when the death returns.

In my daydreams, and nightmares, I either feel my last friends die in my nonreality, or I wait for it in reality. I know their deaths are coming and I know I can't stop them from coming. I've tried to help them, but they don't trust me anymore. So all I can do is wait for death to take them.

I know Neil, Daniel, or Olivia are next.

But I'm so afraid to lose them I choose to live in this dark fog now because it hurts so much less here while I wait.

CHAPTER 21

Waking to Neil sliding in bed beside me, I can't remember what day it is, or even when I last moved actually.

I feel like I've been in his bed forever, and though he doesn't mind, I think I know it's time to get up soon. I know I need to get out of this purgatory grey now, but it's just so hard.

The days have blended into one, and time keeps flashing by without the struggle it should take to get from one moment to the next.

And still, I don't understand anything anymore, no matter how much time passes.

"Daniel is on his way, honey. I have to leave for work now, but he'll be by soon to make your breakfast, okay?" He makes me breakfast?

Wait... Neil cooks me dinner every night and makes me eat, and Daniel makes me breakfast and forces me to eat, I think. When did that happen?

"Samantha, I have to tell you something, but I don't want you to get upset, okay? I have your pills here so you can breathe, honey."

My pills? Yes. I always take pills now. I take pills, and I sleep, and I cry. What else do I do? I can't remember anything except nothing.

I have to wake up now I think or I'll ruin my whole life forever.

Trying to sit up, Neil helps me lift and leans me against the headboard. Feeling a little nauseous, my head spins from moving, but focusing my blurry eyes on Neil I need him to know how much I love him.

"Have I ever told you how much I love you, and how beautiful and *straight* you look in a suit?"

"Yes, you have. Every morning actually," he grins for a second then turns his eyes away from me.

Looking at Neil's sad face, I panic instantly. "What's wrong? Oh, *no...* is Daniel dead?" I gasp as he turns back to me.

I think I just spoke to Danny. I think I just called him again. I call him all the time. And I call Neil and Olivia, too. I think I call them hourly, maybe. Do I even wait an hour? I think I just spoke to him a few minutes ago and he was okay, but...

"Samantha, I just told you Daniel will be here any minute. And he's absolutely fine."

"Then what *is* it?" I yell already shaking.

Grabbing me in a tight hug, Neil moans against my head. "Please, Sam. Keep it together for me. *Please,* baby? I need to talk to you."

Okay, I will. If that's what Neil needs from me, I can do it. I have to keep it together for Neil because he asked me to do something to help him, and I want to help my friends so they don't die again.

Because they're going to. I saw death coming late last night. I saw it, and I felt it all around me. Death was everywhere again.

Convincing myself to stay calm, I try to slow my pounding chest and my shaking hands. Neil is here, and Daniel's on his way. But Olivia...

"*Olivia*!" I scream as Neil jumps like I shocked him on the bed.

Oh God, *no*! Already moaning, I can feel it. She's not okay. Something happened to her. I *know* it. I saw Death last night on the balcony warning me.

"Is she dead? Did she kill herself?"

Screaming in pain, my whole body reacts to the news. I can't believe I've lost another one. I can't believe she's dead, too. I kept calling her to make sure she was okay. I called all the time to be there for her if she needed me. I begged her Matt to wake her if she was sleeping, and I begged Olivia to tell me when she was sad.

Moaning at my loss, I pull at my hair and try to catch my breath.

"Samantha! Olivia's not dead! Fuck, baby. *Stop!* Olivia's alive. She was just hurt last night. She was mugged after she left work. But she's alive," Neil moans fighting my hands as they hit my chest to make it beat right again.

I hear Neil and I know what he said but the panic is still so hard to fight. I can't stop feeling like everything is suddenly very wrong again. I know he said she's alive, but I don't really *feel* like she is.

"Samantha! Look at me. Look. At. Me," Daniel says sternly grabbing my arms from Neil as I try to focus on him.

"*Danny?*" I beg as he nods in my face. Kissing my forehead, he seems to exhale my tension for me. "Is Olivia dead?" I know he won't lie to me. He can't lie. Daniel's an angel, and angels don't lie. They just tell a little fib once in a while, but I don't think he will this time.

"No, Sam. Olivia is alive. She was hurt last night, but she's going to be fine, I promise. Sam? Can you hear me? Olivia is okay. You can even call her later if you want."

Shaking my head to clear it, I try to focus my eyes on Daniel better. He doesn't lie to me, so I don't think he's lying this time. "Olivia's alive," I whisper feeling out the words. "She didn't kill herself," I nod to myself.

"No. Olivia didn't kill herself," he says leaning against my forehead again with his own to protect me from Neil's bedroom.

Okay. I'm okay.

Taking a deep breath with Daniel still only inches from my face, I look at his ice blue eyes as he pulls away from me, and I exhale fully. My chest is already loosing up, and my hands aren't shaking as much as they were.

Wow. I think I just had a panic attack. Actually, I think I have them all the time now. Thinking about it, I'm pretty sure I have panic attacks whenever something feels wrong inside me, which is all the time now.

Strangely, I feel almost clear right now looking at Daniel watching me breathe my way back.

Turning my head, Neil is still sitting on his bed in his gorgeous work suit waiting for me to resurface I think.

"I'm sorry," I moan as tears fill my eyes. I think I say sorry all the time now, too. Like daily or multiple times a day, or all the time, I think. "I think I'm having a hard time right now," I whisper to Neil giving me his classic *no shit* face.

Laughing at Neil's face, I feel almost normal right now, and I kind of like it. Sometimes I miss feeling like me because I wasn't so bad before.

"I used to be pretty awesome before, wasn't I?"

"Yes. You still are," Neil smiles, but we both know it isn't true anymore.

"Don't lie to me. I know I *used to* be pretty awesome. Just like I also know I'm not awesome right now. I'm not stupid, Neil. I'm just mental."

Feeling a little stronger suddenly, I need to figure out this newest trauma around me. "What happened to Livi?" I ask as calmly as I can.

"She was mugged leaving the store last night but she's okay. She's just bruised and beat up, but she made it back to her apartment afterward to call the police."

"Where is she?"

"She was at her parents' house when I heard an hour ago, but I think she wants to go back home this afternoon," Neil speaks quietly like he's struggling with the thought of tiny Olivia being hurt, just like I am.

"She was mugged?" I ask as something slowly falls into place when they both nod.

What is it? What was I supposed to do? Coffee and *cookies!*

"Neil, you have to go get her. Or you have to make her parents keep her if she won't come with you. You *have* to."

"Sam..."

"Listen to me. I know what happened." With a conviction straight through to my soul, I know the truth. I just *know*. "Matt beat her up. I know it. And she was going to tell me. We were having a coffee/cookie date and she was going to talk to me so I could help her," I say as Neil shakes his head no like I'm wrong.

"Neil, I'm dead fucking serious. I don't know how I know, but I do. Just like her boyfriend in high school did, Matt is hitting her and that's why she looks bad. *That's* why she's scared all the time. Matt's hitting her and breaking her, and she's getting so thin and depressed and she *will* kill herself soon because she's too afraid all the time and she can't get away from him, and she's tired of men hurting her I think."

"She was mugged, baby. That's all," Neil interrupts me. "The police are looking for the guy who stole her purse. And Olivia gave a description-"

"She's *lying*. Go get my key. Look in the half drawer of the old desk her dad gave her. It's a hidden drawer like they had in the old days. Go look! I promise you'll find her stuff in there. I know it," I cry because he's still shaking his head like I'm wrong. But I'm not wrong.

"*Please...* Go look in her desk, Neil. Or *Daniel!* Please go look. Neil has to go to work, so you can go look. I'm fine here. *Please*?" I beg. "She was going to tell me that Sunday but-"

Jolting, I remember that Sunday suddenly. I feel the blood hit my face, and I watch Allan fall slowly to the ground. I hear the loud bang, and I feel the warmth hit my face as that one tear of his falls down his cheek.

Moaning, I see it all so clearly my chest hurts. Shaking, I pull at my hair to make sure the clumps of Allan are gone. Touching my cheeks, I scrub away his blood from my face with shaking hands.

"Please get off my face. I don't want you in my hair anymore, Allan..." I beg Allan, but he never leaves.

"Here, honey," Neil whispers putting something in my hand. "Take this," he says lifting my hand to push a pill past my lips. Lifting a glass to my mouth, Neil forces me to drink as the liquid dribbles down my chin onto my chest.

Remembering in this moment little Olivia, I see her almond eyes and sweet little mouth crying as she held me in her arms after Allan's funeral. She's a little porcelain doll. She is tiny and fragile, and she's going to be broken soon if I don't save her in time.

"She's *not* okay. Please go check the desk drawer for her stuff. She wasn't mugged, and I have to help her before she's lost, too. I have to *save* her, Daniel," I cry as the world starts fading around me. "Please?" I beg.

"I'll go right now but only if you sleep, honey." Looking at Daniel, the relief is so overwhelming, I exhale a cry smile at my angel.

"Thank you. I have her house key with the red plastic thing on it in my purse. And the key to the drawer is in the pen slot in the top drawer. She doesn't hide the key very well," I laugh thinking so clearly of the placement of her desk and its contents.

I even teased her once about having an old fashioned desk with a cool secret drawer at the back, but then the key to that very secret drawer right in plain sight in the pen slot. Olivia just grinned and shrugged at my observation.

"She's *not* okay, Daniel. And I have to help her."

"We will. Go to sleep, Sam, so I can go to her apartment," Daniel pushes until I give into the darkness dragging me back down to settle deep in my chest.

*****

"Why the *hell* did you tell her now?!" I hear Daniel vaguely as I try to fight falling asleep completely.

"I *had* to. She was going to call Olivia as soon as she woke up, not get an answer, and lose it again. Just like she does all fucking day *every* fucking day when one of us doesn't answer quickly enough."

I'm sure Neil's right. I remember when my boys don't answer their phones right away I panic. I know if Olivia doesn't call me back after my texts I panic. I think I even panic if my dad doesn't answer me when I call him- not that I call him often, but I think I do once in a while, and I usually panic because he doesn't check his phone all the time like we do.

"You could have told her something else. You could have said Olivia's phone wasn't working, or she lost it and was getting a new one or something, Neil. You didn't have to tell her Olivia was hurt. She can't handle any more upset," Daniel says angrily.

"*I know what she can handle, Daniel,*" Neil growls back. "You never lie to her, so why ask me to?"

"Because she needs some peace until she gets better," Daniel chokes up. I can actually hear the distress in his voice.

Where the hell are they standing? Everything sounds so clear, like they're right here in Neil's bedroom with me.

"I'm doing everything I can," Neil says softly and I can almost feel his dark eyes begging Daniel to understand. "I'm trying everything I can to help her."

"But she's not getting better. And I think it's time we got her outside help, Neil. I know she doesn't want it, and I know you want to give her whatever she wants, but we're not helping her anymore. It's been over a month, and she hasn't moved unless we move her. She's out of school, and she won't get her chance again. She's losing everything."

"No, she isn't!" Neil snaps making me flinch.

"Neil, just hear me out for a second. I'll help you in any way I can with her always, but what are you going to do in the long term? Can you afford to support her forever? I know you want to, but she has no more coverage and her meds alone are hundreds a month. Plus all the Psych visits, and everything else. Neil, can you really do this? Can you take on this kind of commitment with her indefinitely?"

Wow. As silence fills the air, I have only 2 thoughts. *Will* Neil support me forever? And, god I *hope* he supports me because without him I have no one.

"Yes, I can and I *will*, Daniel. I'll figure it out. I've thought about all my choices here, and I'm figuring out what I can do long term. I'll fucking marry her if I have to so she gets my spousal benefits," Neil says choking an awkward laugh. "I *love* her Daniel. She's my soul, and I'll *never* abandon her. I already hurt you more than I ever thought I could love and hurt someone, and I won't do it to her. I can't hurt her like that when she's been so good to all of us for so long. I don't want to hurt her any more than she's already hurting," Neil says sadly and I feel my heart break again.

"I know you don't. Do you think I do? I love her, Neil, almost as much as you do. But we need to try something else now."

When they stop talking, I'm sure they've left the room so I can't hear them. I never hear them speak like this, and I didn't realize how hard everything must be for them with me. I didn't mean to be a burden to Neil, I just didn't know what else to do. I don't know how to get better, and I don't know what will make all of this crazy stop.

My life is getting out of control, and I finally realize I hate it.

"I'm exhausted, Daniel," Neil suddenly cries into the silence as I force myself to stay awake as hard as I can.

Listening to Neil clear his throat to get it together, I feel so sorry for all he's going through with me, I want to get better for him so he doesn't sound like that ever again.

Choking out the words, Neil continues. "Her mother calls me every fucking day, and I have to fight that crazy bitch to keep her away. Her dad begs me to let him help, but Sam doesn't want him around. Olivia is getting worse, and I thinks Sam's right about her and Matt. So I'm going to fucking *kill* him if he's hurting Olivia. And I know Sam's not getting better, Daniel. I *do* know that. *Fuck,* I can just look at her and see she's not getting better, but I don't know what else to do," he exhales so hard I actually feel it in my own chest.

They're in Neil's room with me. How strange that they would have this argument when I can actually hear them. Or maybe I need to hear them, so they don't argue anymore. I don't know what to do, but I think this is a good thing for me somehow.

"*Please* Daniel... She's everything I have, and I'm afraid I'm losing her this time for good," Neil cries.

Waiting out the silence, I hear Daniel whisper an 'I'm sorry', but the silence continues.

I think they might be hugging. I *wish* they were hugging. Maybe if they hug each other they'll get back together and I can finally breathe right again. Maybe if Neil and Daniel fall back into place with each other I won't be so afraid of losing them all the time. Maybe if I know they're together, this murky grey I'm drowning in won't seem so dark anymore.

"Okay. For starters, we'll let Dr.Berney come over to talk to her to see if she needs help outside of here. He was quite taken with her, like we all are," he laughs a little. "Especially after the Heather freak out she had. And I think he truly wants to help her, Neil," Daniel says softly.

Listening to their soft voices, I feel like maybe they're okay now. So if me talking to someone gets them back together, I'll talk to anyone. I'll even speak my crazyass mother if it'll help, I almost laugh.

  Closing my eyes tighter, I try to sleep when they finally leave Neil's room together.

*****

  When I finally wake up again, I decide I need to get myself back together. I don't want to be broken anymore. I *can't* be broken anymore. My boys need me, and Olivia needs me, especially.

  I have to help them, and fix them, and make everyone who is left okay now.

  Stepping into Neil's shower, I clean away all my slumber. I breathe as deeply as I can until I feel less foggy. I shave and shampoo my body until I feel like Samantha again.

  Walking back to Neil's room for clothes, I see *all* my own clothes hung up in his closet. Wow, I didn't know he had moved everything in. I thought maybe he'd grabbed some clothes for me, but I had no idea he packed up everything. He even gave me the nice black hangers he loves so much.

  Staring at his closet I almost choke up but hold it in so I don't start with all the crazy crying again.

  I've moved in with Neil and I didn't even know it. He took me in because he loves me. Smiling, I know I am Neil's soul. Just like he told my mother, I know we're a packaged deal. And we've each proven it time and time again.

  Standing in Neil's closet, I know what I have to do, and I'm going to do it. I'm going to get better again so I can give Neil back his Samantha.

CHAPTER 22

Waiting in Neil's living room for Daniel to return, I haven't taken any pills, and I've tried really hard to stay sane. I forced myself to not call Neil and Daniel each and every time the urge hit. Like every few minutes since I got out of the shower. I even made myself eat a few crackers with juice while I waited, to help the shaking and nausea I'm struggling with.

I know Olivia is going to need me to be strong for her, and I will be.

"How was Olivia?" I yell from the couch the second I hear the door open.

"I don't know. You were right about the hidden drawer, though," Daniel says shaking off his coat. "All her ID and makeup and even her phone was in it. But when I went to her parents' to ask her about it, she denied everything. She told me that stuff was her *extra* ID in case of an emergency. She even tried to tell me her phone was her old one, but I know her new phone," Daniel says huffing. "I was with her when she bought it a few months ago."

"What did you do?" I ask practically bouncing with fear.

Shaking his head, Daniel breathes, "Nothing. It was too soon, and she was breaking my heart. I could see she was scared, and she looks so awful, Sam I didn't want to push her too hard. When I left it was close to 7:00, and she looked so exhausted, I decided to leave her alone today."

"But we have to *help* her!" I gasp jumping up from the couch a little dizzily as I lean against the wall for support. "We should go get her. She needs to be around us until she feels safe again."

"She's staying at her parents' for a few days she told me, so I let it go. For *now*, Sam. I'll go back with Neil tomorrow, and we'll talk to her and to her goddamn parents if she won't listen to us. Okay?"

Looking at Daniel's resolve, I try to stop freaking out. He's trying to help, and he will help. I know he will. So if she's safe tonight at her parents' house, I'll have to trust him and Neil to talk to her tomorrow.

"You look good, honey," Daniel says taking my hand.

"I showered," I grin making him laugh. "It's amazing what a little water can do for a girl. With shampoo and a razor, I instantly turn human, too."

Watching my eyes, I can tell he's cautious with me. I can see it, and though it's meant well, I don't want it anymore. I need us back.

"Good?"

"Sure," he replies softly as he pulls me onto the couch with him.

"I'm okay, Daniel. Well, I'm getting better. I'm sorry for another funk. I just couldn't really get past Allan doing what he did. And I felt like he was still on me no matter how many times I showered which really freaked me out."

"I can't even imagine. Please don't apologize, honey. We're all good."

"Are we?" I ask sadly. I want us to be, but I know I'm wearing on them- I'd have to be. It seems like I've been babysat for so long now, I don't know how they can still stand me.

"We'll always be good. You're my girl, Sam. And I adore you- no matter what happens. Okay?"

Squeezing his hand, I breathe a little *okay* as he tugs me into his arms. Lying back on Neil's comfy couch, Daniel swings his leg over my head like he always does and pulls me in so I'm between his legs lying against his chest.

Crossing my arms over my chest, Daniel holds me tightly as I snuggle in. This is my second favorite place to be and he knows it.

"I've missed you so much," he whispers in my ear causing me to shiver and laugh.

"I'm sorry. This one was really hard."

"I know it was, and you never have to apologize for anything. Nobody can even imagine what that was like for you."

"It was *really* hard, Daniel..." I moan trying to tell him more. I think I need to tell him everything so he understands. "Um, Allan was so scary at first, but then so like his old self, and somehow I started getting the Allans confused, and then I was almost happy or content or something with him until the police showed up."

"I'm sure you were just struggling with what was happening around you and trying to make sense of everything," he tries. But he's wrong. There's so much more.

Turning in his arms, I sit up so he can see me. Waiting for a second to collect my weird thoughts, I need to explain more.

"I wasn't just struggling with him being there, or forcing me to stay with him, I actually kind of liked it. Well, not liked it, but it was comfortable, and I needed to feel like that again. We even snuggled on the couch and talked like we used to before the police arrived. And it wasn't so bad between us."

"Sam, he had a gun and forced you to stay with him."

"No, not at first. I didn't even know about the gun until the end. He just talked to me."

"And hit you. And made you stay there while he raged at you about *you* fucking up your relationship, which you didn't." Daniel pushes I can tell to help me understand, I think. And I do see what he means, but I also know what I felt at the time.

"It didn't feel like that after he calmed down. I didn't feel so lonely and confused."

"*Lonely?* When have you ever been lonely, Sam? None of us ever leave you alone, even when you desperately wish we would," he grins. But it's not the same thing.

"I slept with Matt," I exhale heavily. "And something happened that was awful and weird, but he didn't do anything wrong. It was just me, and I freaked out, and I wasn't sure what happened, but it can't be what I think I saw because it wasn't real. But it felt real, like when Heather came to me in the lecture hall. But I know it wasn't real, it just *really* felt real. So I'm not sure *what* happened anymore. But then the Allan thing happened, and Allan came to me after too, so I'm not sure it wasn't what I think anymore."

Admitting, well *half* admitting the truth feels a little better than having it all sit on my chest. I'm not sure if he understood any of that, but still, I can't tell Daniel what I saw or he'll probably have me committed, I almost laugh. Fuck. I'm almost losing it again, and I need to stay strong.

"Do you want to tell me what happened between you and Matt?" Daniel asks gently. "Matt was very tight-lipped about whatever happened earlier that night with you and the police. But he did let Neil know something bad happened to you, and he thought maybe you needed some help," Daniel whispers softly like he's afraid I'll freak out.

I don't freak out though. I'm lucid enough right now to *know* I need help. I also know I need to talk everything through so it makes sense.

Sitting back against his chest, I don't know how to start, or even where to begin. When *did* everything start changing for me? *What* happened to me?

"Have you spoken to Matt since that night?"

"No. He's called me a few times but I hang up on him. I, um... I have to tell you something though."

"Okay," he whispers lifting me from his chest again so we can look at each other.

Shaking myself, I just speak. "It's really big, and it started everything I think. I can't really explain it, but somehow Matt is important in all this."

"In all what?"

"Everything that has happened since last year."

"How?" Daniel asks waiting for me to continue. "Just talk to me, Sam," he pushes when I struggle to speak.

"Um, before Heather did what she did- when I was with Matt, I saw something. Well, he *was* something. No, I guess I imagined something. I don't know..." Trying to find the words, it's so hard to explain and describe. I can't quite get them out because even I know they sound messed up.

"Sam, just say it. I'm right here, and I'm not leaving." Taking my hand, Daniel waits with his blue eyes searching my face, almost willing me to speak to him.

"After I had a second orgasm with Matt, which is probably *why* I saw what I did. Well, I hope it was," I laugh nervously. "Um, Matt turned into a freaky, long black-tongued, scaly like demon monster." There. It's out. *Whew.*

Waiting, he keeps looking at me like I'm joking, or not explaining right, or like I'm insane. Whatever he's thinking, I know I need to explain myself better

Speaking before he can, I ask, "I was okay back then remember?" *Was* I? Maybe not. I know I suffered from depression after my accident, and I know I suffered from time lapses even then because I barely remember that summer, but I vaguely feel like I remember living through it.

"Sam..."

"Wait, Daniel," I breathe as he nods in silence. "Okay. I don't think I was *perfectly* okay at that time, but physically I was much better by then. I wasn't sore anymore, and my leg was healing though still in the cast, but I was better. I was starting school, and we were all still so close and everyone loved everyone, and Heather was alive, and I'm sure I was totally sane then I think. Wasn't I?"

"I think so. You seemed fine, or like you had recovered from the accident."

"I think so, too." My friends were still alive and okay. And Neil and Daniel were still kind of together, and fighting to stay together. Things were strained, but not totally over yet.

I have to think. There's something I'm not getting here. There's something that's just to the side of me and though I'm reaching as hard ask I can, I'm not quite getting it. But I know it's there waiting for me to understand.

"What happened that night with Matt, Sam?" Daniel asks trying to bring me back to our original conversation.

I can tell he's trying to keep me focused which I actually appreciate. My brain is too scattered to keep focus right now as I try to understand what I'm trying to understand.

"Okay. As I said, Matt turned into a monster right in front of my eyes. Like a horrible, scaly, black demon thing, and I couldn't get him away, but then he suddenly wasn't a demon anymore. Um, like in the blink of an eye, he was gorgeous Matt again. But I panicked, *obviously*, and I needed to get away from him."

"Samantha, you've experienced these hallucinations before," he says gently. Nodding, I know he's right. But it wasn't *until* Matt came into my life.

"It was Matt who did it," I say plainly as my reality hits me smack in the face.

"How could-"

"Look. Matt turned into a monster, and then he wasn't. And then I convinced myself I was just having a second orgasm loopy moment."

"I've had 2 orgasms before, and never had a hallucination, Sam."

Laughing, I burst out *lucky you* as he smirks. "I know that isn't what you meant, but *I* don't. I've never had 2 orgasms, plus I was drinking that night so I thought somehow I just zoned out or something. Which honestly made me feel way better at the time. So, I pretended I was fine, Matt and I eventually went to sleep, but then Heather showed up."

Did she show up? Yes. I know she did, but that part seems so long ago, like *years* ago. Not just 4 months ago. "Um, then everything happened with Heather, and she died because of-"

"She *killed* herself, Sam. She was emotionally unstable and she killed herself," he pushes.

"Whatever. It's the same thing in the end. She's dead," I nearly cry but hold it in.

Whispering, Daniel asks me what I know to be the absolute truth suddenly staring me right in the face. "So you think Matt has something to do with Heather's death?"

"I *know* he does."

Exhaling, Daniel is trying to understand me, I can tell. But he doesn't understand. He thinks I'm still mental, and I don't really blame him. I *know* I'm mental, but not about this. About this, I know I'm right.

"So what happened the night before Allan…?"

"The exact same thing. Except it was after the first orgasm. Matt had just finished making me, *um*…" I pause.

Wow. I'm actually embarrassed talking to Daniel about this. The man who has seen me naked, washed my body, loved me endlessly without so much as a pause himself. The man I love only equal to Neil. And for some reason I feel horribly embarrassed discussing all this suddenly.

"I can't believe how red you are," Daniel grins which helps release some of the discomfort I was feeling.

Nodding, "I'm surprised myself. I didn't think there was anything I couldn't talk to you and Neil about. Even my lady parts," I laugh.

"Sam… just talk to me. Matt made you come and then what?"

"Ah, he became the demon again. But this time I screamed and tried to fight it, and I kicked at it and hurt it, but…" Shaking my head I try to remember clearly what happened.

"But it was Matt."

"Yeah. Somehow I calmed down when he held me tightly against my mattress so I wouldn't hurt him or even myself I think, and I was going to explain I wasn't crazy while he waited for me to speak, but then the police showed up."

"Shit… *really?*" Daniel asks looking stunned *and* embarrassed for me.

"Yeah. So Matt and I had to explain what happened separately until they eventually believed no sexual assault took place because I guess when I was screaming at the monster a neighbor called the police. But then Matt left with the police when it was all explained. And it was awful, and I felt really bad for him at the time."

"*At the time?*"

"Yeah, but then the Allan thing happened after the monster came to me, just like the Heather thing happened after the monster visited. So now I know what really happened, and I don't feel so bad anymore getting Matt away from me. Actually, I'm pretty sure Matt did it to both of them," I admit, knowing the truth. I know Matt is somehow involved in everything that's happening to me.

"Sam... that is *completely* illogical. Matt had nothing to do with either Heather or Allan's suicides. He couldn't possibly. Never mind the fact that you were hallucinating for some reason we need to look into."

"Nope. He killed them," I say fiercely so Daniel understands.

"Matt made Heather commit suicide *alone* in her locked apartment, and Matt killed Allan in front of you with a gun? But neither the police or Neil saw him come or go?"

"No, he didn't *commit* the murders, but he made *them* do it to themselves."

"I think you're grasping to find a reason for their deaths because it's too horrible for you to accept that you've had 2 people you love kill themselves in less than a few months."

"What about you then?" I ask a little angrily. "You lost Heather. And you *used to* love Allan. Why aren't *you* freaking out like I am then? Huh? I know. Because you haven't been with Matt. *That's* why."

"You can't honestly believe-"

"There's more," I jump in quickly to stop him from doubting me. "I saw Matt last night before Olivia was hurt."

"When?" He practically yells. "You were here all night with Neil. Weren't you?" Daniel asks sounding a little angry, like maybe Neil wasn't watching me or something. But he was.

Suddenly laughing, I know what I'm about to say is crazy, but I also know it's the truth. I know it because he was here.

"*Sam...?*"

"Um, when Neil and I were watching t.v. last night I felt creeped out suddenly. Like *super* creeped. So I looked past Neil and I saw Matt standing on the balcony smiling at me."

"Sam, there's no way," Daniel shakes his head.

"He was, Daniel. He was standing there. And when I jumped totally afraid I looked away and then I saw him again through that mirror," I say pointing to the side of us. "And Matt was the demon again. But when I quickly looked back at the balcony Matt blew me a kiss looking like himself before he walked right off the balcony. And I KNOW that's crazy. But it happened," I exhale hard waiting for Daniel to freak about me being crazy. "I'm not crazy, Daniel. He was here."

"On Neil's fourth floor balcony?"

"Yes."

"Did Neil see him?"

"No."

"Because he wasn't here."

"No, because I started shaking and crying, and Neil jumped up to get my meds, and he eventually calmed me down and carried me to bed. But it was real."

"Honey... I'm telling you that didn't happen," he says taking my arms in his hands to force me to stare at him.

"It *did* happen. Matt was here and that's how I knew one of the three of you left were hurt this morning."

"No, you didn't. Neil woke you up and told you about Olivia."

"But I called you and Livi in the middle of the night when I woke up for a bit, didn't I?"

"Yes, but you always call us now," he exhales hard. "Sam, nothing happened last night. And Matt wasn't here."

"Yes, it did. And he *was*. Olivia didn't kill herself last night, but she was hurt and if I don't help her feel better- if I don't help get her away from *her* Matt she'll kill herself soon because she doesn't know how to help herself, and she's too afraid to keep living like she is."

"Honey, listen-"

"Matt was warning me when he came to me last night as the demon."

"Sam, he wasn't *here!*" Daniel yells as he stands quickly in front of me making me jump. "Think about it. If Neil was right here he would've saw him too. Never mind there's no way for Matt to suddenly be here then gone from the fucking balcony!"

When Daniel silences after his sudden explosion, I feel myself start shaking from the shock of his behavior, not from my weird thoughts anymore. Daniel has *never* yelled at me before. He doesn't yell, period. So I know I'm pushing him too far, and testing him too much.

What the hell *happened* to me? Christ! I used to be fun and normal and have friends and a life. I was going to be a goddamn doctor, for fuck's sake. And now I'm just so unhappy and confused, I'm hallucinating and struggling all the time with everything around me.

  Admitting on a rush the truth to my angel, I finally exhale all the confusion and pain I feel.
  "I need some help, Daniel. I think… Um, I'm afraid I'm next."
  And that's the truth. I'm scared I'm getting so messed up I'm going to kill myself soon.
  Feeling my tears slowly fall, I decide not to run and hide. Daniel isn't my mother, and he won't care or hate me or mock me if I cry. He's Daniel, and he loves me.
  "I'm really sad," I suddenly choke. "Um, I'm confused, and scared, and I'm seeing things and feelings things that aren't real even though I'm pretty sure they're real most of the time. And I'm really scared, Danny," I burst into tears as he hugs me. "I *need* help before I die, too."
  "*Oh,* Sam… We'll get you help," Daniel moans leaning back down to me. "Tomorrow even. I'll set up an appointment for you, and me or Neil will take you out of here. You're good, Samantha. I've got you," he breathes into my hair as I cry. I can actually feel myself relax in his arms as the pressure and fear lessens a little. "I won't let anything bad happen to you, honey. I promise."
  "The last 9 months has been really hard," I whisper again as he nods against me.
  "I know it has. It's been awful for you, and so unfair, and just a tragedy. But one day it won't hurt so much, Sam. You just hold on to me, and I promise one day you won't hurt like this."
  Weeping in his arms, Daniel is everything in the moment between my life and my death

  Slowly pulling away from Daniel, I know what I need. In this moment with my beautiful cherub, I know what will make me feel alive again. So in a desperate sounding whisper I beg, "Will you dance with me?"
  And he doesn't even pause. As usual.
  Standing up with a smile all for me, Daniel pulls me to my feet and walks to Neil's iStereo. Choosing my 'favorites list' he and Neil programmed what feels like years ago, the music starts as Daniel moves Neil's table

right against the opposite wall, and extends his hand to me with another beautiful smile before we begin to dance.

When 'I'll stand by you' begins, completely random on my playlist, it is everything in this moment.

Oh god, I *love* this man. He is everything to me. He is light, and love, and everything good in the world. He is an angel and I love him with everything that's left of me.

Singing Queen's 'Love of My Life' softly to each other as we dance, I feel so sad, but kind of happy, too. In Daniel's arms, I almost forget how much shit is going on with me, and how much help I need to get better.

When the next song, 'My Love' by Sia begins, I'm done. Crying softly in his arms, Daniel holds me tightly as he dances us around Neil's living room together. He doesn't acknowledge my tears, and he doesn't hold back his love because I'm weak. He doesn't love me any less for not being a tough cookie anymore.

Dancing the darkness away while Sia sings sadly about her lost love, and the strength he gave her when he left, I am strengthened by Daniel's voice whisper-singing to me everything alive and beautiful between us.

Crying, I slowly realize the grey has faded, and I am bathed in Daniel's light once again. There is no sadness drowning me, and there is no fear holding me down.

"I love you Daniel, so much," I whisper as he sings about Sia's love in my ear. "Um, I need you," I say nervously.

When Daniel stops moving to look at me, I look into his beautiful eyes and suddenly choose life.

"Can you please make love to me so I know I'm okay? I need my beautiful cherub to show me I'm not crazy. I need to know if the monster will come back," I smile embarrassed by my request, but sure of my decision. I need to know.

I can feel in every part of my soul Daniel will keep the demon monster away. I know he'll keep me safe, and I know no one will die today. I just need to be sure I'm okay in this moment.

"Samantha?" He asks obviously confused, but as I stare in his eyes, I nod yes with my certainty. I need Daniel to help me move past this living nightmare.

This is my choice.

CHAPTER 23

Walking slowly into Neil's room, Daniel holds my hand to keep me sane. This is my choice...

It might not be his, but he's willing to be with me to show me I'm okay. Daniel is willing to give himself to me because he loves me enough to want me to *be* okay.

Turning to me, he whispers, "Are you sure you need this?" And I'm sure.

Quickly pulling off my sweater, I can't quite make eye contact with him, but I'm sure. Slipping my jeans and underwear from my body, I'm sure. Standing before him, I've never been so sure of anything in my life.

Waiting silently naked in front of Daniel in the darkened bedroom to give him time to decide, he leans down and sweetly kisses away all my wait and embarrassment.

At some time or another Daniel has seen me naked, but not like this, and not in this context. But thankfully, he doesn't panic at my very naked nudity, nor does he seem to mind.

Pulling his own clothes from his body, he keeps our lips as close as possible and he touches me often to keep me in this moment with him.

For one awkward moment, after he raises his own sweater overhead, I feel the intimacy between our naked bodies, and though I want to cover myself quickly, I don't. I wait for him to look at me before making his final decision.

"I love you, Sam," he whispers against my lips as I wrap my arms around his neck for a deeper kiss.

Kissing Daniel is everything I knew it would be. It's lovely, and natural, and sweet. We don't fight with our tongues, and we don't fight for dominance of the kiss. Everything moves between us at such a natural pace, I'm swept up in the light of his eyes and the beauty of his smile.

Easily, we kiss each other to Neil's bed, until gently, we touch each other's bodies. Learning the feel of Daniel while he touches my own skin makes me relax in his arms.

Daniel is so stunning, my hands explore his soft, smooth skin, and my kisses deepen with my need.

Once in a while with awkward humor we laugh through any nervousness we experience until we make it to the inevitable together.

"What do you need, honey?" He asks lying between my opened thighs, holding my face sweetly in his palm.

Blushing, I almost giggle at the awkwardness of his question until he moves his body against my own until I moan. "I need to have an orgasm so I know if..." *monsters really exist* "... I'm okay."

"Tell me how you need me. Through penetration, or through oral sex?"

Oh *god*... I should be dying right now, but there doesn't seem to be anything between us he can't handle. Pulling myself together, I breathe *oral* as he once again smiles and nods before kissing me deeply.

When I suddenly panic and wonder if he even likes doing that to a woman I gasp pulling away from our kiss mortified. "Unless that grosses you out?" I accidentally yell in his face.

Shaking his head with another adorable grin, Daniel says, "Not hardly, Sam. I just *prefer* the dick," he says like Olivia would as we burst out laughing together.

Lowering back to my mouth for another long, stunning kiss, taking my breast into his hand, Daniel eventually moans in my mouth as I arch closer to him. Moving down my body, he takes my nipple into his mouth, and I arch further. Sliding his hand down my body, his fingers gently enter me, and as I gasp he straightens to watch me.

Moving against his fingers, my eyes open and close to his eyes always watching. With encouraging smiles and quick kisses on my lips, Daniel pushes me calmly into pleasure.

When he decides to take me further, I'm already panting. Arching and moaning, Daniel easily lowers himself between my legs and as he breathes against my body, I cry out for him.

Kissing my body softly, his fingers continue to penetrate me as his tongue teases me breathless. Moaning, my hands grasp his hair as I pull him closer to my body. I need more, and I need to know for sure.

"Danny... *Please*," I beg. "I need more," I whine with shaking legs and a pull deep in my stomach.

Lapping at my body, I feel myself climbing. Pulling at him, I feel myself straining. He's so good, I know it's coming soon. I know I can reach the place I need to experience, and though scared of what could happen, I honestly know it won't.

Daniel is the angel in this life.

Feeling him move harder inside and around my body, I'm at the precipice when he growls inside me until I come undone.

Screaming and grunting my release, I try to focus on him but my eyes close as the shudders force their way through my body. I'm in agony and ecstasy at once, and I'm okay.

Quickly opening my eyes, I search for it, but I see only Daniel raising up my body, kissing my stomach softly, eventually lifting higher to nuzzle and linger on my breasts.

Daniel is the only one here with me, and I know I'm not crazy.

Crying out, I breathe our reality. "I had my orgasm and it's still just us."

Nodding with a smile while reaching for Neil's bedside drawer, Daniel sits on his shins to roll a condom on. Watching me closely, I know he's afraid there's more. I can tell he's nervous I'm going to freak out, or need to stop. But I don't need to stop. I know nothing is going to change between us with this. I can feel it.

He'll always be my Daniel.

"Are you sure, Sam?" He asks with patient eyes and the gentleness I adore.

Smiling, "I'm okay. But it's your turn now. So show me what ya got," I tease. I feel so much lighter inside. I'm lighter than I've been since I was 18. I'm lighter suddenly than I've ever been. God, I don't want to ruin this feeling of happiness ever.

Grinning, he teases right back. "You're the first woman I've slept with since I was 21, so my moves may not be *female* specific anymore. But I'm sure I'll figure it out."

"Yup. I'm sure you will," I giggle until he kisses me silent.

Bending back low, with his body between my legs, Daniel holds my cheek with one palm as he positions himself for entry with his other hand. Moving slowly, I feel the first pull of penetration, and as I smile at him to continue, he whispers, *I love you* against my mouth.

Buried deep inside me, neither move, but we both feel it I think.

There are no words needed between us. There is a silent acceptance, and almost a peace that covers us as we adjust and wait for movement.

In this moment, I feel so happy, tears fill my eyes, and I want to scream, 'I'm not crazy!' I want to giggle and laugh, and tell my angel he healed me. I want to remember this moment for eternity.

No one is going to die in the morning. And I don't have to be afraid of living anymore.

"Thank you so much," I cry in relief as a tear slides down my temple.

*****

Suddenly looking at Neil standing in his bedroom doorway, I freeze and panic. Looking at the clock I see its after 9:00, and Neil *always* returns from working on Saturdays to catch up after 9:00 if he hasn't blown off the gym. I *knew* that, I just didn't think about it.

"Oh *GOD!* I'm sorry!" I yell across the room. *Shit!* "Ummm. This is *all* my fault! I needed to know if I was crazy," I say as he stares at me and my explanation like I'm exactly that- *crazy*.

"Shut up, Samantha," Neil whispers in shock I think. Staring at Daniel, Neil moans in a hoarse voice, "If you need to be with her to come back to me, then take her. Be with her. But *please*, Daniel, be with me too. I still love you, and I *miss* you," Neil suddenly cries.

Watching Neil beg Daniel, and seeing the pain on Daniel's face shatters the peace I felt. It shouldn't be like this. *I* shouldn't be like this. Slowly, pulling the covers back up my chest, I barely breathe for fear of breaking their moment.

Trying to push Daniel away from my body, he refuses to pull out of me. He is inside me while Neil stands there unmoving like we've broken him.

"Don't move, Sam," Daniel whispers still not looking at me.

"I'm sorry, Neil. But I love her, and she needed me. I wasn't choosing between you, because I can't," Daniel says so sadly, there's a palpable agony in Neil's bedroom.

"Then don't choose. Be with us both if you have to," Neil whispers as another tear rolls down his cheek.

After his desperate offer there is nothing but silence around us. I can't believe what I'm hearing. And I can *NOT* believe what Neil is offering. I don't know what to do or say, so I stay deathly silent.

Slowly pulling out of me, Daniel covers my body with the comforter before standing naked in front of us. With slow movements, Daniel seems to be asking permission to walk closer to Neil. And he gets his permission with an audible sigh as Neil nods his head yes just before Daniel makes contact.

Taking Neil's face into his hands, Daniel looks deeply into his eyes, wipes a single tear away with his thumb, then kisses Neil slowly.

Watching them silently, the shared kiss is so beautiful, I can only stare with wide eyes. It is a kiss of love and devotion between two lovers. It is a kiss I have never known personally.

Watching them, the sudden pain in me is too great to hold in. My heart aches and my body is shaking with the need to know love like theirs. I want to be them in this moment with someone of my own. I don't want to take Daniel from Neil. I've *never* wanted that. I've only ever wanted someone of my own to love like they do.

Turning away, I fight the sob that wants to break free of my chest. I fight the agonized sobs that want to scream from my heart. And I fight the pain that threatens to break me again.

I am alone. And nobody loves me the way Neil and Daniel love each other. Not my mother, not Allen, not Heather, not even Matt.

No one has ever loved me like that, and I will never help break it.

"What is it, *Samantha*?" Neil sneers like he hates me. Though given the circumstances he just found me in, how could he possibly not? Shit, *I* hate me. "*Jealous*?"

Shaking my head no, I fight with the absolute last of my strength to not cause a scene. I can't do this, and I *won't* do this to them. This is their moment, and I won't break it. I don't want to be here, and I don't want to know this.

"Samantha. Look at me," Neil demands as I turn my head away from Daniel pulling on his jeans beside Neil.

Giving all I can back to the man who has been there for me every single day since he found me shell-shocked and alone in my new dorm room, I can only apologize.

"I wasn't trying to take Daniel from you. I would *never* take Daniel from you. I was just trying to come back from the grey for you, and-"

"For *ME*!?" Neil yells actually vibrating with his anger. "If you *dare* say anything like YOU fucking the love of *MY* life was for me I'll-"

"*Neil!* Let her explain!" Daniel jumps in to help me I think.

Turning on Daniel, Neil looks shocked, and hurt, and betrayed by both of us. Standing there looking between us, Neil is paralyzed by his upset. I can actually see how hurt he is and I wish I could fix it.

"I needed to find out if I was okay so I begged him to help me," I moan so he understands. "Daniel didn't want me- he *doesn't* want me. He was only doing what I begged him to do so I could be sure."

"Sure of *what?*" Neil growls like he wants to be done with me and this entire conversation.

Lifting my head to look at Neil one last time, I know I can't tell him what I thought was going to happen. The demon didn't come, and they'll both survive tomorrow morning. I know they will.

Whispering an absolute, I need Neil to get it. Finally. I need him to accept and know and choose right. I need him to make the right choice in this life.

"Daniel is your angel to love, Neil. But I can't talk right now or I'm going to lose it," I barely whisper. "This wasn't about anything other than I needed to be sure I was okay. So Daniel helped me that's all. He doesn't want me like he wants you, or even love me like he loves you. And I would *never* take him from you like that."

Glaring at me, Neil sneers his own absolute. "Of course you wouldn't *take* him from me. Get over yourself you selfish fucking *Psycho*!" He bitch slaps me with words more effectively than Monica and Allan did with their hands. I can hardly breathe from the new reality I'm facing.

"I am so sorry you saw this, but I needed to know if I was going to see death again." God, I wish I had all the right words so he could understand.

"Neil, we can all talk about this in the morning," Daniel tries to ease the growing tension between us and I could just kiss him for still trying to help me.

Smiling at Daniel, I immediately look at Neil and see the hatred all over his face as he watches me. Jolting, I realize I can't smile at Daniel ever again or Neil will hate me more.

Oh, *god*... I've lost them both.

In one night of desperation I realize I made the choice that sealed my fate. I can't love Daniel anymore because Neil hates me now. And Neil doesn't love me anymore because I still love Daniel.

"You almost got that *ménage* you've always wanted," Neil growls, and as the breath bursts from my chest in horror I know he truly believes that was what this was about. He couldn't be more wrong, but he'll never believe me if I explain, so I don't even bother trying to explain when he's this angry.

Pulling the comforter tighter around me, I stand to leave.

"Where are you going?" Daniel asks softly.

"Um, I'm going to go. I'll just go-" *where?* Where the *fuck* can I go? My mother's is a painful torture for me. Olivia is a mess at her parents'. Allan is dead. Heather is dead, and her mom hates me for being better than Heather anyway.

I have nowhere to go in the world. Except back to my old apartment to my old life with blood all over my face and hair.

"You can spend the night here. But that's it. Tomorrow morning you need to get your shit, and get the *fuck* out," Neil snaps making me jump and shake at his hard tone.

"Neil... You and Sam need to talk about this. We *all* need to talk about this. I was right there with her. This wasn't all her, and I won't let you beat her up over something I was more than a part of. Tomorrow morning we'll all talk."

"Not a *fucking* chance! After all I've done for her? After I helped her when I found her in that fucking dorm, assaulted and fucked up. After years of waking to her screams and nightmares, and holding her while she got her shit together-*this* is what I get? Too bad, *Danny,* but I'm not talking to her *EVER* again!" Neil turns on Daniel. But Daniel doesn't back down, even as my own confusion hits me so hard I don't understand what he's saying anymore.

Assaulted and fucked up? I was *NEVER* assaulted. I was just fucked up. Why does everyone lie about me like that?

"We'll all talk in the morning or I'm leaving *with* her. Period, Neil. Nothing between you and I magically righted itself tonight because you're pissed at her. So we'll *all* talk in the morning. *Understood*?" Daniel states the demand and though Neil looks like he's about to out bitch him, he surprisingly nods once before leaving the room.

"You can sleep in here tonight with the door closed! And don't come out. I can't stand to fucking look at you!" Neil yells one last insult before storming out of his bedroom.

"I'm sorry..." I moan to Daniel's back.

I didn't think this through. I didn't think about the consequences of sleeping with Daniel. I didn't think about what I was potentially

destroying when I begged Daniel to help me. I just needed to be sure.
  "It's okay, Samantha." When he says my full name, he's clearly telling me it isn't okay. He never calls me that, and the sound of my full name alone is enough to make me scream in pain. "We'll all talk in the morning. But I'm going to try to talk to him now- to explain what happened. *Before* he does something stupid again. Good night," he says leaving the room with a sad little smile.

  When Daniel closes the door quietly to be kind, it has the opposite effect. If he had slammed the door in my face, I wouldn't have felt his upset and disgust with me more clearly than I did when he walked away closing the door quietly behind him.
  Daniel is gone.

  Sitting back on Neil's tainted bed, I shake and panic thinking of all I've lost.
  Crying, I can't help but realize, nothing in life can destroy you faster than your own choices...

CHAPTER 24

After sleeping off and on for a few broken, sad hours, I know I have to leave. My head is pounding from crying and from lack of sleep, and I'm horribly nauseous. But mostly my heart is killing me from everything going on around me- everything *I've* caused.

I took pills once in a while through the night when the darkest grey I've ever known started to close down on me. And I took some of my pills when the panic started to make me scared and paranoid. But I always stayed quiet.

Wherever Neil and Daniel are, hopefully is where they should be together. On the couch, or on the floor, I don't know. Last night I took what little comfort I could picturing them holding each other as they try to mend their beautiful relationship.

Dressing quickly in a pair of warm sweats and running shoes, I pull my hair back in a ponytail and stuff all my purse contents into my hoodie pockets to leave.

Maybe when Neils at work tomorrow he'll allow me to come back, just one more time to collect all my things. Hopefully, he'll give me one last kindness, like the hundreds he's given me since the day we met.

Hopefully.

After having the quietest bathroom break ever, I slip into the living room to all I've ever wanted. Daniel is holding Neil tightly against his chest on the couch exactly where they should be. They are together, and hopefully on their way back to each other.

Watching for only seconds, I turn to leave but catch Daniel's eyes open quickly. Staring at each other, his eyes look almost eerily blue, but when he smiles and nods once I know I'm forgiven and it's time for me to go.

The soft light from the bay window is stretching across Daniel's face and hair, making him glow in the early morning light. His face is perfect, and his eyes are so expressive I feel his love for me straight through to my soul.

"I love you," I whisper.

Watching Daniel start to move, I quickly shake my head no. He can't move. He *shouldn't* move. He is where he should have always been.

"Please tell him for me how much I love him. Tell him until he *finally* listens," I smirk as Daniel nods and smiles again. Neil is so damn stubborn, it'll be a hard task, but I trust Daniel to try to make Neil see the truth.

Feeling my tears fall, I watch one single tear slide down Daniels's cheek and I know I'm seeing our end.

"You will always be my white knight Danny, no matter where I end up. Please love him forever so I can finally let go," I say smiling for the last time as he nods his head, pulling Neil a little closer to his chest.

I will never see them again. We're done. The two loves of my life have found their way back to each other, finally. And I'm going to walk away forever, so they can love without me 3rd wheeling my way through their life together.

Closing Neil's door as quietly as possible, I exhale everything I've ever felt was wrong in my life, and I make the choice to start again.

Walking down the street, the cold air freezes me to my core but I keep moving forward. The morning is dark and sad, and so lonely as I walk, I can only breathe deeply the cold and take it into my soul.

I've never felt this devastated, or lonely in my life.

"*Samantha!*" Neil yells from the street behind me.

Crying harder, I don't want to look at him. I won't hurt him again, and I don't want to be a burden to him anymore. I don't want to see his face hating me, and I don't want to face our ending just yet.

I *can't* accept our ending yet.

"Sam! *Wait!* Turn around for me!" He yells getting closer.

Looking across the street, I suddenly see Matt as I jolt to a stop. Smiling, Matt waves his hand at me and calls my name as well.

Shaking my head as I stop to look at Matt, I'm so confused again I can't even move as Neil gets closer to me.

What the *hell* is happening?

"Samantha! Open your eyes, Sam! Look at *ME!*" Neil screams, but I'm stuck staring at Matt motioning for me to come to him.

"*Samantha!* Make a choice! Come on baby. Stay. With. *ME!*" Neil cries.

What?

Turning, Neil seems so sad as he approaches me with his hands raised he looks almost afraid I'll freak out if he touches me. But he's sobbing in the street begging me to stay. *Why?*

Oh, *god...*

Walking backward away from Neil, I can't do this anymore. He shouldn't even be here. He should be sleeping in Daniel's arms.

"I don't know what to do!" I scream as my head whips back to see the demon monster smiling at me. The monster who looks like he's been waiting for me. The huge, black tongued, scaly demon who has been tempting me. The devil in low-rise jeans.

Spinning back toward Neil, all the dark confusion suddenly rights itself and the world opens up to me on a gasp.

The purgatory grey has lifted and I'm bathed in the light of hope.

I know what I have to do.

Hearing the depth of my reality suddenly spin louder and louder until the sounds make sense all around me, my eyes quickly open, and the answer opens my chest until I breathe deeply for the first time forever.

When I feel the shock of darkness clear completely from my mind, I see all I've ever been. Lying on the ground in Neil's arms, I know my reality.

Spinning through the darkness that I've seen, I gasp and stare at Neil. Oh, *god...*

I know this reality now. I was allowed to see. I am still awesome. And I am still a tough cookie.

But *this* is my end.

I'm not crazy, and nothing bad has happened yet. I am NOT crazy.

I'm just dying... Thank *fuck.*

"My rib has punctured my aorta I think," I choke out suddenly as my reality surfaces clearly. "I can't be fixed, Neil. There's not enough time to fix me," I wheeze in Neil's arms.

Listening to all the people around us with the sirens singing gently in the background, I stare at my Neil and know.

"Sam, *please*," he begs louder than the heartbeat of fear and confusion pulsing through my body and mind.

With no more pain, and with my lungs suddenly clear, I finally have my chance to make it all right.

"Don't tell Allan I was meeting him tonight. He needs to live out his life with Monica so he can finally move on. And help Heather find herself before she fades away. She has to stop looking for randoms to love her, and she should work in a shelter or as a counsellor for children so she loves herself as much as we love her. She's too kind and good a person to be wasted. Make sure she knows she's better than me."

"Stop. Don't *do* this!"

"Where's Matt?" I panic looking around us to all the people watching me die.

"From last night? I don't know, why?" He begs confused.

"When did you meet him?"

"Yesterday at the gym when I invited him to join us last night."

"Is he here?"

"No... *Why?*"

"Um, stay the hell away from Matt. Okay?"

"Okay. But I don't understand."

Smiling, *I* finally understand though. "From cock to clavicle," I laugh when Neil looks at me like I'm crazy for real this time. "Matt was temptation. He was the test for me. And I failed, Neil."

"Sam, *please?* I don't understand," Neil cries louder, shaking himself as he holds my shaking body in his arms.

Matt was the temptation to fight to stay. I was given my chance. But my fight has to end now so everyone else can live.

I have to make a choice...

"Listen to me. I've seen it all play out, and I know what happens if I stay. Dr. Danieli and Professor Neilly- it was *always* the two of you with me. And I know how my story ends now."

"No, you don't!" Neil screams. "You don't know anything." Shaking me again Neil moans, "We were just jogging. This isn't the end for you, Samantha."

But I don't have time to listen to his denial anymore.

"Keep Olivia away from her Matt so he can't hurt her. He's bad and he's going to break her if she stays. Make sure she dumps him today like she said she was going to."

"Sam…" Neil moans.

"Neil, you have to tell my mother I forgive her for what they did to me when I was 18. Tell her I turned out okay anyway. Tell my mother god did *not* save me so she stays crazy but tell her I said she has to stay clean for me or I don't forgive her. And tell my dad I said thanks for always trying to parent me, even though it was really hard to with my mother the way she was."

"*Fuck,* Samantha. Stop. *Please…*"

"And *love* Daniel. He's our white knight, Neil. He's everything. He is love and kindness. And he was my angel, Neil."

"Daniel can still hear you, honey," he moves the phone closer.

"Don't be mad at Neil for this," I gasp through the speaker. "He loves you… more than he loves even me," I grin to a sobbing Neil. "Danny…" I cry as I try to breathe. "…You are the love of our life. And I need you to promise me you'll take care of each other. You have to promise to smack the shit out of Neil if he ever tries to screw up your relationship."

"Sammy, *please!*" Daniel screams through the phone.

"Neil, don't *ever* cheat on Daniel… And I promise he'll love you forever. I've seen it," I say with a smile because I know the truth of their love now. It's real, and it's forever.

"I won't," Neil whispers.

"I have to go. I've made the right choice… *finally*."

All the choices I saw were wrong, and everything went wrong. I can't stay here anymore. I know I have to go. I have to die so everyone else can live.

"I'm going to always remember dancing with you, Daniel. I'll hold those memories with me always. *Wherever* I end up," I whisper to his ragged moaning in the phone. Smiling, I realize I'm no longer being tested or punished, so I'm finally free to just dance now.

"God, I'm going to miss you," I cry in Neil's arms listening to Daniel cry out through the phone for me to hold on still. "Thank you for finding me and loving me and for making me awesome, Neil. I love you so, so much," I cry with a sad smile.

When Neil suddenly stops sobbing like he finally understands what I'm saying, I know it's time. Looking at his beautiful eyes loving me in the end, I really do feel at peace now.

"I saw it all, and this is the right choice, Neil. I have to go now…" I whisper knowing with certainty that this is the death I must live.

Inhaling as deeply as my broken chest will allow, I say what needs to be said.

"*Love* Daniel. It's always been him, Neil. And with Daniel, we've finally found our happily ever after."

"*Sam!* Please don't leave me," Daniel screams so sadly it should break me. But my heart doesn't hurt anymore, and my mind is totally clear. I'm okay now that everything has worked itself out.

"Promise you'll love Neil, and I'm still here with you. Promise me that, and I'll never leave you, Daniel."

Pausing, Daniel finally croaks, "I promise, Sam," as I exhale.

That is all I was waiting for. That was what I needed to hear.

Now I can let go.

"Samantha," Neil whispers holding me tighter to his chest. Looking at his dark eyes crying for me Neil says all I've ever wanted to hear with the softest, sweetest voice I've ever heard in my life.

"You're my *soul,* honey. And I will cut a bitch for you. Forever."

Nodding as a final tear slides down my face, I know he's finally letting me go.

"What time is it?"

Looking at his phone quickly, Neil whispers 7:42 just as I do. Because I've always known. *My* life ends at 7:42 so they can all live.

Choices…

  I have my closure. And I know my end. I saw my life play out, speeding through my frightened eyes in a madness I couldn't understand. My future was there, but it was too dark to live with. And I don't want to linger here in this purgatory grey of bad choices and indecision anymore.
  Exhaling for the last time, Neil kisses my life away.
  Closing my eyes to the feel of Neil's lips pressed against my own, I'm ready to finally let go now.

  This is my choice…

EPILOGUE

Life! We've been long together
Through pleasant and through cloudy weather,
It is hard to part when friends are dear-
Perhaps it will cost a sigh, a tear;
- Then steal away, give little warning,
Choose thine own time;
Say not Good night,- but in some brighter clime
Bid me Good Morning.
A.L. Barbauld

Sitting in the front row beside Sam's dad, Neil is hunched over his own stomach while Daniel cries softly behind him with his hand on Neil's back. Holding Neil together, Daniel feels nothing but the pain of his own loss, knowing this loss is absolutely destroying Neil inside.

Samantha was just like Neil, only better Neil has said a million times over the years. Picturing Neil still holding her as she slipped away, it was obvious to all who watched in the street how much he loved her.

There was something about Sam that made everyone love her. Maybe because of what her mother did to her at 18, or maybe she was always like that, no one can say for sure. But she was the kind of person you wanted to love because she gave you all of her love first.

She was loving, and caring, and fierce, and beautiful, and so smart. She was a treasure in their lives, and Neil may not recover from losing her. Then again, none of them ever will.

Watching a crying Allan walk away with Monica and his parents, everyone can see how much Allan loved her. He just didn't love her enough when she was alive to not hurt her. Sadly, Allan actually lost her before the rest of them did. But watching him hurt now, and seeing his regret was so awful, even Neil shook his hand at the funeral and wished him and Monica well.

"I can't keep doing this," Neil suddenly cries jumping up from his graveside chair. The priest stopped speaking long ago to allow the mourners to grieve, and the few family members left are just waiting around for something to signal they can finally leave.
"We need to get out of here. I'm fucking *dying*," Neil moans in Daniel's ear as Mr. Newman watches Neil with the shocked sadness only the parent of a dead child can know.
"I have to go, Mr. Newman. I can't sit here looking at the ground anymore," Neil says sadly before hugging him. Holding Mr. Newman tightly, Neil promises to keep in touch before spinning out of his hug.
Daniel will never forget Mr. Newman walking up to Neil, taking his hand and leading him right to the front row beside him. He'll never forget watching Mrs. Newman cringe either, though amazingly she didn't speak or acknowledge Neil's presence, thank god.
Turning to the girls, Neil grabs both Heather and Olivia's hands and starts pulling them away from the gravesite.
"Let's go somewhere else."
"I've got some vodka in my purse," says a crying, desperate Olivia.
"Good enough. Can you drive, Daniel?" Neil asks likes he's on a mission.
"Sure. Where to?"
"The grasslands behind our old campus. That's where Samantha used to go when she was in school, freaked out by what her mother did to her"
Walking back to Neil's jeep, all four pile in quietly, deep in their own thoughts and memories of Sam until Heather suddenly blurts out, "Her mother is such an *asshole!*"
After a second of silence among them, Neil finally bursts out laughing.

"I *know*. As if Sam would be caught dead in- Oh, *SHIT!*" Neil yells making them all jump and laugh hysterically. "Jesus *Christ!* I *am* as tacky as Sam always said I was. *Fuck*, I didn't mean to say that," Neil laughs from the front seat shaking his head. "It was just so weird to see sexy Sam in that long grey moomoo dress," he continues as Daniel takes his hand to soothe him down a little.

"It's too bad we weren't allowed to dress her," Olivia adds. "I loved that sexy as hell red dress she wore Saturday night."

"Me too. I was totally jealous of her in that dress. Especially with her sexy red lips and blue eyes," Heather admits.

Turning to Heather, Daniel smiles. "You shouldn't have been jealous of her, you look *gorgeous* in red, baby."

Smiling back, Heather nods a *thanks* to Daniel before he starts the car.

"Remember when she danced Saturday night to her sex song? That's the visual of Sam I'm going to always keep. She was so sexy, and funny, and happy that night. God, she loved dancing. Especially with you," Livi adds as she touches Daniel's shoulder from the backseat.

Grasping her hand, Daniel can only nod. Thinking about their last dance breaks his heart over and over again. They were so awesome together, and they both knew it. Thinking about her giggles when he dipped her low makes his chest hurt so badly, Daniel has to fight his own tears so Neil doesn't start crying again. But it's hard.

Neil has been all over the place for 3 days now. Laughing, crying, sleeping, dreaming, and talking to Sam. All the time, actually.

If it wasn't so sad hearing Neil tell her each and every single thing he's doing from one moment to the next, almost like he needs her to still be there listening, Daniel would be afraid for Neil's own sanity.

But Neil is aware of what he's doing which takes some of the fear out of it. He just doesn't want Sam to feel like she's not a part of his life anymore, he says. So he keeps telling her what's going on so she doesn't miss anything if she's still around listening.

  Sitting in the grass, Neil inhales deeply before making his announcement.
  "Okay, since I was with her at the end, Samantha told me a few things that we have to do. She died thinking they were important, so we have to *make* them important. Okay?" When everyone nods, Neil braces himself to continue.
  Though Daniel was there by the phone hearing everything Sam said as well, Neil still feels like he is the keeper of Sam's dying wishes because he kissed her lips when she exhaled her last breath and died in his arms. Daniel was there, too, but he lets Neil have his closure, however he needs it.
  Crying softly, Neil shakes his head clear, and explains his Samantha's final wishes.
  "Okay. Heather. You need to find yourself quickly, and we'll all help you. Whether it's working for a shelter or getting a degree in counselling for children, you have to do something special, because as Sam said, 'you're too kind and good a person to waste.' No more looking for love in the arms of randoms, because love isn't going to happen for you that way. And you need to love yourself like Sam loved you, so you can feel as special as you are to all the rest of us."
  Crying her eyes out, Daniel pulls Heather in tight and kisses her head as she struggles to deal with Sam's sweet words about her.
  "And Olivia, you are NEVER to go back to Matt. For whatever reason, Sam was convinced he would hurt you, and she was so afraid of you being hurt she made me promise to keep you away from him. No matter what."
  Nodding, Olivia quickly agrees. "I wouldn't take him back anyway, but I think I know what she meant. Matt was already a little weird with me and he was so much bigger he scared me a few times when he was all possessive and demanding," she admits on a long exhale.

"Okay. Good. But *what the fuck,* Livi? You should've told us about that, or got the hell away from him sooner. Seriously," he glares.

"Neil. She's away from him now," Daniel pushes until Neil finally nods staring at a crying Olivia.

"And what about you?" Heather asks with almost a twinkle in her eye. "What did she want *you* to do?"

"Nothing like that, Heather. *Christ...* you're dirtier than I am," Neil laughs as Daniel takes his hand.

"I'm to never cheat on Daniel. Which I won't. But she made me promise her, even though I know I never will. No matter what," he whispers to a smiling Daniel.

"Well, that one's too easy!" Heather whines. "Who *would* cheat on Daniel? He's to die for. Ooops. *Shit.* Sorry," Heather giggles at her death comment as Neil laughs again.

"Sam told me Daniel was my forever, and as long as I didn't cheat Daniel would stay with me and love me forever. And Daniel agreed he *would* love me forever if I didn't cheat on him. So even when things are tough, I'm going to learn to work on our relationship instead of me being me and cheating. And Daniel promised Sam he'll work hard on our relationship and smack the shit out if me if I ever even think about cheating. *Right*?" Neil turns to a nodding Daniel with a smile.

"So there you have it. We each have a thing, and Samantha was dead serious. *Fuck!* I did it again," Neil bursts out laughing with Heather. "I swear to god, if I make one more dead reference about my girl, somebody please punch the shit out of me."

"Okay," all three say at the same time, and that's it.

There is no more laughter, and there are no more tears. For now. Sam spoke from the grave, and they all love her too much to not listen.

"God, I love her. She was *everything* to me," Neil whispers as a single tear slides down his cheek.

Choices…

ABOUT THE AUTHOR

Sarah Walker lives in Canada with her American husband and their son.

In her real life, Sarah is a devoted mother, (semi)devoted wife ☺, and an absolute junkie for coffee, dark chocolate with sea salt, and high heels.

www.authorsarahannwalker.com

Sarah can be found on Facebook
www.facebook.com/SarahAnnWalkerIAmHer

Amazon
http://www.amazon.com/author/walkersarahann
http://amzn.com/e/B00AW22K56

Goodreads
https://www.goodreads.com/Sarah-Walker

and
Twitter
@sarahannwalker0

Made in the USA
Middletown, DE
15 June 2015